FROM
SHADOW
TO
FLAME

RYAN KIRK

OLIVER-HEBER BOOKS

FROM SHADOW TO FLAME

RYAN KIRK

OLIVERHEBERBOOKS

PROLOGUE

Endless grasslands stretched below Edam as he flew, clutched in the claws of the largest dragon he'd ever seen. Tears ran down his cheeks, carving small valleys in the layers of ash caked upon his face. The flames of his city reappeared every time he closed his eyes, so he kept them wide open even as the wind whipped across his face and ripped his tears away.

The Elders claimed they spoke with the dragons. That the dragons heeded their orders and obeyed their will. Edam wished for many things at that moment, but first among his wishes was that he could speak to the dragon carrying him. He would shout questions at his captor and demand answers.

But the dragon held him too tight to shout, and there was no connection between him and the dragon. Edam couldn't speak to it any more than he could a bird or a deer. His questions burned in his throat, but there was no point in asking them. Nothing would answer.

Why had the dragons that supposedly served them attacked? Why hadn't the Elders' shouted commands had any effect?

Edam made the mistake of closing his eyes. For less than a heartbeat, he was back home, watching the fire spread as the dragons dropped flame across the city. Screams piled upon one another like children in a wrestling match, filling the streets with cries of agony. Countless infernos trapped hundreds, if not thousands, of people in their homes.

Not Edam. He'd woken up from his dreamless slumber in the middle of the street. He never walked in his sleep. Yet tonight, of all nights, he'd walked to safety. He stood helpless as he watched the home he'd grown up in burn. Though he couldn't hear their screams, he assumed Mother and Father were within. They weren't in the street with him.

He'd still been standing in the street when the shadow descended from above, lit by flames from below. Edam only noticed a moment before the dragon struck. Then the dragon had him in its claws and he flew over a sea of fire.

The dragon had taken him out to sea. Edam's bitter thought was that in a city full of burned citizens, he would be the only one to drown. But the dragon had held tight and turned, carrying him over mountains and to lands filled with mysteries.

Edam opened his eyes and saw the endless prairie was closer than before. The dragon landed, putting Edam down as gently as if he was a thin-walled pot. Then the dragon flapped its wings and took off, pressing Edam's body against the inhospitable soil as it launched into the air.

Voices shouted after the dragon. Screams of incoherent rage, followed by weeping. Heavy feet hurried through the grass. Soft murmurs passed between the two who knelt beside him, though they sounded distant and hollow, as though their voices had echoed down a long empty hallway.

Two pairs of warm hands turned him gently over. Slowly, he realized the voices were speaking to him. He blinked and his spirit found its way back into his body, finally catching up to him after the long flight. His arms and legs were cold. He sat up and wrapped his arms around his chest as he shivered.

"I'm sorry, son. There's no extra clothing here. There's

nothing at all, if my eyes don't lie. Best you sit up and move around. It's helped the others."

Edam forced his eyes toward the speaker. He was a middle-aged man with glasses and a kind face. His cheeks were round and ruddy, and he wore sleeping clothes that cost as much as Edam's father brought home in a month. A merchant from the central districts, most likely.

Under any other circumstance, Edam would have sneered and stomped away from the man. Father claimed the merchants were at the heart of every problem the land faced and Edam had never seen any evidence to the contrary. But today wasn't a normal day. He wouldn't be dragging his feet on the way to school this morning, wondering if he would get recruited for the war. He wouldn't be napping during class and trying to sneak a kiss from Marta on the way home. And under the cold light of the tonight's moon, he couldn't summon the vitriol he normally reserved for rich merchants.

Edam nodded at the merchant's suggestion and sat up. The second person beside him was a girl a few years older than him. She shared the merchant's round face and expensive taste in nightgowns, so he assumed she was his daughter. Her eyes were bloodshot and her cheeks tear-stained, but she kept close to her father.

Edam almost punched her right in the nose.

It wasn't fair that she had her father at her side. Not after all the suffering the merchants had caused.

He drove his fist into the ground instead and pushed himself to his feet. He jumped around a few times, surprised how good he felt after being forcefully transported from the street outside his home to, well, wherever this was. The ankle that had bothered him the last two days felt as good as new.

After warming his body, he took stock of his surroundings. The impression he'd gotten from the air was only strengthened now that he was on the ground. Grasses stretched for miles in every direction, for as far as the eye could see. It was as if he was on the wall of the city looking out at the sea, but instead of white-capped waves, all he saw was heads of grass.

He and the merchants weren't alone. Other citizens stood and sat in the grass, their empty gazes reflecting Edam's hollowness. Some stumbled around as if drunk, but no one moved with purpose. It had been stripped from them with all their possessions.

"What happened?" he asked the merchant.

"No one knows. The story is the same for everyone here. We were fast asleep, then woke up in the middle of the night, either on our roofs or in the street. We're all from different neighborhoods, but all were on fire when we woke. Then the dragons came, swept us up, and deposited us here."

Edam looked around again, this time taking the measure of those the dragons had saved from the fires. He saw merchants, elders, and children of various ages. One young man who had the arms and look of a blacksmith's apprentice stood next to a thin youth who kept squinting. He saw scribes, craftsmen, farmers, and weavers. Almost every occupation had its representative, except for one.

"Are there any guards?" Edam asked.

The merchant's eyes narrowed in thought. Then he, too, looked around. "You know, I don't think there are."

Edam resisted the temptation to ask why. The merchant wouldn't know any better than him.

There was a commotion as several of the survivors pointed to the sky. Edam twisted to follow the direction of their gaze and took a step back when he saw the shadows approaching. He clenched his fist and looked for something nearby to throw. He noticed he wasn't the only one.

Unfortunately, the empty fields lacked for decent artillery. Edam could do nothing but stand his ground as the dragons approached like a plague of enormous locusts. He let his eye drift across the sky as he attempted to guess their number. He'd rarely seen more than one or two at a time before, and he'd never guessed there were so many in total. There were hundreds, at least.

They landed by the dozen, depositing one or two people at a time, then taking off again. The scene Edam had just lived through repeated for hundreds of new arrivals. Edam searched the fields for the familiar uniforms of the city guards or the Lord's army, but there wasn't one to be found.

He wandered with no particular purpose, listening to the story repeat. Every survivor had been asleep in their bed. They'd woken up to flames and an unexpected flight.

Edam looked at the sky. He'd watched the dragons burn his home with his own eyes, so why go to all this trouble to save so many?

No explanations made sense, but the ones that came closest dealt with the Debru. The war had stretched on for years, but the latest news from the front was that they had almost won the final battle, the one that would drive the Debru from their world for good. Had the dragons decided their human allies were no longer necessary?

Edam shook his head. The story didn't add up.

The earlier arrivals tended to the new arrivals, but it wasn't long before fingers once again pointed to the sky. Another flight of dragons, smaller than the last, deposited a group of survivors and took off once again. Edam guessed there were several hundred survivors milling about. No one had tried to take command of the situation, but Edam wasn't sure what there was to take command of. Before they'd faced a death in the flames. Starvation was a much slower demise.

As the flight of dragons left, sharp eyes caught sight of an enormous shadow approaching. All dragons were large, but the one that neared was at least twice the size of the others.

Edam had never seen its like. From the way those around him retreated one unconscious step at a time, he wasn't alone.

It landed before them. Though it stood nearly a hundred feet from the closest citizen, it towered over the humans. It stood on its powerful legs, but it raised its head until it touched the sky.

Edam was certain it was about to speak, though before tonight he would have sworn such a feat was impossible. It stood like a speaker about to address a crowd, but all it did was roar into the sky. The sound vibrated Edam's bones and crushed the air from his lungs. He felt compelled to take a knee, but he refused the command, if it even was one. Many around him did, though.

When the roar ended, the world was perfectly silent. Growing up in the city, there was always noise. Even at night, the drunks staggered home as the night watch patrolled dark alleys. Once Edam's ears stopped ringing, he was certain he would hear a whisper from the other side of the crowd.

A wave of–something–passed over him. He couldn't name it, as he'd never felt it before. It was like a gust of wind, except it had a weight, a presence he couldn't explain. After the wave passed, he understood the world in a new way. When he looked at his new neighbors, he saw strands of light flowing between them and the world. They were all connected, though they'd never realized it before. Many others joined him in studying the intricate web of light that danced beneath their feet.

Tears fell down his face for the second time that night. It was beautiful, made even more so because he understood how fleeting it would be. The elder dragon spread its wings and took to the sky, turning away from them like a disappointed father leaving home for good.

The sight left a bitter taste on his tongue.

They'd been betrayed.

The elder didn't see it that way, of course, but did a betrayer ever? Edam knew it wouldn't matter, but he swore to himself that he would never trust a dragon again.

The dragon sped away, gathering speed as it flew. Edam snarled and spit at the ground, cursing his feeble body. Had he the strength, he would bring the elder down with his bare hands and make it answer for its crimes.

It disappeared into the darkness, and Edam cursed it again.

Already, he began to forget. The flaming city was the first to vanish from his memories, swept away like dust before a broom. Others soon followed. Eating meals with his mother and father. Going to school and learning about the history of his land. Playing with friends on crowded streets.

Some remained. Father had taught him how to start a fire, and that lesson lingered even as Father vanished. Mother had taught him how to cook, and her methods and recipes stuck firmly to his rapidly emptying memory.

New knowledge and skills leaped to replace those lost. He learned how to hunt and forage. He could identify which plants were safe to eat and which helped wounds heal faster. It was as if he'd grown up learning the information, as though it had been locked in a vault deep within his mind. The knowledge had just been waiting for a key.

Nothing else rushed in to fill the void left by his memories. Whenever his thoughts turned toward the past, they were gently turned away. What had come before tonight didn't matter.

The first rays of the morning sun rose in the east, shading the horizon with deep hues of purple and pink. Many of those around Edam were gathering into groups, and he did the same. He joined with the man and the girl that had first welcomed him to his new home.

Together with his new family and hundreds of others, they walked toward the sunrise, eager to begin their new lives.

Elian imagined the large tree as a Belog and launched a punch at it. Adani sped through his limbs in an endless loop, racing like a waterfall that had no end. He stopped his punch a hair's width away from the trunk and growled. Practicing against trees did nothing to calm the turbulent storm raging in his chest. He growled again and snapped a kick at the trunk. Like his punch, he pulled it before striking the bark.

The gathering grounds of the Hawks was sacred ground, and he wouldn't defile it with his frustration. The trees had done no wrong and deserved none of his ire.

He took a step back and clenched his fists. Last night he'd asked Harald for permission to join one of the patrols the Hawks sent out beyond the borders of the gathering grounds. Harald had finished chewing the stew in his mouth and pretended to consider the question before denying Elian's request. He'd said something about Elian needing to be present for the daily council meetings, but Elian hadn't listened to anything that came after the "no."

Elian grimaced at the memory. He'd stomped away from the fire soon after and no one had followed him.

He looked around the small clearing he had claimed as his own, seeking something he could hit. Unfortunately, the gathering grounds provided few options. Majestic oaks, wide enough to carve a room into, surrounded him. They'd been old when his father had been a child, and Elian couldn't bring himself to unleash his frustration upon them as he had the younger trees in the grove outside the village when he was younger.

In his mind's eye he saw the smoke and the dust clearing after the battle with the Belog. Harald was on his knees, bloody and broken, his right arm sheared clean off just below the shoulder.

He cried out but choked the sound off lest someone hear. He swung a fist wildly as tears gathered at the corners of his eyes. Another punch followed and then another. There was nothing to hit, but Elian fought as though he was surrounded by enemies.

The moment passed and the tears faded from his eyes. His legs felt as though someone had come in the night and stolen the bones from them. He leaned against a tree and wiped his eyes dry.

He forced himself to repeat one of the forms Alec had taught him as he'd started his journey with the Bears. The movements were simple because they were meant to focus adani more than strength. The goal was to move through the routine with speed and balance. He'd found the routine a foolish waste of time at first, but now that he understood his gift better, the point of the task made more sense.

Elian breathed in deep, feeling the adani flood into his body with the inhale. Following Loken's advice, he gently directed the adani into his limbs and sealed it into a loop. He punched the air and rejoiced in the speed of his fist. Adani moved down into his torso as he twisted and prepared his kick. It passed through his torso and dropped into his leg as he delivered the kick, his foot snapping through the air.

Adani remained in his legs as he found the next position. He planted his feet, squatted down, and leaped into the air. The jump took him to the lowest limbs of the enormous oaks. He resisted the temptation to grasp the limbs and he dropped to the ground. His powerful legs absorbed the landing with ease, and as he stood, he directed the adani back into his arms for a series of punches.

His troubles fell away as the routine consumed his attention. Matching the flow of adani to his body's needs required his complete focus today, but Alec assured him that if he trained long enough, most of it would become second nature.

The crack of a twig on the path leading to his clearing pulled him out of his moving meditation. He stood up straight, released adani, and wiped the sweat from his brow. Most everyone here moved like a ghost, so his visitor had wanted him to know he wasn't alone. He turned to see Harald standing at the edge of the clearing. Tera hid in the shade half a dozen paces behind the giant warrior, the shadow that never left his side.

Elian's eyes were drawn, as they were every day, to the stump where Harald's right arm had used to be. Loken and Brittany had worked together to save his life, and the stump had healed well under their careful ministrations. Adani couldn't bring the limb back, but it could give Harald another chance at life.

Elian's stomach twisted at the sight, but he forced himself not to avert his gaze. That missing arm was his fault. He didn't have the right to look away.

Harald saw the direction of his gaze. "It's feeling much better," he said.

Elian looked down at his feet as shame flushed his cheeks.

Harald waited for a response, but when none was forthcoming, he said, "I was able to sense some of your training. Saw some of it, too. You've improved considerably in the last few days."

Elian kept his gaze firmly fixed on his feet, hoping Harald would believe he found few things more interesting than the gathering ground's dark soil. "It's still not enough."

Harald glanced back at Tera, as though pleading for help. Tera remained still and expressionless and Harald sighed. Elian hoped Harald would simply turn around and leave him alone. As Harald's new second, he already spent too much time around the leader, reminding him of his failure. Surely the giant understood Elian's suffering.

Instead of retreating, Harald stepped into the clearing and took a seat on a limb that looked like it had come down in a storm. His weight settled heavily on the thick branch, but thankfully it didn't snap. "We need to talk, Elian."

"What about?"

"You."

Once again, Harald waited for a response. When he understood Elian wasn't going to give him one, he scratched at his beard with his left hand. "You seemed eager and prepared to accept the mantle of second when I gave it to you after the battle, but since then you've done nothing except hide in this clearing and train. You've been present in the council meetings, but your voice goes unheard. Do you no longer wish to be my second?"

"I don't deserve to be your second."

"You agreed with my reasoning when we first spoke about it. What's changed?"

Elian swallowed hard. Both he and Samora had always considered Harald an incredible leader, not just because of his control of adani and prowess in battle, but because of his ability to both understand and inspire those who followed him. Surely Harald understood Elian's heart. But if he was going to make Elian say it out loud, so be it. "You lost your arm because of me. Because of my weakness and my foolishness. Whatever good I've accomplished pales in comparison to the harm I've wrought."

Harald chewed on his lower lip as he thought. "You truly believe that, don't you?"

"It's not hard to believe that which is true."

Harald stood up. "Then come with me."

Arguing would do him no good, so Elian obeyed. Harald set a

brisk pace along the thin path that led away from Elian's clearing. Elian trotted behind, followed by Tera.

He studied Harald's massive back as they walked. Even with the loss of his arm, Harald's sheer size was intimidating. He still controlled more adani than half a dozen average adanists. Underestimating him in a battle remained a quick shortcut to an early death.

All that had remained the same about Harald, but there was also no denying the changes that had come over him since the battle a week ago. Before, he'd always been ready with a quick smile and a hearty laugh. He smiled less now, and when he did it was with tight lips. His laugh had all but disappeared from their evening meals, leaving a silence none of the Bears or Hawks knew how to fill.

All because Elian was a fool who'd thought he was a hero.

Harald led them out of the trees and into the thick grass that denoted the beginning of the edge of the gathering grounds. He didn't slow but continued in a straight line toward the boundary. All Bears and Hawks had been prohibited from leaving the grounds unless they were part of a patrol, but Harald stepped over the boundary and into the deadlands without pausing.

Elian hid a grimace as he followed Harald without question. His body had gotten used to the steady flow of adani from the gathering grounds over the last two weeks. Leaving it behind made him feel like a shell of a man.

Harald came to a sudden stop and spun on his heel, so he faced Elian. "Why are you responsible for the loss of my arm?"

"If I hadn't been consumed by the Belog's shadow, you would have had more strength to fight the Belog. When I was possessed, you showed me mercy, even though it cost you."

"Did you cut off my arm?" Harald asked.

"No."

"Did you force yourself into the battle against my wishes?"

"No, but—"

"When you escaped the power of the shadow, did you run and hide? Did you leave me behind to fend for myself?"

"No." Elian understood Harald's points well enough, but no argument would convince him Harald wouldn't have been better off with Elian absent from the battle.

Harald didn't pause in his assault. "And what do you mourn? It's true that I can no longer fight in battle the same way that I once did. I doubt I'll ever attain the same coordination with my left hand that I had with my right, but what does that matter?"

He waited, and Elian knew he wouldn't be able to avoid answering. "It matters because you can't use a bound spear or sword in your right hand."

"True enough, but a warrior isn't defined solely by what weapons they possess. A true warrior's legend is created when others witness what they're capable of despite their limitations."

"You told me you wanted me to be your second because you couldn't fight the way that you once had."

"And that's true. A leader needs to be up front in the thick of the battle, and that's no longer where I'll be most useful. I can't inspire by dropping adani on enemies from a distance, but you've shown me you can take my place. In time, I believe you'll even surpass me."

The knot in Elian's stomach had grown tighter and tighter as Harald spoke. It finally snapped, igniting a fire that burned hot enough to burn all the oaks in the gathering ground to ash. Before, he would have fought to control it, but he was no longer sure he could. "Don't you hate me for what I've done to you? You've lost everything because of me!"

"I've lost nothing because of you," Harald said. He didn't raise his voice, and his calm only stoked the flames in Elian's chest.

Elian's jaw worked, but no words could escape his constricted throat. How could Harald be so blind? It was as though Elian had taken his sight and reason along with his arm.

"A warrior grows old, Elian. They adapt or they die. My days on the front lines were numbered whether or not this battle happened as it did. When we get too attached to our abilities, we lose our chance to grow."

Elian's hands opened and closed into fists.

The corner of Harald's mouth turned up into a smile. "I didn't think words would convince you, which was why I brought you out here. You've always required a more—forceful approach. I didn't want our discussion to do any harm to the gathering ground."

Harald spread his legs, digging his feet into the loose soil of the deadlands. He lifted his left arm and took a fighting stance. "If you can defeat me, I'll let you choose your path. Otherwise, you'll be my second, not just in name, but in truth. Are we agreed?"

When Elian hesitated, Harald said. "You believe you've taken something from me. I'm telling you that you haven't. There's an easy way to discover the truth of the matter. If you win, then you're right. But if you lose, you need to understand you've taken nothing and that your moping has been childish."

Elian attacked before he realized he'd made the decision. He lacked the focus his training had achieved in the clearing earlier that day, but adani responded naturally to his commands. It looped within his body, which was still full after the long days of rest in the gathering grounds.

He punched at Harald's face, expecting that he'd end the fight in one blow. Harald bound a shield and blocked Elian's punch. Fist met adani, and for a moment, Elian wasn't sure who would triumph.

Harald's shield held and kept Elian a short distance away. A hammer appeared in Harald's left hand, and he swung the weapon at Elian's chest.

Had the blow connected, Elian feared his chest would have been turned into soup, but Harald was slow with his left hand,

and the hammer had never been his weapon. Elian took a few quick steps back and evaded easily.

Harald was undeterred. He let the momentum of his swing twirl him around, and Elian realized Harald had never expected to connect. He cursed as Harald's spin picked up speed, the hammer at the end of a long arm. He looped more adani into his legs and shifted right.

Harald released as the hammer came around. His timing with his left hand was a little off, but with a brief nudge of adani he corrected the hammer's angle. It sped toward Elian's chest.

More by instinct than by choice, Elian looped all his adani into his right arm and swung at the hammer. He knocked it from its path as he slid to the side. It brushed across his shoulder and flew toward the gathering ground. Elian tried to catch it, but he was too slow.

He needn't have worried. Harald unraveled the hammer's weave even as he formed another in his left hand. He ran forward, reminding Elian of a bear rearing to attack.

Elian stumbled a few paces back before he found his balance. The fire in his chest had settled from a raging inferno to hot coals, burning as though banked by a smith prepared to forge a new sword. He lashed out at Harald's side with his foot.

Harald's shoulder moved as he instinctively tried to deflect the kick with an arm he no longer possessed. Elian's kick struck true, and Harald went flying to the side. The giant's enormous body skipped once across the sand before he rolled to his feet, a wide grin on his face.

Harald threw the hammer, but Elian slapped it away. The impact sent vibrations from his hand all the way to his elbow.

Harald charged again, this time with a staff in hand. Elian backed up a pace. Harald was an incredible spear fighter, so the staff would be comfortable in his hand. Sure enough, Harald stabbed out when he came close. Elian stepped out of the staff's path and Harald responded by snapping the staff at him. Elian blocked the blow with his forearm, but his arm went numb.

He answered with a fist, driving it hard into Harald's stomach. It landed solidly, but Harald braced himself and kept his feet. Harald twisted. Elian prepared for him to whip the staff at him again, so he wasn't prepared when Harald's foot came up and caught him in the side.

He skipped across the loose soil twice before finding his feet. He looked up in time to see a storm of staffs soaring through the air and dropping toward him. They landed with bone-crushing force. Elian endured the blows with crossed arms. As soon as the last one struck, Harald charged yet again. The enormous man's fist caught Elian in the stomach and lifted him off his feet. Elian coughed but couldn't find his breath. He collapsed to the ground on his knees as he wrapped his arms around his battered torso.

The fire in his chest burned still, but not because of Harald.

Why was he always such a fool? He'd allowed himself to wallow in self-pity and act like a child. Harald had lost an arm, but at least he hadn't lost his wits.

Once he recovered his breath, he said, "Now I'm not so sure I deserve to be your second after how I've acted."

Harald's smile reminded Elian of the larger-than-life leader he'd first met. He'd lifted his shirt and was examining the bruises forming across his torso.

A familiar pang of regret bloomed, tightening Elian's throat. He didn't doubt, after that display, that Harald would find a way forward. But the man had been born to fight. There was no doubting that.

Harald let his shirt drop. "We all make mistakes, but it takes courage to admit as much. I want you as my second. I need you. Will you?"

Elian swallowed the stone in his throat that prevented him from answering. "I will."

2

Samora wandered through a world of beauty she hardly understood. Webs of adani carried fragments of her spirit farther than she'd ever walked, farther than she'd ever dreamed of walking. The strength contained within the newly born gathering ground propelled her to places forgotten for generations.

As she often did, she followed the tangled web through the deadlands to Elian. A week ago, she'd checked on him and the Debru had been preparing for an attack with two of their Belogs. Now the Belogs and the Debru were gone, but Elian remained. The knowledge unleashed a storm of emotions she barely succeeded in containing. She should have been by his side, but she was proud of what he'd achieved.

Today, as had been true for the last several days, she found him in the gathering ground that Karla told her had belonged to the Hawks. Harald and his small party had found both the lost clan and their ancestral homeland.

She lingered longer than was necessary on Elian. As usual, he trained by himself. She felt the flow of his adani, rushing through his limbs like a river threatening to overflow its banks in the spring. It was such a change from the sense of him she was familiar with. She tried to imagine how the shift had come about, but every imagining made her heart ache.

She should have been by his side.

His improvement was necessary, though. They'd need that strength, and sooner than most expected. She was tempted to stay and observe. Sensing Elian with adani wasn't the same as fighting next to him, but it was the closest she could come, at least for a while. She longed for his steady presence and constant attention. Being around him was easy, and at the moment, she'd give nearly anything for something to be easy in her life.

She pushed aside the dream and turned away from her brother. Her adani received a small boost from the distant gathering ground, allowing her to push her spirit just a little farther than it would otherwise go. It didn't take long to reach the true reason for today's search.

The Debru circle had grown considerably since yesterday. At this distance, she had no way of knowing how close it was to completion, but she feared the day grew near. The circle along the western frontier had already stopped growing, an ominous detail Samora fretted over whenever she wasn't worrying about Elian. She feared the one on the frontier was ready. The one closest to Elian wasn't far behind.

The more she surrounded herself with adani, the more sensitive she felt to the subtle changes in its ebbs and flows. The Debru circles pulled adani towards them, changing it to something darker, something foreign to this world. Beyond that pull, though, she felt a more subtle flow directing her toward the circle on the frontier.

Samora wasn't convinced that adani had a will of its own, but she believed it obeyed an order, a pattern embedded in the world itself. Her neighbors might call it fate, but that seemed too simple a term. All she understood was that trusting it served her well, even though now it wanted her in the one place she longed never to return to.

Samora let adani return to her. She lingered in the trance for a few moments longer. Here the world made sense. The terrors that haunted her waking hours shrank from her presence. It was hard to let go, and getting harder every time, but eventually she did.

Returning to the world made Samora feel as though she had lopped off a limb. Even her mundane senses, such as sight and taste, were dulled by adani's departure. She opened her eyes and stretched her arms high overhead while her pupils adjusted to the light. The sun shone bright today, and her eyes watered as they adjusted. She wiped the tears away as she stood.

"You crying again?" Karla asked.

Samora fixed the older adanist with a glare, but she failed to put any emotion behind it. Since Karla had fought off two Belogs in Samora's defense, Samora figured she had earned a lifetime's worth of forgiveness for her sharp tongue. "Just blinded by the sun."

"Whatever you say," Karla said. The smile faded from her face. "Though, truth be told, I worry about you. I'm not sure I've ever known anyone to spend so much time using their adani. I know you've got a gift, but I fear you're pushing too hard."

"Careful, Karla. You keep on like that and I might start to think you care about me."

A single sharp laugh echoed across the gathering ground. "Care about you? I'm only worried that the sharpest sword we can wield against the Debru is going to chip and break because it didn't know when to stay in its sheath."

"A sword's no good in its sheath," Samora argued.

Karla conceded the point as she rose from her seated position. She moved well, especially considering the number of years Samora knew she carried. Still, and Samora wasn't sure if it was just her imagination looking for something that may or may not be real, but she swore Karla didn't move as well as she had used to when they'd first met. All the best healers among the unified clans had checked on her after the battle, and all had claimed there was nothing wrong.

Samora wasn't so certain, even though Lenon told her she was making something out of nothing. Karla had channeled more adani than any living being in her desperate fight against the Belog. There had to be a cost.

"You've got that look again," Karla said, a hint of warning in her voice.

"I worry about you, you know, especially now."

"You've got much bigger problems to worry about, girl. And a handful of them are from your village. Don't you think it's about time we return? You can't sit out here and avoid them forever."

Karla referred to Gabe and Henk. Those two had been causing trouble, but Samora wasn't ready to think about them yet. She pushed them out of her mind, took a deep breath, and basked in the glory of the gathering ground.

It didn't yet possess the same majesty as the gathering grounds of the Wolves. Before it had been a gathering ground, it had been the site of one of the Debru's dark circles which had choked the life from the area. Trees had crumbled as if they were made of dust. The grass became brittle and frail. The infusion of previously trapped adani from Samora's healing had restored much of the life to the grass, and when Samora ran her fingers through it, it was now as soft and pliable as any bed.

The trees would take time to recover, though. Seeds that had been buried in the ground now sprouted into small saplings. Even with adani's help, it would be many years before the trees rivaled the ancient growth that dominated the heart of the Wolves' gathering ground. Samora could only begin the healing process. Time would be responsible for the rest.

Still, a sense of peace lingered over this place, made all the more potent because Samora remembered what it had been before. If it had been possible, she would live her entire life here, undisturbed by the events and suffering that plagued the world.

But if she did that, it wouldn't be long before the troubles visited her. One could only flee from conflict for so long. She took one last look around her little sanctuary and then nodded to Karla. "Let's do it, then."

———

THERE WAS little recognizable left of the village Samora had grown up in. It seemed impossible that so much change could overtake a place in so little time, but there was no denying the evidence before her eyes. The village she'd known was no more.

The most marked change was the sea of tents that now surrounded the village. Most bore the markings of the Hounds and the Wolves, but a decent number belonged to Bears. For the most part, the tents of each clan remained separate, but exceptions were numerous. After the battle with the Belogs, the councils of the unified clans had decided the village would serve well as a new location for a semi-permanent camp. The clans faced a host of difficult decisions, and the village offered a convenient location and plentiful supplies to aid in the discussion.

That decision meant that a fair number of the fields she had most frequently wandered growing up were now pathways between tents. Bare patches of ground had been cleared for the number of campfires each clan required. In time, the wandering clans would pick up their shelters and wander again, but for the moment, they looked more like an invading army, surrounding the land's worst-defended village.

Samora and Karla weaved their way through the tents to find their way to Henk's home, where they expected to find the elder waiting. The camp was full of life. Warriors and families moved in all directions. Some carried wood or a cooking pot filled with water from the nearby stream. Others carved up the meager fresh game the land provided. Still others mended clothes ripped and torn after too long on the trail.

One and all would pause briefly when they caught sight of the two women. At the very least, they'd nod their heads respectfully, but most dropped into a bow. It didn't matter which clan they passed; the response was the same.

Samora returned each bow in equal measure, too uncomfortable to do anything less. She'd told the story of turning the Debru circle into a gathering ground more times than she could count. Some days it felt like she'd done so at every campfire and in every conversation since the battle.

Some part of her recognized the enormity of what she'd done. It was the first time someone had dealt a meaningful blow to the Debru since the legends of old. Had it been anyone else, she would be bowing, too. But it didn't feel right when it was her. She'd done nothing more than try to save her village. She was more lucky than heroic.

Karla, on the other hand, deserved every bit of praise she received. Few adanists could stand against a single Belog alone, and no one had faced two and lived to tell the tale. If not for Karla, they'd all be dead.

As they made their way through the camp, Samora found it helpful to believe the warriors were bowing only to Karla, and that she was simply in their way. It was false, but it kept her cheeks from bursting into flame from the embarrassment.

Her discomfort took on a new shape as they passed from the tents to the permanent buildings of the village. Samora had only been gone for a matter of weeks, but the buildings looked as though they had aged years in her absence. Children and adults alike were thin and haggard, and Samora's sharp eye detailed all the small repairs that needed doing. The people and buildings might have been the same as those she left, but they'd been changed by their trial as surely as she'd grown in her time with the Bears.

They didn't make it to Henk's house, because he found them first, Gabe following close on his heels like a hungry pup. Samora cursed silently and forced her hands to relax. It wasn't Henk's fault that the village had endured the suffering it did, but he had been the one the orders had come through.

She reminded herself that if it had been Elian corrupted by shadow, she would have been more forgiving. It almost worked.

Henk's eyes narrowed when he spotted her. He strode directly toward her, almost knocking a passing woman off her feet. "Samora, thank goodness you're here!"

When she had first returned to town, Henk had hidden himself from her. Now, he ran toward her every chance he got. She'd almost preferred him when he was possessed by shadow.

She slipped into old habits, bowing toward him and not saying a word.

Henk almost put a hand on her arm but was stopped in his tracks by her glare. The deterrence only lasted a moment before he launched into his latest plea. "Samora, you need to speak to them on our behalf. They've become so vicious; they won't even let me sit at their meetings. Just now, Gabe and I requested another audience, and they demanded I return to the village. They even gave me an escort."

Samora fought the urge to roll her eyes. The battle was won, but barely.

Henk, of course, didn't notice, and took her silence as permission to continue. "They say they are going to stay for the foreseeable future, but they can't! It's a violation of all the agreements the clans have made." Henk pointed west, as though unsure Samora understood what he meant. "They're supposed to be out there, protecting us from the Debru. Not here, tempting the Debru toward us."

Karla interrupted Henk's monologue. "You'll agree these are extraordinary times. When the pacts were formed, no one anticipated the Debru advancing as far as they have."

"Which is even more reason for all of you to be out there!

How many thousands of acres are you surrendering because you're too scared to fight?"

Karla didn't move, and Samora was glad of that. If she did, Samora expected Henk would be visiting the healers to mend several broken bones.

Henk focused his gaze again on Samora. "You're the only one who can help us. I'm still not sure why, but they respect you. If you tell them they need to leave, then they'll leave. You're the one who can remind them of their pact: Food for protection, that was always the deal. If they stay here, we won't be able to grow our food and they won't be able to protect us. I don't know why I'm the only one who sees this."

Gabe chose that moment to become a part of the conversation. "I see it too, sir. And you're right. If there's anyone they'll trust, it's Samora. I've known her since we were both children, and she's always been the most responsible of her family."

Karla's hand on Samora's shoulder prevented her from unleashing the beating Gabe so richly deserved. When Karla spoke, her voice was colder than a winter's gale. "You two are in luck. We were coming to the council meeting today to express the same sentiments. We also believe the clans need to move again. So, rest assured, we'll present your case, even though you're wrong on one count. The Debru won't attack because the clans are here. They'll attack because humans live here, and they mean to see us all wiped out."

Henk shook his head so vigorously that it was as though he believed he could bend reality to his will. "I know that's what you Bears believe. But we've not seen that here. This village has only been attacked once before, and it was after their family moved in." Henk pointed to Samora.

Karla's hand clamped down tighter on Samora's shoulder, her grip so firm Samora winced. "We understand your concerns and we'll bring them to the council," she said.

Henk gave a satisfied smile. "See that you do. You can

convince them to leave. There may even be some extra food in your pack when you depart. It would be the least I could do for a friend."

Henk and Gabe turned as one and walked away, leaving Samora stewing in a pit of old but familiar emotions. If she left the village yesterday it wouldn't be soon enough.

Karla squeezed her shoulder once more before letting it go. "You good?"

Samora nodded.

"Good. Because you and I have a much bigger battle to fight against the councils. Let's get there before they start."

3

E lian stood with his feet shoulder-width apart in a small clearing within the Hawk's ancestral gathering ground. He had his eyes closed to help focus his attention on the adani looping through his limbs. It raced faster than he could follow, but there was no need. His only task was to shape the loop and allow adani to follow.

It wasn't surrender, exactly, but he was learning there was an ease to the process. When he tensed, either in body or mind, the speed of the adani slowed and his strikes weakened.

The sensations never failed to fascinate him. For years he had pushed and shoved adani around and called his minor triumphs success. After all this time, it was so much easier than he'd thought. All he had to do was let go.

Sometimes that sequence of thoughts led him down dark paths. How much more could he have accomplished if he'd learned earlier? How different might life have been?

But the question that haunted his nightmares reached even further back into his past. If he'd learned these skills early enough, would Father still be alive?

He knew that pondering such questions did him little good. The past was unchangeable, and what was done was done.

Easy enough to say, but impossible to accept.

His body slid into motion. He'd practiced Master Heinrick's forms so often they barely required thought. He cut, parried, stabbed, and evaded, flowing from one movement to the next with a speed he doubted even Harald could follow. The sword in his hand felt like an extension of his body.

He stopped when he heard familiar footsteps softly approaching. He sheathed the blade, opened his eyes, and smiled, because it was always a treat to speak with Capricia.

She stopped at the edge of the clearing and offered a quick bow. He understood his position as Harald's second merited the respect, but after what the two of them had endured together, there was no need for the formality.

"You never need to bow to me," he said.

"You're the Bears' second. Battles have been fought over less disrespect."

He took a few steps toward her, wishing she would have entered the clearing. "*You* never need to bow to me. If not for you, I wouldn't have survived that scouting expedition. When you bow, it makes it feel like we aren't friends."

Emotions passed quickly over her face, but they were too quick for him to decipher. He didn't understand Capricia as well as he did Samora. Yet. Someday he hoped it would be different.

"Is that what we are?" she asked.

There was an edge to the question Elian hadn't expected. Instinctively, he'd almost said yes, but her tone brought him up short.

"At the very least," he said.

It wasn't the most truthful answer he could have given, but it was close. She cocked her head slightly to the side, studying him as though she was a hawk and he a field mouse. The moment passed before long, and she straightened. A coy smile played across her lips. "I'll try to remember not to bow to you, then. But I'm here on behalf of Kati. She and Harald are meeting with their councils, and your presence is required."

Elian's heart sank a bit at the news. Not because of the councils. Those had been nearly daily occurrences since the battle. Because the only reason Capricia had come was because Kati had told her to.

There was little point in moping about. The sooner he arrived at the council meeting, the sooner it would end, and he could return to his training. He felt as though his journey thus far had brought him to the entrance of an undiscovered cave. He stood only at the entrance, unsure of how deep this new way of knowing went. All he was certain about was that he could spend the rest of his life exploring the depths of adani.

Harald had extracted a stronger promise from him, though, so Elian stood to follow Capricia. He looked once around his clearing and wished, not for the first time, that Samora was near. She was smarter than him and faster to understand everything about adani. If she was here, he was certain that his own progress would be twice as rapid.

"Where were you just then?" Capricia asked.

He liked that about her. She wasn't as sensitive to his moods and thoughts as Samora was, but she was more aware than most and was kind enough to ask if he was well.

"I was wishing that my sister was here." He gestured to the enormous trees that surrounded them. "If I encounter a problem on my journey, like this forest, my answer is to grab an ax and start chopping a path straight through. My sister would find a small game trail and reach the other side long before me."

"She seems like someone I would like," Capricia said.

"The two of you would get along well, I think. Hopefully you'll have the chance to meet her soon."

Capricia didn't take offense at the suggestion, which Elian

took as a good sign. He couldn't say for sure what she thought of him, but at least she wasn't running away.

Capricia brought them farther north than the usual clearing where council meetings were held. The trees were much thicker here, the canopy letting little light through even though it was the middle of the day.

"Where are you taking me?" Elian asked.

"Where Kati told me to," Capricia answered. She came to a stop and pointed ahead. "This is as far as I take you. Follow the path for another hundred paces or so and you'll come upon a small clearing. Everyone else should already be there."

Elian frowned as he heard a hint of jealousy in her voice that, combined with the fact that she wasn't allowed to proceed, meant this council meeting wouldn't be like the others. Most were held in a large clearing close to the center of the gathering ground, near where the Hawks had set up their camp. It was a space with plenty of fallen logs and a handful of stumps that provided ample seating. It was also open enough to accommodate all those in both clans interested in listening.

This place, Elian surmised, was considerably more private.

He offered Capricia a short bow in thanks for her service, and the way the corner of her mouth turned up in a smile reminded him of his instructions to her earlier. With his elevated status, he no longer needed to bow to her, but he'd spent so much of his life bowing to everyone, the habit was hard to break.

He stood there looking like a fool for a long moment, and she said, "You best be going."

"Right," he said as he bowed again. Then he grimaced as he realized what he had done. He shook his head, started to apologize, then thought better of it. He summoned what meager scraps of dignity he still possessed and hurried forward. Capricia turned her back to him to stand guard on the path.

Whatever was happening, Harald and Kati really weren't interested in making this a public affair.

Elian reached a small clearing and slowed to a stop. Most council meetings involved no fewer than a dozen participants; this one only had four. Kati and Loken sat next to one another in the grass. Harald and Tera sat across from them. Harald gestured for Elian to sit beside him. Elian did, but his mind still raced.

He, Harald, and Tera represented almost half the Bears' fighting strength in this area. They were outnumbered by the Hawks by more than ten to one, and yet in this small council, they had the advantage of numbers.

This might be the first council more interesting than his training.

Harald was about to start the council, but Kati spoke before he formed his first word. "Thank you for joining us, Elian. You're here today as Harald's second, and there are weighty matters for us to discuss."

Elian frowned even as he nodded. Of course he was here as Harald's second. That was the only reason he was invited to any council. Why would she feel the need to remind him?

His best guess was that she wanted to ensure he'd stay focused. He'd made no secret in the past of his lack of patience for the endless debate, and his mind often wandered back to training. Harald had lectured him on it, too.

Kati said, "The reason we're gathering as a small council is to speak about the proposal Harald has brought forth. He's spoken of it at times in the large council meetings, but it's never been considered seriously. In our more private moments, he's confessed that he feels strongly about the issue, but I thought it best to discuss it here, first. There's much at stake. Harald?"

Harald nodded. "I believe the Hawks and the Bears should unify under the Bear banner."

Loken's eyebrow rose at the proposal. Elian wished he understood the healer better. He'd unlocked many of Elian's new abilities in only a brief time, but he kept himself almost as closed off as Samora.

Harald continued. "My reasons are simple. The Hawks have fought well these past few months, but the fight has claimed too many lives. You're on the brink of collapse, and I would hate to see the clan decline further. Kati and I could be bonded, and the clans made one. The Bears could use the fresh blood, too."

Loken looked like he'd been made to swallow something sour. "You would strip away our pride?"

"That's not my intent. The Hawks deserve all the honor and praise the clans can offer, but there is no honor in dying alone. It is to the benefit of both clans."

"What do you think of this?" Loken asked Kati.

"I can understand Harald's reasoning, and the selfish part of my heart desires the union. But I do not know how to ask my people to give up their history and their pride."

Elian couldn't remain silent any longer. "What are you saying? That you would rather die than fight under a different name? That's foolish!"

Harald cut him off with a sharp gesture. "You grew up in the villages, so you wouldn't understand the pride the clan adanists carry within. Her point is a reasonable one."

"No, it's not. I might not understand the pride of a wandering clan, but I understand the value of a life. Who cares if one is a Hawk or a Bear, so long as they can bind a spear and kill the Debru? It is not our names that live on, but our deeds."

Elian expected a reprimand, but none came. Loken stared at his feet while Kati tapped her fingers against her knee. Harald and Tera shared a knowing look that Elian didn't think he was supposed to see.

"What?" he asked them.

Kati turned to Loken, who thought for a moment longer and then nodded. "It could work."

Elian looked between those who had gathered. He felt as though he was playing a part that he didn't understand. Beside him, Harald had a slight grin on his face and Tera seemed satisfied, which was as close to smiling as she ever came.

Before Elian was forced to ask again, Kati nodded to Harald. "Let's do it."

Harald, in turn, spoke to Elian. "Sorry to keep you in the dark like this, but the four of us have been attempting to solve a problem that has no easy answer. Kati and I agree that our clans need to unite, but there are many among the Hawks who will feel strongly about such a unification. Loken here was party to our discussion, but his complaints aren't much different from those we'd face among an open council. We're hoping to use you to argue our case before them, much as you just did."

"Why?"

"Because you're not one of us, but you're respected by all. Word of your deeds has spread, and no small number of adanists have seen you with the dragons. There will be those who believe that Kati and I argue out of self-interest. Our relationship has been no secret, and people have speculated about our possible bonding for longer than you've been alive. That, combined with clan pride, may make it difficult for others to accept our proposal. We hope you'll remind them all of what truly matters."

"You could just tell them this is what's necessary," Elian said. The set-up seemed too elaborate for a problem that seemed so simple.

"If we did, we'd spend more time fending off challenges to our leadership than we would actually leading," Kati said. "I agree your way would be easier, but I can't risk dividing the fighting spirit of my clan. Our enemy has to be the Debru and only the Debru."

"Will you do it?" Harald asked. "Will you let your frustration and rage shine before the large council like you did here? I know it goes against your nature, but we need your spirit now, more than ever."

Harald was right that the suggestion went against Elian's

nature. He'd spent most of his life striving to control his emotions. Excess feeling filled his limbs with adani and created even stronger feelings in response. It was only during the battle with the Belog that he accepted he might need to release his emotions. It seemed far easier to do so in the heat of battle than while sitting in front of a large council.

But if Harald believed it was needed, Elian would follow. The giant warrior hadn't led him astray yet. He nodded.

Harald grinned from ear to ear and pounded him on the back so hard Elian worried a lung was going to come out. "I'm glad to hear it," he said.

4

Karla straightened out the sheath on Samora's hip, then nodded her approval, ignoring Samora's obvious sighs of discomfort. Samora felt more as though she was being prepared for battle than a council meeting. She now wore two knives at her hips and carried a tall walking stick that could double as a staff.

"You're making me look ridiculous," Samora said.

"Only because you're used to wearing rags. Argue all you want, but now you look like you belong at a council. It may not matter to you, but it will lend your words an extra weight."

"You'd think saving them from a Debru circle and a pair of Belogs would carry enough."

"You would, but that isn't how this works. Have you practiced what you're going to say?"

"Yes, Mother."

Karla glared briefly, grunted, and took a step back, inspecting her work one last time. "Your rudeness aside, I would have been honored to have a daughter like you."

Samora looked up from her feet and met Karla's steady gaze. They locked eyes for a moment, then Samora offered a bow of her head. "I'll try not to let you down."

They walked beside one another as they passed through the last tents to the heart of the Hounds' camp. Stones from the fields had been arranged in a circle two paces across. The ground within had been cleared and filled with wood from the nearby grove. The flames already reached higher than Samora's head. The warmth wasn't needed today, but Tiafel argued that all important matters deserved a fire, and so a fire had been lit.

Karla and Samora weren't late, but most of the council had already arrived. Each of the three clan leaders had selected two members of their individual councils to serve as part of the unified council. Samora found the arrangement reasonable, but it had been the result of days of constant argument. Both the Hounds and Wolves believed they deserved more seats on the council than the much smaller Bears. Samora couldn't guess what Warran had done to keep the number of seats even, but the current agreement was more a tentative truce than a lasting pact.

The council voted on every meaningful decision, with a simple majority carrying the day. Unfortunately, because the members of the clans always voted together, the votes all ended up either being six against three or unanimous. Samora hoped for a unanimous judgment today, but she'd be fortunate if she found six votes in her favor.

Logs and stumps had been organized around the fire, but no one sat. The unspoken hope was that no unified council lasted so long the warriors felt the need to sit.

They passed through a light ring of guards, who mostly served to ensure no prying ears wandered too close to the conversation. The guards bowed and let them into the council without a word. When the councilors saw them, they bowed, too. Blood rushed to Samora's cheeks, but she kept her gaze high and returned the bows. They found an empty gap in the circle and took it.

Karla leaned close as the others returned to their conversations. "A few weeks ago, you'd have collapsed on your knees under the weight of so much attention."

"The day's still young. It might happen once the argument begins."

Two Wolves entered the ring from the west, deep in conversation. Warran was the last of the unified council to arrive. His eyes drooped and his step was slower than Samora was used to seeing. He'd been Harald's second before Elian because the two were close, and Warran's grasp of what the clan needed to survive day-to-day made up for Harald's weakness in the area. But Warran would be the first to admit he was eagerly awaiting Harald's return.

Tiafel, who served as the unofficial head of the unified council, started. "No point in circling around the problem. We need to plan, and we're running out of time to do so. Everyone has opinions, so let's hear them."

Lenon, the Hound's best healer, turned to Samora. "You've been casting out adani daily to keep track of Harald and the Hawks. Are they returning yet?"

Samora shook her head. "They've hardly left their gathering ground since the battle."

"Do you have any sense of when they're planning to return?"

She shook her head again. "All I can tell is where their adani is. Beyond that, I know nothing."

Lenon continued to press. "Is there anything holding them there?"

"As best as I can sense, no. Their battle eliminated most, if not all, of the Debru in the area. The Debru circle west of them has almost completed growing, though."

A handful of tense looks shot around the council at her mention of the circle. She thought she saw one of the Hounds roll her eyes, but she might have imagined it.

Lenon addressed the group. "Whatever we decide, it must be with the knowledge that Harald and the Hawks won't be a part of it."

Aldo, the leader of the Wolves, said, "I still believe we need to consider the possibility of making our new boundaries permanent. We were already stretched thin before this last invasion, and with Harald and the Hawks playing out west, I'm not sure we can maintain the old border."

Warran, thankfully, argued against Aldo's plan. "As annoying as I find Henk, he's got some good points. If we retreat all the way to this village, we'll be sacrificing a lot of farmlands. That makes me uneasy."

"I'd rather lose farmland than lives. Thanks to Samora, we have a gathering ground to fall back to here. It's the strongest position we have."

Samora listened as the argument went back and forth. It was the same argument they'd held at almost every council. The council argued about resources, strategy, and the terrain, but Samora heard a different argument, unspoken but truer. Many among the wandering clans wanted to stop wandering, while others remained true to the pact their ancestors had made.

The clans needed to resolve the argument, but not today.

Samora took a sudden step forward, interrupting the exchange between Aldo and Warran. All eyes turned to her as the leaders went quiet. Her knees quivered.

"We need to attack the Debru circle in the Crows' old territory," she said.

She didn't miss the looks that passed between the other council members. They weren't that different from the looks she and Karla had shared when speaking with Henk. They humored her, though, because of what she'd done for them.

"I believe that the circles are gates that will allow more Debru to come to our world. When I fought the last one, I sensed a Vada waiting on the other side. It won't matter where you set up your defenses if the Debru are allowed to pour in."

Aldo was quick to argue against her. "So you've said, but you've also claimed the circle on the frontier has been 'complete' for days now and nothing has come through. I agree we'll need to take action on the circle in time, but right now it hosts the largest concentration of Debru forces that we know of. I understand that you believe the circle is a gate, but I have yet to see the evidence that will make me risk my warriors."

Samora bared her teeth at Aldo. The Wolves' leader had yet to find a single cause worth risking his warriors over, and she began to wonder if he ever would. "If we don't attack, we risk allowing a Vada to enter our lands without opposition, with a large group of Debru nearby. What more reason could you need?"

Warran tried to act as a peacemaker. "I'm aware that Samora's claims are extraordinary, but she hasn't misled us yet. It's worth taking her seriously."

Aldo turned on Warran. "I am! I don't doubt that the girl has sensed something, nor do I doubt that the gate is a problem we'll need to face. But I'm not going to throw my adanists into a battle unless I'm sure we can win it with minimal casualties. Look around! These camps hold the majority of the adanists left on the front. If we fail, humanity falls. We can't simply launch this attack because she has a bad feeling."

Instead of arguing, Warran nodded.

Samora pressed her lips together so she wouldn't swear at the leaders. But she couldn't hold back everything that needed to be said. "You can't keep hoping for something to change. It may seem like wisdom to keep retreating, to sacrifice land to protect lives, but you're trading away any chance at victory for a slow death."

When Aldo looked up at her, his stare was flat and lifeless. Samora prepared another argument, but Karla gently nudged her arm and she fell silent.

"Thank you for your opinion. The council will take it under advisement. Is there anything else you haven't told us that would influence our debate?"

Samora gritted her teeth. They already knew about the gates and the Vada. She'd told them everything she thought would convince them to act. Only Karla's presence by her side prevented her from lashing out pointlessly. "No, sir."

Aldo nodded sharply. "Good. We'll be certain to inform you of our decision. Thank you for your time and advice."

Samora looked around the circle for an ally, but even Warran could do nothing but stare at his feet. She shook her head, then bowed deeply, holding the bow far longer than was necessary. Several of the leaders cleared their throats while others shifted from foot to foot. She continued to hold the bow for several long moments more, then straightened, turned on her heel, and left the council behind.

KARLA DIDN'T SPEAK until they were well away from the council circle. "What are you thinking?"

"They won't act. If we're going to destroy that circle, we'll need to do so alone. Can we?"

"Honestly? I'm not so certain. We were more than lucky when we took down the first circle. The Debru weren't guarding one approach and underestimated us terribly. They won't make the same mistake again. Your own searches have shown their preparation."

Samora was forced to agree. Adani reported that the Debru had completely encircled the new gate and the Belog roamed constantly around it. The behavior stood in stark contrast to what they'd observed beforehand, when the Debru were as good as dormant when not actively marching to a destination. "There has to be a way though, isn't there?"

"If there is, I haven't thought of it yet."

"I'll return to the gathering ground and examine the Debru circle thoroughly. There has to be something I missed."

Karla shook her head. "It's not a terrible idea, but it's not as if you haven't explored every step of grassland around that circle. We need a better plan, though I don't know what that is."

"Are you giving up?"

Karla didn't rise to the bait. "You know better."

Samora's cheeks flushed, and she looked down at the ground. "I'm sorry. I just can't believe that we're forced to sit here and wait for the Debru to make the next move."

They reached Samora's tent. Samora held the flap open and gestured for Karla to join her. "Want to discuss it?"

"Thanks, but no thanks. There's a young Wolf who desires a visit, and if there's not going to be any fighting, I know what I'd rather be doing."

Samora's eyes narrowed. "Not Aldo's son?"

Karla gave her a mischievous grin and a shrug before turning away and walking toward where the Wolves were camped. Samora watched her go, then ducked into the tent.

She sighed as she pulled off her boots. The sounds of the camp easily penetrated the thin hide of the tent, but they were muffled enough she could pretend she was alone. She lay down on her bed and stared up at the ceiling as though she'd written the answers to her questions there. A lone tear formed in her right eye, and she wiped it away. The clans were supposed to solve her village's problems. They were the wandering clans! How many nights had she and Elian listened to their mother recount legends of the traveling warriors?

She let her mind wander, hoping it would guide her somewhere productive. Unfortunately, it did little except run in circles, hopping from Elian to the gate, to her frustration at the unified clans. Eventually she sat up and stretched. Sitting here and moping did little good. Perhaps Mother would have some useful advice.

Samora stood, but as she was putting her feet back in her boots, she heard the sound of footsteps outside her tent. "Who's there?" she asked.

"Aldrick, ma'am. We met earlier. I'm a scout for the Wolves."

Samora vaguely remembered the man. He was the scout who'd first discovered Karla and Samora after their first battle with the Belog. He'd not cared for Karla, but that seemed an attitude most of the Wolves shared. Samora stepped out of the tent

Aldrick stood a head taller than Samora. His hair was cut close to the scalp, and though he looked to be about Samora's age, the scars across his body told of a much more violent history than Samora's. He was all muscle and sinew, but what struck her most was his gaze. It was open and honest, genuine in a way Samora, now used to dealing with the elders, hadn't seen in some time. "How can I help you, Aldrick?"

"Nothing you can do for me, ma'am. This is about how I can help you. Orders just came down from the council. You and Karla are both to have no fewer than two guards at all times. The council is concerned about your safety."

Samora arched an eyebrow. "Are they, now?"

Aldrick nodded, no trace of duplicity on his face. "Yes, ma'am. I got my orders straight from Aldo."

The scout looked around and frowned. "Is Karla around?"

Samora almost snorted at the trouble that was about to ensue. Aldo already detested Karla for enticing his firstborn. He couldn't have chosen a much worse time to attach a guard to her. Samora kept her face even and shook her head. "We went our separate ways after speaking to the council. I'm not sure where she wandered off to."

"What about you, ma'am? You look like you're about to go someplace."

"I was about to visit my mother."

"Then please allow me to accompany you. Another adanist will meet us soon."

Samora didn't see any point in arguing, especially with Aldrick. The poor scout was just following orders, and he seemed decent. "Of course."

He followed a few steps behind her as she left her tent. She tried to ignore his shadow but didn't have much success.

She silently cursed Aldo and the council. It wasn't enough for them to dismiss Samora's information and warnings. They also ensured she couldn't act on her own. A Vada approached, and she was nothing more than a captive of the clans.

5

"I'm still not sure why you think people will listen to me instead of you. You're *Harald*, and I'm just the strange adanist you've been watching for the last couple of months." Elian and Harald sat alone in the clearing he used for training, waiting a bit for everyone attending the council to settle before they made their appearance. Harald claimed they would gain more attention if they arrived last. Elian considered the late arrival rude, but he wasn't about to contradict the giant man in his dark mood.

Harald glanced up before turning his gaze back down and trying to cow the ground into submission with his glare. "It's not just about who you are, but who you aren't. We've discussed this."

"It seems foolish. They should be paying you far more respect than me."

"I agree. But some days, people make less sense than animals, so here we are. Are you ready?"

"I suppose. I'm still not convinced this is a great idea."

"We need to unify. If there was another way, I'd take it. I don't think it makes much more sense than you do, but what I think doesn't matter. I still haven't figured out how to bend reality to my will."

Harald stood and gestured for Elian to follow. "Come on. They should be prepared by now."

Elian stood, but before could follow Harald, he felt a tremor pass through the land. His heart skipped a beat. "Did you feel that?"

Harald nodded. "I've heard stories of quakes. They shake the land, but they only last a moment. They aren't worth worrying about."

His explanation didn't sound nearly as convincing as Elian wanted it to be. They stood still for a moment. Harald grinned nervously. "See? There was nothing to worry—"

A second quake struck, more powerful than the first. Elian shifted his feet wider to keep his balance. He shot a questioning glance at Harald. "You sure this isn't something to worry about?"

Harald wasn't paying him any attention. His gaze had gone distant, focused on nothing in particular. His jaw dropped open. He blinked and his gaze shifted to Elian. Before he could speak, terrified cries rose from the Hawks' camp. They turned in unison and sprinted through the trees.

They arrived to find a camp in chaos. Most Hawks had gathered in the large clearing that hosted the open councils, but now several ran in random directions. Elian saw wide eyes and slack jaws throughout the crowd. Two young men to his left had their knees tucked in tight to their chests, their arms wrapped around their legs as they rocked back and forth.

"Harald, what's happening?" Elian asked. A week ago he'd seen the Hawks boldly attack a Debru encampment guarded by two Belogs. They weren't the type to hide in closets or cower from a threat.

When Harald didn't immediately respond, Elian turned to look at him. The Hounds' leader had shut his jaw, but he breathed heavily through flared nostrils. Elian's blood slowly froze in his veins. They were sensing something through adani, something so terrifying it sent veterans running for a place to hide.

"Harald?"

The giant reached out and put his large left hand on Elian's shoulder. He didn't squeeze, as he was fond of doing. If anything, it felt more as though Harald was leaning on him. Fingers tightened on his shoulder, but not so hard that Elian felt the need to wince or squirm away. "Vada," Harald whispered.

Elian looked to the west. Most of the gathering ground stood between him and the distant circle, so he saw nothing.

He was frustrated that he couldn't sense what the others felt, but on the other hand, he was the only one with his head still firmly attached to his shoulders. He shifted his weight so he could look directly at Harald. "What do we need to do?"

Harald continued to stare west. His hand trembled on Elian's shoulder.

Elian reached up and slapped Harald across the face. The blow was hard enough to snap Harald's head back around. Harald glared at Elian, which was good enough for Elian's purposes. "Sir. What do we need to do?"

Harald looked around, but this time he looked for something specific. "We need to find Kati. If it were up to me alone, I'd run, but this is her gathering ground. Have you seen her?"

Elian looked left and right, but she wasn't anywhere in the circle. He shook his head.

"Where's Kati?" Harald bellowed.

Most adanists were too consumed by their own fears to notice Harald, but at least two heard and answered. They both pointed west. Harald bolted back through the trees with the grace of a deer. Elian cycled adani through his limbs and followed.

They passed through the whole of the gathering ground and emerged in the meadows that formed the western boundary. Kati stood there alone, staring west. Harald and Elian stopped beside her.

The western sky had darkened, but in no way Elian had seen before. The darkness was contained, no more than a mile in diameter, but it was absolute, as though a giant hand had come and pulled all the light from the air. As Elian watched, a ripple in the air passed across the deadlands, disturbing the loose soil as it passed. It struck the boundary of the gathering grounds and continued without pause, blowing the grass as though in the midst of a powerful storm. The ripple passed over them, freezing both muscle and spirit. Elian wrapped his arms around his chest to warm up, but it did little to help.

Kati gritted her teeth. "Just when we did something worthwhile, too."

"What are you thinking?" Harald asked.

Kati didn't answer for a long while. Elian was about to repeat the question when Kati blew out a long breath. "I don't see how we have any choice. We'll need to retreat."

"That's weeks across the deadlands, pursued by that thing," Harald said. He squinted as he focused his attention west. "And it's brought friends, too. A lot of them."

"You think it's a poor decision?"

Harald shook his head. "There are no good decisions. The way I see it, we're already dead. So long as we're here, we can at least hurt them. Once we enter the deadlands we won't even be able to do that."

"I refuse to be the last of the Hawks," Kati said.

Harald's throat bobbed as he swallowed hard, but he said nothing.

Kati wrestled with the decision, then swore again. "It might not pursue us."

Harald grunted. "It's already approaching."

Kati closed her eyes. When she sensed the same, she grabbed onto Harald for support. She faltered for a moment, and it looked like she might cry. She steadied herself with a deep breath and straightened her spine. "Then a fight it is."

She leaned close to Harald and held onto his arm. Elian looked away, feeling as though he was intruding on a private moment.

He almost jumped when Harald spoke to him. "You could try running. I don't know what the Vada knows about what happened here, but you might be able to escape. It might not notice you."

"I'm not leaving you to die," Elian snapped.

"There's no shame in it. If I could run, I would. It's not as though your presence is going to change the course of the battle, and you're one of the only adanists they don't notice. Any Debru that knows better is dead," Harald said.

Elian's angry retort caught in his throat as he heard Harald call him an adanist. It was a small detail, but it was a title he'd worked for his whole life. Unfortunately, granting him the title probably had the opposite effect than Harald intended. He checked his surroundings for inspiration, but the gathering grounds stood as still and silent as always.

"There's no way for us to defeat them?" Elian asked.

"There might be a way, but the Vada's strength is far beyond my own. Right now, it feels far stronger than a Belog, and it's still miles away. I could hit it with the most powerful spear I have, and I don't think it would even annoy the beast," Harald said.

"How did our ancestors beat them?" Elian had heard plenty of stories, but now that he was thinking about them, he realized how light on useful details they were. Perhaps Harald and Kati had listened to a more helpful retelling.

Kati's answer was sharp enough to cut flesh. "Ask a dozen adanists and get a dozen answers. Some say adanists used to be stronger generations ago. Others believe it wasn't that they were stronger, but that they had a better grasp of adani than we do. The short answer is that we don't know."

"We need to arrange the defenses. Both Hawk and Bear are close to bolting if we don't organize them soon," Harald said.

The pair of leaders turned back to the east, but Elian didn't follow them. Harald shot Elian a questioning glance.

"I'll stay here for a bit. I'm going to try something," Elian said.

"Nothing too foolish?"

"Time will tell, but I'll be careful."

Harald nodded and disappeared back into the woods with Kati. Elian made sure they were gone, then turned west. He wasn't ready to believe that all hope was lost. He knelt and placed both his hands in the grass of the gathering ground.

"I'd never hear the end of it if you were here," Elian said, thinking of Samora.

He closed his eyes and focused his attention on the adani flowing through his body. When he'd been carried by the dragons, he'd felt the way in which they'd connected. He hoped it wasn't much different than with the gathering ground. He shoved his adani deep into the ground.

It bounced back as though attached to a string. Elian grunted as the impact twisted his insides. His adani complained at its abuse, and he felt as though he was failing the most basic binding lessons he'd been taught back in the village.

He cleared his thoughts with a deep breath and prepared to try again. He knew better. Adani didn't like to be shoved or pushed around. It flowed, and true strength came from harnessing that flow instead of fighting against it.

Elian cycled some of his adani into the gathering ground, treating it no different than if it were another limb. The adani cycled smoothly so long as he didn't try to control it too much. He dripped more adani into the web pulsing beneath his hands and watched in wonder as it became part of the gathering ground's cycle.

The boundaries between him and the gathering ground faded,

though not quite in the same way as when he'd been in contact with the dragon. He tried to extend his adani farther, but it still didn't obey his commands. He licked his lips and considered his options.

Elian imagined the dragons far to the west, far beyond the deadlands. He held their likeness in his mind as he pleaded for help. Adani shifted under the gathering ground, but Elian couldn't track the patterns of the shift. He imagined the Debru advancing on the gathering ground and silently shouted for help once again.

He felt a fool. For all he knew, he was shouting into a void. But it was all he could think to do. He repeated the process twice more, thinking first of the Debru and then of the dragons as he pleaded for help. Maybe adani could carry the message. It was a slim hope, but the only one he could hold onto.

Elian stood and fixed his gaze westward. The circle of darkness had spread, and it had grown closer. No gusts of wind and force followed the first, but a cold wind blew a steady stream of frigid air across his skin.

He turned away to find the others. The Debru were coming, and it was no time to be alone.

6

Samora found Mother working in a small herb garden on the south side of their house. The sight made her pause. Harvest was completed, but the first snow hadn't yet fallen. Even so, the nights grew cold and Samora was impressed Mother's herbs had lasted this late into the season.

Mother was in a squat, and Samora noted the ease with which she stretched to pluck weeds from the soil. She was well into her fourth decade, but was untroubled by the aches and pains that afflicted so many of the other women in the village. She picked a handful of herbs with efficient movements, sorting them into bowls that she would later bring into the house.

Samora couldn't count the number of times she'd sat cross-legged outside that garden helping Mother tend to the plants. When she looked at her mother now, she could almost forget everything that had happened. She felt younger, as though she'd just come home from hunting with Elian and the world made sense.

The moment passed. The village she'd called home was now surrounded by the wandering clans, and they wouldn't leave anytime soon. Eventually, Aldo's fears would become reality and the Debru would attack. She'd hoped to save the village by enlisting the help of the clans, but in the end, the village would die regardless.

Mother must have either sensed Samora or caught movement out of the corner of her eye, because she twisted and nodded at her daughter. "Go on in. I'm just about finished."

Instead of going into the home, Samora squatted beside Mother and picked the weeds. It made her feel like a child again.

And maybe she still was. As soon as she struck difficulty, she ran to her mother's embrace. She pulled a few more weeds then stood as Mother finished picking herbs. Mother's sharp gaze caught sight of Aldrick standing guard. "New friend?"

"Aldo's worried about my safety. They're keeping guards on me so that I'll remain safe."

"Kind of them." Mother's face revealed nothing, but Samora knew she wasn't fooled.

Samora picked up a few of the bowls and followed her mother in. Aldrick made to follow, but Samora shook her head. "I don't need an escort inside my home, thank you."

She shut the door behind them before Aldrick could protest.

Mother arranged the bowls on the table. "Ruffle some feathers?"

"At the unified council this morning I suggested the clans make haste to attack the circle in the Crows' territory. Not only was my suggestion ignored, but I also earned a constant escort for my trouble."

"Were you thinking of running off with Karla again?" Mother asked.

"The thought occurred to me, but Karla pointed out that the Debru have learned from our last attack. They're on guard, and I don't think even Karla can get us past them. So, at the moment their caution is a bit unnecessary."

The women took seats at the table. "You're troubled by the

council's decision," Mother said. It was half a question and half an invitation to share.

Samora didn't need much encouragement. "I understand their reluctance well enough, but if we don't act soon, it'll be too late. We'll lack the strength to do anything against the Debru."

Mother nodded along as Samora spoke, but that was all.

"Do you have any suggestions?"

Mother smiled and shook her head. "You know quite well that Jace and I left that life a long time ago. Even when we were with the clans, it wasn't as though we were invited to council meetings. We were just another pair of adanists in love. I wish I could help you, but your problems are far beyond anything I had to face."

Samora blew out a long breath. "You still give good advice."

"Then I'm afraid you're stuck with the same lessons I taught you when you were younger. Find the thing you can do, then do that thing."

Samora grunted. She'd heard variations of that advice plenty growing up. She wasn't sure what she'd hoped to gain from coming here. Some clarity, perhaps. But Mother spoke true. Both she and Father had been middling adanists before they decided to leave the clan. The thought curled up the corner of her lips.

"Something funny?" Mother asked.

"Elian was so disappointed when Harald didn't know Father's name. It wasn't as though you'd ever lied to us, but he was convinced, despite everything you said, that Father was more well-known than he was. He really struggled to accept that Father wasn't the legend he'd built in his thoughts."

She frowned as she spoke. There was something there, a tug she recognized as adani guiding her, but she couldn't quite bring it to life. Something about the difference between illusions and reality. She couldn't see how it applied to her problem yet, but the hint was there.

"Your brother was so focused on what he wanted to be, and

what he wanted life to be, that he sometimes forgot to see what is."

"Do I need to learn the same lesson?" Samora asked.

A look of surprise passed across mother's face. "What do you mean?"

Samora tapped her fingers against the table. "What if I'm no different than Elian? What if I have become so consumed by what I think I know that I'm missing something obvious?"

"If you were missing something obvious, I would hope one of your companions would have noticed by now."

Samora shook her head. "But that's exactly what I'm talking about. The wandering clans are filled with incredible warriors, but they're just as much a slave to tradition as the rest of us. Most of them have spent their entire lives running whenever the Debru appear in numbers. It's what they're taught to do. What if their tradition blinds them more than most?"

She felt herself nearing the cusp of revelation. There was something there. Something no one had considered. But just when she felt like she was close enough to touch it, her stomach twisted as a wave of adani passed through it. She clutched at her stomach and looked at her mother. "Did you feel that too?"

Mother's tight-lipped nod was answer enough.

The tension in her stomach eased and she sat up straight. The tension of it reminded her a little of when an adanist extended their adani to learn more about their surroundings. But this had been far more powerful, and edged with something else, a sensation she couldn't quite describe.

A moment later, more adani passed through her, just like the first. But this time, stronger and clearer. Her legs went weak as she looked up to mother. Mother's expression was a mirror of her own. She whispered the name that was on both their lips. "Elian."

Mother's confirmation shattered Samora's indecisiveness. She stood so quickly she knocked a chair back. She put her hand on mother's shoulder as she passed by. "I'll find out what's happening, and I promise you I will get the clans to act."

A tear formed in the corner of Mother's eye, but she nodded as she wiped it away with the back of her hand. Samora understood a little of what mother felt. For weeks she'd been able to track Elian with the assistance of the gathering grounds, but even that had felt like a distant and meager effort. She still didn't know nearly enough about what Elian experienced.

And now, with no warning, this. The wave that had just passed through had carried Elian's adani, and for a brief moment it had felt like all three of them were in the same room together. A family reunited after too much time apart.

She strode through the door and was surprised to find that the camp was not in chaos. A handful of people wandered between the village and the tents. But they did so without hurry.

Even Aldrick looked surprised to see her. He had found a patch of grass in the sun and was laying on his back, with one knee crossed across the other and his hands behind his head. He tilted his face and squinted toward her. "Something wrong?"

"You didn't feel that?"

"Feel what?"

Samora's thoughts raced. If she wanted to know more, the quickest route would be back to the gathering grounds where she could extend her adani and search for her brother. That would take time she wasn't sure they possessed, though. She bit her lower lip. She'd assumed at first that if both she and Mother had felt the same wave of adani, the others in the camp would have as well. If they hadn't, convincing them of anything was going to be far more difficult. Considering the rejection she'd just experienced from the council, it might be downright impossible.

"Is the unified council still meeting?" she asked.

Aldrick rolled to his feet and shook his head. "Aldo gave me my orders after the council had disbanded for the day."

"Do you know where Warran is?" Samora asked.

"No. But I assume he would be back among the Bears."

Samora took off in that direction, sprinting between the tents as though chased by a Belog. Aldrick swore and then gave chase, but his footfalls rapidly receded as Samora wove her way nimbly around the tents. She shouldered one woman aside and almost slammed into a child chasing his friends in some game. She danced around the child and resumed her sprint. No doubt Karla would tell her to relax and enter the Bears' camp with a calm and dignified air, but Samora didn't have the time or the patience. She almost knocked over a young man carrying wood but dodged at the last moment. She breathlessly apologized, then turned the corner and almost ran straight into Warran's back.

The Bears second gave her a look that silently asked if she had lost her mind. She bent over and put her hands against her knees for support as she fought to catch her breath.

"Where's Aldrick?" Warran asked.

That a question about Aldrick should be his first put Samora on edge. She'd never spent the time to understand him. Some days he acted as though he was one of her greatest supporters; others he acted as though they'd never met before. Of the members of the unified council though, he was the only one likely to listen to her.

"Did you sense the adani that just passed through here?"

His eyes narrowed. "I don't know what you're talking about."

Samora's heart sank but she wasn't deterred.

"Mother and I just felt adani pass through the camp. They're from my brother. I'm afraid he needs help."

The last part was nothing but a guess, but she could think of no other way to ensure Warran's consideration. The Bear's second might not care much for Elian, but Elian was with Harald, a man who certainly commanded Warran's respect.

"I've neither felt nor heard of such a thing. Are you certain?"

Samora hadn't yet caught her breath, so all she could do was nod.

Before Warren could respond, Aldrick burst onto the scene behind them. Like Samora, he was breathing heavily. "I'm sorry, sir. She ran off before I could stop her."

Samora's fists bunched up against her pant legs. Aldrick had nothing to apologize for. She'd only come to speak to the second of her adopted clan. It was hardly against any rules.

Before she could snap at him, Warran raised his hand for peace. "It's alright. Did you sense the wave of adani she speaks of?"

Aldrick admitted that he had not.

Warran looked between Aldrick and Samora, then spoke to Aldrick. "It's fine. Please give me and Samora a moment to speak together."

Aldrick obeyed, leaving Samora and Warran alone.

"Stand up straight," Warran said.

Samora did, taking a deep breath. She was pleasantly surprised to see the concern in Warran's gaze.

"Even if what you say is true, what do you expect out of me? Harald and your brother are weeks away at best. Whatever they need help with will be long decided by the time we arrive."

"I don't know, but we have to do something," Samora said.

Warran grimaced. "I wish there was more that I could do to help you, truly, but Harald taught me a very important lesson once: a warrior can't fight every battle that comes their way. The best warriors don't even try. They save their strength for the fights that matter, and as much as I want to help Harald and Elian, this fight doesn't matter to us at this time. There is nothing to be gained because there is nothing we can do. I would rather save what influence and sway I have for a fight that makes a difference."

Samora snarled, her frustration at the clan's inaction breaking through her efforts to rein it in. The reasonable part of her mind knew there was nothing Warran could do, but a more primal part wanted something to strike, and so she lashed out before reason could regain control. "I didn't know the clans had so many ways to justify their cowardice."

Warran's spine stiffened as the compassion dropped from his face. When he spoke next, it was as the leader addressing one of his own. "I'm sorry, Samora, but whatever trials Harald, Elian, and the others are facing, they'll have to face them alone."

❦ 7 ❦

E lian watched as the darkness on the horizon grew larger, equally fascinated and horrified by the mysterious event that crawled across the sky. The longer he stared into the west, the more he felt that someone had come and painted the air itself black. While the shape of the darkness remained roughly locked, it bent, wobbled, and extended as it moved, as though the air was a malleable liquid.

He wondered what Samora would make of this but was glad she wasn't around to find out.

Motion in the corner of his vision pulled his attention from the sky. Capricia stood beside him, looking as though she'd rather be anywhere else. Elian chose to believe her expression was due more to the terrible shadow advancing across the land than it was his presence.

"How are you holding up?" he asked. He regretted the question as soon as it escaped his lips. It was obvious how she was holding up. Her face was pale, and she couldn't look west long before turning away and studying anything else.

She took no offense at his efforts, though. She shrugged in a courageous attempt to appear nonchalant. "I'll confess that I'm curious to see a Vada in person. Some of the legends claim they're shapeshifters, while others claim they're giants. I suppose we'll all know before the end of the day."

"I wish I had some fraction of your courage. I keep standing here thinking I'll figure out how to win this fight. But then every time I realize there's nothing I can do, and I'm not sure if I should cry or wet my pants."

She snorted. "If it makes you feel any better, I believe both of those methods have been tried today, though with lackluster results."

Elian laughed. Given what was approaching, the knots of worry he'd tied himself into unraveled, and he found it was easy to say what was truly on his mind. "I'm sorry we didn't have more time together. I would have liked to have known you better."

She nudged him with her shoulder. "Then you better figure out a way for us to survive this battle."

She walked away before Elian could respond. He watched her go, and with every step, the smile on his face faded a bit more. Once she had disappeared back into the trees, it was gone. He turned back to the west and stared at the approaching shadow as he tackled the problem of the Vada with renewed determination.

Unfortunately, all the determination in the world wasn't going to help him defeat the enemy that approached. He'd sent out his call to no response and hadn't come up with anything more useful since.

He was still trying to imagine a creative solution when he heard the shouts of the others as the first Belog crested the hill and pointed its long arm toward the gathering ground. Less than a heartbeat later, dozens of Debru came over the rise and charged. Elian had forgotten how fast they could move. Their clawed limbs rushed across the soil without tiring. A handful of dark spears formed in the Debru's hands as they launched them at Kati's assembled warriors.

Elian watched the spears fall. A few were thrown too short, but most arced high enough to reach the defending adanists. As soon as they reached the boundary of the gathering ground, though, they began to dissolve. Elian watched, losing track of all else. The bound shadows unraveled and dissipated, a dark reflection of the time Samora had bound a spear of adani and thrown it into the Debru circle.

Judging from the expressions of some of the nearby Hawks, Elian wasn't alone in his surprise. He looked back at the Belog and clenched his fist tighter around the hilt of his sword. He didn't doubt the task would be difficult. But maybe they had more of a chance than they thought.

The Debru were undeterred by their spears' lack of success. They hurried forward as quickly as before. The adanists who stood at the front line of the defenses looked to one another and back to Harald, who lay on his back casually in the grass behind them. He hadn't even bothered to rise to a sitting position. The Debru were less than a mile distant, but Harald gave no orders.

Elian couldn't decide if the giant was incredibly brave or incredibly foolish.

Finally, Harald stirred and rose. He stood and stretched as though waking from a long nap. He casually flicked his wrist, and an enormous spear of bound adani appeared in his left hand. Elian had witnessed Harald's techniques before, but this one possessed a strength beyond Harald's earlier efforts. Like them all, he drew on the adani from the gathering ground and shaped it to his purposes.

Harald took a deep breath, then let out a frightful yell and whipped the spear into the air. It arced across and down, speeding through the sky like an oversized arrow launched from the land's strongest bow. The Debru saw it coming, but the speed of the spear left them little time to react. They broke ranks and split apart, but the spear came crashing down like vengeance from the heavens.

It struck with the force of more than a dozen normal bound spears. There was a flash of light and then a wave of pressure. Elian closed his eyes against the flash, and when he opened them again, dust hung in the air like curtains. For a moment, he dared to hope that Harald had killed the entire charge with a single throw. Then the adanists on either side of him formed their own spears and launched them into the cloud. A moment later, the first of the Debru broke through only a hundred paces away from the gathering ground's boundary.

Kati and Harald had argued intensely about the final defense of the gathering ground. She had wanted to place all her warriors at the edge of the boundary to prevent the Debru from laying a single filthy claw within the Hawks' sacred territory. Harald had reminded her they would be far more effective if they hung back closer to the trees.

Elian was grateful Kati had eventually acquiesced. Harald's positioning meant the Debru spears couldn't reach them, and it meant that when the battle occurred, the fight would happen on land favorable to the humans.

More adani spears followed the first wave. Elian could do little more than watch as the golden spears pierced the dark creatures. Some of the stronger adanists threw spears that passed clean through their targets, and in one case, impaled another Debru running behind the first.

The Debru did all they could to avoid the onslaught but dodging one spear usually meant leaping into the way of another. The adanists formed spears and threw them without delay, sending a constant barrage of deadly projectiles at the charge. The sheer amount of adani was the greatest defensive outpouring Elian had witnessed from a wandering clan.

The last of the Debru died two steps within the gathering ground, impaled by no fewer than four bound spears that all found it at once. It died without a sound.

A wide grin spread across his face. There had been dozens of

Debru. Enough that if they'd attacked under other conditions, they would have likely overwhelmed the entirety of the Bear clan. But thanks to the added strength of the gathering ground, the Hawks and the handful of Bears had made short work of the invaders.

He sensed more than heard Harald's presence behind him. When his leader spoke, his voice carried none of the joy Elian felt. "Now the real battle is about to begin."

"That wasn't the beginning?"

Harald shook his head. "Barely a half-hearted attempt to measure our strength, I think. The Vada has plenty of friends behind that rise, and we've only glimpsed the very tip of the spear."

Elian swallowed hard.

Harald pointed toward the western horizon, where a dense bank of clouds had formed and obscured the Belog that had been standing there prior to the charge. The cloud grew and expanded until it billowed over the hill and raced toward the gathering ground. The clouds were much darker than the ones that had almost overwhelmed Harald on their journey here.

Elian couldn't decide if he was glad he couldn't sense the numbers of Debru or not. "How many Debru are hiding within that cloud?"

Harald's eyes narrowed. "Perhaps forty to fifty Debru. A handful of Moka and two Belogs."

Elian swore under his breath. That was about the same size of the force the Hawks and Bears had marched out to meet a week ago. They'd won that battle, but at significant cost, and only thanks to the timely arrival of the dragons, and there'd been no Vada there. The flicker of hope burning in his chest dimmed as the cold winds of reality threatened to completely extinguish it.

Harald laid a hand on his shoulder. The giant's presence calmed the worst of Elian's fears. The only sense he got of

Harald's worry was a slight tremor in his leader's palm. "Straighten your back and face it head on," Harald said.

Elian obeyed and forced himself to look forward. Harald responded with a tiny nod. "It's a good way of fighting any battle, but especially battles like this. Someday, everyone will be looking at you, and the way you act will be so much more important than anything you say."

"Don't you think it's little soon to be giving final advice? I plan on being your second until you're old and gray and Kati has to feed you your meals by hand. Maybe even long enough so that she has to chew your food first so you can gum it down."

Harald chuckled and removed his hand from Elian's shoulder. "Yeah, I think you'll do just fine."

Harald took a few steps back and bound another of his massive spears. He thrust it high, drawing the gaze of every eye in the gathering ground. Then he roared and launched the spear at the heart of the approaching cloud.

The spear punched through the cloud, leaving a hole a dragon could have dropped an ancient tree through.

Unfortunately, the hole closed and healed as soon as the spear passed through, and for one terrible moment, Elian feared Harald's attack had completely failed. Then the cloud bulged and expanded as golden rays of light shone through fresh cracks. The cloud strained to contain the force of Harald's strength, but the cracks only widened for another heartbeat before the cloud gained control and returned to its normal size. Elian couldn't see for sure, but he didn't doubt more than one Debru had lost their lives to the strike, even if it hadn't done much visible damage.

Harald grunted. "I thought that would be more impressive."

A few adanists formed their spears to follow his lead, but Harald waved for them to wait. "Save your strength until they reach the border."

The Hawks took the suggestion like a bitter pill, but they obeyed.

Harald looked meaningfully toward Elian and nodded. Elian drew his sword before he could remember how dangerous his position was. He held the sword up high as he cycled adani through his body. It didn't attract the same attention Harald's spear did, but he thought he noticed a few of his companions stiffen their spines and ready their bound weapons.

Then the cloud struck the boundary of the gathering ground, and the battle began in earnest.

The dark mist penetrated farther than Elian had expected, but as it fought to gain purchase in the gathering ground it began to dissolve, exposing several Debru. Their red eyes glowed as they broke from cover and bounded toward the adanist front line. Elian shouted and ran to meet them.

His steps were light and quick, but before he met them, dozens of bound adani spears, daggers, and darts passed him and struck the Debru. Two near Elian fell dead, but the one closest was merely grazed. It formed a sword of black shadow, though the construct lacked the solidity Elian had come to expect from the Debru's bound weapons. Elian cut down with his sword. The Debru blocked, but its bound sword barely slowed Elian's cut. He sliced through sword and Debru as though they were no more substantial than a wispy cloud.

Elian leaped several paces across the battlefield at another Debru searching for an adanist to kill. It turned in time to block Elian's strike, but like the Debru before it, its bound weapon did next to nothing against Elian's sword. It fell without a sound.

An adanist's choked-off cry caught Elian's attention. A cluster of Debru had penetrated the front lines, and though their bound weapons couldn't stand against the edge of Elian's blade, they were substantial enough to cut through flesh. The adanist who had cried out clutched at his neck as blood pulsed through his fingers. He took a step back, meaning to run, but before he could escape a second Debru drove its dark spear through the man's chest. The adanist's eyes went wide as his grip on his neck loosened.

One of the adanist's companions, a young woman with blonde hair that reminded Elian of Kati, cried out and stabbed her bound daggers deep into the Debru's skull. It crumpled to the ground, dragging the fatally injured adanist with it.

In her grief, the companion didn't notice the other Debru preparing to strike. She pulled her daggers out of the dead Debru and stabbed it again as tears clouded her vision.

Two long steps brought Elian to the battle. His sword brought down two of the Debru before they realized they'd been flanked. The blonde's companions protected her from the one shadow sword that cut at her neck. The Debru gnashed their teeth and swiped their claws at the adanists, but they were caught between Elian and the front line, and for once, they were weaker than their opponents.

Elian ensured the adanists were safe before leaping to the next battle that needed his help. Up and down the line the same basic story repeated. Several Debru reached the front lines, and the Hawks couldn't escape without casualties, but the fight was nothing like previous battles. Instead of several adanists gathering to kill one Debru, it required two or three Debru to bring down a single adanist. The fight felt like it had barely started when Elian realized there were no more enemies for him to test his steel against.

He came to a stop and looked down at his blade. It was coated with the blood of slain Debru, but he hadn't suffered so much as a scratch. Everywhere he looked, the adanists had the same look on their faces, like a condemned criminal given a second chance at life. Elian's blood pulsed through his veins. The gathering grounds had always been a vivid green, but the trees seemed more alive as their extensive roots soaked in the Debru's blood. The scents of the forest smelled sweeter than before.

Elian thrust his bloody sword high and roared. Bears and Hawks alike joined him with their bound weapons, their combined voices rattling in his chest.

He lightly bounded back to the center of the line, where Harald waited with a slight grin on his face. He seemed entirely too impassive for the victory they'd just won.

Harald dipped his head toward the western horizon and Elian's heart dropped. The shadowy clouds remained, as thick as ever. The unnatural blot of dark behind the cloud continued to grow bigger and approach. "It didn't send any of the Belog or Moka. Either it was some sort of test, or it feels like it can dash its forces against our defenses without concern for its losses."

"We're strong here."

Harald nodded. "We are, but I fear not strong enough. You did well, though. Several people are alive today who wouldn't have been if not for your help. That's something to be proud of."

Elian was about to criticize Harald's defeatism when the darkness stirred. His heart dropped into his stomach. "Oh. Even I can feel that."

Harald's voice boomed. "Get back into the trees!"

The adanists obeyed without question, leaving Elian and Harald alone in the meadow. "Are you sure? Perhaps there's a way to still fight."

Harald turned to follow the others. "There's a time to stand and fight, even when the odds are against you. But knowing how to choose the right battle is important. This is one we can't afford to fight. Come. It will be here soon, and our best hope is to be behind the barrier."

Elian took one last look west, then followed Harald. They entered the trees and Harald gestured to Kati. A barrier of golden light sprang up around the trees, their last line of defense.

Elian cleaned the blood off his blade before sheathing it. Every face was turned toward the barrier, but he couldn't bring himself to look. Even its glow made him think about that night in the village when he'd cowered behind Mother's barrier as Father fought a Moka.

Almost every day since then he'd told himself that if such a fight came again that he would be the one standing outside the barrier, fighting against the encroaching darkness. Now he finally had some fraction of the strength he needed to wage that war, but he was still behind the barrier, hiding with the others.

He gripped the hilt of his sword tightly and turned. He knew there was nothing he could do out there, that he'd be a fool to stand alone against whatever the Vada was about to bring, but some part of him still wanted to fight.

Quiet mutterings tore Elian's attention away from his own difficulties. Elian followed the gazes of his neighbors and saw a crackling sphere of darkness swirling in the sky. The adani cycling in his body fled from the sphere, pushing back into his spine. He couldn't tell how far away the sphere was, but he didn't think it was close.

Those more sensitive to adani were on their knees, tears streaming down their faces. Dark lightning flickered across the surface of the sphere, spinning faster with every nervous breath Elian forced past the lump in his throat. Giant cracks of lightning erupted from the sphere, walking across the deadlands like angry giants. Each bolt lingered, as though the lightning savored the contact with the loose soil.

The sphere moved slowly at first and then faster. The few adanists on their feet started running, but Harald stood next to Kati and put his hand to the ground. Several other adanists joined in, pressing palms into the rich soil of the gathering ground. They channeled their adani into the barrier Kati had created. Thanks to their efforts, the adani running beneath Elian's feet shifted from a that of a steady stream to that of a mighty river, and the barrier glowed brighter, rivaling the sun. He squinted against the glow.

The dark sphere fell from the sky faster than a boulder dropped from a dragon's claws. It passed through the boundary of the gathering ground without slowing and crashed into the meadow. Elian was thrown from his feet as the land bucked him into the air like an untamed horse. He cracked the back of his head against a tree and his vision swam. Blinding lights and a deafening roar made his head feel as if it was being squeezed between Harald's bicep and his forearm. He closed his eyes and held his hands over his ears, but his actions did nothing to ease his suffering.

He dared to crack open one eye, just in time to see the golden barrier erected by Kati and Harald flicker and die. A wall of dust, uprooted grass, and broken branches raced toward him, slamming him again against the tree. Blackness threatened to consume his vision, but he grunted and forced his eyes open. When he coughed it felt as though his chest was on fire, but he couldn't hear a thing.

He stumbled to his feet, looking around to see if anyone else had survived. The forest, which had welcomed him even in its quietest corners, now felt haunted. Trunks and branches were covered in the fine ash that fell from the sky. The world had gone dark and only shadows moved. He called out, unable to hear his own voice.

A mound of ash moved at his feet, and he yelled. The one-armed giant blinked, and Elian recognized Harald. He reached under Harald's armpit and pulled the leader to his feet, ignoring the fire that burned even brighter in his chest. Harald looked at him, his eyes blank, and Elian pushed him farther east.

They stumbled at first, then ran, a river of filthy humanity. He glanced back, but the trees blocked any sight of his enemy. Harald tripped over a root and Elian caught him. Soon they were sprinting along the paths like frightened deer. The ground rumbled under his feet, but he didn't see anything approaching.

They emerged on the other side of the forest to find more ash-covered survivors in varied poses of disbelief.

Elian let Harald slump against a tree. He sought the adani that had flowed so freely just moments ago, but it no longer pooled under the gathering ground. Before long, this vibrant refuge would be another part of the featureless deadlands that surrounded it. All because of one attack.

The hope he'd held just moments before felt foolish now, a child's naïve dream. He couldn't stop a Vada any more than he could hold back a thunderstorm.

He felt sick, as though the dust had coated the inside of his stomach. He bent over and put hands to knees. Despair made his vision swim. He should fight. He'd always told himself it was better to die with a sword in his hands, but what difference did it make? Death was death, regardless of how it came.

A tall, thin woman with gray hair came to kneel beside Harald, and it took Elian too long to realize it was Kati, her blonde hair hidden underneath a layer of dust and grime. She leaned her tear-stained cheeks against his shoulder. He shifted and wrapped his arm around her and held her close.

Elian turned away; the sight too raw. He walked away, crossing the old boundary of the gathering ground. Thick grass gave way to dead soil, but Elian felt no change.

Something pulled on his adani. He first thought it was the Vada preparing to let loose another attack, but the feeling wasn't the same. That had pushed his adani away. This attracted it. He looked to the sky, where dozens of dark shapes approached.

He blinked, then squinted, sure the new arrivals were some desperate attempt by his imagination to spare him from the inevitable. But the silhouettes grew larger, and Elian's eyes went wide. Others took note, but the arrival of the dragons did little to pull the survivors out of their despondent lethargy.

The dragons gave the Debru wide berth, circling around and dropping toward the survivors. The first dragon landed, the same one Elian and Capricia had helped rescue from the Debru earlier. It bent its head down and Elian reached for it. When he touched the dragon's snout, he let his adani flow into the dragon. It shared its intent with Elian, and he nodded, tears coming close to overwhelming him. "Thank you."

Harald and Kati had risen and were only a few paces away. The other survivors stood further back, trapped between the Debru and the dragons. Every eye was turned to him.

"They're here to take us home," Elian said.

"Not to fight?" Kati asked.

"They lack the strength."

Kati's hand tightened on Harald's. Ordering the retreat would be no different for her than if Elian walked away while his village burned behind him. She handled the loss better than he would have. She turned to the survivors. "The dragons will help us leave this land. Prepare to climb on."

Elian told the dragon they agreed, and the enormous creature raised its head and roared. Dragons that had been circling came in for a landing, and Elian was the first to climb up. The dragon took to the sky before anyone could follow. Elian shouted, but the dragon didn't slow. It circled high above the gathering ground as the surviving Hawks and Bears climbed onto their saviors.

Elian's eye drifted to the western side of the gathering ground. The meadow was a crater. The blast had destroyed everything it touched until it struck Kati's barrier. Debru stepped lightly through the destruction, unprotected by shadow but unconcerned about the dragons circling nearby. The unnatural darkness waited beyond the rise in the land, still out of sight. Elian strained his eyes for some glimpse of the Vada, but it remained hidden.

He took some small comfort when he saw that none of the Debru seemed too concerned about pursuing the surviving adanists. They spread out slowly through the gathering ground but didn't seem interested in either the humans or dragons.

The last of the survivors climbed upon a dragon and Elian sensed his dragon asking where they should go. Elian didn't know the state of the frontier since they left, so he told the dragon to take them to the one place he knew was safe.

Elian smiled bitterly. After all this, he was finally going to bring a clan back to his village.

8

Samora ate supper quickly that night. Normally she enjoyed sitting and eating with the clan, but her frustration with the clans lingered, and the food tasted bland whenever she thought of Elian fighting alone without help. She pretended not to notice as her neighbors' conversations slowly excluded her. She forced herself to finish her bowl before excusing herself from the meal. Her fellow Bears let her leave without inquiring after her, knowing she often preferred solitude and silence.

She wandered away from the campfires, her feet taking her in whatever direction they pleased. She hadn't made it far before she heard Aldrick's hurried footsteps behind her.

"Sorry, I didn't realize you were planning on eating so quickly."

Samora took pity on the young man. He believed his duty was to protect her, and he looked queasy from finishing his food too fast and running after her. "I'm sure Aldo wouldn't have minded if you finished your meal. I just wanted to walk outside the camp for a bit."

"He'd have my head if he found out. With everything that's

been happening with the Debru, he made it clear I wasn't supposed to let you out of my sight, especially if you leave the protection of the camps."

Samora nodded in mock agreement. "Well, I wouldn't have told on you. I feel bad I made you chase after me."

"It's no problem, truly."

She'd been considering returning to the gathering grounds, but now that Aldrick was here the temptation vanished. She wasn't ready to share them with just anyone. Instead, she wandered through the fields. Harvest was done and the soil would lie fallow until spring. She crouched down and scooped a handful of dirt into her palm. It wasn't as rich as the adani-laden soil of the gathering ground, but it was good land that had been carefully cultivated by generations of farmers.

It was just dirt, but it had kept her family alive since before she'd been born. Much of the food grown here was sent to the wandering clans to aid them in their fight. Aldo and the others looked at the soil and only saw the dirt. They rightfully claimed it meant so much less than the lives of their adanists. Samora agreed, but they needed the land, too. It was the cultivation of the fields that had allowed the wandering clans and the villages to grow. Without it, humanity would slowly fade away.

She didn't know how to protect it.

Samora stood and brushed the dirt from her palm. Her eyelids felt heavy, and if her mind would ever settle, she was certain she would sleep for days. Unpleasant dreams meant her sleep rarely offered the respite she craved. She walked north, keeping the camp close so as not to alarm Aldrick any more than necessary.

Adani stirred in her core and brought her to a stop. The shift had been subtle, no stronger than a puff of wind that rustled the leaves, but she was certain of what she'd felt. She cast out her adani but found nothing that she wouldn't expect.

Aldrick saw the specks in the sky before she did. He grunted and pointed, and she saw what had caused her adani to react. They approached from the west and Samora's heart skipped a beat at the sight. The last dragon she'd seen had brought a Belog to kill her, and they were coming roughly from the direction the Debru were camped in. She turned to run and warn the camp, but the shifting flow of adani within her core brought her to a stop. It pulled toward the dragons, too strong to be denied.

Aldrick was halfway to the camp before he realized she wasn't following him. He gestured frantically, but she shook her head. "Go ahead and warn them. I...I don't think they're here to harm us."

Her guard's eyes leaped between her and the camp, but then he turned his back to the camp and came to stand beside her. At her questioning look, he said, "I figure they'll see the dragons soon enough. Aldo told me to keep you safe, so here's where I'll stay."

"You don't have to," she said.

"I know."

The warmth in her chest burned some of her exhaustion away and the quick pounding of her heart took care of the rest. "Thank you."

Aldrick's prediction came true soon enough. Horns sounded throughout the camp as the lookouts caught sight of the dragons. Samora smiled as the camps became a chaotic mess. Against the Debru they would have been prepared for battle in moments, but none of them had trained to fight against an army of dragons. She walked forward, only to be stopped by Aldrick's concerned hand on her shoulder.

"If I'm right, I'd rather be a bit farther from the camp, so I don't get caught up in whatever defenses they're preparing."

Aldrick looked unconvinced, but he loosened his grip on her shoulder.

Samora found a place well away from the camp and waited.

Shouts came from behind her, but she ignored them. Adani was clear. She was supposed to be here.

The first dragon spread its wings as it descended. A lone rider sat on its neck, just ahead of its wings, smaller and grayer than any Debru she'd come across. The dragon landed as softly as a feather and settled peacefully into the field. Its rider half slid, half jumped from the neck. He was caked in dirt and blood, but his gait was familiar. When he spoke her name, her knees went suddenly weak.

"Elian?"

Then she was running, her steps wobbly. Her right foot sank in a patch of loose dirt, and he was there, catching her as she fell. He held her so tight it was tough to breathe, but if not breathing was the price to pay for this moment, she would pay it gladly.

The moment passed too soon. He broke off the embrace first, leaving her cold and filthy. His eyes took her in, and though his attention was familiar and welcome, it was different than before. Sharper, somehow, and deeper. Then he smiled and he was the brother she'd left behind. "I swear you've gotten taller."

"You come back leading an army of dragons, and that's the first thing you have to say?"

He shrugged, but her question had brought him back to their situation. His smile fell and he gestured to the flights of dragons coming in for landings. "We found what was left of the Hawks and their gathering ground in the deadlands. There's too much to explain, but we were attacked by a Vada earlier today and had to retreat. We have many who are injured."

For a moment, all she could do was stand there and stare at the place where she thought her brother stood. She'd felt some of the changes in him from a distance, but his new abilities with adani paled in comparison to this new maturity. She shook her head to clear it, then nodded. She had so many questions, but for the moment, they could wait. "I'll speak to the unified councils. Your adanists will have the healing they need."

Elian nodded and turned his back on her. He raised his hand and made a series of gestures she couldn't decipher. "Dismount and assemble. Find those with the most serious wounds and prepare to move them. If you're not seriously injured or helping someone who is, let's form a gathering point. It's going to take a bit for the clans to figure out what to do with us, so let's not make it too hard on them."

The adanists hopped to Elian's orders. He turned and saw her watching and a sudden, sheepish look crossed his face. "Harald and Kati gave everything they had to form a barrier against the Vada. They're alive but unconscious, so someone had to take command."

All she could do was nod silently. Aldrick tapped her shoulder, and she glanced back. He gestured to the camps, where Aldo, Warran, and Tiafel had gathered with the full might of their clans.

She took a deep breath, straightened her spine, and went to convince the others to help provide the healing she'd promised her brother.

SAMORA RESTED her forehead against the corner of Mother's house. "Aldrick, I promise you, there's nothing for you to fear. I'm going to go inside and speak with my family. We've got so much to catch up on. Then I'll probably fall into my bed and not move again until the sun is high in the sky. There's absolutely no need for you to wait outside our door."

Aldrick looked around as though afraid someone was about to catch him abandoning his duty. Bags hung under his eyes and his gaze was distant.

"Thank you for helping today. It was more than I could have asked for, but you need rest, too, and my mother's house is probably one of the safest places in the world. We're surrounded by dragons and more adanists than have ever been gathered in one place. You can rest."

Aldrick's promised companion hadn't shown up today, but her guard hadn't left her side since she'd run away from him that morning. He nodded. "I'll be here at first light."

She answered with a weak smile. "I'd expect nothing less."

She watched him turn and shuffle away, then took another moment to collect her thoughts before entering. Elian had sent word that he would stay at Mother's for now, and though she wanted to sleep for a day, her brother came first.

Samora knocked on the door and entered. Mother and Elian sat across from each other at the long table Father had built two years before he'd died. The top of the table looked like a battlefield, filled with empty bowls and dirty plates. Elian noticed her staring at the mess and grinned. "Mother made sure I didn't go hungry. I meant to leave you some, but I'm afraid my stomach was too susceptible to temptation."

Mother pushed her chair back and stood. "He might not have saved you anything, but I kept a small loaf of bread in reserve. He never was good at sharing his food, and you look like you could use the sustenance."

Samora nodded gratefully and sat down in her customary seat.

"How did the healing go?" Elian asked as he poured her a glass of Gabe's latest fermented creation. She took a long pull and coughed. The drink was probably better for lighting fires than it was for consumption.

"One of the Hawks had died in flight and her companions hadn't noticed. One more died before we could save him. A handful will need a few days of healing and rest before they'll be ready to fight. Everyone else should be ready to resume training tomorrow."

Elian bowed to her. "None of us can thank you enough. What about Harald and Kati?"

"Kati will be fine. She'd burned her body to a crisp from the amount of adani she used in your fight, but she responded well to the healing. Their healer, Loken, is incredible. If not for his efforts, I'm not sure any of us could have saved her."

Elian nodded his agreement. "He is impressive. He's the one who taught me how to cycle my adani so I could use it. What about Harald?"

"We're still not sure about Harald. Frankly, I'm not entirely sure how he's survived this long. Has he talked to you about his injury?"

"In what way? He's told me that I shouldn't feel sorry for him."

Samora poured herself another drink and tossed the whole cup down her throat. "The wounds to his amputated arm aren't just physical. The spears that impaled him spread shadow through his body, too. Loken has been helping keep the shadow at bay, but he hasn't been able to dispel it completely. We've all tried, and we can reduce it, but it won't let go. It's either more persistent than the shadow that affected you, or you were able to expel it because of the unique way your body handles adani. Harald isn't so lucky."

Elian's face paled. "I never knew."

"Loken told us that only he and Kati were aware, but he said the two of you had become close. Harald didn't want others to know. He needs his adani to fight the shadow and keep it contained. When he used so much to protect against the Vada's attack, it left him more vulnerable to the infection. We've beat it back, but we gave both him and Kati medicine that will keep them asleep for a while. They both need the rest."

Elian rested his fists against the table and stared at his empty plate. He looked as though he was on the verge of tears. Loken had spoken true. "Is there any way to cure him?"

Samora's expression was answer enough for her astute brother. "There might be, but we don't know it. I'll search for one, though."

"Thank you, again."

Samora nodded and tore small chunks from her bread and chewed them slowly. She washed down the bites with sips of Gabe's concoction. She fixed Elian with a look, and it was as if no time had passed. He understood without being asked. "Are you sure you want to hear everything now?"

She gestured to her bread, which remained mostly whole despite her best efforts.

"Right. I suppose we have some time."

Elian helped himself to another pour and settled back to tell his tale. He started at their parting and spent most of his time recounting the battle against the Belogs. His story ended that morning, when they'd been attacked by the Vada and run with their tails between their legs. In exchange, Samora told him how she had met Karla and how they'd healed one of the circles.

A scowl settled on her face when she told Elian of the unified council's failure to act. She appreciated that he didn't defend their decisions. Instead, he looked at her the way he always did when trying to decipher what she was thinking. "What's your plan?"

"It's not much of one. But you've got dragons, and if what I saw earlier today was real, you command them as you would an adanist."

Elian shook his head. "There is no commanding a dragon. But we have reached an agreement."

"Would they help us?"

"All I can do is ask. I still haven't figured out exactly how they stand in relation to the Debru. They helped us in this most recent battle, but they haven't done much in the past."

The answer was unnaturally reserved for her brother, but she was more concerned with the circle that needed destroying. "If we can cooperate with a handful of dragons and recruit a few volunteers, we might have the strength to launch an assault on the other circle. I know Karla would join us."

Elian leaned back in his chair and twirled his empty cup mindlessly. Samora waited for Mother to lecture him on the importance of keeping all four feet of the chair on the floor, but she watched him with the same undisguised interest Samora did. Elian acted as though he was ignorant of the attention. He raised the cup to his lips, realized it was empty, and placed it gently on the table. Then he nodded to no one. "I need to speak with the council."

"Why bother? Their decision has been made."

"True, but that was before we returned with the dragons. It's possible we'll receive a warmer welcome than you."

"By the time they finish arguing among themselves, we'll have more than one Vada to fight against."

"They'll need to be persuaded, then. It's important the clans fight together. A victory today that divides us further tomorrow is no victory at all."

Samora couldn't fight the smile that played at the corner of her lips, even though it came at the cost of losing the argument.

"What?" Elian asked.

"Who are you and what have you done with my brother?"

Elian's cheeks flushed and he stared at the table. "I had to learn some hard lessons in the deadlands. You understand better than most the strength the Debru will bring to bear. It's possible the council won't listen, and we'll need to act alone, but I don't want to risk the clans' unity if I can help it."

"You'll need to speak to Warran, then."

Elian's eyes darted to the half-empty jug of Gabe's liquor and his hand started toward it. Then he exhaled and pulled his hand away. "I'd hoped to delay that conversation until Harald rejoined us."

"If you want Harald to live, he'll need to sleep for at least another two days."

Elian nodded, then slapped his hands on the table and stood. "So be it. Where are the Bears camped?"

"South side of the village," Samora responded.

Elian placed his hand on Samora's shoulder as he passed. "It's wonderful to see you again."

"Likewise."

He strode toward the door. "Don't bother waiting up. You look like you could use the rest, and this might take a while."

9

Elian looped adani quickly through his limbs and through his head. The pleasant fuzziness he'd enjoyed while drinking with Samora vanished with the blink of an eye. He grunted softly and turned his head quickly. His vision remained sharp and focused, and dizziness remained nothing more than a distant threat. Tera had told him the technique would work to clear alcohol from his mind, but he hadn't really believed her. He'd have to thank her when he saw her.

He was tempted to take a detour through the grove. In the past it had served him well as a place to think and burn off the emotions that had threatened to overwhelm him. But there was nothing to think through, and he wouldn't hide from his feelings any longer.

He followed Samora's instructions to the Bears' camp. As he'd suspected, the fire at the center of the camp was roaring and almost all the adanists were still gathered, passing around small jugs of liquor and toasting their surviving friends. He remained in the shadows for a bit, observing the celebrations like a ghost. Alec and Brittany sat shoulder to shoulder, their faces red from the heat of the fire and the burn of the liquor. They looked more relaxed than they had on any night since they'd followed Harald across the deadlands.

Elian didn't see Tera or Warran at first. They weren't among the celebrants, and he only found them when his eyes studied the shadows beyond the ring of fire. They were deep in hushed conversation with one another.

Elian worked his way through the tents so he could approach them from the darkness. He didn't care about surprising them, but he was in little mood for a celebration and didn't want to ruin the night for others. It didn't take long to join the two Bear veterans. Tera bowed slightly at his arrival, but Warran only fixed him with a hard stare.

He'd always gotten along well enough with Warran when they'd traveled together, and he respected Harald's former second, which made all of this harder.

"We need to talk," Elian told Warran.

"You just finished speaking with your sister, I assume?" Warran asked.

Elian nodded. "I need to speak to the unified council tomorrow."

"I can't say for sure, but you'll likely be wasting your breath. They aren't ready to launch an attack on the Debru."

"Will they ever be? I haven't spoken to the dragons yet, but my hope is that they'd aid us. We'll never be stronger than we are now, and Samora says we don't have much time."

"And I'm inclined to believe her, even before your arrival with news of the Vada far to the west. Unfortunately, I don't think it matters much to the others. Frankly, even if Abram himself were to step from those gates and lead us, I'm not sure the other elders would follow."

"Then what must be done? I refuse to stand by passively while our lands are stolen from us, and we're driven before the Debru like cattle."

"The only possibility I can think of is if Harald presents the case. He's always been able to persuade the others, though, given the nature of his injuries, I'm not sure that's still true."

Elian stepped close to Warran. "He hasn't become any less of a leader because he lost his arm."

Warran wasn't intimidated. "You and I may believe that, but the other elders in their fear will latch onto any excuse not to listen to him."

Elian retreated a step. Warran wasn't his enemy. "Besides, if we attempt to wake him, it's likely he'll suffer. Samora told me he needs to sleep for at least two days before she feels comfortable attempting to wake him again."

"Brittany told me the same. She was quite insistent," Warran said.

The veteran warrior stood up straighter and squared his shoulders. "There's also the matter of our positions. Tera told me that Harald wanted you as his second after the battle. Is this true?"

"It is. I didn't want the position, but he was quite persuasive."

A rueful grin crossed across Warran's face. "He can be that, can't he? You'll have to learn your own tricks to keep him on a straight and narrow path, just as I did."

"You're not upset?"

Warran chuckled. "Elian, I've never for a moment wanted to be Harald's second. I was a good choice because he needed someone who could think beyond the next meal and the next battle, but I've never inspired other adanists the way he does. Tera spoke highly of you in your fights against the Belogs to the west."

Elian had come prepared for a fight, so Warran's easy acceptance caught him flat-footed. He fumbled with his words for a bit before saying, "That's very kind of her, but it feels like there's more that I don't know than what I do. Harald convinced me to be his second, but I'll need all your help so I don't make too many mistakes."

Warran smiled. "You've already learned a lesson it took Harald years to learn, so don't be too hard on yourself."

"What lesson?"

"How to ask for help. Don't worry. You have the entire strength and wisdom of the Bears behind you."

The belt that had been tight around Elian's chest from the moment they landed back at the village loosened a few notches at that. He bowed deeply to Warran and Tera. "Tomorrow, if I fail to persuade the council, will you join me in marching to battle against the Debru?"

Warran shook his head, and the belt tightened again, making it difficult to breathe. What good was the Bears' support if it was so conditional?

"It's what Warran and I have been discussing," Tera said. "And it's not because we don't want to help, but it's because we have a better idea. You still see strength in unity, do you not?"

Elian nodded.

"Then try this, instead," she suggested, and she laid out her plan for the next day.

ELIAN WOKE the next morning feeling more refreshed than he had in weeks. The strength of the gathering ground had nourished his body and spirit, but it still paled in comparison to Mother's cooking and his familiar bed. He'd argued last night that he should spend the night with the Bears, but Tera and Warran had insisted he return home. The Bears would be too hungover the next morning to remember where he slept, and it was good for him to spend time with his family. So he'd returned home, after a slight detour to visit the dragons.

He retraced his steps to the Bears' camp, where he found Tera and Warran waiting for him.

"The council will start shortly. Are you ready?" Warran asked.

Elian was. In a way, he felt as though he should give thanks for the Vada's arrival. Now that he'd seen the enemy's true power firsthand, it forced everything into a new perspective. Before, the idea of standing before so many elders would have set his heart racing. Now he recognized the foolishness of fearing something so meaningless. The Vada had wiped away his doubts and shown him the only path that mattered.

Warran had Elian lead them to the council, and when they entered the large ring of elders, Elian watched everyone's eyes take note of their arrangement. Without saying a word, they'd made clear the new order of leadership among the Bears. A ripple of muted conversation passed through the crowd, but Elian paid it little mind.

He didn't bother to join the ring in the place left open for the Bears' council. He strode straight into the center. They may listen and agree or not, but at the very least, he intended to bring a reckoning. The muttering around the ring grew louder, then crested and faded like a flock of birds flying past. Elian turned slowly, meeting the eye of every elder present.

None of them had known he'd be joining them today, so they'd taken no precautions to keep their meeting secret. Last night a handful of Bears had gone throughout the camps, whispering into sympathetic ears, so there were more observers today than usual. Warran's plan, so far, had worked. Now it was up to Elian to do the rest.

He finished his slow spin and began cycling a little adani through his chest and throat. Another technique Tera had imparted on him last night before he'd returned home. He cleared his throat and spoke, his voice carrying not just across the ring, but to every ear listening beyond.

"Some of you know me already, but many don't. My name is Elian, and I'm the adanist Harald personally selected as his second while we battled both Belogs and a Vada in the west. I am the one who speaks with the dragons, who called them to our aid in our darkest times. Unfortunately, Harald suffered grievous wounds in our last battle, and as such, remains unconscious in the healing tents. I am in temporary command of the Bears while he heals."

Murmurs around the ring threatened to become shouts, but Elian continued so they wouldn't have the chance to drown out his voice.

"I tell you as much only so you know who I am. Today, I come before you not as the leader of the Bears, but as an adanist who refuses to surrender our lands to the Debru. I do not presume to speak for Harald, but I like to believe that if he were here, he would be standing by my side in agreement. As many of you know, the Debru are nearing the completion of a gate to bring more Vada into our lands. This honored council has debated long and hard about how to respond to this threat. It is no easy decision. The gate is well-guarded and the chances of a Vada appearing soon are higher than I care to admit. The council, in their wisdom, has decided to set their lines here instead of attack the Debru."

Elian looked around the circle. Most of the elders looked like they were ready to bind spears and impale him where he stood, but no small number of adanists beyond hung onto every word.

"I offer no judgment on the council's decision, for it is not my place. Instead, all I offer is an alternative. This afternoon, the dragons and I will take off and attack the Debru. My sister, Samora, who turned the Debru circle nearby into a gathering ground, will seek to do the same with this gate before it lets a Vada through. It is a dangerous task—perhaps the most dangerous the clans have undertaken in my lifetime, and trust me, I understand what that means. But I am convinced that if the Vada are allowed to use the gate, our resistance is ultimately doomed."

One of the elders finally worked a question in. "So, you're in command of the Bears for one day and you'll order them all to a certain death?"

Elian shook his head as he said a silent thanks to Warran. Such had, more or less, been his idea, but Warran had convinced him of his foolishness. "No, sir. It is not my place to give such an order, even though by right I may. I told you, I'm speaking not as the leader of the Bears, but as a simple adanist. My offer is open to all, but I compel no one. Karla, Samora, Tera, and several Bears have already answered my call, but there are many Bears who have volunteered to remain here and guard my home village. I bring opportunity only. If you are tired of running from the Debru and giving up land, join me when the sun reaches its midpoint. I and the others will gather by the dragons, to prevent the Debru from taking any more land than they already have."

Elian bowed deeply to the circle. "Thank you for your time."

Then he strode out through the stunned crowd before anyone could shout questions after him.

"It was well done," Warran said. "It's a shame Harald wasn't around to see that. He would have enjoyed the spectacle."

"Now let's just hope it works," Elian said.

ELIAN WALKED among the dragons as though he had something important to do. He pretended not to keep checking the position of the sun. It crawled toward the midpoint slower than it ever had before. Samora hadn't arrived yet, but Karla was busy befriending a dragon while Alec and a handful of other Bears kept a respectful distance.

Tera remained behind him like a shadow. "You shouldn't worry so much. If I know the clans, you'll have as many riders as you can handle."

"I hope so. Otherwise I'm going to look like a real ass ordering the Bears into the fight."

"You'd be better served riding off alone, fighting a low-risk skirmish, then returning," Tera said.

Elian smiled, though Tera couldn't see it. "That was a joke, Tera."

"Ahh. Perhaps you should stick to fighting, then, and leave the jokes to me."

Elian snorted and turned around. Tera maintained a straight face for a moment, then briefly chuckled. "No point in worrying, is all I'm saying. You've done what you can, now we wait to see what happens."

Elian looked beyond Tera to the village and the surrounding camps. A mass of warriors had left the tents. Several were armed, but all looked ready for battle. "Looks like we don't have to wait to see."

He thought the sight would let him breathe easy, but as he watched them approach, he realized he'd just traded one weight for another. They'd believed in his words and ideas.

Now he had to lead them to victory.

🦎 10 🦎

Samora woke after Elian and stretched out in her familiar bed. It was as good a night as rest as she'd had in a while, for which she was incredibly grateful. The day promised to be a decisive one. Either they'd push the Debru back or lose the war.

She padded out of her room to find Mother in the kitchen, staring with vacant eyes at the fire. Mother startled as she came out. Her eyes were rimmed with red, but she stood stiffly at the fire, occasionally stirring tonight's stew. Samora went over to her and embraced her. The stiffness in Mother's spine melted and she sank into the hug. Fresh tears followed the trails earlier ones had left.

"We didn't want any of this for you," she said as she pressed her cheek against Samora's shoulder. "We used to laugh about how glad we were that we didn't have famous names, that nothing much was expected from us in battle. Your father was happier in his days here than he ever was with the Spiders."

Samora held her mother. It was the first time she'd offered such support. Even after Father's death, Samora had only seen Mother cry when his body was buried in the dirt he'd spent so many years cultivating. After that, there'd only been dry eyes and an endless procession of chores and work.

She didn't know what to say. Anything she could offer, her mother already knew.

Mother took a deep, shuddering breath and pulled away. "Promise you'll do all you can to come back to me?"

Samora nodded.

"Then get out of here before I embarrass myself further. I'll expect you both for supper."

"Did Elian's plan work?" Samora asked.

Mother's laugh was bitter. "Oh, it worked. Your brother always had a penchant for trouble, though he's never stirred up anything like this. The elders are furious, the camps are full of arguments, and my tears aren't the only ones falling this morning. But he's got his war."

Samora nodded again. "He's really grown, hasn't he?"

"More than I thought possible. Bring yourselves back, and good luck."

Samora bowed to her mother and stepped out the door.

Mother's summary had been a bit understated. As soon as Samora left the boundary of the village she stumbled straight onto the chaos Elian had unleashed. She heard no fewer than three arguments between the tents, each coming from a different direction. The normal patterns of the day were disrupted as groups of people stood together and held hushed conversations. Her presence drew a fair number of stares, some of which were kindly, but many of which were not.

She ignored them all as she walked to the healing tent. She'd barely crossed the threshold when Brittany blocked her way.

"What do you think you're doing here?"

"I came to check on everyone and see if there was any way to help."

Brittany crossed her arms. "According to your brother, you're supposed to be traveling to the circle today. I don't think you have any strength to spare for healing."

The words were true enough, but they carried an edge Samora hadn't expected. She stared at Brittany, wondering if it was best to pick this fight now or wait until later. Given that she might not have a later, the decision was a simple one. "What's wrong?"

Brittany flared her nostrils. "I've always told you Harald doesn't value human life enough. Since Warran took command, I haven't had to bury or burn any more of my family. Now your brother is back, and less than a day later the Bears are marching off to war. I thought you and he were better than that."

Samora retreated from the verbal assault. She stammered half an apology, then stopped. She shook out her hands and breathed deep. "You're right. They ride today on my word, and I wish it were different. If I knew of another way that guaranteed every Bear returned to their tent tonight, I'd take it in a heartbeat. But if we don't fight today, we might not have a chance tomorrow."

Brittany formed her hands into fists and thrust them down by her side. "Just come home with them."

She turned on her heel and stalked off down the line of cots. Samora made to follow, but Brittany fixed her in place with a hard stare. She nodded, then left the tent.

She was still contemplating Brittany's dismissal when she reached the dragons. Her slow paces came to a stop as her eyes took in the sight. More warriors than she'd expected had answered Elian's calls. They were organizing themselves into groups and being assigned to dragons. She spotted Elian speaking with a handful of adanists she didn't recognize. She headed his way.

His discussion with the adanists ended just before she reached him, and he greeted her with a grim smile. "You slept well?"

She nodded and gestured to the collection of adanists that had gathered.

"More than I expected, too, but with their help, we might just have a chance. Are you ready?"

She didn't even have to nod. He could still read every nuance of her expression.

"You and I will ride together. How close do you need to get to the circle to affect it?"

"Closer is best."

They were interrupted by a young woman who came around a dragon and stopped when she saw Samora. She carried herself like an adanist, and the way her eyes lingered on Elian made the purpose of her visit clear. Instead of her original plan, though, she simply bowed to Elian. "I came to wish you well," she said.

Elian's cheeks flushed the same way they had used to when Sara had paid attention to him. "Thank you."

They stared at one another for a moment before Elian remembered they weren't alone. "Capricia, this is my sister, Samora. Samora, Capricia. She's the Hawk who kept me safe when we scouted the Debru circle out west. She's the one who helped me save the dragons. Without her, none of this would have been possible."

Samora bowed. She'd wondered, when Elian had told that part of his story last night, but now his feelings were obvious. "I'm honored. If you'd like, I can give you and my brother a moment."

Capricia smiled. "I appreciate your kindness, but I was only coming to wish him well." She turned and left before either Elian or Samora could invite her to stay. Elian watched her walk away until she was out of sight. When she disappeared around a dragon, he returned to himself.

"When we return, we can all spend some time together. I think you'd like her."

Samora nudged him with her shoulder. "You know she wasn't coming here just to wish you well, right?"

"She wasn't?"

Samora laughed out loud. "I hope you're more observant than that when you lead us into battle."

Elian still looked confused. "What do you think she wanted?"

"If you can't figure that out on your own, I'm not sure there's anything I can do to help you."

A moment later his eyes went wide. "Really?"

"Really."

"I'd hoped, but I wasn't sure. It wasn't like we had a lot of time together after the battle. Mostly because I was struggling to understand what had happened to me. I—"

Samora shook her head and Elian silenced his running commentary.

"Right. We need to win this fight first. Thanks."

"And when we get back, I think you should spend some time with her. I'm happy to meet her as well, but I'm not the one she wants to spend time with."

Elian nodded, then turned to the dragon he'd been standing next to. "You ready to fly?"

"Absolutely."

BY THE TIME Samora felt comfortable flying on the back of a dragon, pummeled by its incredible well of adani, they were close to the circle. They flew high to avoid the spears and ropes of the Belog, and from this altitude, the mass of Debru standing guard around the circle looked insignificant, like ants scurrying around the corpse of a freshly-killed creature.

The Debru had spotted them. A handful of shadow spears had been thrown into the sky, but even the Debru's muscular frames and powerful command of shadow couldn't reach the heights Elian's assorted adanists soared through. The Debru ran around the circle, though Samora noted none stepped foot within the ring of dead grass that marked the gate's boundary.

"Are you seeing or sensing anything we should be concerned about?" Elian asked.

"I can't search far with adani up here, but I don't see any reason why your plan won't work."

Elian nodded. "Then would you be so kind as to throw the first spear?"

"Have someone else do it."

Elian turned back to look at her, and when he saw the expression on her face he nodded. "Sure."

He raised his hand and gestured toward Karla, who rode on a dragon next to them. Karla formed a spear so bright Samora was forced to turn away. Riding on the dragons gave the adanists a boost similar to if they fought upon a gathering ground. Karla held the spear high, then threw it down. For a long moment it sped alone, but then it was joined by others, falling from the sky like deadly rain.

Even from afar, the destruction was unlike anything Samora had witnessed. Every adanist drew on the dragons' deep wells of strength, so every spear was among the strongest they'd ever formed. Moka and the Belog cast protective shadows over their charges, but the spears poked holes in the shadows and cast them aside like tattered blankets. The Debru scattered under the assault, leaving only the Belog to hide under its shield of shadow.

Those shields became targets for every adanist in the sky. As the Debru were cleared from the field, the dragons descended and allowed the adanists to become even more accurate. The Belog shield began to resemble a dark porcupine, its sharp bristles made of glowing adani spears.

When Elian had first told Samora of the plan he'd created with Warran and Tera, she'd doubted it could work. And for some time, she remained convinced they weren't strong enough. Adanists dropped enough spears to level her village a dozen times, but the Belog still stood without problem.

In time, though, their advantage became clear. She'd underestimated the strength of the dragons. Their ability to fly, combined with the strengthening effect they had on adanists, changed the shape of any battlefield completely, and she was glad of it. Though she hated to admit it, Aldo had understood the dangers of this assault far better than her. On foot, she wasn't sure how many of their adanists would have survived.

Elian and the dragons remained patient. They remained high, and adani dropped from the sky like a deadly waterfall. They didn't approach the ground until the Belog finally lay still on the ground. Just to be safe, Elian had Karla punch an enormous spear through its chest. Then he signaled for the others to stay in the sky while he and Samora landed. The dragons and adanists circled high above, keeping them protected.

"Would you prefer for us to stay or leave?" Elian asked.

"Stay, please. I might be able to use the dragon's strength to aid me, if it doesn't mind."

Elian closed his eyes and his lips moved silently. After a moment he opened them and nodded. "He agrees."

Samora bowed toward the dragon. "Thank you."

She sat cross-legged on the ground. She put one hand to the soil and the other on one of the dragon's claws.

"Good luck," Elian said.

Samora nodded, closed her eyes, and released threads of adani into the land. The circle pulled them from her with surprising strength, but she held onto the threads as they were hauled toward the center.

The ground rumbled gently. She ignored it. If there was any trouble, she was certain Elian would keep her safe or let her know if they needed to leave.

She remembered well her lessons from her first battle with the circles. They weren't conscious, exactly, but they possessed some basic level of intelligence that protected them from intruders. In their first duel, Samora had learned that she couldn't force her way past the defenses. She had to trust in adani to find the way.

She did so now, allowing the threads to drift and unravel as they would. The threads became thinner and thinner, winnowed down to just a point of adani that danced through the defenses of the circle. When she feared they would be whittled down to nothing, she pulled the smallest fraction of the dragon's strength to reinforce her own. The point of adani grew back into a faint thread. Curved shadow blades emerged from the heart of the circle, but her countless threads danced through most of the assault. At least one blade struck and bounced off one of her reinforced threads.

It was all going better than she expected until every one of her threads froze in place. She reinforced them with more adani from the dragon, but nothing happened.

The previous circle hadn't done anything similar, but the threads of adani didn't seem to be in immediate danger, so she relaxed as she considered different options. She tried directing the adani, reinforcing it with even more of the dragon's strength, and pulling them back toward her. Nothing caused the threads to budge a hair.

Then she felt it, lurking somewhere within the center of the circle. The power she'd felt before. Not corporeal yet, but coming close, exerting its will through the circle.

A Vada was coming.

Elian sat on top of the dragon and looked out over the battlefield. Dozens of dragons flew in the air with warriors who'd answered his call. They effortlessly maintained a perimeter hundreds of paces away from Samora, allowing her to heal the circle without interruption. Debru, either desperate or brave, tested the perimeter, but their efforts had become a sort of sport for the adanists. Any Debru who came close was hunted down from the air, inevitably the victim of two or three spears reinforced with dragon adani.

It was such a change from the battles they knew. Debru had always been the hunters and adanists the wily prey. Now, for the first time in their generation, the Debru were scattered and hunted by adanists. By itself, that was almost victory enough.

Almost.

Closer to him, the ground around the circle was as torn up and dead as the land within. Their bound spears had wiped out all that had been living here. For a moment he was back in the Hawks' gathering ground, staring at the forest destroyed by the Vada's attack. His throat constricted at the memory, but he swallowed hard. What he had done was different.

He couldn't deny the effectiveness of the tactics they'd devised. Tera was primarily to thank, though she would claim no honor in public. To be able to attack from up high without risk was a change that would shift the course of history.

So long as the dragons continued to cooperate.

He couldn't fault them since their paths had crossed, though. They'd turned the course of the battle outside the Hawks' gathering ground and saved them again when the Vada appeared. Now they were here helping them make short work of the Debru. When he returned with every warrior that had left, the war would change.

Distant thunder pulled his awareness back to the present. A handful of Debru had charged the perimeter together, but all they'd earned for their efforts was a mutual death. Hoots of victory echoed across the sky and Elian smiled. Whatever joy he felt at the shift of fortune was nothing compared to the release the adanists of the wandering clans must feel.

The grin faded as he looked down at Samora. He couldn't see her well from where he sat, but she seemed pale. She'd claimed the first circle hadn't taken her all that long, and Karla had supported the claim. She'd healed that circle quickly enough that Karla had been able to keep her safe alone. How long had this been? It felt as though they'd been here for a while.

He gripped the dragon tighter. It didn't much matter how successful the attack had been if the Vada was still able to emerge.

As he stared down at Samora he felt a shift in the adani running through the dragon. It had been a strange sensation, sharing the dragon with Samora as she fought against the circle. She manipulated adani with a subtlety and surety he didn't sense from other adanists and put even his newfound skills to shame. He pulled adani hand over fist, as though hauling an enormous bucket of water up from a well. Samora sipped at the power as though sampling a new, delicate tea.

Suddenly, though, she pulled more adani than before. He wanted to call down to her and ask why, but he didn't dare interrupt her concentration.

The center of the circle, about a hundred paces away, convulsed, reminding Elian of a child dramatically sucking in their belly and then extending outward as far as it would go. Brittle grass and cracked trees rose and twisted like waves on a lake caught between a rushing wind and rocky shore. When the ground settled, three new Debru stood near the center, squinting into the bright light of an unfamiliar world.

Elian dropped from dragon and was halfway to the boundary of the circle before he stopped. Bound adani was little good within the circle, and if he attracted the circle's attention, the shadow would infect him again.

His hesitation crumbled as the Debru spotted them. The other adanists were next to useless within the circle. Even if the shadow infected him, he'd cleansed himself before and could do so again. It wasn't as immediately deadly as poison. But the simple truth of the matter was that if he did nothing, Samora would soon be dead.

He leaped into the circle and drew his sword, meeting the Debru halfway between the center and the boundary. He cut down at the first, who bound a sword of shadow and blocked the cut. Elian pressed his attack, but the Debru surrendered ground easily, parrying or dodging Elian's cuts. The other two Debru never slowed. They passed to either side of Elian, their eyes firmly fixed on his sister.

Elian swore, but the moment he turned his attention away from the first Debru, it launched its own attack. Elian skipped back and chased after the other two Debru, looping a massive amount of adani within his legs. His burst of speed caught the pair by surprise, and he cut down one before it could turn and defend.

The other formed a shadow spear and successfully blocked

Elian's sword. Elian struck again, but the Debru slapped his sword away. He glanced back to see the first Debru forming several bound spears. Elian's eyes went wide, and he dove to the side as the first ripped through the space he'd been standing a moment before. Two more spears kept him running, but the Debru held the fourth spear with a confident grip as he took aim at Samora.

Elian stomped his foot into the ground and slid to a stop. He looped all the adani in his body into his legs as the Debru brought its arm back and launched the spear. Elian leaped.

The spear punched into the right side of his chest, spinning him around like a child's rag doll thrown violently away. His sword dropped from his lifeless arm as he crashed and tumbled across the ground. He lay motionless, grateful he felt nothing. He willed his body to move, but all he accomplished was rolling from his stomach onto his back.

The first Debru walked up to him, yet another bound spear in hand. It snarled as it raised the spear for the killing blow. Elian sought adani's strength, but his body and mind refused to cooperate.

An enormous shadow passed overhead. Elian flinched away. When his sight returned to the Debru about to kill him, he noticed the top half of his enemy had vanished. A moment later the legs tumbled backward.

Elian groaned as feeling started to return. His chest felt like someone had placed dozens of heavy, burning stones upon it. He levered himself up with his left arm. His vision swam as he sat up. He looked left and right for the other Debru, but it was nowhere to be found. He twisted farther and saw Samora was unharmed. She remained in the same pose, her attention fully on the battle in the circle.

His saviors flew close to the ground, worried expressions visible on their faces. He waved weakly, then stood and retrieved his sword with his left hand. He was a fool. Using the dragons hadn't occurred to him.

He stumbled toward his sister, but as he came closer, he saw the battle she fought was no less intense than the one he'd just survived. Her eyes were pressed tight together and her teeth were gritted. He swallowed hard and looked at his own wounds.

The sight made him sick, but he'd expected worse. The spear had carved a hole in his chest, but it didn't go much deeper than the muscle. He looped adani in the area to begin the healing process.

He passed Samora without word, then shuffled the last few steps to the dragon. Adani rushed through his limbs when he placed his hand on the dragon's scales, aiding in his healing. Now that he was connected to the dragon, he felt the massive amounts of adani Samora was pulling. Her battle was even more intense than before, but he lacked the skill to even sense her struggle.

"I don't know what to do," he admitted.

The dragon's adani responded. As it had when they'd first met, it showed him what he couldn't sense. His breath caught in his throat as he understood the nature of Samora's battle. She fought a Vada as it attempted to rip through the thin boundary separating their world from the Debru's home world.

Thanks to the dragon's perception, Elian understood the duel in a flash of insight. The Vada's strength dwarfed Samora's, even with the dragon's assistance. The only reason Samora had lasted as long as she had was because the Vada fought its side of the battle through the boundary that separated worlds. Unfortunately, the Vada continued to shred that boundary, and as the boundary weakened, the Vada could bring more of its strength to bear against Samora. That was why the amount of adani she pulled from the dragon had gone from a trickle to a raging river.

It wouldn't be enough, though. The dragon and Samora both knew it. The Vada lacked its ultimate power, but not for long.

Once it was fully physically present on this world, there was nothing Elian knew that would stop it.

Elian sensed something from the dragon as it followed his thoughts, but the hint was quickly obscured, and Elian wondered if he'd simply imagined it. Before he could investigate further, he sensed the Vada redouble its assault on Samora and the dragon. The attack forced the dragon to break its attention away from Elian.

He opened his eyes and pulled a small amount more of adani into his body. The hole in his chest remained, but some of the muscle had been rebuilt. He pulled his hand off the dragon and tried clenching his right fist. It opened and closed, though it lacked some of its normal strength.

He turned back to the circle. For the moment it was quiet, but there was no telling how long that would last. Elian chewed on his lower lip.

The air above the center of the circle turned the same inky darkness that had haunted his nightmares since they'd fled from the Hawk's gathering grounds. They didn't have much time, but what could they do? Adani remained next to useless within the circle, robbing them of the one meager weapon they possessed.

Samora groaned and nearly pitched forward.

The darkness in the air above the circle took on a new shape and texture, with the deepest shadows forming near the ground. The air itself seemed to bubble and boil, slowly taking on the shape of a small human. Elian sensed its power through his own useless senses. It still lacked the strength of the one outside the Hawks' gathering ground, but its power grew by the moment.

Samora screamed and the dragon behind Elian sagged to the ground. Their joint assault broke the shadowy figure apart, but it slowly started to repair itself.

Elian ran away from Samora until he was in open fields. He waved at Tera and gestured for her to land. She did.

"Get off," Elian said.

She shot him a dubious look, but she nodded to the other adanists and they dismounted so fast it was as if the dragon was on fire. Tera was last, and she fixed Elian with a hard, questioning look.

"Protect my sister. The Vada is almost through, and if all looks lost, do everything you can to get her safely away from here. She's likely the best weapon we have against the Debru, and I won't lose her here."

"What about you?"

"I'm taking your dragon."

"Why?"

He didn't bother with an answer. They didn't have time. He strode past her, but she grabbed his arm and stopped him. She nodded to the hole in his chest. "You're wounded. I'll do it."

"Adani is next to worthless in there. If any sword has a chance where I'm going, it's mine."

"You can't attack a Vada alone."

"I'm not. I'll have the dragons, you, and all the wandering clans behind me."

She swore under her breath but let go of his arm. "I'll protect your sister until my dying breath."

Elian gave her a quick bow, then hurried over to the waiting dragon. He climbed on, let his adani connect with it, and shared his plan with it. The dragon considered for a moment, then took to the air. Elian considered that agreement enough.

They circled once while Elian pulled as much adani as he dared into his body. He looped much of it into his chest, healing what he could before the attack. The dragon gained considerable altitude as it circled, then dove toward the center of the circle.

Elian felt as though his skin glowed with the vast rivers of adani running through his limbs. He looped it, guiding it into ever-tighter patterns that made him feel as though he could run for months. He inched his feet higher on the dragon, until he was almost in a squat.

The Vada's reformation continued, growing faster as more pieces of its body came together. Samora's face was in the dirt now, but the Vada still seemed to be fighting against an invisible force Elian couldn't sense. Its face formed last, and it wasn't the face of a small man, but a human child. Its eyes were empty and lifeless, but as the dragon raced toward the Vada, the pupils began to form.

The dragon reached the bottom of its dive and leveled out. Elian stood a bit taller and drew his sword. They passed through the boundary of the circle, but they flew so fast it barely affected the dragon.

Elian leaped as the Vada's eyes finished forming. Its eyelids closed, and when they opened, it woke into the full extent of its power. He was in the air when he saw the Vada's first flicker of awareness, and then his sword passed cleanly through its neck.

12

Samora knew the fight was lost long before she lost it. No matter what tactic she tried, she fought against a power that made the bottomless wells of adani the dragons drew on feel like a drop of water in a lake. She poked and prodded with adani while fighting off the shadow blades the circle sent after the threads. She wrapped the Vada in the dragon's adani, but it shrugged off the bonds as though slipping off a loose pair of pants.

Though her battle happened within the realm of shadow and adani, she sensed the Vada fight to assume physical form. Its strength pressed against her mind and made focus nearly impossible. She lost several of the threads closest to the heart of the circle as her attention wavered.

The dragon dumped more adani through their connection, burning her channels from the inside out. She screamed until the back of her throat was raw, but the dragon's effort succeeded in interfering with the Vada's rebirth in their world. The victory was a temporary one, but perhaps it would give Elian and the others time to flee.

The Vada began to reform and Samora felt her grip on the duel loosening. Her body felt as though she had carried a heavy stone for miles, and her arms and grip were weakening. She made one last effort, but by the time the strand of adani reached the Vada, it was too late.

It walked upon their land, its strength indescribable. Elian had warned her, and though she had believed him, she'd hadn't understood until now. She still held the threads of adani, but they no longer tried to advance toward the circle's center.

Then the power winked out, as though she'd imagined it. She opened her eyes and saw that she had fallen forward. She pushed herself up in time to see a young boy's head fall from his shoulders, a surprised look on his face. Elian stood perhaps seven or eight paces away, the edge of his sword dripping blood.

The boy's body collapsed and Samora's adani surged toward the circle's center. Two threads were unraveled by the circle's defenses, but one slipped through, and the moment it touched the edge of the circle's core, the circle unraveled and the pent up adani flooded the area.

The wave of adani struck her with a physical force that almost knocked her backward. She'd channeled so much adani through her body that her body wanted nothing to do with more. She let it pass through her, pleased the dragon that had befriended Elian seemed much rejuvenated by the wave.

She wobbled uncertainly to her feet, but after a deep breath she trusted her balance enough to stumble forward. Her body felt heavy, as though she now carried the dragon on her back instead of the opposite. Elian turned as if he was in a trance, but when he saw her, he came back to himself. He looked at the new corpse and a shiver ran through his body.

When she stopped beside him, she saw that his tunic had a large hole over his chest. Some of the skin had healed, but she could see muscle under half-healed flesh. He saw that she noticed, but she sensed he'd rather not speak of his wounds. She promised she'd make him see a healer soon, but for the moment, she turned to the corpse. It took her several tries to get the words past her constricted throat. "Was that the Vada?"

Elian nodded.

"It's just a boy, though."

Elian shrugged, equally at loss for an explanation. "There's no doubt about what it was, no matter how it appears."

The heavy weight of the battle, combined with the exhaustion of the fight, crashed into her all at once. She sagged against him, barely noticing how he winced. He supported her with his wounded arm as tears streamed down her face.

She couldn't stop looking at the corpse, crimson blood pooling on the ground next to where his neck had once been. She swore she saw a finger twitch, but couldn't be sure it wasn't her imagination, or the wind moving the body. The face, which now stared blankly at the sky, reminded her of the young boy she'd almost run into in the camp the day before.

She knew it was the Vada. She'd felt it form and felt it die. Her mind knew.

Her heart didn't.

"He was a child" she said.

His whole body stiffened, and he pushed her gently off him. At the former boundary of the circle, dragons were landing and adanists began to flood toward them. He shot her a hard look. "*It wasn't a child.*"

Then he turned his back and went to greet his warriors, the conquering hero he'd always dreamed he would be.

THEY'D FLOWN separate dragons on the return journey. Elian had claimed the dragon he'd befriended was exhausted and only capable of carrying one. It might have been true, but Samora didn't argue. Her upper back and shoulders were sore where adanists vigorously congratulating her. She'd been embraced by strangers and pulled from celebration to celebration until Karla had finally rescued her. The veteran adanist had taken her away without a word and silently sat with her among the dragons.

Once they'd returned to the camp, Samora had made a straight line for home. She'd closed the door, told Mother they'd been successful, and that Elian had returned safely, then hidden in her room. She fell asleep on her bed before her mother had time to harass her with questions.

Her sleep was deep and dreamless, and when she woke, it was to the sound of two soft voices from the dining room. She pulled the blankets higher over her head and ignored the conversation, but eventually her stomach rumbled and the smells from the kitchen were irresistible. She flung the covers off and joined the others.

Mother hosted Karla at the table, and from the snippet Samora heard as she entered, Karla was filling Mother in on the details of the battle. Karla nodded to Samora, then said, "He ended up killing the Vada a moment after it physically entered our world. He was respected before, but he's a living legend now. There's only one other adanist who's ever killed a Vada alone."

"Abram," Mother said. The pride burning in her eyes made Samora's stomach crawl, but before she could leave, Karla kicked one of the chairs out so Samora could sit.

"Of course, none of it would have been possible without Samora. She fought the Vada singlehandedly for a long time, and if not for her efforts, Elian never would have stood a chance. Unfortunately, her battle didn't receive the same attention. We couldn't sense it from the air and there was nothing to see. All that I know about her struggle came from Elian," Karla said.

"I'm proud of you," Mother said to Samora.

Bile rose in her throat, but she swallowed it back down. She closed her eyes and took a deep breath, but the headless boy stared back at her.

She knew what it was. There was no doubt. And yet her body

rebelled at the memory of what had happened. What she'd been a part of. She managed a short, hesitant bow, and then for the first time heard the commotion outside.

"What's going on?" she asked.

Karla answered. "A celebration the likes most have never seen. This morning the clan leaders believed we were flying to our deaths. Instead, we have a new gathering ground, we defeated a Vada, and scattered the handful of remaining Debru, all without losing a single life. That's because of you and your brother. In one day, it feels as though we've changed the course of decades of war."

Samora met Karla's eye. "Is that how you feel?"

"War's not over, but it's the greatest victory I've ever witnessed, and as you well know, I've been alive for a long time."

Karla's sharp eye didn't miss the way Samora turned away. "It's the Vada's form, isn't it? Elian told me you took it hard."

Samora nodded.

"Legends say the Vada can take whatever form they please. I don't know why it took the form of a young boy, but I know that the way something looks doesn't always tell us what something is."

Samora swallowed and nodded. She didn't want to say more in front of Mother. Karla must have sensed something of Samora's dilemma because she said, "Truth be told, I came to fetch you. There's a lot of people wanting to see you, too."

The thought of leaving the house made her legs turn into blocks of ice. "It was always Elian who wanted recognition. It's better if I remain, I think."

Karla grunted. "It wasn't much of a request. It comes straight from the clan elders. If you ask me, they're worried about the authority your brother is about to wield. They want to honor you and hopefully diffuse his influence a bit."

Samora couldn't help but bitterly laugh at the absurdity of the situation. "They want to use me to steal the honor my brother has rightfully earned? They're fools if they think I'll cooperate."

Karla failed to find the humor in the situation. "What your brother achieved is greater than the victory alone. If he so desired, a word from him might upset generations of tradition. I don't care for the timidity of our elders any more than you, but I understand some of their concern. I fear your brother is leading us into unexplored territory, and some degree of caution is warranted. Truthfully, I'm worried that by the end of the night he'll attempt to set himself above the unified council."

"He'd never do such a thing."

Karla's eyes glittered like knives. "Wouldn't he? Wouldn't you? As different as you are, you both tend to act how you see fit, regardless of what permissions you've been granted."

Mother smiled at that. "I'm glad someone else finally understands the struggle I faced for years. But be that as it may, they've always acted in the interests of the clan."

"I don't doubt that, but the decisions facing us aren't so simple. There's a time for action and a time for deliberation. I fear your brother will steal the latter from us."

Samora sighed. "I don't think you have anything to fear, but I understand. Besides, I suppose it would be rude to my brother to miss his celebration." She paused. "It's a good thing they sent you. You're probably the only one alive who could convince me to leave the house right now."

"Then it's a good thing I'm the one who asked."

Samora bid her mother farewell, then stepped outside with Karla. The scene that greeted her was even more raucous than she had expected. Giant bonfires licked the sky to the west and north. Karla might have worried about Elian, but Samora wondered if the festive clans would burn down the village. Children ran freely between the homes and tents, and men and women danced in every clearing to the beat of the drums.

Karla scouted a quiet route for them to take, sticking mostly to narrow paths deep in shadow. It didn't take her long to interrogate Samora.

"What is it about your brother's actions that disturb you so, regardless of the Vada's form? You know well what it was, and you're no fool."

Samora searched for the answer to that question. Karla's claim was true, but that didn't diminish the sorrow beating in her chest. "I never imagined my brother would be the sort of person to kill a child with such ease."

Karla shook her head vehemently. "But it wasn't a child, and even you saying as much makes the idea stick in your head. It was a Vada, one that had come through this portal to destroy all life. If anything, we should praise your brother's decisiveness. I suspect that if he had hesitated for even a moment, the Vada would have killed him and ended this war before the next eighthday."

"Is it really so simple for you, too? Don't you see how twisted this fighting has made us all?"

Karla stopped and stared off into the darkness ahead. She worked her jaw for a moment, and then turned slowly around to face Samora. "Are you mad at your brother for what he did? Or are you furious at yourself for what you're unable to do?"

Samora's mouth fell open and she retreated half a step, as though Karla's calm words were an assault. "Why would I be mad at myself? This is about Elian."

"And the louder you proclaim it, the more certain I am that I'm correct. You know that if your positions had been reversed, if you had held the sword and been responsible for killing the Vada, its form would have caused you to hesitate and doom us all. Somewhere deep within your spirit, you know you would have failed."

Karla's accusations hammered against Samora's heart like a blacksmith beating a sword into shape. She stammered for a moment but couldn't articulate a response. This wasn't about her; this was about Elian being willing to kill a child without blinking.

Karla turned with a snort of disgust. "Think on it. It seems to me, from where I stand, that there is a part of you that finally understands the weakness inherent in your pacifism. Don't get me wrong, girl. It's a lovely ideal, but until you grow up, you are almost as much a danger to us as the Debru."

SAMORA HAD BEEN to celebrations before. Growing up, the village had always held small feasts every eighthday, and threw two larger celebrations on the last day of harvest and just before the first day of planting. But those celebrations had always felt more like a leisurely ritual than a true celebration. They marked time and served as doors from one week and season to the next.

She'd seen something of the wandering clan's celebrations as well. Like the clans themselves, they were rowdier affairs, with less order and structure. She thought, perhaps, that the celebration that awaited her was of a similar nature, although perhaps greater in size due to the number of unified clans in the area.

What she discovered instead was something entirely different. There was ale and liquor, dancing and song—all of which she expected. But there was also nudity and coupling, and fights between warriors that she was sure would destroy both tents and friendships.

Karla led her deeper into the chaos, unfazed, as Samora reconsidered her decision to follow the adanist. The acts she witnessed grew wilder until they passed some sort of unmarked barrier. The shouts and licentiousness faded behind them, and she reached the bonfire where all the elders of the unified clans sat and drank. She looked around the circle and noted that Harald and Kati weren't among the celebrants. Their absence didn't surprise her, but she missed them all the same.

Then her eyes landed on Elian, sitting on a chair which had been placed on top of a table so that he sat above all others. The sight of him brought back memories of the battlefield and the boy's corpse.

She shook her head. The Vada's corpse. It had been a Vada.

She forced her eyes up and to her brother, looking for any change in him, some sign that he'd become a cold and brutal man.

While the others in the circle drank freely and often, Elian took only the smallest of sips. He smiled at the jests and antics of his companions, but the smiles never reached his eyes, which watched the others like those of a hawk pursuing a field mouse across the grasslands.

She couldn't decide what to make of the thin evidence, but her time to think

Unfortunately, she had approached too close, and the choice was taken from her. Elian spotted her, and his somber face broke into a wide smile. When he stood on the table, she saw that he kept his balance without problem. He raised the cup in his hand high, and it splashed so much liquid she knew it must have been nearly full. "My sister has finally arrived. To Samora!"

Every pair of eyes in the circle turned at once, and she stood frozen as though impaled by a dozen Debru spears. She knew she should force a smile onto her face, but she couldn't find one, and so she bowed deeply to the circle.

Given what Karla had told her, she had expected Elian to be upset that she would appear and steal any fraction of the glory he had basked in. Instead, it seemed to her as though he was the only one in the entire circle genuinely pleased to see her. When she rose from her bow, she saw him gesture her closer, and it was as though he pulled her toward him the same way he pulled adani toward him.

The circle hushed as he gestured for their attention.

"I have been honored by the gratitude and respect shown to me by everyone here," he said.

He sounded sincere, but his observations didn't match Samora's. She looked out across the circle and saw a group of scared elders. They weren't just scared of the Debru anymore, but feared their own warriors and this man who might steal their assumed authority.

Elian continued without a hint of a slur in his voice. "But I tell you that what I accomplished today is nothing compared to what my sister achieved. The only reason I could strike at the Vada was because she first held fast to it. She was the one who fought it as it strove to break into our world, and it was she who weakened it so that I could cut it down with mere steel. I hear my name on the lips of the celebrants, and I will not deny that I take pride in the role I played, but seeing my sister tonight reminds me that the only reason we won this fight is because we fought it together. It is my hope, and my most fervent desire, that this is the lesson we all take from tonight."

He paused, and Samora found herself greatly conflicted. The man behind her wore the face of her brother and inhabited his body, but he hardly seemed the child that lived in her memories. She knew somewhere there was a path of stories that led from the child she knew to the man he'd become. She knew the rough shape of those stories, but because she hadn't been with him when the crux of his change had occurred, this new Elian was almost as unreal to her as the legends Father had told when she was young.

From the tone of his voice and the steel in his gaze, she knew he spoke with clear intent, but she couldn't guess his ultimate aim. Did he hope to unify the clans so he could command them, or did he simply hope for greater cooperation?

She might not know her brother's mind, but she read the mood of the elders well enough. Her brother was not among friends. They may not be enemies, not yet, but they were no more friends to him than Gabe had been a friend to him when they were little. Elian might have won glory today, but he'd lost any chance of sitting at this council as their equal.

Elian squatted down beside her and whispered softly into her ear. "I'm sorry they made you come. Were you hiding at home?"

Samora nodded.

"I know you would have preferred to stay there, but I am glad you are here, because I was starting to feel very alone."

He stood and smiled, but Samora knew it for a lie, and it was almost enough to bring a matching smile to her face.

He had changed, but some part of him was still the Elian she knew. The same brother who would do anything in his strength to protect her. No matter where their paths led, she promised herself she'd do the same for him.

13

E lian woke as the sun poked its first tentative rays of light over the horizon. The light streamed in through the east-facing window. It rose slowly, as though afraid the adanists would shout it back below the tree line. Elian stood by the window and watched the sunrise over the silent camp. If he didn't know better, he'd have said there wasn't a soul within miles, but the truth was that he might very well be the first awake.

His head was clear, despite the increasingly aggressive efforts of the adanists to get him to drink a silly amount of liquor last night. When he'd tired of the elders he'd wandered the camp, and his back was sore from the vigorous congratulations he received. Secretly, he wondered if the adanists had some sort of quiet bet between them to see who could slap him hardest before his spine cracked.

He hoped he hadn't robbed them of too much mirth the night before. They all deserved to celebrate their achievements, but every sip of wine had been bitter and the food bland. He'd smiled and said what needed saying, but his thoughts had been for the days to come. Tantalizing possibilities danced before him, tempting him with the promise of unbelievable futures. All he had to do was reach out and grab them, for no one else would.

He licked his lips and stretched. He ran through all the forms he'd been taught, from the earliest ones Master Heinrich had instructed him in.

The camp was finally starting to stir by the time he finished his morning training. The movements hadn't helped him answer any of the challenges he faced, but he felt better for it. He glanced over to the sword resting in its sheath in the corner of the room but made no move toward it. He flexed his fingers, then opened the door and stepped into the living area.

Mother tended the fire near the center of the room, heating up some of last night's stew. "Breakfast will be ready soon. Why don't you wake up your sister?"

Samora's door opened and she stepped out. Her hair looked like it was trying to run away, but the glare she gave Elian told him the paths of wisdom and silence ran in parallel. "Your sister is perfectly capable of waking herself up, thank you very much."

Elian took comfort in the familiar routine of preparing the table for breakfast. He set clean bowls on the table while Samora collected the carved spoons. He ate eagerly, finishing his bowl before either of the women were halfway done.

"Do you have someplace to be?" Samora asked.

"I was hoping Harald would be awake. I'd like to speak to him."

Samora's look questioned why, but she didn't ask out loud.

Elian put his spoon down. "There's a couple of problems that are bothering me. Harald might be able to help."

Samora nodded. "Maybe you should check on Capricia, too?"

Mother's eyebrows rose past her bangs. "Who's Capricia?"

Elian grunted and stood quickly. "Well, I should probably get going, then. Lots to accomplish today." He gave the women a short bow, then hurried out the door. His sister's and mother's soft laughter followed him outside.

He'd barely gotten the door closed when he noticed an adanist hurrying over to greet him. The man's face was familiar, but Elian couldn't name him. They embraced like old friends and the warrior congratulated him on his accomplishments, then continued stumbling south. He looked and smelled like he hadn't slept the night before.

It didn't take long for him to realize traveling among the village and the camp was going to pose a problem. He couldn't go more than a dozen paces before he was interrupted by a stranger who wished to congratulate him, or a warrior who wanted to hear his account firsthand. Elian was only three houses away from his when he considered returning for a wide brimmed hat that would cover his face and allow him to walk in peace.

Tempting as the possibility was, he rejected it. The thanks and welcomes were genuine, and they needed to see him. It felt wrong to hide from the honest questions and congratulations of the other clan members. He was proud of what they'd accomplished, and he saw that pride mirrored in the faces of almost everyone he passed. People had forgotten the feel of hope, and now they latched onto it like the still-drunk adanists seeking out a morning ale to save them from their hangovers. If he could provide some sliver of that hope, the delay was well worth it.

Elian reached the healing tents much later than he anticipated. His arrival was preceded by a commotion, as was everything he'd done since returning home. By the time he had bowed to the last of his well-wishers, the sun was a quarter of the way into the sky, and its light fell squarely upon an angry healer with her arms crossed.

In a way, Elian was pleased to finally come across someone who wasn't bowing to him or slapping him across the back. But try as he might, he didn't know why Brittany was angry with him. He gulped and asked, "What's wrong?"

She didn't answer but instead kept her arms crossed, tapped her foot, and tried to stare holes into his chest.

"Brittany?"

"I can't decide whether I should hit you or embrace you," she said, still tapping her foot and staring at him.

"You're welcome to do either, but if you're taking opinions, I'd much prefer the embrace."

Her nostrils flared, but then her stern expression broke. In the end, she ended up doing neither. She just stood there and continued to glare at him. "Did you know? Did you know it would be so successful?"

"No." He was tempted to stare at his feet, but that no longer felt like an option. He forced himself to keep his chin up. "I had hoped and planned, but I didn't know. I just knew that it needed to be done."

Brittany chewed on her lower lip and then thrust her chin toward the back of the tent. "He woke earlier than he was supposed to, and he's been entertaining visitors all morning already, despite my wishes. He's been wanting to see you, but make it quick and don't excite him. He needs his rest."

She turned on her heel and walked away. Elian watched as she attended to a different patient, then followed in the direction she had indicated.

He'd never stepped inside a wandering clan's healing tent, and he walked slowly among the wounded. Most within were from the battle in the Hawks' gathering grounds. Some had lost limbs, while others suffered from maladies less obvious. Elian forced himself to see them, to not hide from the consequences of battle.

Most were asleep, which allowed him to walk among them without causing too much of a disturbance. The sight of the wounded illuminated the source of Brittany's anger. Outside, they celebrated his victory, but the price was paid here, beyond the sight of most. He swallowed hard, adding the knowledge to his growing, and nearly overwhelming, list of uncertainties.

Harald's bed wasn't hard to find, as Kati sat next to it, her long blonde hair shining like a beacon in the darker recesses near the rear of the tent. She looked up when he approached and smiled. "The legend himself. We've heard of nothing except you since we awoke."

Elian took a stool from beside a nearby empty cot and sat down next to Harald. "I'm sorry. No one should have to endure such torture."

Harald reached out with his hand and Elian grasped it. It was the first time Elian didn't feel like Harald's hand suffocated his own. His voice was scratchy but strong. "It's good to see you and great to hear what you've accomplished. Is it true?"

"I suppose it depends on what they're telling you, but probably yes."

"Will you tell me about it?"

"Someday every word, I swear. But Brittany made me promise that I wouldn't excite you and that I wouldn't stay long."

Harald groaned and was about to make a comment when Elian said, "Besides, as much as I'd like to celebrate with you, I came here today with a different purpose. There are matters that I wanted to talk to you about."

Some of the mirth faded from Harald's eyes, and he nodded. Somehow, he appeared formal even as he lay recuperating in bed. "You're my second. Ask away."

"Is it true about the shadow within you?"

Harald nodded.

Elian looked down at his hands. He licked his lips and spoke softly so that his words wouldn't carry. "I feel like a pretender who doesn't belong. I don't deserve the praise they're heaping on me."

He held up a hand to forestall Harald's objections. "Before the Vada appeared, I fought a few Debru within the circle. I was barely able to use my adani, and they almost killed me. Everyone outside this tent is celebrating because they believe I'm some incredible warrior. And I want that to be true, so they can believe in something that's real, but it's a lie. Without adani, I'm nothing. Without the dragons helping me, I'm nothing."

The words poured out of him like he was a pitcher of ale tipped over in last night's celebrations, and once his rant finished, he felt just as empty.

He ran his free hand through his hair and stared hard at the grass underneath Harald's cot. "For the first time, I'm in a position where I might be able to help, but it sickens me to know that what they believe isn't true."

Throughout Elian's confession, Harald had never let go of his hand, and now he grasped it even tighter. "Look at me, Elian."

Elian forced his gaze up and almost flinched away from the intensity of Harald's stare.

"There's no one to fool, Elian. Every Bear alive watched you training with Alec and knows where you came from. They don't need you to be some perfect myth from legend. They need someone strong enough to show them a way forward."

Harald let Elian's hand go as his voice lost some of its volume.

"Even I feel like a pretender sometimes, so know that you're not alone."

"You?"

Harald nodded. "I like to imagine even Abram felt like one at times. You can't control the stories that are told about you, but so long as you never lay claim to something that isn't true, you'll be fine."

"You make it sound easy."

"I make it sound simple, which it is. There's nothing easy about it, but that can be said for almost everything in life."

Elian nodded. "Thank you. I have many other questions, but not many that need to be answered today. There's only one other thing, something that worries me almost as much as the Vada that remains."

"What's that?"

Elian opened and closed his fists. "When we were fighting in that battle, I saw the difference the dragons made. We couldn't have accomplished what we did without their help. It's possible, even though I don't yet know how, that when we work together, we can drive the Debru completely from our lands. But you know the legends, probably better than I do. The dragons are ancient and have watched the Debru steal our territory and kill our clans for more years than I've been alive. So why is it they are only helping now?"

Harald's gaze traveled over to Kati, and they shared one of those silent looks that said so much more than Elian thought a look could. She gave the barest hint of a nod, and Harald said, "We were wondering if that had occurred to you yet."

"You've thought about it?"

"Ever since you came riding back on one. Warriors in the past have searched for the dragons, but none has found them."

"They wouldn't. They live so far to the west there's no chance we'd stumble upon them without a years-long search."

Harald's raised eyebrow indicated the knowledge might have been something he would have enjoyed learning earlier, but he didn't chastise Elian for holding the information back. "Regardless, there's a reason why we've long thought the dragons dead. Because if they were alive, why wouldn't they help? Now that we know they live, it raises the question again, and now the answer matters more than it once did."

"Do you have any ideas?"

"You're the one who summons them to battle. I've only ridden on one once, and I was near delirious for most of the trip."

"The legends don't provide any clues?"

"None that I'm aware of."

"So, what should we do?"

Harald scratched at his beard. "It seems to me that what *you* should do is go and ask them. The group of dragons that carried us from the gathering ground are still here, right?"

Elian nodded. "They've made what appears to be some sort of

nesting area north of the camp. They're the same ones that carried us into battle against the circle."

He hesitated, then said, "I can't say I'm excited to ask too much. They strike me as private creatures."

"Which is all well and good, but if we are allies, we can't keep secrets from one another. They're intelligent. Befriend them, and ask what needs to be asked."

"What if they don't like the questions, or refuse to answer?"

"Then that's an answer, too. Regardless, we need to know where they stand if we're going to know how to fight this war. And as far as I know, you're the only one talking to them."

Elian stood. "You get some rest and take care of yourself. I'll see you again soon."

"You will. Be careful, though. You're walking a path none of us has before, and we don't even know what dangers to watch out for."

❧ 14 ❧

Samora woke up the next morning to find Aldrick sitting on a bench outside her house. His face was turned toward the sun, his eyes were closed, and there was a gentle smile on his face. She tried to hurry away before he noticed her, but he was so relaxed, and she hesitated. As she did, he opened his eyes. "Good morning, ma'am."

"Good morning to you, too. I had thought your orders had ended." He hadn't followed her to the battle or any time after, and Samora had figured the elders had turned their full attention toward her brother.

"For a while, but I received a new set," he said. His brows were furrowed, as though pondering one of life's great mysteries.

Samora walked away from him, and he hurried to catch up and walk by her side. "Where are you going?"

"To the gathering ground."

"Why?"

"Because I have many questions and the gathering ground is the only place I might find them."

"May I accompany you?"

The question brought Samora up short. "You've never asked for permission before. Are you saying I have a choice now?"

Color flushed his cheeks, and he stared down at his feet. "You knew, didn't you, that my assignment was never about protecting you?"

She stared at him as though he'd just explained to her that the sky was blue and the sun rose in the east.

"Right. Of course you did. But you see, I didn't. I believed Aldo spoke true, but I didn't see what a fool I was until last night when he summoned me again."

Samora resumed her walk and Aldrick kept pace beside her.

He continued, "Last night Aldo ordered me to stay beside you no matter what. He ordered me to report on your movements and take note of everything you said and who you said it to. I feel a fool, but it was only then I realized the true purpose behind my orders."

"And?"

"And I'd like to ask your forgiveness. We've all heard the stories. I know what you and your brother did, and Aldo wants me to spy on you so that he might know your next moves before you tell the clans. It's not right."

"If you feel so strongly about it, why are you still here, following me?"

"Because I want to do what I originally promised. You and your brother might be two of the most valuable adanists among the wandering clans, and after striking the Vada down, I can't help but think you've made yourselves targets. I'd like to help protect you."

"And report my movements to Aldo?"

"Not if you don't want me to."

Samora waved a hand. "Tell him what you like. It's not as though I'm trying to hide. My brother and I want what we've always wanted, a life free of the Debru. If you'd like to help us, we'll be grateful for your strength."

Aldrick bowed deeper than was necessary. "Thank you, and once again, I'm sorry."

"If I'm being charitable, I would say that Aldo is only doing what he thinks is best for the clans. My brother and I bring change, and that can try a man's courage."

"And if you weren't being charitable?"

"I'd be saying much more unkind things."

Aldrick smiled, and Samora wondered if having some protection besides Karla wasn't such a bad idea after all.

SAMORA ASKED Aldrick to wait at the boundary of the gathering ground. He started to protest, but Samora cut him off. "It's nothing personal, but it's easiest for me to send my adani ranging wide if I'm the only one within the boundary."

She pointed to a young elm that stood close to the center. "Besides, I'll just be there, so if there's any danger, I won't be too far away."

Aldrick gave the elm a stare that made it seem like it was closer to a dozen miles away than the few hundred paces it was. "Very well. I'll keep watch from here."

"I appreciate it. It might be a while."

"I didn't have anything else to do today, and it's much quieter out here than it is in the village."

He wasn't wrong about that. Despite having a gathering ground within a quick walk's distance, the land was barely visited by anyone besides her. Karla had pointed out that the new gathering ground posed several difficulties for the wandering clans' traditions. Up until a few weeks ago, the number of gathering grounds had been set, each the sacred home of one of the wandering clans. Now there were two additional, but no one knew who they belonged to.

Samora found their avoidance foolish, but she didn't spend

much time attempting to convince them otherwise. It meant she had the gathering ground largely to herself.

She left Aldrick to find a comfortable spot to rest and observe as she stepped within the gathering ground she'd made. The transition from open prairie to gathering ground wasn't as pronounced a sensation as when she'd visited the Wolves' territory, but it seemed to grow in strength as the days passed.

In some ways, the birth of the gathering ground reminded her of nurturing the garden she and Mother had kept outside their house growing up. The gathering ground was like a young plant that had just broke through the soil to stretch into the sun. It needed care, protection, and sustenance until it was strong enough to grow on its own.

The gathering ground needed the same. It pulled adani, much like her brother, and even, she admitted with a grimace, like the Debru circles. It differed, though, in that it returned adani to the world, too. She felt the flow under her feet, like gentle waves lapping at her toes.

She reached the elm at the center of the gathering ground and placed her palm against its warm bark. The flow of adani was strongest here, and for a while she lost herself in its currents. It warmed her from the inside out and soothed away aches, pains, and worries. The temptation, as always, was to let herself get lost in adani forever. She slowly extracted herself from the gentle flow and looked around. She was delaying and knew it, but she treasured the moments of peace the gathering ground gifted her.

Samora turned her back to the tree and sat down beside it. She placed her hands against the ground, closed her eyes, and pushed her adani out and into the world. Thanks to the gathering ground, her adani was carried away on the vast, incomprehensible web of life that spread across the land.

The village and its new inhabitants were brightest against her senses, but she ignored them and pushed further out. Next, she found the second new gathering ground, younger even than the one she sat in. It felt young and fragile, but still healthy. No Debru lurked nearby, so she used that gathering ground to collect most of her adani and send it further on.

The journey across the deadlands was a more difficult one. Adani didn't travel through the broken soil as easily as it did closer to home, but Samora pushed on, aided by two gathering grounds. She hoped there might still be some fragment of the Hawks' gathering ground she could use to boost her adani further, but when she reached it, there was nothing there.

Her throat tightened as she searched nearby. She neared the limit of her reach and couldn't believe there wasn't anything to latch onto, but her search was fruitless. As near as she could tell, it was as if the gathering ground had never existed. Whatever plants and animals had called it home were dead.

Without the aid of the Hawks' gathering ground, she wasn't sure she could reach much further, but she tried anyway, searching for the last known Debru circle. It didn't take long to find. Debru crawled around it like ants building a new home, their numbers far too great for Samora to count. She wouldn't have been surprised to find there were more Debru out there than the clans had fought in the past year. Their numbers made Elian's last victory seem pathetic in comparison.

She slowed the racing of her heart. They had Elian and the dragons. Not all was lost.

Her adani recoiled as it brushed against the Vada. All Debru, from Belog down, felt as shadows against her senses, but the Vada was darker yet. It was a darkness that stole all light and heat, sending a shiver down her spine even though she was weeks of travel away. The Vada sat at the heart of the Debru circle, swirling in darkness and attempting a working she couldn't identify.

It felt a little as though it was digging and ripping, tearing through the fabric of adani to plant something else. Samora wasn't sure she wanted to know what, but the clans needed to know the dangers they faced. She pushed her adani closer, straining near the edge of her ability to get a clear glimpse of the working.

The Vada noticed her presence. She sensed its attention on her adani and tried to flee, returning to the gathering ground as quick as thought.

The Vada was faster. In less than the blink of an eye her adani was trapped and held in place by needles of shadow. She called and pulled at her adani, but the Vada laughed at her efforts. It pulled her in close, then opened its mouth and swallowed the thread of her adani whole. Samora just had time to scream before her awareness was ripped away and she felt nothing.

WHEN SHE OPENED HER EYES, she didn't know how much time had passed. Perhaps only a heartbeat, but perhaps much more. She screamed, but no sound escaped her throat. Frozen air stabbed icy needles into her bare skin, but no light, sound, or feel provided any clue as to her location.

She could sense it, though, watching her like a child playing with a new toy. It laughed, the sound rippling through her ribs and shaking her spine. She grasped for adani, but none answered her call.

The darkness around her faded into a time and place she had no knowledge of. The Vada showed her a land of tall buildings, many that contained enough rooms to house her whole village. Men and women walked on hard paths between the buildings, and though it was night, lanterns illuminated the paths with a light that never flickered. She floated above the scene, somehow knowing nothing about it but understanding all that mattered. Her gaze flicked from sight to sight.

Their clothes were nothing like the rough-spun fabrics she and the others wore. Buildings were made of stones and metals, shaped with far greater skill than any smith of their age.

The night grew silent, and then the dragons came. Adani-fueled flames lit the buildings on fire and killed hundreds, if not thousands. Whole villages perished in less time than Elian needed to cook a steak. A few defenders launched bound adani at the dragons, but none were strong enough to leave so much as a scratch.

She was dropped, not of her own accord, among a group of the defenders. She didn't understand their language, but their sense of betrayal was clear to her eye. A long streak of flame washed over both her and the defenders, but she didn't feel any of the heat of their deaths.

She was pulled back into the sky, where she saw something she couldn't explain. The dragons destroyed, but they saved, too. People walked from their homes as if in a trance, only to wake up, witness the destruction of their homes, then be scooped up in a dragon's enormous claws.

Samora wondered where they went but didn't have to wonder long. She was pulled along with them, yanked by a string she couldn't see. She ended in a field and watched as the great elder dragon wiped the memories of those who survived.

The vision faded to black, and she was once again in the clutches of the Vada's shadow.

"You lie!" she shouted into the blackness.

The Vada laughed, insensitive to her distress. Or worse, reveling in it. She struggled to find any hint of adani, but she felt as helpless as Elian must have when he was a child. Then, suddenly, it let go and she was once again in the trance so familiar to her. Her adani retreated from the Vada faster than one of Karla's lightning strikes, and when it finally returned to her, she opened her eyes with a gasp.

Aldrick was beside her, a hand on her shoulder and a worried look in his eyes.

"Are you hurt?" he asked.

She shook her head. "No, but we need to find my brother right away. I don't think the dragons are our allies."

🎇 15 🎇

Elian sat at the table in his home, feeling very small even as words of his deeds spread from lip to ear like wildfire. Harald, Kati, and Karla sat at the table alongside him and Mother, while Aldrick stood against one wall with his arms crossed. Harald alone made the room seem tiny, as though someone had designed the house a few sizes too small.

Elian didn't know why Samora insisted Aldrick join them. This meeting was supposed to be for only those most trusted by the siblings, but Samora had been firm, and Elian didn't know the scout well enough to say otherwise.

The scout was the least of his worries, now. Every word Samora told of her story felt like Elian's worst nightmares coming true. Not only were the dragons fickle allies, they had a history of treachery. His sister always insisted she didn't know if what she'd been shown was true, but she claimed it had felt real to her, and Elian was inclined to believe her. It answered some of the questions he'd been wrestling with, too.

Samora finished her story and the room went silent.

Eventually, Elian felt as though they were waiting on him. Harald and Kati were still recovering, and had only left the healing tent because Harald had threatened to tear it down if Brittany didn't stand aside. Karla was strong but had cut her ties with the clan. That left him. He cleared his throat.

"We need to find a way to find out if what Samora saw was true. It's certainly possible the Vada is lying."

"Or that the dragons are," Karla pointed out.

"Or both," Kati said. "There's no way of us knowing."

Elian thought quickly. "Perhaps there's some sort of test we could give the dragons, something that would prove once and for all if we can trust them."

Samora nodded. "We could—"

Harald cleared his throat, and the room went silent again. "We could spend all day creating elaborate plans, or we could ask them."

"But what if they attack us like they did in Samora's vision?" Elian asked.

Harald shrugged. "I think if they were going to attack us, they would have done so already. But if they're biding their time for some reason, I don't think we lose much by confronting them right away. It's not as though we'd defeat them with a few weeks of preparation."

All eyes in the room drifted toward Elian.

"What?" he asked.

"You're the one who's been able to communicate with them."

Elian realized why they were all staring at him. "Oh."

Samora raised her hand. "I'd like to try speaking with the dragons, too."

"We don't both need to take the risk," Elian said.

Harald disagreed. "She might be onto something. For all we know, given the way we communicate, it may be best to try with two people. Who knows? Maybe it's harder for them to lie if there's more than one mind connected with them."

Elian looked for some excuse. He might be a fool, but he believed that if the dragons attempted to attack him, he had some small chance of surviving and escaping. Samora would have none. Gifted as she was with adani, she couldn't fight her way out of a tent.

It was a poor excuse. As Harald had said, if the dragons decided they were going to attack, it would mean the end for the whole village, not just him.

He nodded. "I suppose there's no point in delaying, then, is there?"

"None at all," Harald agreed, and the matter was decided.

———

THE DRAGONS HAD SET up their own camp north of the village, though it bore little in common with the camps of the wandering clans now surrounding Elian's home. They dug up huge tracts of soil to settle their massive bulks in, and they spent as much or more time sleeping than they did being active. Every so often one would stand, spread its wings, and launch itself into the sky. It would return later in the day, blood painted across its jaws.

Also unlike the clans camped around the village, the dragons didn't eat the cattle or pigs raised by the farmers. Elian didn't have much patience for the elders of his village, but he understood their fears about the clans remaining for much longer. The clan's hunters did what they could to ease the burden of their presence, but the land had been picked clean of prey long before the clans arrived.

Elian and Samora stood together and watched the gathering of dragons. Elian could feel it in his feet when one nearby stirred, and he was reminded once again of the immense strength they wielded. He glanced over to ensure Samora was ready, then made his way through the field toward the dragon that he'd rescued from the Debru. The dragon rested near the center of the field, and it fixed him with a hunter's gaze as he approached.

Samora already knew how Elian "spoke" with the dragons, so she joined him in placing one of her hands against the dragon's neck. He looped adani through his arm and hand, then let it connect with the dragon's circling adani. Strength rushed through his limbs, but he wasn't interested in it today.

Harald had told him to befriend the dragon, so he tried, no matter how much embarrassment rose to his cheeks. "My name is Elian. Do you have a name?"

The dragon rumbled, and though it said nothing, Elian sensed it was annoyed with the question.

So much for that, he supposed.

Elian hadn't yet figured out how to best communicate with the dragons. So far, simply speaking to them as he would a human had worked well enough, but he always wondered how much of his meaning was lost in their unusual exchanges. There was nothing to do but ask the question that had brought him here.

"Why are you helping us, truly?" he asked.

After a time, a vision appeared in his mind's eye, the same one he'd been shown earlier, of humans and dragons marching and flying into battle together.

Samora's sharp intake of breath stopped Elian from asking the dragon again.

"What do you see?" he asked her.

"Notice their clothes."

Elian hadn't paid much attention to the humans' attire before. It didn't look like any he'd seen before, but little else seemed important. "What about them?"

"It's the same style of clothing the humans wore in the scenes the Vada showed me. I think this is from the past."

"Is that true?" Elian asked the dragon.

The dragon rumbled.

"Do you also think that means 'yes?'" he asked Samora.

"It does."

"You fought with humans before. Did you betray them?"

Another rumble, this one much deeper. Another vision appeared, this time of the dragons carrying humans away from a burning city. Samora's breathing grew heavier and Elian didn't need to ask. This was also what she'd seen before, except with less context.

The Vada hadn't been lying.

"Why did you betray us?" Elian asked.

A series of visions flashed before him. Humans building new settlements after the betrayal, the dragons keeping close watch from high overhead. Then a final flight to the west once the dragons were certain the humans would survive.

Elian shook his head. "I don't understand. Why care for us after you killed so many?"

To this, the dragon had no answer.

"Can we trust you now? Or will you kill us again?"

The dragon sat silent, as if it were indifferent to Elian's opinions. And it might have been. The visions were the dragon's own, meaning it had lived hundreds of years. That it bothered with Elian at all was a wonder.

"We need to know more," Samora said. Her calm voice soothed the sharp edges of Elian's worry. "We know so little of our history, and our leaders are nervous. If you want us as allies, you need to remind us of what has been lost."

The dragon shifted under their touch and the flow of adani shifted within. It didn't stand, but it felt as though it prepared to lash out. Elian tensed, but Samora's adani remained as still as a lake under calm skies.

Then another vision, of the dragon in flight. Underneath there were mountains and villages that were larger than anything Elian had believed possible. The hard paths were overgrown with weeds, but the buildings stood taller than trees and were made of materials Elian didn't recognize. The vision was accompanied by something more, part offer and part question.

Samora deciphered it first, and Elian suffered a pang of his old childhood jealousy. In this, he thought he might be best, but Samora overtook him here, too. "You want us to come with you? So that we might understand?"

That higher-pitched rumble. *Yes.*

Samora responded before Elian could. "We need to consider it carefully. Give us some time to confer with our elders, and we'll return shortly."

The dragon rumbled again, leaving Elian and Samora with a new dilemma.

ELIAN DRAGGED his feet as they left the dragons' field. Samora noticed and stopped, gazing at him quizzically. Elian swept his arm back, gesturing toward all the resting dragons. "I should be the one to go, but I don't want to. If I leave, the clans will go straight back to their bickering, and by the time I return any chance I have of making a difference among them will be gone."

He feared Samora's judgment. Who was he to think that his absence or presence could matter so much? He'd been fortunate in one battle, and now he thought the fate of the clans hinged on his presence.

Her biting comments never came. When he found the courage to look up at her, she was watching the dragons more than him.

"Am I wrong?" he asked.

She thought a moment longer, then shook her head. "Hard as it is for me to believe, I think you're right. The clans need your voice in their councils, and they will hear it more clearly now than later. If you left, that would be lost."

"What do we do, then? We'd be just as foolish to ignore the dragon's offer."

Samora looked back at the dragons. "I should be the one to go. I sensed how you speak with them, and I think I can do the same. It doesn't come as naturally to me as it does to you, but it should still work."

"Your confidence doesn't exactly inspire."

"Nobody can cycle adani through their body with the ease you can, which is what allows the dragons to speak to you so easily. But I can do so well enough to make myself understood."

Elian had witnessed the truth of her claim firsthand, so he didn't doubt she'd be able to speak to the dragon. His worries were of a different nature. "If you leave, we'll lose our ability to know what the Vada is doing."

Samora bit her lower lip. "That's true. Karla can send her adani out a long ways, but not quite as far as I can. You'd lose that if I left, but she'd still be able to warn you long before the Vada arrived."

"But I don't only want to know when it is coming for us. I want to know everything we can learn about the Debru so that we can plan."

"Do you think it matters that much? We know their ultimate goal, and with the dragons, you might be able to scout the Debru from the air. I don't think I'm as useful as you think I am."

Elian narrowed his eyes. "You're the only adanist who has ever created a gathering ground, as well as the only one that destroyed a circle. If anything, I should be the one leaving, because you're far more useful than I."

Samora scoffed. "Try making that argument in a council meeting. Nobody made a throne for me to sit on."

Elian's eyes went wide. "Wait. Are you jealous of me?"

Her answering look made him feel like he was stupid. "Of course I am. I mean, it's mostly pride, but there's jealousy there, too. Always has been. You've always been faster and stronger, and you never stopped trying to master binding, long after most children would have given up."

Elian grunted.

"What?"

He scratched at the back of his neck. "It's just that I've always been jealous of you. Ever since you were little you've been able to master adani with such ease. I wanted to have your abilities, but no matter how hard I tried, I could never come close to you."

"And I felt like I'd never catch you."

Elian let out a low chuckle, still feeling like a fool. "I'm sorry for any suffering I've inadvertently made you endure."

"I could say the same."

Elian took a deep breath. "We can't let the opinions of the council sway our decision. If you can learn how to speak to the dragons, do you think others could, too? Is there someone else we could send?"

"I'm not sure. You should know, it's hard for me, as difficult as sending my adani all the way to where the Vada is camped. It's possible someone else may be able to communicate, but I'm skeptical."

There was something else she wasn't saying. Elian heard it in her voice but couldn't guess what it was. "And?"

Samora blew out a long breath. "And truth be told, there aren't that many people that I would trust. We need this knowledge, and the people in our house earlier today are about the only ones I'd be willing to send."

Elian completed her thought without problem. "And all of them have roles to play here. Karla is probably the only other choice that makes any sense."

"And she has the distinction of killing a Belog all on her own. You're going to want her in any fights to come."

Elian grimaced. "You're assuming I'm going to be the one staying."

She shrugged. "You've started something here. You led an assault with adanists from all the wandering clans. They'll listen to you more than they will me."

"But putting that aside, who do the clans need here more? All I can do is swing a sword, but you're the one who can heal circles and create gathering grounds. Not to mention safely keep an eye on the Vada."

"None of that matters that much. We can't attack the Vada and the circle, not anytime soon. All I can do is help keep an eye on it, but even that's not safe. After last time, I'm not sure I'd want to get close enough with my adani to sense it. You'd be served just as well, or maybe better, by sending scouts on the dragons."

She smiled, but Elian could tell she was trying to display courage she wasn't feeling. "Besides, it's not like I'll be gone for that long."

Elian agreed with her arguments, but still didn't want to see her go. She should be away from the front lines, as safe as any human could be. "Is this what it felt like when I went west with Harald?"

She nodded.

"I suppose it's only fair then, isn't it?"

She grinned, and this time it was real. "That's one way to look at it, I guess."

They resumed their journey home, and Elian had a thought that made him smile.

Samora noticed and waited for him to explain.

"I'll agree that you should be the one to go, but on one condition."

"What's that?"

"You're the one who has to tell Mother."

16

Silence echoed loudly around the room as everyone stared at her. Harald stuck his pinky finger in his ear and twisted it around. "Say what, now?"

Samora shot him a glare that, unfortunately, didn't cause him to suffer any harm at all. The giant man tipped his chair back on its two rear legs. It was a testament to Father's skill that the chair didn't immediately break under the man's weight.

Harald turned to Mother, who took Samora's announcement without much reaction. He pointed first to Samora, then to Elian, who stood leaning against one of the walls. "Did both your children always have this problem of running off into danger?"

"It's a more recent development," Mother said.

Harald returned his chair to all four feet. "Why not take a larger party and scout whatever it is the dragons have to show us?"

Kati answered that question. "Because we need everybody here to defend the villages. There's no point risking more people than necessary."

"But what if it's a trap?" Harald asked.

"Then it's good we're only sending one adanist to die. There's no force we could send that would match the dragons."

"I might match a dragon," Harald said.

Kati scoffed. "So you've often claimed."

"I'll go with her," Karla said.

"We need you here. Samora and I already talked about this," Elian said.

"Oh, did you? Did your sister mention I'm not particularly fond of orders?"

Elian set his mouth in a firm line, and Samora saw a hint of their mother in his expression. "It's not an order, but we need your strength here for when the Vada attacks."

"No, you don't, and you'd know it if you used that mind of yours for more than a few moments at a time. Would you say I'm as strong as five Haralds?"

Elian shook his head. "No matter how strong you are, you're not five Haralds."

"Thanks," Harald said, acting more indignant than he was.

"And if you'd had five Haralds against the Vada's attack, would it have mattered?"

Elian's face fell, which was answer enough for Karla.

The ancient adanist ticked points off on her fingers. "First, I wasn't planning on staying here much longer. Too many people. Second, your sister's adventure sounds like the most interesting experience I've heard about in a while, and that's saying something after all we've been through this last year. And third, someone needs to protect her and makes sure she returns home. That might as well be me."

Elian looked around the room for help, but there was none coming. Everyone else was diligently avoiding getting pulled in. Finally Elian looked to Samora, but she just shrugged. She hadn't been sure Karla would be interested, but it would be good to have her.

Elian realized the battle was lost and offered Karla a short bow. "Thank you for protecting my sister."

A cough from the opposite side of the room drew everyone's attention to Aldrick, who sheepishly raised his hand. "I'd like to go, too, if I could."

"Why?" Elian asked, clearly dumbfounded.

"I don't want to be part of Aldo's schemes anymore. I think that what Samora is doing is important, and I'd like to help how I can. Karla will protect her well, but it seems to me there's no harm in having another person helping, right?"

Elian looked lost, and he turned to Samora for guidance. They hadn't expected anyone else would be interested in joining Samora, but she found she didn't mind the idea of companionship. She nodded.

Karla interrupted before Elian could give his final answer. "You sure you can ride with me?"

Samora remembered all too well their rude initial greeting, but now Aldrick seemed properly shamed. He bowed to Karla, even if he grimaced as he did so. "Yes, ma'am."

"Then it's decided," Elian said, "so long as no one else suddenly wants in."

He waited expectantly, but when no one else added their voices, he relaxed. "Let's get them ready to go, then."

THEY GATHERED and took off later that night. There were farewells that lingered longer than necessary and embraces and bows aplenty, but eventually Samora, Karla, and Aldrick were all positioned on the dragon's back. They'd been provisioned with almost two weeks' worth of supplies divided up among three heavy packs, and Samora felt about as prepared as it was possible to be.

She connected with the dragon, letting it know that she and the others were ready. She thought she felt a small rumble of discontent, but it was hard to know what was real and what she imagined in their exchanges. The dragon lumbered to its feet, then spread its wings and launched itself into the air, powered part by the massive strength of its wings and part by its mastery of adani.

Samora had only ridden on a dragon once before, and that had been to and from the battle with the nascent Vada. She'd been so distracted on the way over, and so relieved on the return, that she'd never really taken the time to appreciate the wonder of flight.

She gripped tightly onto hand-sized scales as the world receded below her. The dragon's flight impressed her with its smoothness. Between the beating of its wings and its manipulation of adani, the flight felt more stable than the boats she'd ridden on before.

As the dragon rose it turned west, but with the moon only revealing a sliver of itself this evening, Samora found her gaze pulled up rather than down. They ascended above the wispy clouds, and it was as though nothing at all stood between Samora and the countless suns above. She stared, enraptured, at the immensity of the sky.

As the sun struggled over the horizon, Samora cast her eyes below. Already they were near the edges of the grasslands. Perhaps five to seven miles away, green gave way to a sharp line of brown. She watched them fly over the boundary to the deadlands with a sense of detachment.

Elian had described his own experiences well, and she'd shoved her adani through the few withered channels that remained in that land, so she knew what she'd experience if they were on foot. Sandy soil, devoid of the thick web of roots more abundant lands enjoyed. A lack of adani, as far as eye and sense could travel.

On foot she might have cried. A life without adani's presence seemed not much of a life at all.

But up above, on the back of a dragon, she felt as though she rested in a gathering ground. The adani coursing through her body made the sight below seem even more distant than it was.

Their flight grew long and the deadlands vast. Though the flight was smooth, Samora's thighs began to ache, and judging from the frequent small adjustments her companions made in their positions, she wasn't alone. She asked the dragon if they might take a break and the dragon reluctantly agreed.

It landed on a rise with a commanding view of the surrounding area. She and the others got off and stretched while the dragon remained vigilant. She glanced up at it. "You were captured in lands like this, weren't you?"

Being as they weren't connected it gave her no response, but she decided it would be best if they didn't rest long. Perhaps the dragons weren't as strong over the deadlands as they were over home.

She dropped into a squat and dipped her hands into the loose soil. It came up easily under her fingers, the small fragments of grass that remained crumbling under her touch. No adani ran near the surface. She pushed her fingers deeper in and sent her adani further down, finally finding a weak thread of life far below.

The absence dug a hole in her heart. As long as she could remember, she'd been able to sense the flow of adani around her. More recently, she'd come to trust to its guidance, and having it so conspicuously absent made her feel a little like she was losing a parent all over again.

"We shouldn't dally here long," Karla said.

"I was just thinking the same. Elian said the deadlands don't extend forever, so perhaps we can rest again in a better place."

Aldrick had nothing to add to the conversation, so they clambered back on top of the dragon and took off again. The distance from the deadlands did little to ease the disquiet in Samora's chest. She stared at the broken ground as they flew over, wondering how far she could trust her senses.

In time she turned her head so she could speak to Karla. "Do we know what made the deadlands?"

Karla shook her head. "They've been dead for as long as I've been alive. We always assumed the Debru were somehow responsible, but I'm not sure if anyone knows."

"I had expected them to feel like a Debru circle, or at least similar, but they aren't. The result is in many ways the same, but this feels like a different process."

"What are you thinking?"

Samora shook her head. "I'm thinking that this is what happens when the Debru have free reign over the land. They squeeze the life and adani out of it until nothing is left."

"Do you understand, then?"

"Understand what?"

"That there can be no peace with the Debru."

Samora swallowed hard. Of course she understood. She'd always known. Why couldn't Karla understand? The Debru had to go, but it didn't mean she wanted to kill them.

It was late afternoon when they finally passed out of the deadlands. The dragon rumbled, and when Samora joined her adani to it, she saw a vision of them landing so the dragon could hunt and rest.

The dragon landed them again on a rise in the land, more pronounced than the rises Samora was familiar with close to her home. The land here rolled like enormous waves. Samora imagined trying to drag a plow up some of the hills and couldn't. Gardens could be grown here, but not fields the size she was used to.

Aldrick stood beside her as she took in the scenery. "Do you think humans ever lived here?" he asked.

Karla grunted behind him as she dropped her heavy pack on the ground. "That's a good question. I don't see any sign, but if

Samora's visions were correct, those humans would have lived here a long, long time ago. Might not be anything of them left."

Behind them, the dragon took off and Karla and Aldrick started.

"It's nothing to worry about. He's just searching for food and then he'll return," said Samora.

"So he says," Karla argued.

"I think if the dragons wanted to kill us they wouldn't go to all this trouble," Samora answered.

"True, unless they've got other plans for us."

"And if they do, you can fight a dragon. That should please you."

Karla laughed out loud. "You know me too well, girl. I've been curious to try my strength against one since the first time I saw it."

Aldrick looked at the older adanist like she was mad. Karla shooed him and Samora away with a wave of her hand. "Now, find us some firewood. It looks like we're camping here tonight, and I'm getting hungry after a long day of sitting on my rear."

THE HILL the dragon had chosen overlooked a small creek that ran across and down the north slope. Trees grew tall near the creek, and Aldrick and Samora grabbed their waterskins and started down. Rain must have passed through recently, because the ground was slippery. More than once Samora would plant her heel and feel it slide before finding sturdy footing. Aldrick led the way, helpfully discovering any particularly slippery spots before she did.

Once they reached the creek they took turns stepping out onto a rock, dropping into a squat, and filling their skins with fresh water. They laid the full skins carefully down, then collected firewood. Samora bound adani into a long golden knife while

Aldrick formed an entire sword. She raised an eyebrow and he grinned. "I only know how to bind a spear and a sword. Spent more time learning how to use them well instead of how to bind different forms."

"Is that typical among the Wolves?"

Aldrick smoothly sliced off several small branches. His cuts were cleaner and better positioned with the sword than hers were with her knife. "Among those of us who intend to be warriors, yes. There are those who want to be healers or hunters, and they might learn some more forms. It's a person's choice."

Brittany's account of the Bears' traditions had been a little different. There, almost all young adanists were encouraged to become warriors, thanks in large part to Harald's influence. She'd endured plenty of grief for becoming a healer, even though she'd saved more of their lives than any warrior.

"Did you always know you wanted to be a warrior?"

Aldrick trimmed another tree with efficient cuts. He'd have enough wood cut for both of them if she wasn't careful. "I did. My father was a warrior, and all four of my grandparents were. I wanted to follow in their footsteps, although I did consider becoming a hunter for a while."

"What decided the matter?"

Aldrick grinned. "Mostly the fact that I was a terrible hunter. I was about as quiet as a summer thunderstorm, and I scared off far more animals than I ever killed. I can bind a spear, but I can't throw one well. It drove both me and my father nearly mad. We'd spend evening after evening beyond the boundaries of the camp and I'd throw spear after spear, but I never got as good as I needed to be. But put a sword in my hand and I'd like to think I'm more than a little helpful."

He gestured to the pile of firewood near his feet, already several times larger than Samora's.

"I can see that," she said.

They gathered the firewood and waterskins and hiked back up

the hill. Aldrick's efforts even impressed Karla, who said, "Maybe it was a good idea we decided to bring you along."

Evening approached quickly, so they got the fire started and made a meal of their provisions. The dragon still hadn't returned, but despite Aldrick's frequent glances toward the sky, Samora wasn't worried. She didn't know how long it would take a dragon to hunt and eat its meal, but she trusted the creature.

She hoped that faith wasn't misplaced.

They were nearly finished with their meal when Karla's ears perked up. Before Samora could ask what she had noticed, she was on her feet and stalking through the shadows. They'd built the fire on the north slope of the hill, where it couldn't be seen for far. Karla walked over the top of the hill and down the south facing slope.

Samora followed close behind, but when Aldrick made to follow her, she held out a hand to stop him. "If you're not very good at being silent, maybe you should stay here. I'll let you know if we go far."

He looked ready to argue, but Samora turned on her heel and left before he could protest. She proceeded slowly, careful not to step on anything that would give away her position.

Karla was crouched in the grass, looking further south. Samora crouched down beside her. She didn't have to ask. Karla pointed, and Samora saw three small shapes trotting along near the horizon. They were miles distant, but it was dark enough that when they turned Samora swore she saw the glint of green eyes.

"What are otsoa doing this far west?" she whispered.

"The very question I've been wondering."

They watched for a moment longer, but the otsoa didn't seem to notice them. They kept trotting further west and eventually fell out of sight. Samora stretched out her adani and tracked them to ensure they weren't about to double back. When she was certain they weren't going to return their way, she allowed herself a soft sigh of relief.

"They're not coming?" Karla said.

"No."

"Did you sense anything else?"

Samora shook her head. As near as she could tell, they were mostly alone in this wilderness.

"Let's hope that's true. If there's one thing I've learned from a lifetime of fighting those creatures, it's that if one of them is near, the Debru aren't usually far behind."

❧ 17 ❧

Elian dragged his feet as he turned the last corner to his destination, each foot feeling like it was tied to a stone. He tugged on the collar of his tunic even though it wasn't anywhere near his throat. His cheeks felt flushed, and he worried that he was starting to develop a fever, but he'd felt fine just that morning. He took a few steps toward the tent in front of him but stopped several paces short. He shook his head, turned on his heel, and was about to walk away when the tent opened and Capricia stepped out.

"Elian?"

He turned back, his cheeks burning. "Hello. I…"

He already felt like a fool, and he hadn't even asked anything yet.

She saved him from himself. "Are you aware that you're a very easy person to sense?" she asked.

"Samora has often told me so," he said, not understanding her point.

She guessed as much. "I'm telling you that I was able to sense your approach, and I've been able to sense you standing out here and hesitating. Most of the people in the camp probably did."

If his cheeks burned any hotter, he feared they would catch on fire. "I see."

She smiled gently. "Rumor is that you're arranging a scouting expedition to the old gathering grounds."

He jumped on the opportunity to speak about anything else. Fortunately, it happened to be the same reason he visited. "That was actually what I came here to ask you about. I'm inviting several adanists from each clan, but I wanted to extend an invitation to you personally."

"Me?" she asked with mock confusion. Elian sensed she knew exactly why he was here but was going to insist he say everything out loud. It was almost the complete opposite of spending time with Samora.

His heart ached when he thought of his sister, but he pushed it aside for now.

"You were a tremendous help when you helped me scout the Belog, and I'd feel better having you with me today, too."

Mirth twinkled in her eyes as he danced around his true reasons. He clenched one of his fists. He'd charged a Vada with a sword, so why did this seem so much harder? He took a step closer to her and said, "And I'd like to spend more time with you, but that time has been difficult to find as of late. The trip there and back will take most of the day with the dragons, and I thought it would be much more pleasant if I could spend it with you."

Her smile shone brighter than the sun. "How can I say no to such an invitation, especially from the hero of all the clans?"

The blood rushed again to his cheeks. "You know better than anyone that I'm as flawed as any other adanist."

"The man who killed a Vada with one cut of his sword? To hear others tell it, you breathe fire, walk on water, and weave adani as though you were Abram's son."

He knew she jested, but he still objected. "You know none of that is true."

She finally showed mercy on him. "I do, but it's quite the treat to listen to how others think of you."

"Maybe someday you'll have to set them straight?"

"Why would I do that? It would be far more entertaining to make up new stories about our scouting expedition to grow your legend even further."

"You wouldn't, would you?"

Her answering grin could have been either confirmation or denial, and he didn't think she'd tell him straight. After making him suffer for a moment, she said, "I'll gather my things. How long before the flight leaves?"

"Not long. I want to be on the way well before midday. The Hawks were the last clan I had to speak to. All I have left is to talk to Kati, and then we'll be set to go."

Capricia half-turned back to her tent. "I'll prepare then and see you soon."

As Elian walked toward the center of the Hawk's camp to meet with Kati, his steps were much lighter.

CAPRICIA SHOWED up well before they were ready to leave. She carried a small sack of provisions and wore the same clothes she'd worn on their expedition to study the Belog. He inclined his head to her, and she looked up at the dragon they were going to ride. "Not the same one we rescued from the Belog."

Elian shook his head. "That one took Samora west."

"Is this one the new leader?"

"I couldn't tell you. As far as I know, they don't have one. Or maybe their leader isn't here. In Samora's visions there was an elder dragon that was supposedly much larger than these, but we haven't seen it. All I know is that I was able to connect with this one and it agreed that it and a few others would escort us to scout the Vada."

The last of the riders arrived and Elian held a quick council with them. The purpose of the scouting expedition was simple enough. He wanted to observe the conditions of the land and observe whatever plans the Debru were forming. He'd asked for volunteers from each of the wandering clans. More eyes meant more chances of spotting something valuable, and he didn't want to play any of the petty posturing games other clan elders too often fell into. This was a chance for them all to work together, and the arrangements he made forced them to adapt.

Three volunteers had been chosen from each of the four wandering clans camped around the village to join him and Capricia. Three dragons would carry one of each clan's adanists, forcing the warriors into a long ride together.

The adanists grumbled quietly among themselves about the arrangement, but no one openly spoke up against Elian. The adanists might hurt each other on the flight, but he hoped to build new bonds between them.

No one had any questions when he was finished, so they mounted their dragons and took to the air. Capricia sat close behind Elian, her arms lightly around his waist. "Just the two of us?" she asked.

"I'll confess I didn't want to share."

She held on a little tighter, and Elian's heart beat just a bit faster.

He pointed out familiar landmarks as the dragon began its journey west. He pointed out the tree that had once served as the farthest point Father had allowed him to travel on his own, then outlined the fields where he'd once worked. It didn't take long for the dragon's incredible speed to leave all of Elian's past behind, and suddenly he had nothing much to speak about.

"Growing up in a village sounds so different than my childhood among the Hawks," Capricia said. She leaned against his back. "Did you like it? There were days when I was young when I dreamed about living in a village."

"Really? I spent most of my days dreaming about being part of one of the wandering clans. You were practically legends to me."

She chuckled at that. "You didn't like growing up in the village?"

"It wasn't that I didn't like it. The days could be long and the work hard, but I was comfortable and well-fed. It was more that I felt like the wandering clans were doing more to serve the village than I was, and were more exciting, too. Village life was largely routine and a part of me wanted to break out of that."

"I suppose we always long for something different, no matter what that is," Capricia said.

Their conversation continued as they explored each other's childhoods, shared stories of their adventures, and discussed the dreams they held for the future. Elian spent more time listening than he did speaking, fascinated by this woman that he'd crossed paths with.

During one lull in the conversation, he said, "You're one of the most curious people I've met. Have you always been?"

"For a few years now, yes. You'll laugh at me when you hear the story, though."

"I'll try not to," he assured her.

"I was out on patrol one day and came across a butterfly breaking free of its cocoon. Have you heard about this?"

Elian shook his head.

"Little caterpillars one day form a cocoon, which usually hangs from a branch for a while, and then a butterfly emerges. I was fortunate enough to watch the butterfly break free, and it made me wonder what happens inside those cocoons. How does one thing become something completely different? The next time I saw a cocoon, I cut it open to find out, and guess what I found?"

Elian didn't have the slightest clue. "Something between a caterpillar and a butterfly?"

"No. Just a thick liquid. There was no butterfly or caterpillar within."

"How is that possible?"

"I don't know. Before I cut it open I could feel the adani at work within, but the weaving was far too intricate for my senses. That moment made me realize I didn't understand a thing about the world, and I wanted to know as much as I could."

"You really would like Samora. She thinks in much the same way, although she started questioning everything younger. I like to say that her first word was 'why?' and she hasn't learned that many since. It sometimes annoyed me, because I was often the victim of her questioning, but now I can see how it's served her well."

"Hopefully it'll serve us well against the Debru, too" Capricia said.

Elian agreed. Now that he'd sensed the sheer strength of the Vada, it seemed more likely that Samora would find a way to defeat them than he would.

The long ride passed in no time at all, and they spotted the inky stain against the horizon earlier than Elian expected. He focused on his connection with the dragon and ensured they planned to approach the Debru carefully. Belogs had proven strong enough to catch dragons, so Elian didn't want to venture any closer than necessary. The dragon wholeheartedly agreed.

They had passed over into the deadlands some time ago, but Elian had thought there was more time before they reached the now-destroyed gathering grounds. He didn't think much of it, though. From up high, the deadlands looked too uniform for him to have a sense of his location. Of course, he'd felt much the same when he'd been walking across them.

"They're closer than we thought they were," Capricia said, confirming his suspicion.

"You can tell?"

"We spent too much time out here when we attempted to reach the gathering grounds, so I have some sense of the shape of the land. The Hawks' grounds are many miles away yet."

Elian instructed the dragon to rise, which the dragon happily agreed to do. He glanced back and saw that the others followed their lead. He'd not paid them much attention on the flight, but no one seemed to have killed one another, so he took that as a good sign.

The additional height allowed them to see farther, and Elian caught his first glimpses of their enemy. The Vada was no longer alone, and he wondered if it had brought other Debru through the gate or if it had somehow called them from across the land.

Either way, the number that approached was great enough to turn his insides to an icy slush. At this distance they were nothing more than dark specks close to the horizon, but if each was a Debru, their war was as good as over. He was halfway tempted to turn around, but he was increasingly convinced knowledge would be their strongest weapon, so he kept them flying forward.

Capricia spotted the otsoa first. She tapped Elian's shoulder and pointed down. He leaned over and saw the creatures trotting across the broken land in ones and twos, ranging far ahead of the main force. More than one pair of green eyes looked up at their passing, but the otsoa seemed unconcerned about dragons overhead.

The otsoa grew thicker the closer they flew to the main body of the Debru, becoming so numerous that Elian considered ordering the dragon down and dropping a destructive wave of adani upon them. He suspected he could kill dozens in a single sweep, but he feared what might happen if they flew too close to the surface. They remained up high and continued their advance.

It didn't take much longer for them to reach the Debru. Once they were within easy sight, Elian had the dragon bank and fly in circles from what he considered a safe distance away.

The sheer number of Debru drew his attention first. What he'd originally thought was a combination of otsoa and Debru soon turned out to be Debru only, and not just Debru. He stopped counting after he'd seen more than a dozen Moka in one small section of the horde. Enormous Belogs towered over the rest of the Debru, scattered evenly throughout the crowd. There had to be hundreds, if not thousands, of invaders. Even with the dragons helping the adanists, Elian considered the Debru's assembled strength overwhelming.

The vast numbers still didn't intimidate him as much as the nearly empty circle that moved with the center of the horde. For hundreds of paces in every direction, Debru of all shapes and sizes were packed shoulder to shoulder as they marched, but the center always remained empty, except for one solitary figure, smaller than the rest.

Elian was too high to say for sure, but it wasn't hard to imagine the Vada taking on the appearance of a young human boy. Elian clutched the scales of the dragon tighter, as though a firm grip might transfer some of the dragon's immense strength to his comparatively frail body.

Capricia tapped on his shoulder and drew his attention away from the center of the advancing army. "Watch the deadlands."

He did, and although it took him several moments to notice what she pointed him toward, he was eventually successful. The land trembled at the Debru's advance, and not just because of the number of feet. Elian couldn't track adani, but he swore he could watch it being pulled away from the land by the mass of Debru.

The land, which he'd thought was already as dead as land could be, became even more so as the horde passed. Whatever small shreds of life had held on through the disaster that had first formed the deadlands now surrendered its final desperate strength. The Debru horde left not just a trail, but a path of destruction, wider and more thorough than any he'd seen before.

Elian had seen enough, and he raised his hand high and circled it above his head to encourage the other scouts to retreat. Then he asked their dragon to leave, and it was all too happy to comply.

Elian's stomach lurched as the dragon turned, a familiar sensation he could have happily gone the rest of his life without feeling again. He turned back and stared at the circle, where the Vada was now too small to see, as a pinprick of darkness floated above the invading army. Elian swore. They had to be too far away; at least a mile separated them from the Vada, and they were many times higher than the highest tree Elian had ever seen. Nothing could travel so far, not even adani bound to such a small point.

Still, it wasn't worth even the sliver of risk it posed. He urged the dragon forward, and it flexed both its wings and its control of adani as it shot forward faster than any arrow.

Elian looked back. The other dragons followed his dragon's lead, and they traveled hundreds of paces with every beat of his heart. The pinprick of darkness continued to hover, and then it vanished.

For the briefest of moments, Elian believed the Vada had given up, but then the twisting in his stomach doubled in intensity, and he realized he'd only lost track of the attack. The dragon he rode on needed no encouragement as it dove hard toward the ground. Elian clutched to its back until his hands turned white, and Capricia wrapped her arms around him so hard he fought for breath. His eyes watered, and he looked back, both to see what was happening and to protect what remained of his blurry vision. He spotted the point of darkness high overhead and allowed himself a moment of relief; they had acted quickly enough, and all were out of danger from the attack. The Vada's shot had missed, its dark power passing safely above them.

The thought had barely finished forming when the point stopped in midair.

Elian swore. He'd never seen a binding controlled so precisely. When an adanist threw a spear, it traveled until it struck something or until the adanist unraveled it. The Vada, it seemed, had a different understanding of what was possible.

For a long moment, the black point hung in the air overhead. Then it bubbled and grew, as though something, or many somethings, were trying to escape. The point exploded, turning into dozens of dark needles that sped toward the dragons and the adanists riding among them.

Elian shouted at his dragon to twist, and it obeyed without hesitation, spinning wildly in the air as deadly black rain fell among the fleeing scouts.

Elian saw nothing except the dragon's back as he clutched onto its scales. Wind and sky became interchangeable as his stomach did somersaults against his spine. Then the dragon leveled out, and he thought he might vomit. He swallowed hard and looked around.

One of the dragons fell freely, its wings and neck snapping in the wind as it dropped like a stone. The screams of the adanists who'd been riding it carried on the wind to his ears, but he could do nothing except watch as they fell to their deaths. They were too low and too far away by the time he saw them.

A violent rumbling from below tore his eyes from the unfolding tragedy, and he turned in time to witness the last of the shadowy darts impact against the deadlands. Each was easily more powerful than Harald's strongest spear, throwing up dust and debris that almost swallowed them whole. Without being prompted, his dragon rose above the rising clouds and sped east.

Elian glanced back again. One of the other dragons had also escaped the attack unharmed, but the other was clearly injured. One wing flapped faster than the other, and although it remained in the air, it wobbled and dipped.

He asked his dragon to slow so they could all remain together. The dragon obeyed, though more unwillingly than it had any of his previous suggestions. The surviving dragons flew in a tight formation, with the injured one taking the lead. Once Elian was entirely sure they were safe, he figured they could land and redistribute the surviving adanists between the other two dragons.

He looked even farther back, and it appeared that no further attacks were incoming. The twisting feeling in his stomach had subsided, and the horde of Debru were almost out of sight.

Elian's anger uncoiled and he swore and pounded his fist against the back of the dragon. He had thought himself a leader, and now a dragon and several adanists were dead.

He didn't have the right to command them.

❧ 18 ❧

Samora and the others kept a watch for the rest of that night and the one following. The dragon returned well after the sun had fallen and settled in as though it had never left. Despite their watch they never spotted any Debru wandering near their campsite. That second day they flew over one pack of otsoa, and they crossed paths with a few more stragglers, but for the most part the land was as quiet and empty as she had expected it would be.

As they flew, Samora couldn't help but learn more about the dragon that carried them west. It didn't like staying connected with her, but their proximity meant she was always close to its adani, and she learned much just by paying attention. The dragon felt young to her senses, almost playful in the way it spread its wings and caught the invisible currents of air that sent them soaring above the clouds. It seemed happy to stretch its wings and fly the entire day, and at times, she swore she caught it thinking about the other dragons, one smaller than the rest.

She wanted to ask him if he was a father, but he continued to keep his distance, gently rebuffing her attempts to connect their adani. She kept listening, but settled for not knowing for the moment.

The second day of travel introduced Samora to the mountains. She'd heard of them in the legends, but never had she thought she would wander so far that she would see them with her own eyes. The hills grew steeper and more varied until tall peaks of granite stood in their way like a wall of jagged teeth. Samora and Aldrick stared with wide eyes and slack jaws, and even Karla gave the sight an appreciative grunt.

The dragon flew toward the mountains without hesitation, and Samora saw firsthand how hard and difficult a land it was. Had they been on foot, she couldn't dare to guess how long the passage would have taken. Days at minimum, but more likely weeks.

Promising paths ended against vertical walls that water rushed over as though fleeing a Debru assault. The trees and undergrowth were thick in places and enormous animals that Samora did not have names for prowled on all fours with predatory airs. Obstacle after obstacle presented itself, and she began to wonder if humans had ever crossed a land so inhospitable.

Fortunately, she didn't have to answer the question with her own two feet. The dragon could have simply flown above the mountains, but he chose to drop lower, flying through the valleys and tilting left and right with the joy of a child running through a homemade collection of obstacles. The humans had little choice but to hold on more tightly.

They crossed over the entire range of mountains on the second day and landed on the hills on the other side. Once again, the dragon chose a hill that provided a commanding view of the surroundings, as though he expected danger that hadn't yet appeared. After they were settled, he left them again, and Samora used their newfound privacy to ask Karla a question that had been bothering her all day. "In my vision, it seemed as though the dragons didn't carry the humans that far from the burning village. No more than a night. How is it that our journey takes so long?"

Karla stirred the coals of the fire before answering. "It is said that Abram's ancestors wandered for generations before settling in the land we now think of as home. Perhaps we have to cover some of that distance as well."

Aldrick had a look of focused concentration on his face. "I'd never heard that story."

Karla didn't seem fazed by this. "That's not unusual. I've lost track of the number of stories no longer told."

The thought bothered Samora more than she expected, and she said, "Why? Stories of the past are how we learn from our mistakes."

"That can be true, but I think that sometimes it's necessary to forget the past."

"Why?" Aldrick asked.

"It's forgetting the past that allows us to face the days ahead."

Samora sensed a story hiding behind that claim, but Karla was in no mood to share, and so she didn't press.

The dragon arrived soon after, silencing the end of their discussion. They rested and took their turn at their watch, though nothing bothered them through the night. Samora wasn't too surprised. Any predator would be unwise to come too close to a dragon and his powerful companions.

The third day dawned clear and cold. A strong wind blew from west to east, and at times Samora swore she smelled something on the air. She couldn't place it, but neither could her companions.

They wrapped their cloaks tight around their bodies and hopped aboard the waiting dragon, who spread his wings and launched himself forward with an eagerness that made Samora certain they'd reach their destination today.

The hilly land continued for most of the morning, and Samora found the undulating landscape subtly mesmerizing.

Karla noticed the change in the horizon first. She pointed forward, drawing Samora's attention away from the land below to their destination ahead. Tall structures with lines too straight to be natural broke the slight curve of the horizon. Considering the distance that remained to travel, their height must have been incredible. As they neared, it became familiar, even though she'd never seen it with her own eyes.

"It's the enormous village from my vision," she said.

"Can you tell if it's the same one, or is it another one that looks similar?" Karla asked.

Samora studied the horizon more carefully, but in the end shook her head. The vision had been too short, and her attention consumed by too many different details. It looked the same, but she couldn't make the claim for certain.

Their approach brought another mystery into view. There was a lake behind the village, a lake that stretched across the horizon from north to south, and farther than the eye could see.

"Have you ever seen so much water?" Samora asked Karla.

"No. But I have heard of this. That's a sea, a body of water far bigger than a lake. And salty too, if the stories are true."

"Salty water?" Samora asked.

Karla nodded.

"Does it go on forever?" Aldrick asked.

"I've never heard one way or the other. But I would guess not. Nothing lasts forever," Karla answered.

The dragon began bleeding altitude earlier than Samora expected. She connected her adani to the dragon and asked why. In response, she saw a vision of the dragon waiting contentedly outside the village. Samora asked if he wouldn't join them, but he was adamant in his refusal.

She asked if he might fly them over the buildings before landing outside the village. The dragon wasn't pleased by the request, but when Samora asked why she didn't receive an answer.

She wondered at the secrets he kept. The connection of adani was more intimate than human conversation. She'd experienced a similar closeness when she'd been in the gathering ground with Karla. She'd learned more about her enigmatic companion in a few moments of exchanging adani than she had in days of attempted conversation.

Her connection taught her that the dragons were creatures of profound emotions, like a deep lake that was still close to the surface but contained unfathomable mysteries underneath. Those emotions didn't get agitated easily, but when they did, the force behind them could destroy enormous villages.

They shared that similarity with Elian. His journeys with Harald had changed him, but growing up, he had struggled to keep his emotions under control. Adani and emotion cycled hand in hand. Perhaps that was why he'd gotten along with the dragons so quickly.

The dragons, though, had learned to keep some part of their spirit hidden while they traded adani back and forth. A dark veil hid memories and thoughts from Samora's vision, and there was nothing she could do to push that veil aside. She was endlessly curious at what hid behind that wall, but every question she asked in that direction went unanswered. All she could do was hope it wasn't anything harmful to her or those she cared about.

After a long deliberation, the dragon agreed that he would fly over the village, but he would only fly high above. Samora didn't mind. There was too much ground for the three of them to explore randomly, so even a bird's eye view of the village would allow them to map out the place and decide where to focus their efforts.

The dragon regained the altitude he had lost and more while Samora explained what they intended. Thanks to the dragon's speed, it didn't take them long to reach the outskirts of the village. The buildings here were more familiar to Samora. The homes, for she thought of them as homes, were bigger, but not that much more so than she would have expected.

As they flew closer to the center of the village the buildings began to grow. Some were two or three levels tall, and their walls and foundations were made of stone rather than lumber. Some had roofs supported by columns, shading the ground in front of the entrance. Others were decorated by stone carvings, their designs too intricate for Samora to make out from her high vantage point.

She had never thought of her house as plain, but she did now. Beauty, before, had always been nature's domain, but now she saw that humans had once reached for it, too.

The ornate carvings and smooth columns contrasted with the signs of the disaster that had befallen the village. Stone was scorched dark where fire had burned out windows, and the hard paved paths of her vision were cracked and full of trees older than Karla. Nature and village fought a generations-long battle, and though Samora didn't think the village would ever be completely vanquished, it was clear nature was winning.

The dragon rose higher as they neared the center of the city, even though he wasn't close to grazing the tops of the buildings. Samora first focused on the buildings, though they didn't impress her after what she'd seen already. Their height was considerable, but they were otherwise much the same as the shorter buildings. The tallest looked to be seven or eight levels tall, judging by the windows.

They couldn't hold her attention for long, though. The buildings had been built around a large open space. From the sky, she couldn't see what the space had originally been. Nature's battle against the village was nearly complete here, and a thick canopy of trees covered most of the square.

Except for the very center. In the center of the square, at the very heart of the city, was a hole.

And not just any hole. As near as Samora could tell it was bottomless, its sides as smooth as polished stone.

"What happened here?" she asked the dragon.

He didn't respond, and her adani was blocked again by the veil it stubbornly kept in place.

"Is it explaining that?" Karla asked.

Samora shook her head. "He's refusing to."

Karla grunted and kept her peace. Samora suspected that the next time they were alone, she'd have plenty of questions Samora wouldn't be able to answer.

The dragon circled the center of the village once, then swooped over the far western side where the sea met the land and the village. On any other day Samora would have been fascinated by the long stretches of sand, the structures that jutted out into the water, and the buildings on the shore. Now, though, her thoughts were only for the hole.

That hadn't been in her vision.

The dragon returned by a slightly different route, but Samora couldn't focus on anything below. Her eyes kept returning to the center of the village. She couldn't see the hole from anywhere except directly above it, but it was all she thought about.

Once they were beyond the outskirts of the village the dragon circled again and settled. They'd barely slid off before he was digging up a small hole in the grass, similar to the holes they had dug in the fields outside Samora's village.

"So, you're not planning on moving much, are you?" she asked.

The dragon pretended he didn't hear her and settled in to rest.

There was still daylight left, and Samora didn't want to waste it. Their supplies wouldn't last forever, and they needed answers sooner rather than later. She asked Aldrick and Karla, and they both agreed, so with little more than a quick bow to the dragon, they began their exploration of the ancient village.

❧ 19 ❧

The potent force of the dragon's adani, combined with the vicious mix of emotions swirling through Elian's spirit, almost made him cry. Had a Vada stood before him, he would have attacked it with bare hands and not a sliver of hesitation. He needed something to hit, but there was nothing within reach that deserved his wrath. Only Capricia's arms around his waist prevented him from turning the dragon around and attacking the Debru army singlehandedly.

The injured dragon's slow pace gave Elian plenty of time to stew over his failure. Night approached by the time they returned, but that didn't stop dozens of adanists from gathering at the edge of the field the dragons used as a home. Each and every one had known that Elian had led three other dragons this morning. Now he returned with one healthy dragon and one injured, his failure laid bare for all to see.

Capricia was silent behind him, and he didn't know what to say to her. He'd thought the scouting would be without risk, but he'd almost killed her, too. She would be right not to want to speak to him ever again.

Elian landed first and collected himself before jumping off to face his judgment. Capricia landed beside him, and he looked at her. "I'm so sorry," he said.

She reached out, took his right hand, and squeezed it. "You have nothing to be sorry for. When you've realized that, come find me."

She let go of his hand and walked away, leaving him feeling dreadfully alone. He longed for the privacy of his room at home, but it felt farther away than when he'd been traveling the deadlands with Harald. He took a step toward the rapidly growing group of visitors but stopped.

The whole flight back, he hadn't spared a thought for the dragons. He didn't know how they related to one another, but he'd been rude not to ask. He pressed his hand against the dragon's neck and connected. "I'm sorry."

The emotion that emanated from the dragon turned his insides to liquid. He thought he'd understood all the different flavors of grief, but he'd only scratched the surface. Brief memories flashed, one after the other, each a tiny drop that, when combined, could fill a raging river.

He often mourned all the time he'd never get to spend with his father, all the experiences they would never share because his life had ended too early. He'd long believed that was the most brutal legacy of Father's passing. The torrent of raw sorrow from the dragon forced him to reconsider.

Perhaps it was worse to grieve a companion of countless years.

He choked and fought back a sob. He couldn't afford to mourn, not with every eye on him. "I'm sorry," he repeated.

The words seemed woefully inadequate, so he added a few more. "We'll make them suffer. I promise."

He placed his forehead against the dragon's scales as memories that weren't his own flooded his thoughts. He endured them a moment longer before pushing himself away and separating his adani from the dragon's. The action left him light-headed, the sudden absence of both strength and memories disorienting.

That wasn't all, though. He'd made another mistake. He'd misjudged the dragons. In his mind, they were creatures. Bigger and smarter than a deer, but fundamentally the same.

They weren't, though. Their thoughts and past remained largely opaque to him, but they possessed the same emotions humans did. Deeper, even. Maybe more human than some of the humans he'd crossed paths with.

"I'm sorry," he said again, this time apologizing not for the deaths he'd caused, but the attitude he'd approached them with. Then he took another stumbling step back.

He found his balance and turned to face the burgeoning crowd. Harald stood tall among them, and Elian made his way toward the giant. When Harald saw him approaching, he broke away from the rest of the crowd. They met, and for a moment, enjoyed a degree of privacy.

"The Vada is on the march with a host of Debru. Far more than we've ever fought before. I thought we were far enough away and safe, but a Vada's attacks can range for miles. One of the dragons was injured and another died."

Harald's mouth set in a firm line. Elian shifted so he could see behind the giant. Adanists and elders from the clans had gathered into groups as the surviving riders returned to make their reports. Elian slid back a step, so Harald's bulk protected him from most of the stares.

Harald's next question caught him flat-footed. "And what about you?"

Elian swallowed hard and exhaled sharply through his nose. "I failed them. I thought we were safe, but I underestimated the Vada. It's because of me they're dead."

Harald didn't deny it. "And it's because of me the Bears find themselves diminished and retreating from the lands we've held for generations."

"But that isn't your fault. You've led the Bears well. Everyone says so."

"Which only means they either have short memories or are too kind. Do you think I've led the Bears for as long as I have without error? And do you also believe those errors haven't cost me the lives of people I've known and loved?"

Elian looked up from staring at his feet. The intensity of Harald's stare almost made him flinch. When he looked into those eyes, he saw the reflection of dozens of wrong judgments. It was as far from the boisterous, carefree legend he'd first met as was possible.

Harald's vulnerability sent another round of shame to Elian's cheeks. In all their time together, he'd never guessed the depths of Harald's suffering. It seemed foolish now, but he had thought Harald was somehow immune to the doubt that plagued lesser leaders. Still, it only confirmed what Elian had already suspected. How could he lead if he couldn't even understand the people closest to him?

"I never should have pretended I knew what to do. Thanks to you, Tera, and so many more, I started to think that I could help drive the Debru away. And you'll always have my sword, Harald, but no more."

Harald's hand landed heavily on Elian's right shoulder. "Do you believe in yourself?"

Elian frowned, not quite following.

"Do you believe the clans would be better off following the council of elders, as they now are?"

Elian wanted to say "yes," but he wouldn't make himself both a fool and a liar. His prolonged silence served as an answer enough for Harald.

"Trust me when I say I know something of what you're going through. After all the years and all the battles, there are still days when I look out at the Bears, assembled to listen to me, and feel like they've bought into a lie, that I'm not the warrior they think I am, and certainly not the leader they believe me to be. It used to bother me more, but now I think it's a good thing."

"Why?"

"Because it reminds me that I'm not infallible. The leaders that pose the greatest risk to their clans are those that believe they can't make a mistake. When I feel like a fraud, it means I won't fall into that trap."

"They died because of me."

"Did you think no one would? The leader of every clan knows all too well the weight you carry on your shoulders. So, too, do all the elders. Why do you think so many are so willing to retreat? You might call it cowardice, and perhaps you're right, but part of the reason is because they don't want to add to the burden they already carry. They don't want to lose any more friends or family."

Elian let that sink in.

"This is one of those moments that has the potential to define you," Harald said.

"As a failure?"

"No more so than any of us. But right now, you have a choice. You can walk from this field, staring at your feet in defeat, and let the elders steal your reputation and your power away, one piece at a time. Or you can address everyone, admit what happened, and still have a say in what's to come. If the Vada approaches, we don't have time or land. It'll hunt us down until humanity is nothing more than a dragon's memory. I know I don't want that, but right now the only one who can get the clans to fight is you, whether you want that responsibility or not."

"I don't want to send any more warriors to their deaths."

Harald let his hand drop. "No leader I respect would, either, but that's what leading a wandering clan means. We fight and die so the villages can live. Now we fight and die so humanity can live. If you stand today, yes, you'll order adanists to their deaths. But if you don't, you might be dooming us all."

The weight of it all pressed the air from Elian's lungs. It couldn't be him. It couldn't.

When Harald let the corner of his lips turn up in a smile, it provided Elian with the first hint of hope he'd felt since enjoying the flight toward the Vada earlier that day, when he'd been speaking so freely with Capricia. "Just know that if you decide to stand, I'll be right here by your side, helping however I can."

"What would I even say?"

Harald shrugged. "Sometimes what you say matters less than how you say it. Remember, you aren't speaking to your villagers. Those who wander know that our fate is likely to die in battle, and though few of us actively seek our deaths, most have accepted their role. It's not death we fear, but a wasted life."

Elian took strength from Harald's confidence. It wasn't that he felt ready to bear any responsibility for the fate of the clans, but knowing he wasn't alone was enough to help him take that next step. "You'll support me, and let me know when I'm being a fool?"

"Of course," Harald said.

Elian bowed. "Thank you."

Harald nodded and stepped to the side, forcing Elian to face the assembled crowd. He straightened his back as he looked out over the assembled warriors and collected his thoughts. Harald had given him the key, he just had to make sure he didn't fumble it in the lock.

He walked forward, Harald keeping pace to his left and a step behind. Elian stopped about a dozen paces away from the first line of adanists. The far edges of the crowd curled in like a claw threatening to crush him, but he stood tall in the center. He didn't bother to hide his face. Let them see that he mourned their dead with them. He took a deep breath and began, speaking loudly enough for most to hear but refusing to shout.

"As many of you have already heard, our scouting party came upon a Vada today. It marches east toward our homelands with a host of Debru and their assorted minions. I wish I could bring better news, but only a fool would deny that we find ourselves in the midst of dark days."

Elian paused to take the measure of the crowd. He sensed the tension of uncertainty and understood how perceptive Harald had been. The clans were no strangers to difficult odds, but none alive had faced a Vada. Even the strongest among them were right to be worried, and in their fear, they would reach out to whoever eased that unspoken fear best. If he'd refused to speak, the elders never would have given him another chance.

"When we finished scouting and turned away, the Vada decided to attack from an impossible distance. That attack took the lives of adanists and dragon alike and wounded another dragon besides. Today, each of the clans here bled, and in exchange for that blood, we know better the Vada's strength. It made a mistake in attacking us today, and we'll make it pay for revealing its abilities too soon. Tonight, let us mourn the loss of brave adanists, but tomorrow, let us plan how to ensure their sacrifice wasn't in vain."

Elian looked from face to face, and most were set in stone. A few offered him small nods. He was glad that Harald stood behind him, providing implicit support.

Harald stepped forward. "For now, we must speak to Firrolw, the Bear widowed by the Vada. But tomorrow, we shall summon a council for all and begin to lay our plans."

The crowd parted to let Harald through, and Elian followed behind, trying hard not to look like he was hiding behind the Bear's leader. As it parted it began to disperse. The fires would burn bright tonight as they remembered the fallen, but Elian wanted nothing more than to hide at home.

"It was well said," Harald said quietly, "but there will be much to do yet. Some will agree with your words while others will be opposed. Tonight, you must wander through the camps and share in their grief and endure their accusations."

Elian said nothing, but Harald noticed him wince. "I know, but it's what must be done. It's easy, at times, to think that because you lead everyone will follow, but a leader is born one believer at a time. Tonight, you'll need to win a difficult battle, and you'll need to win it over and over. But you'll need their hearts if you wish to command their strength."

"It's the only way, isn't it? If we want to fight the Vada."

Harald nodded. "To fight the Vada, and to live well."

20

Samora, Karla, and Aldrick walked abreast as they wandered deeper into the ancient village. They moved slower than they should have, but there was much to see and Samora didn't know where the answers they sought would hide. If she had to guess, it was at the hole in the ground near the center of the village, but she didn't know.

Or maybe she did. Ever since seeing the hole from the air, it had become almost the sole focus of her thoughts. The more she thought about it, though, the more uneasy she became.

If they'd made a straight line for the hole, they could have reached it and looked around before nightfall, but instead they took a slow, meandering route through the outskirts of the village, pretending something important might be found in one of the homes.

All the small buildings along the outskirts were most certainly homes. Many had been too damaged by the intervening years for Samora to want to enter, but a few survived nature's slow moving but inevitable assault.

They stepped in carefully, as though hunting wary prey.

A glance told Samora that it had been many, many years since humans had lived here. Dust covered every surface, and intricate spiderwebs hung in every corner, the spiders glaring angrily at the intruders.

They wandered through the home, and although it was very different from the home Samora had grown up in, it was still a home. The dining room table had been constructed with joinery Samora hadn't seen before, but six chairs sat around it, the same number that were around her table back home. The bowls were bigger and better than what she was used to, but they'd once fed hungry mouths, too.

If she'd had the time, Samora believed she could have gotten lost in the ruins for years. There was much to learn here, better ways of doing things that would help the villagers and improve life for all. Unfortunately, none of that would matter if they didn't find a way to stop the Debru.

They wandered through the house for a bit, but all were driven by the same sense of urgency that pulled Samora away from her investigations. Aldrick and Karla were waiting for her by the broken front door, and they stepped out together.

The path between the homes was wide and flat. Once, it had been all stone, but it hadn't fared so well in its battle against the wild. Seeds had landed between the cracks in the stones, and as the generations had passed, trees had risen and shoved the stones out of their way with trunk and root alike. The explorers picked their way down the street, eyes open for anything out of the ordinary.

It wasn't long before they reached the edge of the fire damage. It wasn't evenly spread out, but there was a marked difference between homes damaged in the fire and those that weren't. In some cases, there was just empty space where it seemed a home should have been. Trees and grasses, unopposed by walls and roofs, had taken over the plots and turned them into small patches of wilderness. Samora scared at least one deer out of its bedding place for the night as she passed.

Other homes had walls that stood but no roof. Samora marveled at an enormous oak that stood tall in the middle of a home, surrounded by walls as though it was trying to protect itself from invaders.

There were others yet that seemed untouched by the fire. Given what she'd seen in her vision and the extent of the damage that surrounded them, it seemed impossible to believe, but it was as if the fire had simply jumped over some houses, as though it had found them distasteful. She wondered if adanists had protected their homes, or if something else had been the cause. They stepped into one such house but saw little different than in the first house they'd visited.

Eventually, nightfall forced them to turn back. They'd made it maybe halfway into the village, and Samora knew, as they prepared to rest for the night, that tomorrow she'd have to confront the mystery at its heart.

Rain swept in from the sea the next morning, so Samora and the others bundled up as they left the dragon behind again. She'd tried to convince him to help, but he remained stubbornly insistent he would not. He seemed perfectly content to bask in the gentle rain.

Through unspoken agreement, they made much better time. Though Samora was certain marvelous wonders awaited in the homes, nothing within would tell them what happened to humanity so long ago. Nothing would tell them how to defeat the Debru.

Their journey that morning taught Samora just how slow she'd kept the pace of the group the day before. She felt like her breakfast hadn't even settled in her stomach by the time they reached the beginning of taller buildings.

The ones closest to the outskirts weren't that much larger than the homes they'd explored the night before. Some were two levels, some were a bit larger, and some even had defensive walls around their perimeter. The fire had done more damage here.

Many buildings had been destroyed, often leaving nothing more than a pile of blackened stone to mark their final resting place. Some still stood, albeit with fire damage, but there were very few that were unharmed.

Samora longed to explore, to uncover the mysteries hidden within, but they'd made their goals clear before they'd left the morning campfire. Today was all about the hole, so they walked past the buildings, as though they were no more interesting than a fallow field.

A surprising amount of wildlife had made the village its home, making Samora think of Elian. If he'd been here, he would have been constantly distracted by the hunting opportunities. The burned-out buildings that still stood provided excellent hunting perches, and any group he traveled with would have eaten like every day was an eighthday feast.

"How do you think they built structures so tall?" Aldrick asked.

Samora wished she knew the answer to that question, although she also wasn't sure it mattered much. Space was one thing her village was never short of. They only needed to figure out how to protect it. She was more intrigued by the walls than the buildings they surrounded. If they built such walls around the village, they wouldn't have to worry about attacks from kettu or otsoa anymore. The walls wouldn't stand against the Debru, unfortunately, but up until recently, the Debru had been a less common concern than the shadowy animals they commanded.

They reached the central part of the village well before the sun had reached the midpoint for the day, and even Karla was brought to a stop by the enormity of the buildings that rose like an enormous forest around them. Seeing them from the sky had been impressive enough, but to be surrounded by them was another experience all together.

"Does anybody else feel like the buildings are leaning over

them, like they're getting ready to fall on top of us?" Samora asked.

"I thought it was just me," Aldrick answered.

Karla grunted. "It's—an unpleasant feeling, being here."

Samora turned to the veteran adanist. The woman knew more about humanity's past than most everyone. "Do you have any idea how they built buildings so tall?"

Karla shook her head. "I heard a legend about a farmer in a village once, maybe two generations back, who wanted to build a bigger place for his growing family, but his home was surrounded by others in the village. A wiser man would have simply built beyond the outskirts of the village, but for some reason, this man got it in his head he could just build taller. Some say he was too attached to his home to leave it; others say he'd always been a fool obsessed with heights. Regardless, he tried to make his house three levels high. Everyone was impressed until the day it collapsed and killed his whole family."

"I hadn't heard that," Samora said.

"Not sure if it's true. I visited the village in question once and didn't see any evidence of it, but I wasn't looking too hard."

They continued deeper into the heart of the village. Some of the buildings were five levels high. Out of habit more than any curiosity, Samora ran the fingertips of her hand across the smooth stone of a nearby building. She stopped after a few paces and placed both palms of her hand against the stone.

Karla noticed the strange behavior and came to a stop. "What do you notice?"

Samora was too distracted by the sensations underneath her palms to answer. She sent adani into the building and the whole structure groaned as though it was an old man getting out of bed after a long rest. Karla and Aldrick swore behind her, but Samora didn't sense any danger. The changes were internal and didn't affect the sturdiness of the building.

Her adani passed through the building with almost the same

ease that it did through the gathering grounds. Far more easily than it did another human. It was similar to many living things but didn't match any exactly.

"Check the other buildings nearby," she told the other two.

She sent another pulse of adani into the building. It didn't groan like it had before, but it almost felt the same as when she sent adani into someone who was wounded, as though dead flesh was coming alive. The comparison wasn't exact. The stone never came to life, but it felt like a close mimicry.

Behind her, the groaning of another building told her that Karla had succeeded in awakening her structure. No third groan followed, and after a bit more study, Samora slowly pulled her hands from the stone and met the other two in the middle of the wide path. Karla's eyes were as wide as Samora had ever seen them, and Aldrick simply looked confused.

He glanced between the two women, who stared at each other in wide-eyed silence. He shifted and fidgeted for a few moments, then asked, "So, what's happening?"

Karla answered for Samora. "The buildings were built with adani. Lots of adani."

"Like a bound weapon?" Aldrick asked.

"No, something different. There are lines of adani running through these buildings, just like there are lines of adani running through your body. They've been starved of adani for a long time, though."

"They're alive?" Aldrick asked.

Karla wasn't as quick to answer as Samora would have been. She turned back and studied the building she had sent adani into and studied it. "Not exactly, no."

"I don't understand. I didn't feel anything different," he said.

Karla didn't respond to that, which seemed like an absolute kindness, coming from her. Samora turned the conversation away from Aldrick before he thought too long on the matter. "The amount of adani used to create these buildings must have been incredible. How much do you think they needed from day to day?"

Karla returned her look to her building, which was just slightly smaller than Samora's. "It ate up my adani like it was barely a snack."

At her questioning gaze, Samora said she'd felt the same.

"So, it stands to reason, quite a bit."

Samora looked around at all the buildings, then thought of all the buildings and homes they'd passed just to get here. "Do you think they all required adani?"

The answer had to be "no." Perhaps all the adani in a single gathering ground could fill a few of these buildings for a while, but it wouldn't be enough for more than some tiny fraction of everything here.

Karla didn't look so certain. "Let's find out. If both of these large buildings required adani, I'm willing to bet most of them did, so let's backtrack a bit and test some smaller buildings."

Samora didn't like the idea of backtracking, as it took them farther away from their agreed destination. She feared that if given half the chance, she would seize it as an excuse to run the other way and never look back.

At the same time, it wouldn't take long, and she agreed with Karla's logic. Not only that, but this felt like a discovery that mattered. If humans had once had access to this much adani, it would have changed almost everything they knew of their history, again. She nodded, and they retraced their steps, testing buildings as they did. It didn't take long for them to confront the honest answer.

Karla stopped first, satisfied with what she'd sensed. "This whole village is like a gathering ground made of stone."

"But if that's true, where's the adani?"

As soon as Samora asked the question, she was certain she knew the answer. She looked toward the center of the village, and Karla nodded.

They turned around again and continued their journey to the heart of the village. They tested a few of the larger buildings they hadn't tested before, but their answers weren't surprising. Dread built in Samora's stomach with every step she took.

Aldrick took up position behind her. "Why the long face?"

She wished, for a moment, that she was as blissfully ignorant as he was. It was no fault of his own. She'd been gifted with an unnatural sensitivity to adani, and Karla had spent more years honing her mastery of the power than anyone Samora knew of. Aldrick had only ever mastered that which made him a strong warrior for his clan. Right now, she wished her own life could be so simple.

"So far, all the buildings we've tested for adani have revealed that adani once ran through them, right?"

Aldrick nodded.

"Karla and I don't know much yet, but we know there was a lot of adani running through these buildings. More than you would find in a gathering ground."

"More?"

"Much more. I don't think the Wolves' gathering ground would fill more than a handful of buildings here at most."

She gave Aldrick a moment to let that sink it, then said, "But we also know that adani isn't anywhere to be found. The buildings are empty, and there's only a little running beneath our feet. No more than you'd find in an empty prairie."

She had to give Aldrick some respect. He followed the thoughts to their natural conclusion. "The hole in the center of the city. Somehow, it's related to the loss of adani."

"It worries me for a couple of reasons. First off, if humans had control over this much adani, how did the dragons drive them out? I've ridden on a dragon and so I've sensed their adani. It's impressive, but it's not this impressive," she said as she gestured to all the buildings.

"And the other reason?"

"If humans had this much access to adani, what would be strong enough to destroy the adani? My first guess would be a Vada, but I'm not so certain. I've sensed them, too, and while they're even stronger than dragons, I'm not sure I believe they're capable of this."

Aldrick thought about it, then chuckled nervously. It only lasted for a moment, and then his face fell until it was as long as theirs. "I see."

It was more an impulse than anything else, but she reached out and took his hand. His eyes darted to her in surprise, but he didn't pull his hand away, and they held to each other tightly as they walked past the last few buildings in the village. Samora saw Karla glance back, but the adanist said nothing.

Either she was as frightened as Samora or she was in a particularly kind mood today.

Samora breathed a little easier as they passed the last of the tall buildings and entered the enormous square at the center of the village. She knew the buildings had stood for hundreds of years and weren't going to collapse the day she walked beside them, but she couldn't convince her body of that truth.

Tall trees, she understood. Tall trees, she trusted.

Without a word, Karla took the lead and Aldrick gently pushed Samora into the middle of their column. She almost objected but quickly realized they had a point. Of the three of them she was the least useful in a fight, so if there was something hiding within this small forest that wanted to harm them, she belonged where she was.

Karla disappeared into the trees and Samora followed close behind. The canopy was thick, and thanks to the clouds that had remained overhead since this morning, the path was dark as night.

Despite the appearance of the place, they encountered nothing more dangerous than a pair of deer startled from their rest. Karla led them out to the other side of the trees just as the sun fought through the clouds and illuminated the hole. As with the buildings, their flight overhead hadn't done the hole justice. From above it had appeared massive. As she neared the edge herself, its size was incomprehensible.

It wasn't simply the diameter of the hole, though that was impressive enough. Samora guessed it was a hundred paces across, with sharply defined edges that served as yet another reminder that no natural process had made this hole. It was the depth and smoothness of the abyss that sent a shiver down her spine.

She'd never considered herself scared of heights, but she crept forward one shuffling step at a time. She imagined the ground giving way beneath her feet and the hole swallowing her without a sound. Aldrick and Karla didn't share her sense of self-preservation. Both walked straight to the edge and peered over.

They hadn't moved by the time Samora arrived. She stopped a pace away from the edge and leaned forward.

It was a mistake. The endless darkness made her stomach queasy as her vision wobbled. She took a step back before she lost her balance and took a long breath. Karla glanced back to ensure she was fine, and Samora nodded. Once her stomach settled, she tried again. Her stomach churned, but she didn't feel close to losing her balance. She studied the walls of the hole first, mostly to avoid staring down.

The sharp edges that defined the boundary of the hole weren't just a surface feature. The hole's walls seemed almost as smooth as glass. Whatever had formed the hole had blasted through soil, stone, and root without a hint of challenge. Not even the best climbers among the clans would be able to find a route up.

She leaned forward until she stared down into the hole, but it told her little. She couldn't see the bottom. It was like the hole swallowed light and offered nothing in return. If she was to fall, she couldn't say for sure she'd ever hit bottom. She retreated a step so as not to tempt disaster.

Samora squatted and placed her hands in the soil. If their guess was right, the center of the village had been a source of incredible adani. She let her adani trickle into the soil, which ate it up even more hungrily than the building had earlier.

"Karla," she said.

The adanist turned and Samora motioned to the ground. Karla squatted beside her, placed a hand against the ground, and did as Samora just had. She grunted. "So, this was the heart of the village, in more ways than one."

Aldrick didn't attempt the same feat. He looked at Samora as Karla stood and asked, "What do you sense?"

"There used to be an incredible source of adani where that hole is. It's been destroyed, but the channels through which it worked remain. Imagine the land underneath the city as the roots of an enormous tree. The buildings have impressive pathways for adani, much larger than human ones, but here they are even wider. It feels as if the whole land we're standing on was a pathway. The amount of adani that must have passed through here is far beyond what I can imagine."

Karla spun slowly, her look distant. "Do you think humans did all this?"

Samora stood and joined the others. "I don't know, but we know who has the answers. It's time to put our questions to the dragon."

21

E lian dreaded the task Harald had set before him. The idea of traveling from clan to clan and mourning their losses felt like being forced to take drink after drink of a bitter medicinal brew. He didn't know if his presence would heal the wounds the Vada had inflicted, and he worried that his being there might make the wounds worse. Following Harald's orders pushed his trust of the giant man to its limit.

He began his tour of the camps with the Bears. They were the closest he had to family in the wandering clans, and it seemed right to begin with them. The Bear killed by the adani had been a woman a few years older than him named Berlotte. Elian hadn't known her well. She'd bound swords with her adani and had fought with the Bears since her childhood. Her husband, Firrol, was already drunk by the time Elian joined them.

Elian expected accusations and recriminations, but when Firrol saw him, he raised his cup high. His slurred words were still clear enough to echo across the campsite. "Berlotte feared we would spend our last days fleeing like cowards as the Debru stole both our lands and our honor. You have no idea how excited she was to follow you to see an actual Vada."

Firrol bowed deeply, and it was as if someone had squeezed the air from Elian's chest. He held up his own cup and forced a toast past his constricted throat. "To Berlotte. May we all be as courageous."

The toast was echoed around the gathering, and everyone drank deeply. Elian made his way through the crowd until he reached Firrol. The man's eyes were bloodshot, and his breath reeked of ale, but he still straightened when he saw Elian approach. Elian reached out and put his hand on the man's shoulder, feeling an awful lot like Harald. "I'm sorry for your loss, friend. Berlotte honored me with her support, and if there's anything I can do to show you that same support, all you have to do is ask. If it is within my power, I'll do it."

Firrol didn't hesitate. "Kill the Debru. Every last one of them, so that those that come after us never have to understand this fear."

Elian nodded. "I'll do all I can. You have my word."

He stayed a bit longer, talking with those who wanted to bend his ear, but he didn't dare linger. The Bears' camp was a comfortable place for him, and too much comfort was dangerous. It invited complacency.

Elian traveled next to the Wolves' camp, where a similar scene was unfolding. He wasn't welcomed as warmly as he was among the Bears, but he repeated the same promises to the mother of the young adanist who'd died as the dragon fell from the sky. Aldo's harsh looks eventually drove him away, though.

When he reached the Hounds' camp, he was intercepted by Tiafel. The old man pulled him aside. Elian followed as Tiafel led him beyond the tents to the empty fields beyond. They watched the stars together until Tiafel cleared his throat. "I never would have guessed you'd cause such chaos that day you first entered my circle. I thought Harald was bad enough."

"It was never my goal to spread chaos. When we first met, I

couldn't see much past helping myself. Now I'd like to help us all."

Tiafel's grunt was bitter. "Few people are more dangerous than the ones who just want to help. I tell all the young of our clan that until you've become a master of your own affairs, there's no point in helping others."

"There's wisdom there," Elian agreed.

Tiafel seemed surprised to find consensus, but Elian continued before he could ask the inevitable next question.

"I won't lie to you and tell you that I've mastered my own affairs, if such a thing is even possible. All I can tell you is that I've seen enough to know tradition is no longer serving us. I understand your caution, respect it, even. But it only means a slow death without hope for victory."

"And you have a plan to change all that?"

Elian shook his head. "All I propose is that we stand and fight. I'm not ignorant. The odds are stacked so high against us it might as well be impossible. But there's a chance that if we fight, we win. That chance, however small, is worth risking everything."

"What if our best hope of success lies in staying alive, in retreating before the onslaught?"

"If I believed that, we wouldn't be having this discussion, would we?" He held up a hand, already regretting his flippant answer. "Tiafel, they're coming to wipe us out. That force is too large for anything else. We could retreat, but I don't think it'll buy us much time, and we surrender the gathering grounds, which are the only places where we have a chance to make a difference. I have a tremendous amount of respect for how you've led the Hounds, but running only delays the inevitable."

Tiafel stood silently, staring up at the stars for a long time. "Did you know, when I was young, that I always expected I would die in battle?"

Elian didn't think Tiafel was looking for a response, so he kept quiet.

"Then I survived all my battles and became the leader of the clan. It forced me to consider a fate I'd never prepared for, that I might die of old age. I think, as I contemplated that idea, it stole something from me. When I was younger, I'd made peace with death, but now that I'm old, I want to keep it at arm's length. Easier to die by the sword, I think, than of the slow passage of time."

Tiafel went silent again, and Elian felt as though something was required of him. "But experience has given you wisdom."

"Has it? Experience has given me experience, but I think the idea that age begets wisdom is a lie created by the elders so that the young will listen to them."

Tiafel sighed. "I don't know if you're right, but I do believe that continuing to retreat would be wrong. You'll have another ally besides Harald tomorrow."

Elian bowed. "I'm grateful. I hope that I'll always be able to rely on your experience. It'll be needed in the days to come."

Tiafel waved him away. "Flattery will do you no good. Go now and spend some time by our fire. The others are waiting for you."

Elian bowed again, then joined the Hounds around their fire. When he was done, he left for the last camp of the night, that of the Hawks. Here he was greeted warmly, the memory of the dragon rescue still fresh in the minds of most. He drank and toasted the fallen, but his eyes were for a young woman he couldn't find. Capricia wasn't at the fire, and Elian worried about what had happened.

Just as he was about to leave, he felt a pair of light hands on his shoulders. He looked up to see Capricia standing over him, a wide smile on her face. "I was wondering when you were going to show up," she said.

"I was just thinking the very same about you."

She pulled him to his feet. A few of Elian's neighbors gave him knowing smiles, but Elian's mind was dull from the drink of four separate fires. He followed her into the dark until they stopped between two tents, and she kissed him.

Her lips were softer than he expected, and what few thoughts he still possessed fled from him like rabbits chased by a hunter. The moment lasted forever but was still over too soon. She pulled away and studied his face. Whatever she saw there, she seemed to find acceptable. She smiled and said, "I realized that if I was going to wait for you, I might be waiting for a very long time, indeed."

Elian tried to respond, but before he could form words she kissed him again, and whatever he was about to say vanished from his thoughts.

When she pulled away the next time, she took his hand and led him toward her tent.

THE NEXT MORNING Harald took one look at Elian and laughed out loud. Elian winced and cupped his hands over his ears.

"I'd heard rumors, but I didn't believe them until now," Harald boomed, loud enough for the neighboring village to hear.

Elian's cheeks burned and he stared at the ground. "Rumors?"

Harald's grin stretched from ear to ear. Elian didn't think he'd seen the giant so pleased since they'd first met. "Yes, rumors."

Elian took a deep breath and sighed. Apparently, there wasn't going to be any hope of discretion. "Is it that obvious?"

"Probably only to those of us who know you well, but yes." Harald clapped him so hard on the back Elian coughed. "I hope you got some sleep last night, though, because the council will be meeting soon."

"Just get me some breakfast and I'll be ready."

Harald laughed again, taking far too much pleasure in Elian's discomfort. The giant joined him for breakfast, though Elian suspected it was the second trip for him. Harald, thankfully, kept his questions focused on the earlier events of Elian's evening. Once the breakfast was finished, they made their way to the Hounds' camp, where the council was to be held. Elders and leaders from each clan were present, but neither Gabe nor Henk had been invited. Elian had asked, but the answer had been firm. Villagers had no place in the councils of the wandering clans.

The council began not long after he and Harald joined. Tiafel silenced the quiet conversations happening around the circle by stepping forward and waiting. Soon, every eye was turned to him.

"We're gathered today to discuss the news Elian has brought back. I assume that everyone here is familiar with what is known, and has confirmed the information with members of their own clan?"

Elian had originally asked for adanists from each clan as a sign of unity, but he hadn't expected they would also be used to confirm his report. The decision had been a better one than he knew. He watched people nod around the gathering.

"Then let's get straight to the matter at hand. A Vada approaches and we have little time in which to act. Who here would speak?"

Tiafel didn't look to Elian, but several others did, and he forced himself to step forward before he allowed hesitation to settle in. He met the looks of those around the circle, then began.

"I believe we only have one option. We should gather our forces at the gathering ground in the Crows' old territory and make a stand there. Between the dragons and the gathering ground, we'll have the best chances for success."

He considered ending there, then continued on. "There are those who believe we should retreat, but I'd caution against it. That Vada has come to wipe us out, and there is no running from it. At best you buy yourself a matter of days. I don't know how good our odds are against the strength the Debru have assembled, but they're the only odds I'll take."

He bowed to the circle, then took his place beside Harald, who stood impassively.

His comments sparked an intense argument between the elders. Elian's proposal enjoyed more support than he had expected, but a vocal minority still believed they might survive if they turned tail and ran.

Tempers rose until Tiafel once again took command of the center of the circle. "I, for one, agree that what Elian says about our retreat is true. We can't outrun the Debru, especially not if we're attempting to evacuate villages at the same time."

"We don't have to evacuate the villages," someone said.

Elian turned to see Aldo step forward into the circle. Over the course of the arguments, he had become the most senior voice calling for retreat. "The wandering clans have served the villages for generations, but if we must choose the ability to fight another day over protecting them, that's a sacrifice we should consider. It's also possible the Vada ignores the villages completely and chases us around the land, where we can pick off its forces in a series of ambushes."

Elian's hands were in fists before he knew it, but Harald's arm across his chest prevented him from leaping into the circle. Harald stepped forward instead, the first time he had asked to speak throughout the council. The elders silenced themselves as Harald glared at them. He saved his last, most venomous look for Aldo, who shrank back before the attention.

Harald's voice rang out over the group. "We've all had disagreements over the years, and I'll not hold another's opinion against him, so long as it's held in good faith. But never in my life have I heard a single soul state so confidently that we shouldn't honor the promises we made the villages."

"Promises our ancestors made!" Aldo shouted.

"And promises that we've renewed year after year with our

blood. No one is bound to a wandering clan. Elian's own parents left the Spiders to work in the fields and raise their children. I've always respected you, Aldo, but I'll hear no talk about abandoning the villages without protection."

He dared Aldo to speak, but the elder suddenly discovered the wisdom in silence and didn't answer.

"Is there anyone else?" Harald looked around the circle. "If so, best we talk about it now. Aldo may be a coward who wants to abandon his duty, but at least he had the courage to admit it out loud. If there are any that feel the same, speak now, lest your secrets tear us apart later."

Harald allowed the question to linger in the air, but no one answered. Satisfied, he returned to his position.

Tiafel still stood in the center, and now he turned to Elian. "I'm inclined to agree with you, Elian. Retreat has kept us alive, but all strategies have their limits, and I fear we are near the end of this one. Only one question about your strategy troubles me. You and the Hawks were camping in gathering grounds when you were defeated by the Vada. What makes this time different?"

Elian took a half step forward. "Dragons and numbers, sir. When the Vada last attacked, we didn't have help from the dragons, and the Hawks and Bears who were camped in the gathering ground numbered less than fifty and were battle-weary. I can't promise a victory, but the gathering grounds give us our best chance."

Tiafel wasn't yet satisfied. "And the dragons? Will they lend their aid, or will they flee at the first sign of trouble?"

Elian thought of his sister, somewhere far away right now attempting to answer that very question. For now, though, the answer was simple enough. "They mourn the loss of their own as much as we do. They'll fight."

Tiafel nodded. "Then I agree. The Hounds will join the Bears on their way to battle."

Elian bowed and stepped back into his place in the circle.

The debate continued beyond Tiafel's decision, but the course of events was clear. Some, like Aldo, remained skeptical even after the decision was made. But no one was foolish enough to think they had any chance of surviving alone.

By the time the council ended, it was decided. The clans would march to do battle against the Debru.

22

They retraced their steps away from the hole, through the dense woods of the park, and between the tall buildings of the village. Samora no longer paid much attention to her surroundings, though. Aldrick and Karla would protect her, and the sight of the hole had sent her thoughts spinning.

There had been no hole in the vision the Vada had shown her, but what did that mean? Had the Vada not known, or had the hole been created sometime after?

It wasn't until she passed the buildings she and Karla had tested that she felt the echo of adani. It was stronger than any she'd felt since they had landed. She stopped and looked around for the source of the strength. "Do you feel that, Karla?"

The woman stopped. "What?"

Samora approached one of the buildings she had sent adani into and placed her hand upon it. "Oh."

Karla hurried over and put her hand next to Samora's. "Feels like your adani to me."

"I didn't use anywhere near that much."

Karla shot her a skeptical look, which Samora answered with a glare.

"Fine," Karla said. She sent a pulse of adani of her own into the building. The stones groaned again, but Samora sensed the pulse and traced it through the building. It looped around on itself and then merged, like two small streams coming together into a small river. Some of the strength bled away, back into the world, but what remained grew stronger yet.

Samora noted every detail of the adani's movement, memorizing the pattern for possible future use. After tracing it for a while, she realized she'd felt something similar before. "This is how Elian uses adani when he fights. He loops it through his body like this and makes it stronger."

Karla grunted. "I'm familiar with the techniques for adanists, but I've never heard of doing this in a building. Of course, I'd never heard of adani in a building before, so I suppose that's not a surprise."

Aldrick split his time between scouting for dangers and watching them. "What's happening?" he asked.

"When we were testing these buildings for adani earlier, we released some into them. It seems they took the adani and are strengthening it," Samora answered.

Aldrick frowned. "That—doesn't seem possible."

Karla nodded along. "If you would have asked me yesterday, I would have agreed with you."

"So, the buildings are getting stronger?" Aldrick asked, still not understanding.

Samora tried to help him. "In a way. There's adani rushing through a few of them now. I can't tell exactly what that adani does. There are lots of places where the lines of adani end. I think it helps keep the building strong, but there's more, too."

"If any adani in a building gets stronger, why wasn't the village full of it when we got here?"

Samora was impressed by Aldrick's questions. They ran in much the same direction as hers. She closed her eyes so she could track the adani more carefully. After a bit, she felt as though she had her answer. "It's not a perfect system. Some of the adani bleeds away, and it feels like there might be a limit to how long adani lasts within. It needs fresh adani every so often to keep working."

Karla nodded. "But this tells us the buildings didn't need as much adani as we thought they did. If they received a little, they would be able to make it into as much as they needed."

Samora opened her eyes and looked around. "It's brilliant, really. A way to make a little bit of adani do a lot of work."

Samora thought of the dragon waiting for them outside the village, and of the humans that had once lived here. "Come on, it's time we put our questions to the dragon."

THEY FOUND him right where they had left him, and Samora wondered if he had moved at all since they had parted ways. The ground around him didn't seem any more disturbed than before, so she suspected the answer was no. He watched them approach with an expectant gaze.

"Did you want to think about this more?" Karla asked.

"No point in delaying. We came to ask questions, and now I think I know what questions I need to ask."

Karla looked between the dragon and Samora, then nodded. "Well, I suppose I'll get a meal cooking, then. Is there anything else I can do to help?"

Samora saw how the question chafed at her. Karla had lived for years as the ruler of her own small world. Her strength and skill had carried her through more decades and trials than Samora could know. Now she was forced to cook meals and escort her across the land. "Thanks for everything, Karla."

Karla waved away her thanks and went to where they'd stacked wood the night before.

Samora turned to the dragon, which still watched her carefully. Though they'd been traveling companions for several days, he still made her uncomfortable. She squared her shoulders and approached him slowly, as though he was a trap about to spring.

The dragon didn't move as she reached out to place her hand against his neck. His scales felt warm under her skin, but not so hot they burned. She reached out with her adani and made the connection that would allow her to understand him. She wasn't sure quite how she wanted to proceed, so she phrased her questions simply. "We saw the city and learned much. What happened? Why did you burn it?"

The dragon settled his massive head in the dirt and closed his eyes. She closed hers as well, and memories unveiled themselves as though they were her own.

She flew overhead and watched the humans build, a vision of a time long past. They'd become more aware of adani and learned to bend it to their will. Shortly after, they'd found the beating hearts of this world, the places where adani had gathered in deep pools of strength. Those places became the sites of their villages, which expanded to become the ruins Samora knew.

She watched as humans developed. Their lives were short, but their brief lives were filled with creativity. They weaved adani into their buildings and into their fields, making their homes stronger and filling their stomachs with food.

Some were envious of the humans' rapid progress, but most were proud. What a human lacked in strength they made up for in discovery and focus, and, as the elder argued, the humans' gain served the dragons well. Many of the human weavings were too subtle to use, but some advanced dragons' abilities, too. The species cooperated and mastered the world.

Then the fabric of the world tore and the first Debru appeared. Soon after, more tears began appearing across the land. Some ripped the land wide open, but others were too subtle for the dragons to discover easily. Dragons blasted the wounds with adani to no avail. Then they carried humans to the rifts, but the first humans to try couldn't close them either.

She watched the Debru march across the land. Watched as humans and dragons banded together to fight the invasion. The battles she witnessed made the ones she'd fought in seem like nothing more than small skirmishes. Hundreds of Debru clashed with thousands of humans. Bound adani clashed with shadow, and when the dust cleared, the only constant was the bodies left behind.

For a time, the human and dragon alliance held the Debru at bay. The two species fighting together were strong, but the Debru were as numerous as the grains of sand on the shore of the sea. Every time the humans and dragons won, more Debru would pull themselves through the rifts.

How did one fight an enemy that could draw on endless reserves?

Humans focused on discovering how to close the rifts. A generation struggled with the problem as their friends and family fought and died to keep them safe, but eventually, they learned how.

Just in time, too. The Debru began pushing hard against the humans, throwing themselves at the defenders as though they understood their window of opportunity was growing shorter. Slowly, the tide began to turn.

She watched through the eye of the dragon as the war shifted against the humans. Wherever the Debru traveled, the land died. Grass and bushes withered and wasted away while trees lost their leaves and branches. Even if humans won a battle, the land they fought upon suffered.

The Debru advanced with a patient, inexorable certainty. They might be pushed back, but with the field of battle stripped of adani, the humans were that much weaker in their next meeting. Each time the Debru advanced, they killed more land and weakened the humans that much more.

The battle must have lasted years, though time was difficult to determine as the dragon flashed memory after memory past her. The Debru overran villages and forced humanity into smaller lands. The enormous villages, like the one she and the others camped outside of, became the last refuges of humanity as the world died around them. She witnessed heroic stands, tragic losses, and more death than she'd imagined possible.

Humans focused their efforts on the closing of the rifts. The dragon had been part of that effort, carrying groups of adanists on his back as they traveled across the land. Closing the rifts was no easy task, consuming most of the adani the warriors possessed with each effort. They refreshed themselves from the dragon's much larger store, but even so, their bodies weakened as they pushed themselves to their limits time and again.

Samora wished she could sense the weaves they used. Unlike the Debru circles, these rifts healed without releasing an enormous amount of adani. It looked more like the adanists would stitch the rift up, leaving the land unchanged from the way it had been before the rift had destroyed it. Unfortunately, the dragon wasn't sensitive enough to adani to track the weaves the humans used.

More memories of battles followed, but Samora encouraged the dragon to move on. She believed she understood the contours of the war, and she'd seen nothing that answered her most important question.

Instead of obeying, the dragon showed her many of the same scenes again. Samora protested, but the dragon's insistence eventually silenced her.

He chose these memories for a reason, but why?

It wasn't until the third time she watched a Vada leap high and slaughter the adanists on top of a dragon that she understood. The Debru killed the humans, then leaped off the dragon to attend to another part of the battle. The dragon played the memory again and Samora understood. "The Debru only cared about the humans."

It was as if someone had slapped her across the face, and she now viewed the world from a slightly different perspective. It wasn't that dragons didn't die in the war, but the Debru didn't care about them nearly so much as they did humans.

"Why?" Samora asked.

The dragon showed her the memories of humanity building the enormous villages. At first, Samora thought it meant to imply it was because of what humanity built, but that was clearly wrong. Then she realized the common thread connecting the memories: the varied ways in which humanity manipulated adani.

Samora swore softly. Something Elian had told her echoed in her head, a sensation he'd shared when the Belog's shadow had infected his spirit. It had feared them, specifically. Was it because they reminded the Debru of the humans of the past?

"I think I understand. Is that why you wanted to wipe us out?"

The dragon skipped forward in time. The desperate efforts of humanity were succeeding. They closed the rifts faster than new rifts opened, stranding the remaining Debru without reinforcements. The war continued, but its conclusion was deemed inevitable, a simple matter of the passing of time.

The elder announced his decision, and the others agreed. Humans had attracted the Debru to the world with their use of adani. Thus, the humans and their ability to use adani were too dangerous. To save the world, the humans had to die.

Samora's stomach felt as though it had caught on fire. The edges of her vision turned white, and she couldn't focus enough to maintain her connection. When she stepped away, there were tears streaming down the side of her face. "What gives you the *right*?" she snarled.

She swore again and stomped away.

The dragon remained still and watched her walk away into the darkness.

❧ 23 ❧

Elian climbed to the roof of his house and settled near the peaked top. From up high, every shout carried to his ear, and there was an impressive amount of shouting. Samora would be glad not to be here. The wall of noise and number of people in motion would have driven her mad. Truthfully, he didn't much care for it, either.

Tents dropped around the village, making Elian feel like they'd been surrounded by a temporary forest that was being cut down. At the rate the tents collapsed, he assumed the wandering clans would be on the move again by midday. An impressive feat, considering the number of people involved.

Closer to home, villagers and clans people alike gathered in the square to divvy up the harvest stores. The division of the food had caused no end of headache. The food was normally allocated and distributed by the villages throughout the winter, allowing adjustments to be made based on the needs of the clans and the harshness of the winter. All of that had been thrown out the window this year.

The first and most pressing of the problems was that Elian's village wasn't the sole provider for so many clans. Both Wolves and Hounds tended to draw their food from villages farther north, and in the uncertainty of the situation, no one had sent messengers north for food while the clans camped outside the village. So Elian's village was already lower on food than expected, and then the clans demanded the full winter's allotment for their campaign.

There'd been no easy solution. The clans' demands weren't without reason. There was little telling what turns their fight against the Debru would take, and they were here, so it made sense to fill their sleds with as much of the harvest as they could carry, but the village needed food, too.

The resulting compromises left no one happy, which Elian supposed was the best they could do. He kept half an eye on the division of food in the square, ensuring it was at least roughly in line with what the elders had agreed upon.

Eventually, though, he couldn't hide any longer. He cycled adani through his legs and leaped off the roof, landing lightly next to the family garden. He knocked on the front door and entered. Mother stood in the kitchen, working the dough that would eventually become bread.

The sight was answer enough for all of Elian's questions. "You decided to stay, then?"

Mother continued kneading her dough as she nodded.

"Why not come with us?"

"For the same reasons I gave before. I'm more useful here."

That was obvious nonsense. "If we succeed, the battle will never reach here, and if we fail, it won't matter whether you're here or not."

Mother gathered up the dough and tossed it into a wooden bowl. She covered it with a towel and turned to him as she wiped her hands clean. "Perhaps it is more to say that I'd rather be here."

"Why?"

"Your father and I left the clans because we didn't want to fight any longer. It was a harder decision for him because he possessed some notable skills, but no one in the clan missed me much. I had some small gift at binding shields, but I was never any good at fighting. I'm proud of you, and it pains me to see you go, but my place is here, waiting for you when you return."

"We need every adanist we can get. Even a single shield might mean the difference between victory and defeat."

Mother shook her head. "If your battle is ever decided by whether or not *my* shield holds, you've already lost."

She stepped forward and embraced him. "I believe in you, and I'm beyond impressed by what you and Samora have accomplished, but this is where I want to be. You might not understand, but please, trust me."

Elian buried his face in her shoulder and nodded. "I don't understand, but I do trust you. I'll miss you, though."

"And I you." She let go and took a step back. "Not only that, but you haven't given me nearly enough time to get to know this young lady who has stolen your heart from me."

"If we survive, I'll be sure that you two have as much time as you want," Elian assured her.

Mother's smile fell and she shook her head. "Not if, but when."

She silenced his protest. "I'm not blind to the odds, but that's not what this is about." She tapped the side of her head with a finger. "It's about what's happening up here. As soon as you let yourself accept the possibility you might not come back, your resolve falters. My master once taught me it was far better to be a fool in battle, because only a fool can fight freely since they don't realize the danger they're in."

"I—suppose I'll be a fool then? But only because you told me to."

Mother's smile returned. "Good. I love you, Elian."

"I love you, too, Mother."

HARALD SCRATCHED at his beard as Elian climbed on top of the dragon. "Are you sure about this?"

Elian ran his hand along the dragon's scales as though he was comforting a friend. Adani tingled beneath his fingertips, even though he made no effort to connect. The dragon shifted subtly, muscle and adani shifting under Elian's palm and reminding him that his meager strength was nothing in comparison.

He silently thanked the dragon for the reminder. It was far too easy, when adanists listened to your commands and whole clans marched at your suggestions, to think too much of oneself. He imagined the dragon twisting his long neck, opening his mouth, and swallowing him in one bite, and all his various illusions of importance faded. He probably wouldn't even serve as a full meal.

"No, but it seems best, don't you think?"

"I agree it's important to keep track of the Vada, but I don't need to remind you what happened last time. We still don't understand the Vada's full strength. It would be easy to fly into the same trap again."

Elian didn't disagree. "We'll fly very high. We don't need to know every detail, just its position and how fast it's moving."

"At the very least, you should reconsider going. If the Vada takes you down, I don't know how well the clans will stick together."

Elian faced the dragon so Harald wouldn't see his reaction, but it didn't matter. Harald had listened to far too many of his complaints over the past few days to not guess the reason for Elian's discontent. "Like it or not, the clans are together because of you. I agree it makes no sense for them to part now, but it's not out of the question if something happens to you."

"What they need to do is the same regardless of whether or not I'm around," Elian said.

Harald nodded and Elian let out a slow breath. They didn't disagree, but Harald took it upon himself to continually remind Elian of the facts he'd rather forget. "I understand. It's important that I go, though. If the dragons sense something, they'll be able to let me know."

"Still don't like you heading out like this," Harald grumbled.

"I'll be wary," Elian assured him.

Harald didn't have any more objections, so he stepped back and allowed Elian to climb on top of his dragon. Elian dipped his head toward the warrior.

Harald stepped back as Elian checked to ensure the other riders were ready. This scouting attempt also required four dragons, but this time, only one rider was atop each. As before, Elian had spread the honors out among the clans, with him representing the Bears. All had been waiting for him, so he connected with the dragon and urged him to fly. The dragon stood, stretched its wings, and leaped into the cloudless sky, launched by muscle and adani working as one.

Elian tracked the shifts in the dragon's adani easily, as some part of his own was captured in the process. As the wings beat the air and the dragon rose, Elian shook his head. "You're a lot like me, aren't you?"

He thought he sensed agreement through their connection.

Elian considered that as the dragon gained more height and they began their journey west. Dragons could bind adani, too, but they tended not to weave anything too complicated. Their methods of shifting adani around within their bodies seemed much more subtle and complex.

The similarity went deeper than the way they used adani, though. It was tough to be sure, but he thought the dragon was eager to scout, to help in the fight against the Vada. He wanted revenge as much as Elian did.

A foreign memory forced its way into his thoughts. A man the dragon had once known long, long ago, who used adani as the dragons did. Whose techniques were closer to Elian's than to Harald's. A new face replaced the first, and then another. All who manipulated adani like Elian.

"Are you saying there used to be more like me?"

Agreement once again traveled through their connection.

Elian rubbed his chin with one hand while keeping his other firmly latched to the scales. The information seemed important, but Elian couldn't imagine why. Even if it was true, almost all the adanists of this age had spent their lives mastering the external manipulation of adani. It didn't change anything about their situation.

His thoughts didn't wander for long. The dragon continued to rise, and soon even Elian was gripping tight. The air this high was cold as it whipped across his exposed face and arms, and he spent most of his time either pressing his face close to the dragon's neck or looking down so that the wind didn't catch him full in the face. From this height he could see that the horizon had a slight bend to it.

The dragon rose even higher, forcing Elian to wrap himself tightly around the neck, both for a secure grip and to enjoy some of the warmth of the dragon's body. He'd seen the land from the sky before, but at this altitude the land took on a different quality. Instead of trees, streams, and tracks, he saw the land as one textured whole.

From this height, the scars the Debru left across the land were more pronounced. Elian saw their track before he saw the main body of their forces. It stretched from west to east, meandering across the land as though the Vada was taking a leisurely, exploratory stroll through a new world. From here it was as wide as his thumb, and he didn't want to imagine how much land that actually was.

The scar ended in a wrinkle in the land, which Elian took to be a small valley. A billowing cloud of shadow obscured every-thing within, preventing Elian from making out any details about the enemy forces. He briefly considered diving lower but quickly decided against it. The shadow wouldn't give up its secrets if he was closer, so there was no reason to take any risk.

He and the others circled for a bit, but the shadow didn't seem to be in motion. Elian considered its position relative to the last time he'd seen the Vada. The Debru were making good time across the land, but they didn't seem to be in any particular rush. Was the Vada so confident it didn't feel the need to hurry, or was something more afoot?

Elian signaled to the other riders that he wanted to continue west. The other riders looked confused by the request, but all agreed to follow him. They followed the tracks for a few dozen miles before Elian asked the dragon to circle again.

Far below, the tracks split. The wider of the two was the one they'd followed, and the one Elian assumed contained the Vada. The other was narrower, but not so much that Elian wasn't concerned by it. He didn't see any Debru nearby, so he and the dragon slowly dropped toward the surface. After a careful descent, they landed next to the split. Elian leaped off the dragon and studied the tracks up close. No small number of Debru had taken the other path.

The other riders joined Elian in his study of the tracks.

"I see what looks like the tracks of several Belogs and who knows how many Debru," one said.

Another, studying the edges of the destruction, added, "There are plenty of otsoa and kettu tracks here, too."

"A considerable force," Elian said. He put his hands on his hips and looked around. "But why split?"

"From up above, it looks like the tracks went north for a time, then curved west. I don't think they run exactly parallel to the main force, but they're heading in the same general direction. Do you think they intend to squeeze us between their forces?"

Elian wished he knew. "It's certainly possible, but why?"

He didn't say the next part out loud, though everyone understood it well enough. The Debru didn't need any special tactics to defeat the clans. All they needed was to advance, and they'd walk right over all opposition.

He considered a moment longer, but guessing wouldn't do them any good. "Let's get back to the dragons and follow this second trail."

In no time at all they were back in the air, following the trail as they gained altitude. Elian's eyes narrowed when he realized this second track had penetrated farther into human lands than the first. Were they moving faster?

He followed the tracks with his eyes and traced the direction to the horizon. This second set of tracks was straighter than the first, and he imagined the Debru rushing to their eventual destination. He wished he knew the land better, so that he could identify where they traveled toward, but they were far from anyplace he could recognize landmarks.

They caught up to the Debru before too long. As they'd guessed, the force was considerable. Elian's heart sank as he counted nearly half a dozen Belogs, at least that many Mokas, and no fewer than thirty normal Debru. Countless otsoa and kettu roamed around the Debru, too.

The Belogs noticed the dragons but made no effort to slow or defend themselves. Elian was halfway tempted to pick a fight, but the strength of shadow was too great. If the Belogs and Mokas worked together, they could simply hide under a bound shield of shadow while the dragons ineffectually dropped adani on it.

Perhaps it was worth it, though, if just to stop them. This force hurried across the land as though they were being chased. Elian flew ahead of them to see if he could uncover their destination.

His heart sank even deeper when he found it. Up ahead a small patch of vivid green grass surrounded saplings that stretched for the sun. Elian knew the area well. He'd saved his sister from shadow here, then later on, killed a Vada as it fought to emerge.

The Belogs weren't that far away, either.

Elian swore and urged the dragon to return to the clans. He had to warn the council before it was too late.

24

Samora flung the pack of supplies onto her back as though it had done her wrong. Aldrick had already packed everything of his and was waiting expectantly by the dragon. Only Karla remained, but she moved among her scattered belongings lazily, frequently casting her eye back toward the abandoned village. Samora kept expecting the adanist to announce that she was going to stay behind, but after a prolonged stare, she'd return to packing her bag.

She bit her tongue hard enough to be painful. She'd already spoken harshly to Karla twice this morning, and both times Karla had agreed to hurry, only to resume a pace most elders in Samora's village would have found slow. Karla also didn't want any help, nor would she speak of the thoughts clearly consuming her.

She finally finished and slung the pack onto her back. She looked at Samora as though she was about to say something, then thought better of it.

Samora grunted, then climbed upon the dragon, kicking her toes into his side harder than was necessary. She doubted he would feel anything, but it calmed the storm roiling her chest for a moment. She took her seat up front, followed by Karla and Aldrick. The moment they were settled, she said, "Let's go."

The dragon's adani stirred itself to life, and though a part of Samora longed to connect and sense the flow through the dragon's body, she refused. They took to the air, enjoying a bright and sunny day, their first since landing at the village. Samora looked back one last time. From here, she couldn't see the hole, but that didn't much matter. With any luck, she'd never see this place again. The dragon's memories twisted humanity's remarkable achievement into a nightmarish monument.

Karla's backward look lasted much longer than Samora's, and she only turned forward once the village was a rapidly shrinking scar on the otherwise unblemished horizon.

Their flight was silent, the remnants of last night's arguments lingering over the day's travel. The silence suited Samora just fine. If they didn't speak until they returned to the unified clans, she wouldn't mind. Unfortunately, Karla wasn't so willing to let the matter rest. They were just flying over the foothills when she said, "There's still so much more we need to ask."

Samora couldn't stop the growl at the back of her throat, but she checked herself before yelling at Karla like she had the night before. "We'll let Elian ask the questions when we return. With what we've learned, he should be able to ask the right ones."

Karla remained gently insistent. "Maybe so, but you're here now, and we have three long days of travel ahead of us. We'd be fools to waste the opportunity."

"You didn't see what I saw," Samora said.

The dragon's adani stirred, as if in response to her anger. Samora ignored it. She stabbed her finger at the dragon's neck. "He was there when they decided that humanity shouldn't exist. When they decided that instead of fighting together, they should kill us."

Karla shifted behind Samora. "But—"

Samora held up a hand while she tried to master her

emotions. Seeing the elder dragon passing judgment on humanity had angered her like nothing else, and she realized it clouded her judgment. They'd argued this in circles the night before, and Samora hadn't made her argument well. Now was her chance to try again. "No. We came out here because Elian needed to know whether or not we could trust the dragons, and we've answered that definitively. We can't."

Karla was silent for a time, but it didn't last. "You said yourself the elder passed the judgment because he thought it was the only way to stop the Debru from attacking. And you forget the dragons didn't kill us all. They saved enough for us to start over."

Samora tightened her grip on the dragon's scales. "Karla, you haven't been forced to see what I've seen. The innocent men, women, and children burning alive in their homes. The dragons, betraying the allies they'd fought shoulder to shoulder with for generations. Perhaps the elder believed their action was justified, but that doesn't change the nature of the act. What they did was evil and horrible, and there's no justification that changes or excuses that. There's no point talking to the dragon, knowing what he's done. Some acts are unforgiveable."

Karla spoke carefully. "I'm not asking for you to forgive them. I'm asking you to work with them, to focus on what is practical. Despite what's happened in the past, the dragons have been a tremendous help to us in the recent weeks. This one has even flown us across the land, and continues to do so, despite your feelings toward him. It's as your brother is always saying: we need to come together, and that includes dragon and human."

Samora weighed Karla's words against what she'd seen and what she knew of the dragons. Then she shook her head. "I'm sorry, but no. Perhaps you're right, but I won't talk with it, knowing what I know. If Elian can stomach what they've done, he can speak to the dragons, but I believe we need to hold ourselves to a higher standard, and that includes our allies."

"But what if the dragon knows something that could help us?

We still don't know what caused the hole. A weapon that powerful might be something we could turn against the Vada."

Samora had thought of that, and she was already fairly certain of the answer. "I think the dragons destroyed it. The heart of that village had grown stronger because of the weavings humanity had laced every building with. Once they killed all the humans, they banded together somehow to destroy the well of adani, so that the Debru wouldn't have a reason to return."

Her reasoning bought her a long period of blissful silence. She was grateful Aldrick chose to stay out of the conversation. He had been a pillar of stability this entire trip, but if she had to endure his questioning, she might go mad.

When Karla spoke again, it was quieter than before. "How certain are you that's true?"

"Reasonably so. It's the only explanation that makes sense. The dragon didn't show me any other creatures that can use adani, and the Debru never fought their way into the village. Even at their peak strength, I don't think humans are capable of what we saw. That only leaves the dragons, and it follows from what they've already confessed to. They believe humans and our use of adani somehow summoned the Debru, so by destroying all traces, I'm certain they hoped to keep themselves safe."

When Karla didn't answer for a long time, Samora turned back to her. "You were placing all your hope on there being another weapon, weren't you?"

Karla nodded, her face long.

"Don't fear on that count."

Karla looked up, doubt and hope warring on her face.

"We might still have questions, but we've also learned enough. I think that village provided us the best chance we have of defeating the Vada. But I'll need your help once we return to Elian."

THREE DAYS of travel passed more quickly than Samora would have expected, especially considering the weight of the knowledge they carried. Their routine was a simple one. They woke early and began their flight for the day. Thankfully, Karla was never as slow on other days as she was outside the village. They would fly through the day, awkwardly eating dried meat out of their packs while the dragon carried them. They didn't stop until the sun was close to dipping below the horizon.

At times, Samora sensed the adani running through the dragon more sharply than usual. It felt almost as though the dragon tried to thrust his adani into her, but she kept him as distant from her as possible. Still, his efforts often caught her by surprise, and when he attempted to connect, she could almost feel his emotions.

An ocean of sorrow lurked within the dragon, but she couldn't bring herself to care. After the atrocities he had committed, he deserved all the sorrow in the world. If Karla felt any of it, she said nothing. On their second night Samora saw Karla next to the dragon, trying to connect with it, but the attempt was unsuccessful. Samora didn't mind. Karla could do what she wanted, and if that meant interrogating the dragon until she was older and grayer, well, it was her life to do with as she pleased.

On the third day of their travel, they returned to the lands Samora was more familiar with. The deadlands fell behind them and Samora felt the closest she had to ease since they'd taken off.

It didn't last long.

They crossed over a wide stretch of desiccated land. The width of the destruction could only mean that the Vada was on the move, nearing their home. They briefly conversed and decided the wise course of action was to give the Vada a wide berth. The information and ideas they carried were too valuable to risk.

They reached Samora's village not long after, but neither the dragons nor the clans were there. Samora briefly considered landing to speak with her mother, but it looked as though events had developed rapidly while she was gone. Thankfully, the tracks of the clan were easy to find and follow, as hundreds of warriors left a trail they could easily see from the air.

So it was that when they returned, they found the wandering clans in the midst of chaos. The sun was halfway between its midpoint and the horizon, and the wandering clans had come to a stop, though no one made any move to set up camp. Dragons lounged on the northern side of the stopped sleds, and the dragon they rode on landed next to them.

Aldrick and Karla jumped off first, with Samora right behind. They were met by the scouts who'd watched them approach.

"What's happening?" Karla asked.

"The Debru sent a force of Belogs, Moka, and more to the gathering ground where Elian killed the Vada. The unified council is debating their course of action as we speak," one of the scouts answered.

Karla looked over to Samora. "What do you think?"

"They need to know what we learned. Gathering grounds are our best weapon against the Debru, and we can't afford to lose them."

Karla nodded, and it was as if the tension that had been sitting between them for the last several days disappeared. "Then let's get there as fast as we can."

The other adanist took off and Samora followed after, leaving Aldrick and a confused scout behind to deal with their packs and the dragon. Karla cleared their path as they ran through the loitering adanists. The elders all stood in a circle near the center of the clans, so it wasn't hard to find them. Karla forcibly opened a space between two of the elders, successfully interrupting an ongoing debate between Aldo and Elian.

Elian's eyes went wide at her appearance, but Aldo looked as though he'd be happy to poke her with a needle of bound adani. Samora ignored the elder and focused on Elian. "Have you decided what to do?"

Elian shot a glare at Aldo, but shook his head. "We can't agree on whether we should risk ourselves to protect the gathering ground or not."

"You should," Samora said.

"Why, and why should we listen to you?" Aldo demanded.

"Because I think I've found a technique that will make us stronger against the Vada, but we'll need the gathering grounds. Otherwise, it's not as effective. They're too valuable to lose."

Aldo waved his hand dismissively at her. "We have no reason to believe you, and even if we did, there are other gathering grounds. We can just retreat to another one."

Elian seemed to grow before her eyes at Aldo's insults. "It's only because of my sister we face one Vada instead of two, and only because of her we even have this gathering ground to defend. If there's anyone we should believe, it should be her."

"Regardless, the point remains. The Belogs are already close, if they aren't already there. We'd be better served retreating to a different gathering ground."

Harald chose that moment to raise his hand and insert himself into the conversation. "There might be some reason to that argument, but this is also the best chance we might get to whittle down their numbers. The Vada sent them ahead, most likely to destroy the gathering ground, while it waited safely behind them. We can't say for sure it will do the same for the next battle."

Aldo shrugged. "We can't say it won't, either."

Elian's voice carried over Aldo's with a quiet authority. "We can argue what we know and what we don't know all day, but the longer we wait, the less likely we are to win. If we delay, the next battle will happen much closer to my village, and that's not a battle I want to fight. We have more freedom now, with the village at our back. I say we fight for the gathering ground. That this is where we stop the Debru advance. How do you all decide?"

The elders spoke, one after the other, the vote racing around the circle. Elian carried the day, though the decision was far from unanimous. Harald took over after the last vote was called. "Choose warriors to mount the dragons. Everyone else can remain here. There's no chance of reaching the gathering ground on foot in the time we have."

The elders broke apart and went to deliver the decision to their respective clans. Elian and Harald spoke quickly, then Harald bowed quickly to Karla and Samora before rushing to summon the Bears.

For a brief moment, Samora and Karla stood alone with Elian in the middle of the chaos, a small island of tranquility as the clans prepared for battle. Elian stared at her as though she was an apparition. "I was afraid you'd never return."

"There are wonders out there. Things I never would have believed if I hadn't seen them with my own eyes."

"You'll have to tell me about them when I return. Are you coming?"

"I am, of course," Karla interjected.

Samora shook her head. "I'll stay here and prepare to help the healers."

Elian nodded, as though he'd hoped for a different answer but didn't expect anything else. "Is it true? Do you think you have a way to defeat the Vada?"

"I think I can make us stronger. I couldn't say if it'll be enough, but I believe the Debru were frightened of the techniques our ancestors understood. It's why they want to kill the humans."

"Sounds like we have a lot to discuss."

"More than you can imagine." She saw him getting ready to say his farewell, so she reached out and grabbed his wrists. "There is something else you need to know."

"What?"

"You can't trust the dragons."

Elian froze at her words. He turned slowly back around. "We can't?"

Samora shook her head. "I wish I had better news, but I don't. They'll help us for as long as they need us to defeat the Debru, so I don't think you need to worry today, but be careful around them. Please. They definitely are not our friends."

Elian looked hurt by Samora's claim, but it was a mark of his trust in her that he didn't argue. He simply nodded and said, "Thanks for warning me. I'll be as careful as I can. You do the same. It sounds like we're going to need your knowledge soon."

With that he broke apart to prepare for battle, leaving her behind yet again.

25

Thanks to Samora's timely return, Elian was able to mount the dragon he'd rescued from the Debru. That fight felt like it had happened a lifetime ago, and he greeted the dragon as though they were old friends. Elian pressed his hands and forehead against the dragon's scales. "Thank you."

The feelings that returned through the connection were complex. Elian could name sorrow, anger, and frustration, but there were more in the mix he wasn't confident he could identify.

"You've been through a lot, too, haven't you?" he said.

Confirmation flowed through their bond.

Elian trusted Samora with his life. If she said the dragons couldn't be trusted, it was with good reason. But as he sensed the currents of emotion flowing through the dragon, he found it difficult to believe. The dragons could have flown away after he'd rescued them from the Debru. Even in the past, if the dragons had attacked the humans, they'd saved some, too.

Elian wished he had more time to speak with the dragon and explore the mysteries of their shared past. He didn't doubt the dragons withheld secrets. He'd sensed and guessed as much himself. Despite that, he still believed in them. Perhaps it was foolish and shortsighted, but he trusted what he sensed when he spoke to them. In time, he was sure he would come to understand them better.

Unfortunately, they didn't have that time today. The protection of the gathering grounds was far more pressing. He checked with the dragon, who assured him it was ready to fly and fight. Elian nodded and waited for the command to leave. After days of feeling like his words would shape the course of clan history, it was freeing to follow someone else's orders for a change. In this battle he was nothing more than Harald's second. The giant warrior settled on another dragon.

Elian wasn't sure how he felt about Harald joining the fight. They could use his strength, but he was still injured and weaker than before. He hid it well, but Elian saw the exhaustion behind his eyes whenever they spoke. When Elian had gently suggested Harald remain behind, though, Harald had given him a glare that made him feel the sudden urge to void his bowels.

Elian hadn't pressed the matter.

Harald gave the signal to fly, and the dragons began to take to the air. They lifted off in ones and twos, joining together in loose formations once they were in the sky. Elian and the other adanists on his dragon were among the last to take off, so once they joined the others, they immediately sped west.

Scouts spotted the destruction before they spotted the Belogs. Smoke and flame rose high in the air, acting like a beacon that called them to battle. Elian's heart sank at the sight. Were they already too late? The smoke was thin and wispy, but the fire grew as he watched. A cloud of shadow drifted behind the smoke, obscuring the forces the Vada had sent to the gathering ground.

Elian gripped the scales of the dragon tighter as they flew faster than any adanist could run. More details came into focus, and he breathed a small sigh of relief. Part of the gathering ground had been devoured by shadow, and the flames would soon spread to more than half the circle, but it didn't feel like they were too late, yet. Green grass on the eastern side of the gathering ground still promised respite and strength.

He looked to Harald for directions. The leader of the Bears rode the dragon with his thighs and knees clamped tightly at its neck while exchanging quick hand signs with the leaders of the other clans. From where Elian was positioned, he couldn't see everything that passed between them.

Then Harald turned to the dragons carrying the Bears. His signals were succinct. He wanted them to drop as much bound adani down on top of the Debru as they could. Elian and the other commanders signaled that they understood, and the battle began.

The Bears joined near the rear of a long line of dragons. Only the Hawks were further back. The Wolves led the assault, which made Elian shake his head. Aldo had fought the hardest to prevent this battle, but once it was decided, he'd insisted his warriors form the tip of their spear. At least Aldo flew on a dragon beside his warriors.

They formed bound spears and knives, all strengthened by the deep wells of adani within the dragons. As soon as they were within range, streaks of golden light fell from the dragons like deadly rain. Their attacks broke against the shadow, which retreated until it formed an enormous shield that protected the Debru from above.

Thanks to his position near the rear, Elian was able to watch as the second and third dragons swooped overhead, their warriors flinging their attacks against the Belogs. As before, the attacks failed to pierce the powerful shield.

The Hounds all attacked the shield at once, four dragons' worth of adanists dropping their strongest attacks on the shield. They succeeded in cracking it for a moment, but it healed as they flew away.

Harald and the Bears tried next. Elian could do nothing but watch, helpless in a battle of bound adani. Harald formed a spear that would have been impressive from any other warrior, but Elian had seen him go bigger. The Bears followed the Hounds' example and attacked all at once, but their attack failed to crack the shield.

The dragons gathered and circled, hopefully out of range of the Belogs. Elian had stared into the shadow as the spears broke against the shield, hoping for a glimpse of what happened underneath the cover of darkness, but he'd seen nothing.

They'd been fortunate the first time they'd attacked using the dragons. The Belog had been unprepared and alone, and the adanists had been able to slowly overwhelm it. That success had given Elian an unreasonable expectation for how other battles would go.

Harald and the others communicated using their hand signals, and this time Elian was in a position where he could see them better. The plan proposed by Tiafel was simple enough. They would approach the dark shield from all directions, dropping the full might of their adani at once.

Elian looked down to study the advance of the shadow. Tiafel's plan was a good one. Their last battle had proven the Belogs' shadows were no more limitless than a human's adani. Supporting the shield had to burn an incredible amount of strength, and if they could crack it, all that strength would be wasted. The only question was whether or not they could break it.

Harald's gestures pulled Elian's eyes back up, and he nodded as he understood his orders. The clans split off in four separate directions, then turned and began another run at the shadow. Adanists bound their spears and prepared to launch.

Shouts from the others were the only warning Elian received. The dragon turned and banked sharply, slamming Elian's stomach high into his throat. He grunted as spears of shadow erupted from the shield, as thick as his leg and thrown almost faster than his eye could track.

His dragon avoided a spear meant for it, but Harald's dragon wasn't so lucky. The spear struck it in its massive chest. Scales fell from the sky, accompanied by the dragon's dark blood, but the dragon heaved itself higher into the air and away from the danger.

The story was repeated all across the sky. Many of the spears missed, thanks in large part to the dragons' quick reactions. But several had been wounded. Elian craned his head left and right, searching the sky for any dragons and adanists plunging to their deaths. As near as he could tell, the dragons all remained airborne, but who knew for how long?

Elian swore. They'd come in high, but the shadowy attacks reached even higher. The dragons and their riders scattered, leaving the Debru far behind and below. Eventually they regrouped, and quick signals passed between the leaders. Elian shook his head and looked down. They were going to have to go down there, but no one seemed eager to make that decision.

From the glimpses he caught of the leaders' signals, it was the exact debate they were having. It was also a debate they didn't have time for. As they circled safely out of reach, the Debru made slow but steady progress through the gathering ground. If they waited much longer, the whole debate would be meaningless.

Elian and the others circled and waited while the argument dragged on. He stretched and cracked his knuckles, one eye always on the gathering ground below. Already the shadow was close to halfway across, and the fires had already spread past the center. He wasn't sure how long it would take the Debru to completely destroy the gathering ground, but their time was running short.

He swore and looked back to Harald, who still gestured quickly at the other leaders.

Elian growled. They didn't have time!

He waited for Harald to look his way. When his leader finally did, Elian gestured that they needed to go down. Harald shook his head and signaled that he should wait.

The shadow grew closer to the center, and Elian imagined the Debru laughing under the protection of their shield as the humans watched helplessly.

He couldn't do it alone, but if he led the way, it was likely others would follow.

Harald was the one who was supposed to make that decision, but the decision didn't look to be coming any time soon.

What good was all the respect he'd won if he didn't use it? Harald, like the others, was too bound to tradition. The clans needed someone who would lead.

Someone like him.

He looked back at the others on his dragon. "I'm thinking of landing. Thoughts?"

All five of them looked terrified by the prospect, but none spoke against him. Elian wasn't foolish enough to believe that meant they agreed, but if they weren't going to speak up, that was on them.

He turned back to Harald one last time, but the argument between the leaders was ongoing. He spoke straight to the dragon, and after a moment of deliberation, they agreed upon the plan. He banked away from the other dragons and dove toward the circle. The riders behind him gasped together, but Elian ignored them. The dragon pulled up close to the ground hundreds of paces away from the edge of the gathering ground, then flew low and fast toward the Debru.

Elian pulled and cycled adani from the dragon, as much as his body could hold. As they neared the circle, he sent a pulse of adani to the dragon, which spread its wings and bled all its speed in an instant. Elian leaped, basking in the sensation of flight as he sailed through the air, the shouts of the other adanists serving as the wind at his back.

He cycled adani through his legs as the ground rushed up to

meet him. His feet struck the verdant expanse of grass and more adani rushed into his body. Momentum carried him forward, but he tucked into a roll and came to his feet and drew his sword, standing alone against the approaching wall of shadow.

The Debru assault looked much more substantial from below. The shield of shadow floated higher than an ancient oak tree, and the shadows underneath roiled with pent-up energy.

He considered, briefly, the idea that perhaps coming down alone had been a rather poor decision.

He turned his eye to the skies above as the shadow of a dragon passed over him. The idea had never been that he would fight the Debru alone, but that he would motivate the others to do what was necessary. The gathering ground would strengthen them in much the same way as riding the dragons did. They'd all be better off on the ground, not just him. He expected the first dragons to drop off their riders soon. They still circled up high, but in a moment, they'd dive down and begin their assault.

He watched and waited, one eye always on the mass of shadow growing steadily closer. It paid him little mind as it gradually chewed up the land. The dragons continued to circle, and he imagined the hand signals flying back and forth between leaders as they planned their assault.

The shadow reacted to his arrival before the clans launched their attack. A pair of Mokas, accompanied by a Belog, stepped from the dark cloud and faced him. Half a dozen Debru gathered beside their leaders and a full dozen otsoa nipped at their heels.

Elian swallowed hard. He'd hoped to provoke a response but hadn't planned on one that was quite so—vigorous. The shield protecting the shadows from above dimmed as the Debru split their attention between him and the destruction of the gathering ground.

He clutched his sword tighter and dug his toes into the rich soil beneath his feet. This was it. Even if the other adanists didn't want to land, the division of the Debru meant they were more vulnerable to the devastating rain of adani the clans could release from above. All he had to do was stay alive long enough for the attack to succeed.

He raised his sword as the various Debru and their dark pets charged, then glanced up to the sky to ensure the dragons were swooping down to attack. He turned his attention back to the advancing Debru, then froze and swiveled his face back toward the sky.

His grip on his sword loosened as his bowels turned to ice. The dragons and the riders upon them weren't coming to help.

They were flying away.

26

Samora helped Brittany prepare the Bears' healing tent for what they both assumed would be a rush of adanists requiring care. She ran a sharp knife down long strips of cloth, preparing the bandages that would soon be soaked in blood. Brittany warmed water over a fire, sharpened her blades, and mixed different combinations of herbs in different cups.

The women went about their work without speaking, with the only exception being when Samora had a question or Brittany had another order to give.

Samora felt as though she was holding in a long breath. When she glanced out the open flap of the tent, she became convinced she wasn't the only one. Her return, followed by the news of the Debru assault upon the gathering grounds, had upended the last traces of normalcy the clans had desperately held onto.

She finished folding the last of the bandages and looked around the tent for anything obvious that needed her attention. As far as she could tell, there was nothing. Brittany's pace had slowed, too. The healer was checking her herbs one more time, but it looked more like she was filling her time than completing anything that needed to be urgently done.

"Is there anything else?" Samora asked.

Brittany jumped slightly at the question. Her eyes flashed briefly, but then she blew out a long breath and shook her head. "All that's left to do is wait."

Samora didn't ask what, specifically, was bothering Brittany. She'd tried earlier and received a dismissive reply. She figured that if Brittany wanted to tell her, she would, but there was little point in pressing.

She hoped that whatever it was passed, though. Brittany had been her first friend among the clans, and of all the people she'd met since, Brittany was still one of the few she felt as though she understood.

Brittany put down the cup of herbs she was inspecting. "I'd hoped, when Elian gained the influence he had, that something would have changed."

Samora looked up but found herself at a loss for words.

Thankfully, Brittany continued. "Under Harald, it feels like we're always preparing for the next battle. I know that it's our role, and it's important, but our lives used to be richer, filled with more than just the fight against the Debru. It's all Harald thinks about, though, and Harald's beliefs have infected your brother."

Samora opened her mouth to speak, but Brittany interrupted her before she began. "I know it's foolish. We're adanists, and if we neglect our duty, it's looking more and more like the Debru will wipe us out. As much as I hate to admit it, oftentimes I find myself agreeing with Elian. Retreating keeps us alive longer, but that strategy won't work forever. Perhaps it's better to attack now and end this once and for all. Maybe the only way to earn peace is through this brutal war."

The memories of the abandoned village far to the west were still rich in Samora's mind, and she wondered if the humans who had fought to defend it had thought the same. Had they believed that if they defeated the Debru, they would live in peace? What would they think, if they could somehow peer into the future and see what had become of their descendants?

She took a few tentative steps toward Brittany. "If it makes you feel any better, I often wonder the same. It seems inevitable that we have to fight, but I keep wondering if there's a better way."

Brittany gestured to the tent and the prepared supplies. "If I'm being honest, I was surprised that you wanted to help me. After all you've been up to, I thought you would be by your brother's side."

"I do wish I was by his side, but only because I want to protect him. I'm afraid I would be more a danger to him than a help, though."

"Considering all you've accomplished, that doesn't seem true."

Samora hung her head. "I've been very fortunate to be gifted with some skill with adani, and I've had teachers like you who have helped me even further along. But I am no fighter, and on the paths my brother walks, that makes me more of a weight to carry than an ally."

"You fought the Vada, though."

"Not because I meant to. I was only trying to unravel the Debru circle as it pushed its way into our world. I never raised a hand against it, otherwise. Maybe I'm mad, but even though I'm well aware of the Debru's aims, I don't want to cause them any harm. I know they'd kill me if given half the chance, but I still don't want to fight them. Did I ever tell you about the first time I fought the Debru?

Brittany's eyes narrowed. "No, I don't think you have. Was it when your village was attacked?"

"It was. A Moka came, accompanied by a large pack of otsoa. To defend my family, I used one of the only weaves I knew at the time, a basic fire weaving. I lit the flame inside the otsoa, burning them from the inside out. To this day, I can hear their screams as they died, smoke pouring out their throats."

She paused to let her pounding heart slow. "I know what the Debru intend, and I know, in my head, that our survival means their death, but I can't bring myself to be the one who fights. Every time I come close, I think of the pain and suffering I inflicted on the otsoa and my body freezes up. Does that make me a coward?"

Brittany watched her for a while, and then her posture softened. "You are many things, but a coward isn't one of them. I'm sorry I brought it up, and I'm glad that you're here to help me. Thank you."

"You're sure there's nothing else I can do?"

"I'm sure. If anything, it's probably best to get out of here for a bit while we wait. In fact, it wouldn't hurt if you were willing to keep an eye out for their return and meet them when they land. Having someone who can sort the wounded before they reach the tent would be helpful."

Samora bowed. "Any suggestions?"

"The ones that matter most are those who are seriously injured but can be healed back to fighting strength. Those who have minor wounds can wait, and if their survival is questionable even with our aid, it's best to move on and focus those we can help, first."

Samora bowed again and left the tent, respecting Brittany's wish to be alone.

When she reached the field the dragons used to take off and land, she found she wasn't the only one waiting. Healers from each of the clans sat and stood around, watching the western sky for any sign of approaching dragons.

Lenon was there, and on any other day, she might have sought his company, but like Brittany, she felt it best to be alone. A copse of trees stood a few hundred paces to the east, so she wandered toward them. They'd provide shade against the late-afternoon sun and protect her from questioning gazes.

She settled down against the trunk of one of the trees, intending to close her eyes and rest, but it wasn't long before she was distracted by the flow of adani through the tree. It was subtler than much of what she'd sensed over the past few weeks, a reminder that the rest of the world continued even as humans, dragons, and Debru wrestled for control of the land.

She rested her palms against the trunk and closed her eyes, lulled into a sense of comfort by the peaceful flow of adani. In her previous life, when her concerns had been so much smaller, she'd often lost herself in such flows for significant parts of the day. Adani rose from the land, crawled up the trunk and stretched to the highest leaves and branches before beginning a slow descent back to the land.

She followed the adani without purpose, content to drift along its current like a leaf caught in a bubbling brook. But as she drifted, she sensed a pattern she hadn't noticed before.

Not all adani returned to the land. Some looped within the tree, caught in eddies within the trunk. It was a miniscule amount, and if she followed it longer, it always eventually returned to the land, maintaining a balance of adani.

It reminded her of Elian and his techniques, as well as the weavings of the humans who had come long before. Inspired, she focused her attention and dripped some of her own adani into the tree. Shifting the flow of adani within wasn't any harder than healing a human. Her alterations were small, but she smiled as she felt them take hold. Adani looped inside the tree, which now grew faster and stronger than before.

The effect wouldn't be noticeable, maybe not for years, but that didn't change what she'd done. Increasing the effect would require nothing more than weaving more loops into the tree.

"Pardon me, I hope I'm not interrupting anything," an unfamiliar voice said.

Samora nearly jumped out of her skin. She'd gotten so lost in the flow of the tree's adani that she'd lost all track of her surroundings. She opened her eyes to see a young man, no more than five or six years older than her, if she had to guess, standing before her. He had long dark hair that was currently hanging loose, and he had a half-smile on his face, as though he understood that life was nothing but a joke and he was one of the few wise enough to understand the humor.

Of course, she figured he might just be laughing at her, but that wasn't the sense she got of him. The fabric of his tunic ended at his shoulders, revealing a wiry arm deeply tanned by long exposure to the sun. His right arm was gone, amputated sometime long ago near the shoulder. When she looked at him, she couldn't decide if he was a dangerous adanist or one of the healers that had been waiting for the wounded to return.

"Sorry to startle you, but I couldn't help but sense what you were doing to this tree, and my curiosity got the better of me."

Samora frowned, not comprehending. The changes she'd made were so subtle even she barely felt them. If he was a healer waiting for the dragons, there should have been no way he could sense her changes from halfway across the abandoned field.

He bowed deeply. "Apologies, again. I forget that even though I know you, we haven't been introduced. My name is Loken, and it's a pleasure to meet you formally."

The name was familiar, but it took Samora several long moments to place it. He was the healer traveling with the Hawks, the man Elian had gone into the deadlands to find. The man maybe most responsible for Elian's newfound strength.

Elian had never given much of a description of the man who'd guided him, but Samora had expected to find someone much older and less intimidating. Loken didn't have even half the physical presence of Harald, but there was an intensity in his eyes that belied his easy smile.

"You helped my brother."

"I would say he mostly helped himself. All he needed was someone to show him where he was going wrong."

"How did you sense what I was doing from over there?"

The half-smile never faltered. "Did you think you were the only human ever born that was so sensitive to adani?"

The questions sent a rush of shame to her cheeks because the truth was that she had. She was very grateful when he changed the subject. "Do you mind telling me what you were attempting with the tree? I've never sensed anyone do that before, and I'm fascinated."

Samora looked to the west, but there weren't any dragons or wounded adanists coming to save her, so she told him. It required her to go all the way back to her journey west with Karla, but Loken hung onto her every word as though it were a matter of life and death. When she finished, he looked up at the tree and she imagined it was with the same gaze she'd stared at the enormous buildings several days ago.

"Can you do it again?" he asked.

She nodded and chose a different tree, deciding it would be most useful to show him the entire process. She closed her eyes, put her palm against the trunk of the tree, and repeated what she had done before. Loken stood beside her, his hand at his side and his eyes open. "Fascinating."

When she was done, she opened her eyes and saw that he had his head cocked to the side, staring at the tree as though he intended to ask it a question. "May I make a suggestion?" he asked.

"Of course."

He still didn't close his eyes, but his gaze went distant, and she sensed the weaves as he made his alterations. He spoke as he worked. "Creating the loop was a clever idea, and it will help the tree create more adani over time, giving more to the land than it takes over the course of its life. You were inspired, at least in part, by your brother, weren't you?"

She nodded, impressed by his insight.

'The only problem is that adani needs to circulate farther than just within a loop. Elian's techniques work well for the purposes of combat, but he both can't and shouldn't loop the adani endlessly. He cycles the adani to gain the strength to fight, but then lets it go so it may return to its normal flow. The more he trains, the more he'll be capable of, but the pattern will hold even as he becomes stronger. The tree, in contrast, can't switch from cycling adani to not, so it needs some way of ensuring adani doesn't get stuck in a loop forever."

The weave he added to hers allowed the smallest trickle of adani to escape from the cycle she'd put it into. The tree still pulled more than it returned, but she could sense the difference after his addition. The adani felt more vigorous than before.

"Why does all adani need to flow beyond one living body?" She knew that adani entered and left the body but had always assumed that most of what cycled within a person remained the same from birth to death.

Loken shrugged. "I can't say why. When I explain it to others, I usually use a metaphor about stagnant water, but that's not really an explanation. All I know is that it's one of adani's properties."

"We still know so little, don't we?"

Loken nodded. "I'm impressed by what you've done, though. The possibilities are considerable."

"I'm hoping that once Elian returns, I'll be able to convince him it should become a key part of his strategy."

Loken nodded toward the west. "Speaking of, it looks like our warriors have returned."

Samora excused herself and ran across the field to join the other healers as they came to their feet and prepared for the dragons' arrival. They all looked to the west as the dragons came in for their landings.

It only took the arrival of a few dragons for the healers to realize something had gone horribly wrong. Samora watched as the adanists lightly hopped off the dragons they rode. None were bloody, burned, or limping. She stood rooted in place as the other healers rushed forward and asked for news of what had happened.

She could guess well enough. If they'd come back without fighting, it meant the gathering grounds had already fallen. Her stomach twisted at the failure. They had other gathering grounds, of course, but the one in the Crows' former territory had been their best opportunity to stop the Debru before they reached her village.

She kept an eye out for the familiar shape of the dragon that had carried her so far across the land, but when he finally arrived Elian wasn't riding. Her heart jumped into her throat.

Everyone had returned without a scratch among them, so where was her brother?

❧ 27 ❧

E lian cursed the adanists who ran, abandoning him against the Debru. There was nothing for it, though. He turned and pulled all the adani he could from the gathering ground. Already it felt weaker than it had before. The Debru's work was almost done, and the clans had done next to nothing to stop it.

The Debru saw the dragons fleeing and ran at Elian faster. Had they been human, Elian imagined they would have been licking their lips in anticipation of the feast to come.

His grip tightened on his sword. There wasn't much point in fear, as there was only one possible outcome to this battle. All he could do was take as many of them with him as he could. He leaped forward, bounding across the gathering ground faster than a deer fleeing the hunter.

He regretted the decision as soon as a dozen bound spears of shadow came for his heart. They formed a veritable wall of pointed doom, and he had no choice but to dive to safety. He rolled and returned to his feet, only to see another half dozen spears flung in his direction. He dove again, barely staying ahead of the attacks.

The Debru made no sound, but he imagined them laughing as

he came face to face with a weakness he'd not considered before. If he could get among them, he had little doubt his sword would kill at least a few Debru before he fell to their shadowy blades. But there was no reason for them to let him close, and no way for him to approach on his own.

He dodged another spear, then scrambled backward as two more dropped from the air. The Debru were playing with him.

At least until the Belog pointed a spear at him. It must have been some sort of command, because the Debru redoubled their efforts. Elian ran, but one of the spears hit the ground near his feet and tossed him into the air and deposited him unceremoniously in the dirt.

Before the final volley of spears took him, an enormous ball of adani flew at the group of Debru. The Belogs formed a shield that protected them from the blast, but it gave Elian a moment of freedom. He scrambled back to his feet and started to run away.

He hadn't made it more than a few steps before an enormous shadow passed overhead, and a moment later he found himself safely ensconced in the claws of a dragon. "Hang on!" Harald shouted.

Elian couldn't do anything but let the dragon carry him, but he felt the sudden burst of speed the dragon put on. His head was outside the dragon's claws, so he could see just how close to the ground they were. The dragon made no effort to gain altitude, and the ground passed so fast and so close to his head Elian began to fear he'd be sick. Grass blurred past him, and he had to twist his head to watch the horizon.

A handful of dark spears flew past the dragon, but none approached particularly close. After they'd flown a few miles, the dragon pulled up and held a more comfortable altitude.

Harald called down. "Are you hurt?"

"No."

"You're a fool, but at least you're a lucky fool."

Elian didn't feel that way. They'd lost the gathering ground and he'd almost gotten himself killed.

The shame didn't last long. He'd warned them! None of that would have come to pass if they'd just followed him. They hadn't lost because of him, but because they were cowards. Once they landed, he would proclaim as much to everyone who would listen, and they would all listen.

It was time for a change to come to the clans, and he intended to bring it.

HARALD ASKED the dragon to land, though Elian wasn't sure why. They hadn't reached the clans yet. But the dragon agreed, dropping Elian none too gently to the ground before landing itself. As Elian tumbled, he saw the wound to the dragon's chest, a sight which cooled some of his temper. The dragon had agreed to rescue him, even thought it was injured.

Elian was just standing up and brushing himself off when Harald wrapped his enormous arm around his shoulder and half escorted, half shoved him away from the dragon and the other adanists.

Elian tried to elbow Harald away, but Harald absorbed the blows without complaint. Once they were far enough away not to be overheard, Harald whisper-shouted at him. "What were you thinking?"

"That we couldn't break that shield from the air, so it made more sense to land."

Elian tried again to break free of Harald's arm, but Harald held him tight.

"Why did you think that?"

"Our attacks from above weren't doing anything, so the only way to defeat them was on foot. If you hadn't run away, we might have saved that gathering ground."

Harald growled. "I thought you had a better head on your shoulders."

"And I thought you had a spine."

Harald's stare was cold enough to freeze a barrel of ale, but Elian's anger burned hot enough he barely noticed. He took a long, deep breath.

"Elian, that shield would have been just as strong on the ground. It's not as if the Debru wouldn't have shifted it lower to protect themselves if we landed."

"Yes, but we could have hit them from both above and below, and on the ground, I had a chance to get among them and thin their ranks. It was the only chance we had."

"I'll grant you that your plan had a chance, but it was a slim one, and nearly impossible to perform. You'll need to remember that the rest of us aren't like you. We can't strengthen our bodies to leap from a flying dragon. The dragons would have had to land, and in so doing, would have made themselves nothing but targets for the Debru and the Belogs. We would have died before we'd even launched a meaningful attack."

It was simple and obvious and true, but it had never once occurred to him.

He swallowed hard as shame rushed to his cheeks. His knees grew suddenly weak, and the massive arm that had been holding him in place now held him up. It also kept sight of his face away from the others. Those watching would have no clue about the emotions Elian wrestled with. They would see nothing more than two friends supporting one another after the aborted battle.

Elian dipped his head in gratitude as more blood rushed to his cheeks. He stared at his feet for several long moments, then shook his head and chuckled bitterly.

"Yes?" Harald asked.

"You're an impressive leader," Elian said.

"True, but what does that have to do with anything?"

Elian took a deep breath and stood up straight. Harald let his arm drop from around Elian's shoulder. "I've been impressed with you since we first met, you know. I've always admired your strength and the way you face challenges. When I dropped into the gathering ground—I did that because some part of me thought it was what you would do if you were in my place. But now I'm thinking about something Samora told me, one of the days right after we'd met. She was impressed, not by your strength, but by the subtlety you possessed."

For once, Harald had no glib response, no quick rejoinder. He chewed on Elian's words for a bit, then asked, "She said that?"

Elian nodded. "She's always had a gift for seeing deeply. It's true of adani and it's true of people."

Harald held his response, giving Elian enough time to shape his words into a form that matched what his heart felt.

"I don't think I'm ready to be your second. Even though I've become more comfortable with the strength adani has granted me, there's too much I still lack. Today we all escaped without harm, but that's thanks to you. What happens next time when my mistake isn't so easily fixed?"

Harald didn't answer immediately, which allowed Elian to pile more evidence on the mountain of his failures. "It's not just the battles, either. I wouldn't think of pulling someone aside from the others and shielding them with my body to protect them from greater shame."

Harald grunted. "I know a fair number of warriors who wouldn't even notice I did that."

"Maybe some of Samora has rubbed off on me, then, but not nearly enough to balance out my weaknesses. Perhaps it would be wise to ask Warran to be your second again."

Harald looked to the west, where the setting sun was setting the sky alight in shades of orange and pink. "Sometimes you remind me a lot of myself when I was younger, though I never had someone like Samora to redirect the worst of my impulses. I was driven by many of the same complaints about the clans that you have. I thought the Bears were too eager to retreat and not willing enough to fight, and I longed for the glory of battle. The whole clan knew my strength, but I wasn't going to be satisfied until the entire land heard of it."

"What changed?"

Harald grinned as a shadow of his old self returned. Elian braced himself for a backbreaking pat on the shoulder, but Harald showed impressive restraint. "Not all that much. I still believe the clans need more songs about me and my deeds, and though I may be one of the greatest fools that lives, I still look forward to battles. Any day we have a chance to make the Debru bleed is a good one."

He paused, then said, "But I have learned balance. A warrior can't win a duel against a skilled opponent by attacking all the time. We can't win this war by charging into battle at every opportunity. It hurt me to order us to retreat today, but it was the right decision."

Elian agreed. "The one I didn't make."

"And you'll learn from that, I trust. The lesson to take away from today isn't that you made a terrible mistake, and you shouldn't be my second. It's that you rightfully realize you still have much to learn, and as my second, you'll be in a place to learn what you need."

"Why not choose Warran?"

"For the same reasons as before. He's one of the best men I know, and if I should die before I can teach you everything you need, I hope you're smart enough to listen to him. But he's not meant to be the leader of a clan. He'll tell you that himself."

"I think you're wrong."

"And that's fine. You can tell me all about it later, once we're back with the rest of the clan. But to that point, don't even think about doing anything like you did today again. Not only did you risk your life, you risked the lives of a dragon and those riding with you. If I don't give you permission to do something, you can complain to me in private all you want, but don't you dare disobey another direct order. Is that clear?"

Elian gulped and nodded. "Absolutely."

"Good. Now let's get back before Aldo starts making plans to take over all the clans. If we're too late, he'll have every adanist running away like we're wolves with our tails on fire."

WHEN ELIAN CAUGHT sight of Samora's glare from the back of the dragon, he almost asked Harald to turn them around and fly him back to the Belogs. He assumed his death among the Debru would be quicker and less painful than the verbal lashing he was about to endure.

They landed and climbed down, and Harald made a straight line to Warran, who gestured him forward. Elian guessed some sort of council meeting was in progress, but he decided it would be best if he was nowhere near. His stunt ensured that anything he said among the council would only cause unnecessary complications for Harald.

There was no avoiding Samora, though, so he stood his ground as though he was part of a shield wall. She stomped right up to him, only stopping once they were almost nose to nose. "You did what?" she demanded.

His cheeks flushed again, and he looked down.

"What were you thinking? Or have you taken so many blows to the head you don't even know which way is up anymore?"

When he didn't answer, she lifted his chin up. "Elian! What were you thinking?"

"I wasn't. Isn't that obvious enough?"

His tone brought her up short. She shuffled half a step back and took a long breath. "I'm sorry. I was very worried, but I'm glad you're safe. Are you hurt?"

"No, but I feel much the fool."

"Well, at least you're in familiar territory, then." She cracked the slightest hint of a smile.

"True enough. I told Harald I don't think I deserve to be his second, but he's insistent."

"What do you think?"

"I don't think I'll ever be even the smallest fraction of the leader Harald is, and I don't see how anyone is going to listen to me after today."

Samora didn't argue or try to comfort him with empty platitudes, which he appreciated. Instead, she challenged him with, "So, what are you going to do about it?"

Thankfully, Elian had been thinking of almost nothing else since they'd gotten back on the dragon, so he had an answer ready. "I'd hoped that you would be willing to help me."

"How?"

"All the skills I lack are ones that you possess. You understand people better than I do, and you're more sensitive and observant to everything in the world. I want you by my side, whether that's at a council meeting or in a battle."

She'd smiled as he'd complimented her on her skills, but her face fell as he finished his request. She considered it for a moment, but he suspected he already knew her answer.

"Anywhere but on the battlefield. I'll help you in as many ways as I can, but I won't fight."

"Why not? I'm not asking you to swing a sword. But ride beside me on the dragons as we fly to battle. Stand behind me on the field to see what I don't. I'm sure that if you'd been with me today, I wouldn't have messed up."

"I don't want to fight. Not like that."

Elian threw up his hands. "What does that even mean? You basically wrestled with a Vada so that I could kill it. How is this any different?"

"It is to me."

"Are you scared? I'm sure we can get a handful of adanists to protect you. Maybe—"

"Not wanting to fight isn't the same as being a coward!"

Her outburst silenced Elian as effectively as a punch that knocked all the air from his lungs. She hadn't yelled at him in anger since she was a child. Since long before Father died.

Her nostrils were flared and her fists clenched, and Elian didn't dare say anything. She huffed once, then turned on a heel and stomped away. Elian reached after her, but she was already several steps away.

He almost called for her, then decided better of it. There was no harm in giving her some space.

He wasn't sure what he'd done wrong. Sure, she didn't like fighting, but he'd envisioned her more as an advisor. He would have done everything in his power to keep her safe and away from the actual combat.

He sighed and kicked at the grass. How could Harald expect him to lead the clan when he couldn't get his own sister to help him?

28

The sun rose the next morning on a cloudy day that perfectly matched Samora's mood. She hadn't wanted to attend the council meeting the night before, but Harald had basically dragged her by her ear. Elian hadn't received the same treatment. He'd been nowhere to be found, and it was probably for the best. Aldo was set on declaring her brother a menace to the clans, and after the foolishness he'd pulled in the battle that day, there were more sympathetic ears listening to Aldo's complaints than before. Harald had eventually turned the tide of opinion, but had Elian been there, Samora doubted her brother would have done himself any favors.

Thankfully, the long night of deliberation had ended with the only reasonable decision being made. The clans would turn around and take refuge in the gathering ground closest to Samora's village.

Samora still would have preferred to eat a wasp's nest, but the Debru left them few options worth considering. The only other plan that didn't result in their immediate destruction was a retreat to the Wolves' gathering grounds, but they were far more distant, and Aldo wouldn't hear of using his clan's sacred ground as their next battlefield.

Samora took some small comfort in knowing that either plan put her village in danger. They either brought the Debru close by fighting in the gathering grounds Samora had created or they abandoned the village completely as they fled toward the Wolves' territory. At least this way Samora might be able to do something if the Debru turned their attention toward her village.

It had also been agreed that Samora would lead an advance group of healers to the gathering ground to attempt to strengthen the lands before the battle. After the long council meeting, she'd run from camp to camp recruiting healers, and only then had she sought out Elian to tell him the full story of what she'd experienced in her travels west.

He'd listened attentively, but his reaction wasn't what she'd expected. She chewed it over as they waited for the last healers to arrive for their departure.

While they waited, she finished recounting her story again to Brittany, Loken, and Lenon. They asked good questions and helped her to consider her experiences out west with new perspectives.

"How did Elian react? As the one who allied us with the dragons, I'm guessing he had strong feelings," Loken guessed.

Samora shrugged. "I would have thought so as well, but he didn't say as much as I expected. He seemed confused and disappointed, and I think he doesn't want to believe that what I saw was true."

"Did he even believe you?" Brittany asked. There was a sharp edge to her question, as though she was looking for a knife she could stab Elian with. Unfortunately for her, Elian wouldn't make it so easy.

"He believed me. He asked a handful of questions, but never seemed to doubt my account. I think he wants to believe there's more to the story that we don't know, that there are reasons the dragons acted as they did that we can't guess at."

"And what if there are?" Lenon asked.

"If you're asking me, it doesn't matter," Samora said.

"Why not?"

"Because they decided to kill the people they fought beside. They destroyed our ancestor's homes, their lives, their skill with adani, and then, after doing all that, they took our memories so we wouldn't know to fear them. I can't imagine, even if they had the purest motivations in the world, why I would trust them after that."

No one spoke into the silence immediately following her outburst. It was Loken who, after glancing around the small gathering, said, "Perhaps the world isn't always so black and white."

"When you destroy villages with thousands of souls within, you've done evil. When that village is the home of the people you've fought shoulder to shoulder with, that's both an evil and a betrayal. I'm not sure how it gets any more certain."

Loken looked down at where his arm used to be. "When I was younger, I was one the strongest adanists among the Hawks. I rose quickly and served at Kati's side. In the midst of a battle against a group of Debru, four of our adanists got separated from the rest of us. Kettu attacked them like flies on a carcass while two Debru cut at them. The battle went well otherwise. Our forces were closely matched, but at the time of my decision, our lines were holding, if barely."

The healer tapped his fingers against a knee. "I decided I wasn't going to lose any of my adanists that day. I left my own part of the line behind and tried to save them. My swords and spears carved a path through the Debru and their pets, but by the time I arrived, it was too late."

He paused and looked up. "Not only did I not save them, but my decision to abandon the line cost the Hawks an enormous number of lives. We very nearly lost that battle, and nearly lost ourselves as a clan. The correct decision that day was to let the adanists die so that the rest of us could live. I couldn't make that decision. My failure cost me my arm, but that was a cheap price to pay."

Samora's heart went out to Loken, but she couldn't agree. "There's a world of difference. You made a mistake. The dragons decided to murder their allies. I don't think the two are similar at all."

Loken didn't press the argument any further, which was just as well. The last of the healers began to arrive, and it was time to fly to the gathering ground.

———

THE DRAGON LANDED the group on the same hilltop from which Samora had first laid eyes on what was now the gathering ground. She remembered well that first encounter with the Debru circle and the way it had felt against her adani. The land had changed almost as much as she had since then. When she'd first encountered the circle, it had been filled with dead and dying grass and brittle trees that cracked and crumbled into dust at a strong wind. Decay had robbed the land of its strength.

No sign of the abuse remained. The grass was rich and green, even though the last month had been largely dry. Clusters of oak trees grew near the shores of the small pond, taller than trees their age had any right to be. An echo of a splash reached her ear as a fish jumped in the pond.

After all that had happened over the last several months, this was still, perhaps, the deed Samora was most proud of. The strength of the gathering ground's adani flowed softly through the rich soil, and Samora smiled as she walked down the hill toward the boundary, which was closer than she remembered it.

When she remarked as much to Karla, the adanist shot her a skeptical eye. "Did you think the boundaries were etched in stone? A gathering ground grows and fades the same as anything else that lives."

Samora said nothing because she hadn't known that. Like so much of the world.

They reached the boundary shortly and Samora issued her commands. The task before them was simple enough to plan but would be difficult to accomplish. She told the adanists to spread out and apply her technique to as many plants living in the gathering ground as they could. Trees and bushes would be a priority, as they seemed the most capable of cycling larger amounts of adani, but if they had the time, Samora would have them establish loops in every blade of grass.

The adanists bowed and jumped to their efforts. Samora watched for a bit, offering suggestions and help as they were needed. Loken, of course, had taken to her technique naturally, and Lenon hadn't been far behind. Brittany needed a bit more practice to learn it, and the other healers longer still. But after each had practiced on a few trees, Samora felt comfortable enough leaving them to it.

She wandered away from the rest of the group and went from tree to tree. The difference in the amount of adani flowing through the gathering ground surprised her at first. All trees could hold a considerable amount of adani, but the ones that grew in the gathering ground had wider channels for adani to flow through. If a normal tree could sip adani from the surrounding land, a tree within the gathering ground drank in enormous gulps.

The amount of adani flowing through the trees proved to be part blessing and part curse. Because the adani enlarged the channels within the tree, the manipulations required to weave the adani into the pattern Samora had created were less delicate, making them more attainable for even the most inexperienced of healers. Unfortunately, with all the adani circling through the tree, it meant that tying the weave in each required more strength than usual. After she had tied the weave into a dozen trees, Samora felt as though she had run to the deadlands and back.

She sat down next to one of the trees, wiped the accumulated sweat from her brow, and took a sip of water from one of the skins they had brought along. She gazed around the gathering ground and decided their labors were slowly paying off.

She let a trickle of adani flow from her fingertips into the gathering ground where it was immediately pulled by the powerful currents flowing underneath. She had always thought of the adani within the gathering grounds like a lake, so deep she could drink for ages and never reach the bottom. Today, that lake fell deeper than before, and it was on the move.

She recalled her adani and opened her eyes. This circle of land was still a gathering ground, but it was becoming something more.

She was still trying to figure out what when Loken came up to her, a questioning look on his face. "Do you sense that?"

Samora narrowed her eyes and shook her head, unsure if he was referring to the powerful currents she had sensed or something else.

"There is something forming underneath us, though for the life of me, I couldn't tell you what it is."

Samora placed her hand against the ground and once again released her adani. As before, it got swept up in the currents, pushed and pulled across the gathering ground, as though caught in violent winds. The rapid motion and lack of control churned her stomach, but she didn't pull her adani back to her as she had before. She let it continue to circle within the gathering ground. As she did, a new pattern emerged.

Near the surface, the motion of the adani was chaotic and

haphazard, jerked randomly to the four corners of the world as the enhanced trees demanded more. In time, she hoped those currents would steady out. But for now, her attention drifted deeper, underneath the raging surface, to a more powerful current below.

As Loken had stated, there was something growing deep beneath their feet. At times, it pushed adani away, flooding the channels running near the surface of the gathering ground with fresh strength. At other times, it would pull, sucking the adani in and wrapping it into a tight weave of incomprehensible complexity. A fragment of her adani got pulled in and was almost immediately lost. Whatever grew was far more intricate and subtle than even the Debru's defenses in their circles.

She continued to follow the adani as it spread out through the gathering ground and eventually returned, each time growing stronger than before. In many ways, it felt as though it was the same as her weave, just more complex and far more effective.

When all her adani finally returned to her body, she opened her eyes to see Loken watching her carefully. "You sensed it, didn't you? It feels like a heart beating beneath the surface."

Wrapped up in the experience as she had been, the label wasn't one she had thought of, but it fit perfectly. Like a heart pumping blood through a body, this heart of adani pumped fresh stores of life-giving energy through the gathering ground.

Her own heart pounded faster at the thought, and her hands felt clammy.

She thought of the abandoned village far to the west, and the hole that had been made to carve out the heart of that village. There was no doubting. Their efforts increased the amount of adani running through the gathering ground. And for the moment, it was what they needed to fight the Debru.

But it looked as though she had inadvertently sparked the creation of something she didn't understand. Something that would give them even more adani to fight the Debru with. For that, she was grateful. But its development spawned a new fear.

If her guess was correct, in times long past the dragons had gone out of their way to destroy a heart just like this one.

She worried she'd just created something that very well might have turned the dragons against humanity all those years ago.

29

E lian bit his tongue and forced himself to listen as he stood with the other clan elders. In the center of the circle a lone scout stood, giving his report from the morning flight with the dragons.

Elian had wanted to take part in the scouting trip but given how poorly he had acquitted himself in their last conflict, Harald told him that the wisest course of action was to remain behind. So now he stood listening to a secondhand account of something he should have seen with his own eyes. He clenched his teeth, sealed his lips, and opened his ears. The scout spoke with short, declarative statements.

"The same group of Debru that attacked the gathering ground in the Crows' territory has now shifted direction. They're making all possible speed toward this gathering ground. If our estimates are correct, they should arrive in approximately two days."

The report sent a wave of quiet muttering around the circle. No one had known exactly what the Debru planned for the next stage of this war. Some had expected this, but most had predicted that the contingent of Debru would return to the main force still surrounding the Vada.

Elian focused less on the direction of the Debru's movements and more on the time that remained. Two days wasn't enough time to create a plan. Two days wasn't enough time to save everyone. Even if Samora's new weavings were working, there was little chance they would increase the strength of the gathering ground as much as the wandering clans required.

The scout continued his report, "As requested, we continued our flight to observe the former gathering grounds, and we can confirm they've been destroyed. Otsoa and kettu were circling the area, so we didn't attempt to land, but the ground is destroyed and there is nothing living inside the circle. It appears even worse than the original circle the Debru created."

Elian winced. It had been a distant hope, but a part of him had wondered if all the destruction the Debru wrought would still not be enough to destroy the gathering ground. He'd known the odds were slim, but the knowledge the gathering ground was gone hurt all the same.

"What of the Vada?" Harald asked.

The scout wasn't willing to meet Harald's gaze. "The main force of Debru is still camped in the same valley. As near as we can tell, they haven't moved at all, but they have created a massive cloud of shadow over their position, so there's no telling their numbers or strength, or if the Vada is still among them. We circled the area searching for other tracks and found none. But we recognize how incomplete that information is. I'm sorry we couldn't do better, but we didn't dare get too close."

Harald waved the excuse away. "You have nothing to apologize for. We are outmatched and you did the best you could."

Aldo looked over to Harald in a rare show of deference. "What are your thoughts?"

Harald shrugged. "The same as before. They're coming for us, but we can take some small comfort in knowing we'll be able to make our stand at the gathering ground. If we pick up the pace, we can make it a full day before them."

Elian expected Aldo to object simply on the grounds that Aldo seemed to object to every idea he or Harald had. But this time the leader of the Wolves kept his lips pressed together as he nodded. If Elian hadn't been convinced of the danger of their situation before, he would have been by that.

The unified council had little else to discuss, so the council ended. Harald went to speak with some of the other leaders. Finding himself alone, Elian made his way from the council circle toward the field where the dragons waited.

Samora's story about her visions and her visit to the west had troubled Elian since she'd told him of it. There had to be something more to the story, some fact or detail her questions hadn't uncovered that would make everything she had learned make sense. Something that would match the sorrow and pain he felt from the dragons.

He didn't doubt Samora's honesty for a moment. But it was difficult to communicate with the dragons, and it was easy to imagine some misstep that had led to Samora's confusion.

Elian found the dragon he had rescued from the Debru resting in the field with all its brethren. He had yet to uncover any signs of a hierarchy among the dragons, and one seemed just as good as the other, but he felt like he and this dragon understood each other well. They'd been through a lot together, so he was the natural choice.

Elian stopped a few paces away from the dragon. It was clear the dragons had little interest in sharing their full pasts with humans, but it was just as clear that humanity needed to know the secrets locked within the dragon's memories. But how did he start? He cleared his throat. "Hey, old friend, how are you?"

The dragon stared at him with the same half-interested expression that seemed to be a permanent fixture upon his face. When Elian connected his adani to the dragon's, it felt as though there was some spark of warmth and kindness there, but one wouldn't know it from a dragon's expressions.

He supposed it was a mistake to expect human facial expressions from a dragon, but the dragon seemed to look at Elian more as an annoying but lovable child than a worthy partner in the fight against the Debru.

When Elian's question failed to elicit any response, he tried another approach. "I've got some questions for you."

He'd already thought long and hard about how he wanted to proceed, so he asked his first question. "My sister says that you held a council in which you decided to kill most of the humans. Can you show it to me?"

The dragon rumbled quietly, and then a moment later, Elian found himself in a memory that was not his own. It was as much feeling and emotion as it was sight and sound, and Elian was almost washed away by the sea of sorrow that accompanied the memory.

It was as Samora had described it. The dragons gathered and the elder proclaimed what must be done.

Elian tried to pull away from the memory, but the dragon's adani held him tightly in place.

"That's enough," Elian said.

He was confronted with another memory. He flew high over an enormous village with tall buildings. Wind and adani held him aloft as he formed the basic weave for fire. His flames washed over the buildings and consumed them, and as he flew through the smoke, all he felt was an emptiness in his heart that no amount of time would fill.

In the darkness between memories, Elian cried out, "Why?"

The dragon didn't answer. Not because he couldn't, but because he refused to. Connected as intimately as they were, Elian knew the answer lurked behind a veil the dragon would not cast aside.

For the first time since he'd learned how to communicate with the dragons, he pushed harder, seeking the answer it held so tightly to. He shoved his adani into the veil, seeking a crack he could exploit, but the dragon fought off his attempts with ease. The dragon tried to shove him away, but he clung to the dragon's spirit as though it was the last remaining weapon on a raging battlefield.

The dragon rumbled and shoved at him again, but Elian's adani danced away and pushed deeper into the sudden gap in the veil. He received the briefest glimpse of a sea of memories, containing far more years than he could have possibly imagined.

The dragons weren't just hiding one memory, but hundreds of human lifetimes' worth. He leaped for the veil again, but then it was all roughly yanked away from him, not by adani, but by a physical force ripping him apart from the dragon. He swore and doubled over as he was forcibly returned to his body. Adani, torn from its natural flows, crashed around in his body as it sought places to settle.

"Are you hurt?" a familiar voice asked.

Elian's arms were wrapped around his stomach, and he rolled from side to side, trying to find a single position that was comfortable.

A large shadow fell over him as Harald squatted beside him. "What's wrong? When I arrived, you were sweating and groaning as you were connected to the dragon and I assumed you were in trouble."

Elian held up a hand. In time, the pain faded and soon he was able to stretch out his legs and lay flat on his back. He blinked up at the sky. "I think I was close to discovering the truth about the dragons."

"Oh. Sorry then."

Elian waved his concern away. "It wasn't going all that well anyway."

Harald helped him to his feet. "Did you want to try again?"

Elian shook his head. "I don't think the dragon is going to let me connect with him for a bit."

Harald at least had the decency to look ashamed. "I'm sorry. I thought you'd gotten yourself into some sort of trouble again."

Elian grinned. "Usually a safe guess. Why are you here?"

"I had come to find you. I was hoping you might help me with something."

Harald bade him to follow. Elian did, surprised that they were walking farther away from the rest of the clans. When they finally stopped, a small rise in the land hid them from the others.

Harald took a fighting stance. "I want you to spar with me."

Even though Elian was uninjured and not plagued by shadow, he took a step back and raised his hands in surrender. Harald would have him skewered by half a dozen spears before he even took a step forward.

Harald understood his hesitation. "No bound weapons. Just you against me."

Elian looked up at the giant whose arm was still as big as the meatiest part of his thigh. "Am I allowed to cycle adani within my body?"

Harald nodded. "As am I."

The part of Elian's mind responsible for his continued survival screamed at him that he was making a mistake, but Harald's offer was too curious to pass up. Very few people could claim they'd beaten Harald at a sparring match. "Deal."

Harald launched himself forward, but Elian was ready. Adani already cycled through his limbs, and he deflected Harald's punch with his forearm, then retaliated with a sharp elbow to Harald's chest.

Harald shifted his weight back, which robbed Elian's strike of most of its power. He used a few jabs to force Elian back, then snapped a kick at Elian's side.

Elian leaned back and let the kick pass in front of him, but his eyes narrowed as the tip of Harald's boot brushed against his tunic. He took another step back. He should have been moving fast enough to avoid that kick completely.

Harald's expression was unreadable, so Elian couldn't decide if the giant was pleased with his effort or not. Elian cycled more adani into his limbs, then approached Harald cautiously.

It was good that he did. Harald launched an assault with blinding speed, forcing Elian back under the sheer volume of blows. He never landed anything cleanly, but Elian was certain he'd wake up with plenty of fresh bruises tomorrow.

Elian cycled as much adani as his body would allow and took the fight to Harald. His leader kept ahead of the first few strikes, but Elian wouldn't be stopped, and eventually Harald slowed. A pair of powerful punches brought the big man to his knees, and he wheezed for breath. Harald held up his hand in surrender. Elian needed a moment to catch his own breath.

"What was that? You've never moved that fast before."

Harald lifted his hand, and Elian took it and helped him to his feet. The leader coughed once, then said, "I've been trying to be more like you."

The statement was so absurd Elian laughed out loud. "That sounds like a terrible decision."

Harald brushed himself off and gestured that they should return to the clans. "I was thinking that it would make me a better fighter when the Debru attack next. It seems likely that the fighting will be close and fierce before it's over, and your techniques seem useful to have."

Elian was flattered at first, but when he thought about the claim for a moment longer, it made no sense. "That can't be all. I've seen you in close combat with the Debru, and there's very little my skills would add."

Harald didn't answer for some time. When he did answer, his voice was slower and more thoughtful. "I've been thinking a lot about what happens after we win. Even when all this is over, I'm still going to have the shadow inside of me to deal with. I don't know if your sister told you, but if I don't find a way to get rid of it, it will kill me sooner rather than later. I'd hoped that maybe, if

I mastered your techniques, I could free myself of the shadow, that maybe there would be a future in which Kati and I can do something different than worrying constantly about the Debru. Maybe we could settle down and raise a few little Haralds."

The thought brought a smile to Elian's face, and he bowed deeply to his friend. "In that case, I'll do everything I can to help you."

30

The gathering ground was as busy as Samora had ever seen it, and it was a sight to behold. The four clans had each staked out their own territories and set up their camps. Given the relatively small size of the gathering grounds, most of the sleds and supplies had been left on the eastern side, outside the boundary. If they won, they could retrieve their sleds after. If they lost, then it didn't much matter.

The idea had been Karla's, and Samora was grateful, both because it was a good one and because it was one less problem she felt responsible for dealing with. One unintended consequence of this gathering ground's origin story was that leaders from the clans kept asking her for permission to do pretty much anything.

At first, she'd been honored they valued her opinion so highly, but it quickly became more of a pain than an honor. They asked about everything, from the boundaries of each clan's camp to whether it was okay for them to erect their tents. If this continued much longer, they'd be asking for her permission to go relieve themselves.

She'd tried to explain they didn't need to consult with her

quite so much, and to her face, they'd seemed amiable enough to the idea. They bowed and nodded at her suggestion but were back again soon after anyway.

Aldrick reminded her that most gathering grounds were sacred territories to clans, and that such mundane uses broke with a whole host of traditions. And although Samora made no claim to the land, all the clan leaders had defaulted to believing it was hers. Samora appreciated the respect shown and found it darkly entertaining that the clans felt it necessary to keep coming to her, a clan-less villager, for permission.

Eventually the pace of the questions settled, and Samora retreated to Brittany's healing tent to see if her friend needed help. She helped Brittany mix herbs and set out the bandages they had prepared before, but thankfully there was little for them to do, as they had prepared much for the last expedition and ended up using none.

When there was nothing left to do for Brittany, she left the healing tent and wandered through the gathering grounds. She hadn't been wandering for long when a strong hand gripped her wrist and pulled her aside. Karla escorted her rather forcefully into an abandoned tent.

"What's all this about?" Samora asked.

"Are you staying for the battle?"

"Why wouldn't I?" The reply came out sharper than she intended. Fortunately, Karla was not one to take offense at sharp words.

"I know how much you detest fighting, and if you stay, there's a very real chance you get dragged into it. Even with Aldrick protecting the healing tent, there's no guarantee he'll be able to keep you safe."

"I'm not asking him to. He should be like you and be on the front."

Frustration quickly passed across Karla's face, but she hid it quickly. It was enough of a clue for Samora, though, to understand something more was going on. "What's this actually about?"

Karla swept her arms open wide, taking in the camp, the gathering ground, and everything that was happening within. "I know you're not going to like this, but I think you should consider running away and finding someplace safe to sit this battle out."

Samora's temper flared as though she was Elian, trying to hold on to too much adani. "Just because I don't want to fight doesn't mean I can't help. I'm more than willing to cast shields or help as a healer for the Bears."

"Sure, and I don't disagree, but have you stopped to think about everything that's happening? This gathering ground is filled with more life and adani than ones that are four times its size and generations older. That heart is granting us more strength than we've ever had, and all of that is because of you. Every advance we've made is one that you've discovered. If we lose you, we lose any chance of fighting against the Debru."

The older adanist missed the obvious point. "If we lose here, regardless, we'll likely lose against the Debru. The other clans aren't large enough to make enough of a difference. So, it doesn't matter if I run or not."

Karla shook her head. "Before I met you, I might have believed that, but I'm no longer so certain. The right person, in the right place, at the right time, might be all that we need. And I'm increasingly convinced you are that person. You're too valuable to risk here."

"That's kind of you to say, but I have a hard time believing that. My place is here, helping to protect my family and the clans."

Karla studied her closely for a bit, before shrugging her shoulders and sighing. "I knew it would have been difficult to convince you, but I had to try."

"You're not leaving, are you?"

Karla's answering smile was grim. "I've told you before, I go where things are the most interesting, and there's no denying that wherever you are has been the most interesting place as of late. So, if you're staying, I figure I am too. I'll be happy to serve along the front, so long as that oaf Aldo doesn't try to give me any orders."

SAMORA ONLY HAD one more task that she needed to complete before allowing herself to rest for the evening, and although it wasn't one she looked forward to, she couldn't afford to put it off any longer. The latest scout reports claimed that if the Debru maintained their current pace, they would arrive at the gathering ground shortly after dawn the next morning. She didn't want to go to sleep with any problems hanging over her head, especially not with her brother.

She wasn't surprised to find Elian with Capricia. The two of them had been spending every scrap of free time Elian could find together, and Samora decided that she approved. She liked the other woman's curiosity, and she liked that Capricia seemed interested in making her brother's life better.

Samora also liked that Capricia had been interested in him before he became the hero of the clans. Elian needed someone who slowed him down and balanced out his headstrong nature, and she seemed competent enough at both.

Elian glared at her when she appeared at the small campfire he was a part of. She wasn't sure how much of it was due to her interrupting his precious time with Capricia and how much of it was due to the bitter aftertaste of the disagreement they'd had when they'd last spoken. But it was that bitter feeling she hoped to overcome. "Can we talk?"

Elian glanced between Capricia and Samora, and Samora said, "It doesn't need to be private. I just wanted to tell you that no matter what happens tomorrow, I will do everything I can to support you."

"Except fight," Elian said flatly.

"If you're relying on me to fight to help beat the Debru, then you have much larger problems," Samora responded.

The comment hung in the air for a moment, and then Elian cracked a smile, although it faded quickly. "I suppose that's true. I appreciate it."

He looked down at his hands, holding a worn teacup. "I can't say that I understand, and I wish I could have your voice in my ear, even during a battle, but I know you'll do everything you think you can."

Samora decided that would have to be enough. "There's something else, too. Something I want to make sure you know."

Elian gestured for her to continue.

"I'm sure you've heard by now that something is growing beneath the gathering ground?"

He nodded. "Some sort of beating heart, right? I can't sense it, but I can certainly sense the power emanating from it. I can pull more adani from this gathering ground than I could a dragon. It's incredible."

"It certainly is. I think that whatever it is, it is similar to what was missing and destroyed from the hole we found outside that village to the west. And if I had to guess, the dragons were the ones who destroyed it."

Elian frowned, but it didn't take him long to understand her point. "You're afraid the same fate may befall our gathering ground."

"It'll keep me up tonight. To be fair, I don't think that it will happen soon. I do trust that the dragons will remain our allies for as long as they feel like we need us."

Elian nodded. "I'll be careful, and thanks for letting me know."

Samora bowed to her brother. "Good luck tomorrow. I'll be in the healing tents with Brittany. And I hope I don't have to see you there."

Elian grinned, and for a brief moment, he looked like the young man she remembered, before all the weight of the world had settled on his shoulders. "Now that's something we can agree on. You take care, too."

Samora couldn't help but feel as though this was the last time she was going to see her brother. The certainty was so strong it almost brought her to her knees. She knew she should turn and leave, but if she did, then that would be it. The last time she saw him.

"I love you, you know," she said.

He looked up, that same smile still on his face. "I love you, too. Get some good sleep tonight. Tomorrow's going to be a big day."

❧ 31 ❧

E lian waited with a handful of other riders as the sun rose the next morning, casting dull pinks across the sky. He sat with his hands pressed into the grass, and when he tired of waiting, he tried pushing some of his adani into the ground. Unlike with the dragons, though, it returned a moment after he pushed it away. Try as he might, he didn't think he'd ever come close to Samora's abilities.

He lifted his hands and brushed them off, then saw the now-familiar silhouette of a dragon off in the distance. He stood and joined the other adanists as they gathered near the edge of the field. The dragon landed with a rush of air and its rider dismounted in a hurry. Elian didn't recognize him, which meant he was most likely from the Wolves. His lips were set in a grim line.

The only authority among the group was Lenon, one of Tiafel's councilors, and the rider bowed to him. "It is as we expected. The Debru will be here soon. They're close enough for us to take to the skies."

"Did you see anything to give you pause?" Lenon asked.

The scout shook his head. "The group is the same one we've

tracked for days now. Half a dozen Belogs, twice that many Moka, and about four dozen other Debru, accompanied by a fair number of otsoa and kettu."

"Still no sign of the Vada?" Lenon asked.

"None."

Lenon looked to the west. Elian was tempted to speak, but he held his tongue. His role had been decided in their councils the day before, and it didn't include this. He waited, along with the other riders, for Lenon to give the order.

After a few long moments of silence, he did. "Mount up, riders. Come back safely."

Elian joined the others in bowing to Lenon, then walked to his dragon. He stopped before climbing on. They'd only communicated once since Elian had tried to force his way into the dragon's memories, and that was for Elian to tell the dragon what the humans had decided and what they wanted of the dragons. That bit of communication had gone well enough, but the dragon's adani had shoved him away as soon as Elian had made his point.

"It's time. May we ride together?"

The dragon rumbled, which sounded to Elian's ears like acceptance. Elian bowed, climbed on, and connected his adani with the dragon's. It didn't flow like it had before. The dragon kept it tightly contained, giving Elian no opportunity to force his way deeper.

Elian grimaced at the lack of trust but couldn't blame the dragon. He wouldn't want strangers rooting around in his memories without permission, either. The dragon launched itself into the air, and Elian held on as they quickly gained altitude. They joined the other dragons and their riders high above the gathering ground.

Tera rode with them today, and Elian was glad for her strength. She was in command of the dragons in the air, so it was her signal that sent the others west. Harald had wanted to join, but the council had overruled him. No one expected this flight to do much, and Harald's strength would be needed for the fights still to come.

They'd argued about Elian's presence, too, but if the unexpected happened and a Belog or Moka wandered outside the shadow's protection, he was the one most suited to bringing it down. He was also the only one capable of communicating well with the dragons, which made his presence invaluable.

The flight was high enough no one expected the Belogs to strike back, and thanks to that altitude, it wasn't long before the Debru advance came into view, a dark, shadowy stain against the land. Their march leeched the adani from the abandoned fields they crossed, leaving a trail of destruction like a scar across the land.

Elian cursed at the sight. Even if they won today, the damage the Debru had done to his home was considerable. Farming would be a much more difficult task next year.

He pressed himself tight against the dragon's neck. "Not long now before this fight begins. I don't suppose you want to tell me about all the secrets you're hiding, do you?"

He didn't even need their connection to sense the adamant "no" in the dragon's rumble.

"Suit yourself, then."

The two forces approached rapidly, but the Debru below seemed unconcerned about the dragons in the sky. After the battle for the gathering ground in the Crows' territory, they had plenty of reason to be confident. But this time would be different.

It had to be.

Elian spotted two scouts less than a mile ahead of the main force of Debru. At least, he assumed they were scouts. He watched them for a bit, ensuring they were alone. Two Debru, accompanied by a pair of otsoa, wandered far ahead of the others. Elian urged his dragon forward until he was in line with Tera. Through rapid hand signs, Elian asked permission to go down and attack the Debru scouts.

Tera looked uncomfortable with the idea, even as Elian glared at her. As Harald's second, Elian should have been able to act as he pleased, but Harald had made it clear, in no uncertain terms, that Elian was to follow Tera's orders while they were in flight.

Finally, Tera agreed to Elian's idea, and Elian asked the dragon to dive. The dragon roared as he dropped drown, as eager to destroy the Debru as Elian was. As Elian and the dragon dropped, dark clouds of shadow rushed from the Belog and Moka to surround the main party's advance. Unfortunately for the two scouts, they were well outside the cloud's protection.

One tried to run for the cover of the shadow, but Elian and the dragon were too close. The dragon bound a sphere of adani that he dropped on top of the Debru as he flew over. Adani blasted the Debru off its feet and flung it back toward its partner. They weren't lucky enough to kill the Debru, but it was certainly hurting.

The dragon picked up speed and Elian filled his limbs full of adani. He leaped at the second Debru, which was too slow to react. Elian drove both feet into the Debru's chest, launching it back. He dropped to the ground but was back on his feet a moment later, charging the Debru with his sword in hand.

Meanwhile, the dragon focused on the first Debru that he had felled with his blast. The scout was rising to its feet when the dragon clamped its enormous jaws on the creature. The attack happened in the corner of Elian's vision, and all he saw was the quick blur of shadow as the dragon passed, followed by the Debru's legs taking a hesitant step forward before collapsing, shorn from the rest of its body.

The second Debru found its feet before Elian reached it. A sword bound of shadow formed in its hand and it cut down at Elian as he neared. He angled his own sword to deflect the cut away, but wasn't surprised when his blade sliced straight through the shadow sword. The Debru held the sword up as though confused, but before it found understanding, Elian whipped his sword across the Debru's body.

He cut across as easily as if he was slicing into a cloud, and the Debru's parts collapsed in front of him.

The dragon touched down beside him, and it took off again even as Elian scrambled to find a position to sit. They took off none too soon, as dark spears, so powerful they could only have been thrown by the Belogs, chased them away. The spears tore up the ground where Elian and the dragon had been, but they were safely away as the spears landed.

He and the dragon were welcomed back into the sky with roars of approval from both the other dragons and the other warriors, but Elian didn't allow himself too long to bask in the praise. There was still too much to be done, and though the adanists of the wandering clans might envy the ease with which he killed two Debru, that feat meant little against the force still approaching the gathering ground.

Tera wasted little time in taking advantage of Elian's victory. She thrust a fist high into the air, then brought it down like an axe, pointing at the enemy cloaked in darkness below. Most of the adanists formed bound spears, the simple weave an effective technique for harnessing the deep well of adani the dragons provided. Two adanists formed spheres, and most of the dragons did the same.

They dropped the first wave of adani on the Debru together. Most in the council agreed the chances of breaking through the combined shields of so many Belogs and Moka were slim, but there was no harm in trying and everything to gain. Even if they didn't break through the shields, the effort of defending against the attacks would use up some fraction of the Belogs' strength. Dozens of weavings struck the shields within the space of a single heartbeat, and Elian was grateful he was nowhere close to the point of impact.

The combined strength of their efforts rumbled in his bones

even as he soared high above the destruction. Wild grasses danced chaotically as powerful gusts of wind ripped back and forth. A pair of unfortunate trees were torn, roots and all, from the ground and hurled hundreds of paces away.

But when the dust settled, the shadow remained. Elian squinted but couldn't see so much as a crack of light in the darkness that continued to stain the land. He swore under his breath. He'd not expected anything different, but to see all their efforts amount to so little still sent a shiver down his spine.

Tera made another gesture and the dragons and adanists began weaving and dropping adani freely. Spheres and spears raced toward the shadow. Some appeared to be swallowed whole while others erupted closer to the surface. Elian's dragon dropped bound spheres, but Elian's usefulness was at an end.

The dragon's control over its adani slackened as it put more effort into the assault, though, and Elian considered another attempt on the dragon's vast trove of secrets. He pushed his adani just a hair deeper into the dragon's reserves and encountered no resistance.

He couldn't bring himself to follow through, though. The dragon was flying into danger with them, spending freely of its stores of adani to hopefully weaken the Debru before they reached the gathering ground. Taking advantage of that sacrifice seemed little better than stabbing the dragon in the back as it fought off a Belog.

He contented himself with watching the assault, which was a sight to behold. The sheer amount of adani dropped might have been greater than any battle the wandering clans had yet fought, and the destruction it wrought was no less impressive for its complete failure.

Given the height of the dragons and the speed with which they flew, it was inevitable that bound spears would sometimes miss their mark. The field surrounding the Debru quickly became more barren than the wastelands, and so much dust hung in the air it was sometimes difficult to tell where the shields of shadow began and ended.

When the pace of the assault grew much slower, Tera called a halt. A handful more spears were thrown, but Elian could sense the weakness of his dragon. It had given everything to support the attack, leaving just enough for them to return to the gathering ground.

The dragons believed the risk posed to them returning tired was acceptable, though Elian wasn't sure exactly how they'd come to that conclusion. It had something to do with the heart growing underneath the gathering ground helping them recover their stamina much faster than they would otherwise.

Elian didn't question their fortune, though. If the dragons were willing to spend as much as they had, it made their odds of success that much higher in the battle to come.

They circled the Debru one more time, and Elian was at least pleased to see the Debru hadn't made any more progress since the attack began. They hadn't killed many, but they'd slowed them down, and that was something. As he watched, though, the shadow resumed its slow march toward the gathering ground.

It was no more than they'd expected, but that didn't take the sting away from the sight. Elian cursed softly again, then turned back with his dragon and flew toward the gathering ground.

―――――

EVEN THOUGH THE council had expected nothing less, disappointment was written across their faces when they heard the report. The assault from the air's only stated purpose was to soften up the Debru and weaken them before they reached the gathering ground, but like Elian, most had hoped for something more. They were used to shouldering disappointment, though, and it wasn't long before they were positioning their adanists for the battle to come.

Elian shadowed Harald as he walked among the Bears. The giant man had spent the early morning selecting the best positions for his adanists, and now he pointed the locations out to Elian as he worked his way through their camp.

The point was to prepare Elian with Harald's strategy in case the worst should happen, a thought which made Elian's skin crawl. He accepted the responsibility of being Harald's second, but it was one thing to ask him to support Harald and entirely another to take his place. Elian memorized Harald's plans, but hoped with all his heart he'd never have to use any of them.

When the thought of losing Harald sank him too deep into despair, he took heart from the quiet courage he witnessed in every corner of the camp. He'd grown up listening to stories of charging into battle against hopeless odds, and he'd imagined bright-eyed men and women surrounded by adani. Today he saw adanists no different than him. They were tired, stressed, and afraid, but they nodded at their orders and took their positions without a word of serious complaint.

Finally, Harald gave orders to the last of his adanists and turned to Elian. "You're ready?"

"As much as I can be."

"I want you to use your best judgment about where you should be. I'm not sure how they'll attack, but do as much damage as you can. Don't be afraid to pick off the Debru, either. The less of them, the more strength we'll be able to bring against the Moka and Belogs."

Elian nodded. They'd discussed it all the night before, as Harald had wrestled with the best way to use Elian. The closest they'd come to fighting the Debru like this was in their earlier confrontation at the Hawks' gathering grounds, but Harald didn't expect the Debru to use the same strategies here, so he'd been uncertain about how to use Elian's unique skills. Unfortunately, they wouldn't know for sure until the battle began.

They took their positions near the center of the western edge of the gathering ground. As when they'd fought upon the Hawks' grounds, Harald had positioned the adanists so they were more than a dozen paces within the boundary.

Then all there was to do was wait, which Elian soon decided was worse than being in battle. Once the fight began there would be little space for thought, but now his imagination had free rein to create all kinds of disastrous futures. It was almost a relief when the shadow crested the rise to the west. Several adanists prepared spears, but Harald held up his hand to restrain them.

This time, there was no foolish charge of Debru, no needless waste of life. Not even a single kettu emerged from the shadow. Elian grimaced, wishing that the Debru were less clever than they were. The shadow rolled forward at a leisurely pace.

He glanced up to see nearly a dozen dragons flying high in the sky above. They'd rested and taken strength from the gathering ground, then returned to the air once the Debru were close. They carried no riders now, but Elian was glad to see them overhead. So long as they remained above, there was at least some chance of victory. Like the adanists below, they held their attacks.

Harald waited to see if any Debru would break from their shelter, but when none seemed eager to do so, he chopped down with his arm and began the battle. Far to the north, Karla was the first to strike, a bolt of lightning descending from a clear blue sky that split the advancing shadows. Elian's bones quivered as thunder rolled over the plains and the shadow shrunk, revealing several otsoa prowling ahead of their masters.

The adanists with spears in hand were ready to take advantage of the lapse in protection. They flung their bound weapons, which pierced the surprised otsoa and pinned their corpses to the ground.

Karla struck again, and this time she was joined by Harald and the other masters of adani. Golden spears of light stabbed into the cloud of shadow from below as lightning cracked into it from above. Dragons joined in the assault as they dropped enormous spheres of bound adani, and the force of the combined attacks very nearly knocked the breath out of Elian's chest.

Perhaps it was due to the attacks they'd already suffered, or perhaps the Debru had some greater strategy he didn't understand, but the shadow protecting the invaders finally retreated, revealing the overwhelming force they'd brought. He counted more Moka and Belogs than he'd ever seen in one place.

Elian's legs went weak at the sight. From the sky he'd been impressed by their numbers. Standing before them, he quailed at their advance. If not for Harald standing behind him, he might have turned and ran.

If Harald felt the same, there was no knowing it from his voice. It carried clear across the field, audible even over the rumbling of bound adani bursting as it dropped upon the Debru.

"They've dropped their shields, friends! Now is our time. Attack!"

❦ 32 ❧

Samora paced around the tent, checking supplies she'd already checked and shifting bowls of clean water from one side of the cots to the other. Brittany sat in the far corner of the healing tent, legs crossed and eyes closed. Samora couldn't imagine how she could sit so quietly, but the sense she got from her friend was that she didn't want to be bothered, so Samora didn't ask.

She'd felt the early morning rumblings of the attack in the distance, and when she wasn't busy helping Brittany prepare, she'd sent out her adani, strengthened both by the gathering ground and the heart below. The combined attack of human and dragon had shaken the web of adani like a string held tight between two fingers. It had weakened the Belogs, but not nearly enough to stop their advance.

When she couldn't take the wait any longer, she put her hands to the ground and sent her adani toward the heart still growing beneath their feet. She didn't understand it, nor did she know exactly how it was connected to the gathering ground. It was unlikely she'd find all her answers this morning, but better to explore a mystery than waste her time pacing like a trapped animal.

Her adani didn't make it far. Darkness pressed upon the gathering ground already, and Samora knew, before the first spear of adani was thrown, that the Belogs had arrived. And there was something else, too, a deeper darkness on the move, but her adani couldn't penetrate the cloud rushing toward them. She recalled her adani and stood. Before she could warn Brittany, thunder rolled over their tent. Samora clenched her jaw shut. Given the clear day, the thunder could only have one source. Karla had launched the assault against the Debru.

More waves of thunder followed the first and the ground quivered beneath Samora's feet. She wasn't extending her adani, but she still felt the way it twisted and pulled around her as more than a hundred adanists called upon the gathering ground to strengthen their attacks.

Brittany's eyes opened wide, and she cursed under her breath. She looked at Samora. "It's going to be hard to focus adani for healing when it's being pulled like that," she said.

The thought hadn't occurred to Samora before, but Brittany was right. "Is there anything we can do?"

Brittany shook her head. "On a different battlefield I might move us farther away, but there's no point here. Be aware of it when you're attempting your healings, though. If someone requires a delicate weave, but their injury isn't life-threatening, it might be best to wait."

Samora swallowed and nodded. The tent's front flaps had been tied open, but they faced east, so they looked out upon a reasonably peaceful scene. It disoriented Samora to look through the opening and see a quiet camp and clear skies while the shouts of adanists came from the west.

The continual twisting of adani made her stomach churn, but it was a small price to pay compared to the warriors who stood against the Debru. She listened to the sounds of adani bursting and releasing its incredible strength, but the Debru never cried out in agony, so it sounded as though it was only the humans who suffered. The ground rumbled constantly.

The first of the wounded arrived before long. Alec stumbled in, grimacing against the pain. A chunk of his upper right arm had been bitten off in what appeared to be a kettu attack. His pale face and distant gaze made him look like a wandering ghost.

Samora jumped to help, eager to finally do something. She gripped his good shoulder firmly and guided him to one of the open cots. She almost had to push him down, but eventually he sat, and she could study his wound. Bloody as it was, she thought she could heal it quickly.

She placed her hands around the wound and closed her eyes. The flow of adani through his arm was a chaotic mess, and she straightened out the channels and flooded them with adani. The push and pull of adani from the battle complicated the matter, but the healing itself was straightforward enough it didn't slow her down.

Without warning, the heart deep beneath their feet beat faster. Adani tore through her channels and filled Alec's arm to the brim. Samora opened her eyes and watched fresh skin displace the infected skin near the edges of the wound. The new skin stretched and reached across the bite, easily visible to anyone watching. No more than a few heartbeats later, adani flowed smoothly through Alec. When Samora let go his eyes were clear and his complexion ruddy. He looked up at her, eyes wide, then bowed deeply. "Thank you."

Without another word he stood and ran from the tent to rejoin the battle. Samora watched him go, her mouth hanging slightly open. Beside her, Brittany cleared her throat. "What just happened? Did the battle make you use more adani than you intended?"

Samora shook her head. "I didn't do anything special. It was just a healing, but as soon as I started, adani flooded me and went through him. It was nothing I did, at least not intentionally."

Brittany looked skeptical, but she didn't have time to interrogate Samora further. More wounded trickled in. Most came in on their own two legs, but two were carried in by friends who left as soon as the wounded were deposited.

Samora lacked Brittany's experience and skill, which meant she saw the less serious of the injuries. The next adanist she helped was a young woman who'd taken a cut along the side of her leg. It wasn't a deep wound, but she could barely stand, meaning she wasn't any use on the battlefield. Samora placed her hands on either side of the cut, and just as before, the moment she began her healing a wave of adani crashed over her and into the warrior. The cut healed in a moment.

Like Alec, the adanist bowed and ran off to rejoin the battle. Samora's throat tightened at the sight, but she had to move quickly to the next warrior, thankfully also suffering from a small wound.

With every new arrival Samora wanted to ask how the battle went. The ground's rumbling had only grown more pronounced since Alec had arrived, and humanity's battle cries were loud enough she could barely hear herself think. She never asked, though. Whatever was happening in the battle, her work was here. It didn't matter if she knew or now.

After healing an adanist with a shallow hole in his chest, Samora looked up to see a fresh commotion at the entrance to the tent. Two burly adanists carried an older woman between them, and for a moment, Samora froze at the sight. It was Rakella, the adanist who Harald had first asked to train Samora. Rakella had been skilled, but they'd parted on poor terms when she'd confronted Samora's pacifism. It was the day after that Samora had started studying with Brittany.

The two of them hadn't talked since then. Rakella had always kept her distance and Samora had never been one to seek out conversations with people she barely knew. If they were ever going to have another conversation, though, Rakella needed a powerful healing.

She looked like she'd taken a shadow spear to the stomach. All the blood had drained from her face, but she still snarled when she saw Samora waiting in the healing tent. Samora was impressed she still had enough strength for that. A part of what looked like an intestine hung limply out of the hole in her gut.

Samora looked back to Brittany, but she had just started a healing that would take longer than Rakella had left to live.

Samora gestured to one of the open cots, and the two adanists placed Rakella on it. They left to rejoin the battle as Samora bent to her task.

Rakella grabbed her wrist, preventing Samora from flooding her with adani. "Brittany," she spat out through bloody lips.

"Is busy. If you want to live, let me go."

Rakella snarled again, but her strength gave out before her stubbornness. She fell back, face ashen, and didn't fight Samora any longer.

Samora bent close, trying to pry apart clothing and organ, grimacing as she stared straight into Rakella's core. She placed her hands around Rakella's wound, but before she could send adani into her body, a violent commotion near the front entrance drew Samora's attention away.

She caught a flash of bound adani as Aldrick's sword cut down at something Samora couldn't see. He shouted to someone else and then the sword cut again. He'd volunteered to guard the Bears' healing tent, even though his place was anywhere but, and Samora was glad for his presence. She'd argued he should have fought with the other Wolves on the front line, but he'd maintained his claim that the most important place he could be was somewhere he could protect her.

Another voice answered Aldrick's shout, and Samora wondered if the threat had passed, but then two small, dark creatures ran into the tent. Samora blinked, wondering if she'd imagined the streaks or not.

A moment later, a kettu launched itself at her head. Instinctively, she ducked and the kettu flew overhead. It landed on an empty cot and bounded off, disappearing from view as quickly as it had appeared. Samora spun, seeking any sign of either of the creatures, but she saw none.

Brittany's eyes tracked the new arrivals, but she continued her delicate work. Her gaze pleaded for Samora's help, and Samora rushed to protect her friend. She wove a shield to protect both healer and patient from the small invaders.

The two kettu appeared together on the other side of the tent. They climbed onto a cot and stared at the group of humans. The one on the left sneered, revealing a long row of deadly teeth.

She glanced toward the entrance of the tent and saw Aldrick's sword flashing again. It didn't look as though he'd be arriving to help anytime soon.

Samora's legs trembled, but she held the shield steady. Two kettu weren't nearly enough to overwhelm her, especially in a gathering ground. They seemed to sense the same because they didn't approach the shield.

Instead, they turned as one toward Rakella, who'd fallen unconscious from the blood loss. Samora swore.

Somehow, Brittany found the focus to speak even as she began the final, most delicate steps of her healing. "Save Rakella."

"If I protect her, they'll only attack you. I can't shield everyone at once."

If she'd learned more of her mother's techniques, she might have been able to. Mother had been able to cast a dome that protected almost everyone in the village, but Samora didn't know the weave.

"Kill the kettu," Brittany groaned.

Why hadn't she thought of that? She dropped the shield and began a new weave. She'd always found fire easy. Two small spheres of fire appeared in the air before her. The weave was an easy one, similar to the spheres of light and force she was fond of. She aimed them at the kettu.

The last time she'd used this technique, she'd formed the weaves inside the bodies of otsoa, burning them up from within. But that had been so many years ago, on the fateful day the Moka had attacked their village. She had no desire to try the same in the much smaller and faster kettu. She'd end up lighting half the tent on fire.

The kettu saw the spheres and leaped, but not to escape. No doubt, they'd been ordered by their masters to create as much death and destruction as possible. They jumped toward Rakella's prone form; teeth bared. Samora shifted her aim and tracked them easily. All she had to do was release them and kill the kettu.

Smoke escaped from the otsoas' mouths as they screamed in agony. They sounded almost like children. Samora covered her ears, but the sound wormed its way deep into her memories, slicing out a scar in her mind that would never heal, no matter how she mastered adani.

The spheres disappeared from Samora's hands as her focus shattered.

The kettu landed on Rakella's cot and snapped their jaws shut. One dug its snout deeper into the wound in her gut while the other closed its teeth on her throat, biting through it in one clean attack.

Brittany screamed, and two bound daggers flew across the tent to embed themselves deep into the kettu. One struck true, stabbing through the kettu's eye into its brain and killing it instantly. The other caught the kettu as it attempted to flee, slicing across the back of one of its legs. It hobbled toward the front entrance of the tent, but before it could escape, Brittany formed a glowing spear easily four times as strong as what was required. She threw the spear, which split the kettu in half with the force of its impact, spilling its steaming guts all around the entrance.

Samora glanced over and saw that Brittany was on her knees, sweat beading down her forehead. The adanist she'd been healing groaned and started to wake. His eyes blinked open and he sat up and looked around. "What happened here?"

Brittany forced herself to her feet and answered before Samora. "A pair of kettu reached the healing tent, but we've taken care of them."

The adanist looked between the two women, then bowed. "Thank you for the healing. Is there anything I can do in return?"

"Take the corpses of the kettu out. I don't want to trip over them as I'm healing anyone. And take Rakella's corpse and put it over there." She pointed to an empty corner of the tent.

The adanist bowed again. He scooped up the largest parts of the kettu that remained and dumped them unceremoniously outside the tent. As soon as he was done and gone, Brittany snarled and turned on Samora. Her eyes blazed with righteous anger, and she stomped toward Samora as though she intended to strike her down.

Samora flinched at the approach. Brittany grabbed her by the collar, then pulled and dragged her toward Rakella's body. She flung Samora down next to the cot and glared daggers into her. She said nothing, but the weight of her silent accusations crushed Samora.

Brittany only turned away when anger started to give way to tears. She strode toward the front of the tent and guided a wounded adanist who had just arrived to a cot. Aldrick glanced in, but he seemed satisfied to see Samora was still alive. His face disappeared as he resumed his protective duties.

Samora remained where she'd been left, not sure where she'd find the will to move her body again. But the short lull in the battle didn't last long, and soon the tent was filling with more wounded. Between healings, Brittany finally said her first words since the kettu.

"Get moving. Our people need healing, and that adanist is going to move the body soon."

Samora took one more look at Rakella's body, swallowed hard, and went to help the next adanist in line.

33

E lian sliced at a Debru who'd wandered too close to him, cutting through the monster with a single swing. An otsoa leaped at him from behind the Debru's falling body, but Elian flicked his sword and cut through it with equal ease.

Though death surrounded him, he'd never felt faster or stronger. His fears had lasted until the moment the Debru had charged through the boundary, but then there was nothing left to fear.

He swore there were moments he felt the heart his sister and the others kept talking about beneath his feet, beating in tandem with his own racing pulse. It sent adani surging through his limbs and he fought as though he had the power of a dragon to draw upon. The Debru moved slowly, as though they were children still learning how to fight. When they attempted to block his steel with their bound shadow, he sliced through their defense with ease. Never before had fighting seemed this easy.

The otsoa's death left him with a few brief moments in which nothing on the battlefield was trying to kill him. He stood tall and looked around. The opening exchange against the Belogs went as well as anyone could have hoped. Once they'd revealed themselves, Karla had directed her full attention on one, sending bolt after bolt of lightning at it. Each bolt shook the land when it struck. The adanists near Karla wobbled on the unsteady ground, and it was all they could do to add their considerable strength to Karla's efforts. Nearly a dozen bound spears struck out at the Belog for every bolt of lightning. By the time it collapsed, Elian had almost felt sorry for the invader.

Across the western edge of the gathering ground, the efforts of Samora and the other healers to strengthen the gathering ground showed their true worth. One Debru, usually enough to challenge four or five adanists, now struggled to fight two. The gathering ground didn't just strengthen the adanists, but it weakened the Debru techniques, too.

Had the fight only been against the basest of Debru, Elian knew they would have carved through the ranks with little difficulty. The Moka and Belogs, though, tilted the balance of power back toward the Debru. The Moka seeded chaos wherever they wandered, and the Belogs absorbed most attacks with ease.

The adanists weren't without their champions, though. Karla was a wonder, her lightning one of the few attacks the Belogs feared. Harald flung spears of adani as fast as he could form them, and Kati's daggers were always true. Even Tiafel and Aldo fought with courage befitting clan elders, though they lacked the strength of their younger counterparts. Tera, fighting not far from Elian, kept the Bears from losing too much ground.

For now, the adanists' lines held, but they were balanced on a knife's edge, and one fatal mistake from either side might end the battle for good.

Elian's study of the battle ended as a Moka turned toward him. It formed a spear of shadow and launched it at his heart.

Elian would have let the spear pass but was all too aware of the adanists fighting behind him. He stepped to the side and brought his blade up, slapping the spear with the side and sending it flying up and away from the front lines. It unraveled as it passed over the gathering ground.

The Moka didn't give him the opportunity to celebrate his accomplishment. It formed another spear but kept this one in hand as it advanced. It stabbed at Elian, who batted the spear aside and tried to step in closer.

The Moka wasn't interested. It swept its spear in an arc parallel to the ground, catching Elian by surprise. He took the blow on his shoulder, and it knocked him to the side. He got his sword up in time to block the next swing, but his steel wouldn't cut through the Moka's bindings.

Fortunately, Elian didn't fight this battle alone. The Moka's greater height made it a perfect target for one of Tera's spears, so all Elian had to do was keep it in place long enough for the veteran adanist to take aim.

As soon as the Moka stood still, a shaft of golden light stabbed into its skull.

The Moka collapsed, and with their commander gone, all the nearby Debru fell into a chaotic panic. Elian hurried back to the adanists fighting behind him, helping to clear the Debru before they broke through the lines. The invaders were dangerous enough on their own, but a wild madness overcame them when a Moka died, making them stronger and less restrained.

He didn't finish the task, though, as a Belog on the other side of the boundary chose that moment to throw one of its giant spears. Half a dozen shields were thrown up between Elian's back and the incoming attack, but they weren't going to be enough.

A new shield appeared between the shields and the spear, stronger than the other shields combined. Even though he couldn't sense it, Elian still recognized Harald's efforts. The dark spear struck the shield like a nail driven into wood by an angry carpenter, and the force of the impact made Elian feel as though someone had punched him in the chest, but the spear unraveled, and the shield held.

"Don't worry about the Belog," Harald called, "the only way it's getting to you is if it risks its neck and comes over to the other side of the boundary."

Elian nodded. The remaining Debru in the area had used the moment of distraction to redouble their efforts. One adanist retreated as two spears struck her at once, one to her leg and one to her side.

Elian cut down the Debru that attacked her first, then helped clear the rest. The Belog tried to interrupt with another spear, but Harald's protection held.

Elian figured it wouldn't be long before the remaining Belogs crossed over the boundary. The longer the battle lasted, the more chances favored the human defenders. They possessed the limitless adani of the heart, and the dragons continued to drop bound adani on the Belogs who remained outside the boundary. For now, those attacks were little more than an annoyance to the giant invaders, but the Belogs' awesome strength was limited, and every bit that they used defending against the dragons was a bit lost for good.

Elian hoped they waited too long. If the adanists could defeat the Debru and the Moka first it would give them much better chances against the Belogs.

Unfortunately, it didn't take too long for the Belogs to reach the same conclusion. They'd already lost one of their number, and Karla greedily turned her lightning onto a second. They marched forward, their giant strides eating up the last of the distance to the boundary.

Elian turned to meet the one closest to him, the one that had tried to kill him with the bound spears earlier. It stood easily twice as tall as him, and as it neared the boundary it formed a long sword of shadow in one hand and a bound shield in the other. It crashed through the boundary, and it was as though every Debru nearby regained the vitality sapped by the gathering grounds.

Elian ignored the Debru, trusting the adanists behind him to defend the gathering ground. The Belog made straight for him, but Elian stood tall as he imagined roots reaching out from his feet that locked him in place. Adani poured into his limbs, and he cycled it throughout his entire body.

The Belog's sword came in fast, sweeping across the ground as though it was attempting to clear a forest in one swing. Elian braced himself and blocked. Shadow met steel and Elian's feet sank into the rich soil as they fought to maintain their purchase. The enormous sword slowed, then stopped as Elian held it at bay.

Unfortunately, Elian's sword could do little to stop the bound shield that rushed at him from his side. One of Harald's spears rushed past Elian's head but was deflected harmlessly away. The shield struck Elian hard, lifting him from his feet and tossing him into the melee happening between the Bears and the remaining Debru. A kettu, which had been nipping around the legs of occupied Bears, jumped at him in a bid to lock its jaws on his throat and bring his campaign against the Belog to an early end.

Elian slapped the kettu away with the back of his hand as he returned, shakily, to his feet. The world wasn't as steady as it had been a few moments ago, but as adani rushed to his head his vision steadied. He looked up at the Belog as it took an eager stride toward him and wondered how, exactly, he was supposed to take the monster down. Given its size, it seemed tremendously unfair how quickly it could move, and its tall stature meant most of its vital points were difficult to reach.

Once again, he was reminded he didn't fight this battle by himself. Tera threw spear after spear at the Belog's face, forcing it to raise its shield up to protect itself. Elian pulled and cycled more adani through his limbs and launched himself into the opening the veteran adanist had provided.

The Belog either saw or sensed him coming, because it

chopped at him with a short swing of its sword. Elian blocked it and kept running. The Belog snapped out its leg, but Elian sliced through it, his sword passing through the Belog's flesh almost as easily as he had the Debru's.

As he passed, Harald joined the assault, hurling an enormous spear for the center of the Belog's mass. It brought its shield down to block, but Elian wasn't about to give it a chance to heal. He leaped at the Debru's back, the tip of his sword pointed at the Belog's heart.

Halfway through his leap, a small wall of shadow appeared. Elian prepared to stab through it, but half a dozen spears emerged and shot toward Elian. He tried to twist away, but he'd been caught in the middle of his jump.

"Elian!"

An adani shield appeared ahead of him, and the spears spent most of their strength against it. The shield shattered, but only one spear made it through. The spear traced a burning line across Elian's back, but it was a small price to pay for his foolish mistake.

Elian stabbed into the wall of shadow, and his sword passed through and into the Debru's back. It didn't penetrate all the way to the heart, but the Belog raised its voice to the sky in a silent cry. Finally, the accumulated damage caused it to lose its balance and fall to the ground, shaking the ground beneath Elian's feet.

Harald, Tera, Elian, and Alec, who had been the adanist who'd come to Elian's rescue, all launched themselves at the fallen Belog, cutting and stabbing as they could. It took the combined efforts of all four of them, but eventually Harald succeeded in driving an enormous spear through the Belog's heart, killing it on the spot.

Elian wiped the sweat from his brow and bowed to Alec. "Thanks for saving me."

Alec bowed in return. "Your sister's already healed me once today, so I figured I should repay your family somehow."

Elian was glad to hear Samora was helpful, but his mirth faded as he let his gaze travel over the rest of the battlefield. The Belog they'd attacked hadn't been the only one that had rushed over the boundary. They struck up and down the line, and where the Hounds should have been, two Belogs working together had pushed deep into the gathering ground. The line had bent around them, and it looked like it wouldn't be long before the line snapped and let the Belogs and all the rest through.

Karla's lightning had stopped, too, and Elian hoped that was due more to the close proximity of the Belog instead of any particular doom befalling her. For the same reason, the dragons no longer dropped bound adani onto the Debru. Any attack from above was as likely to hit an adanist as an enemy. The dragons still flew and snapped at the Belogs, but that was the limit of their help. With some of their strongest forces limited in the aid they could provide, there was little holding the Belogs back anymore.

Harald's evaluation of the situation was the same. He pointed in the direction of the two Belogs. "That's where we need to be."

Elian caught his breath, then nodded. He tried to take a step toward the Belogs, but his feet refused to move. Before, determination had kept him rooted in place, but as he watched one of the Belogs sweep three adanists aside with a single cut, his brief bout of courage failed. A second attempt to move resulted in a small, shuffling step forward.

Then Harald was at his side, and his mere presence melted the ice that had formed in Elian's joints. He spoke softly, so that Alec and Tera, standing behind them, wouldn't hear. "It's always hardest when they aren't attacking you. It allows you to think that someone else will do what needs to be done."

Elian swallowed hard and nodded. They'd defended their position well already. How much more could the clans ask from them?

He knew the answer, though. They could ask for everything

and more, because the clans were all that stood between humanity and extinction.

"Ready?" Harald asked.

"I am."

So long as Harald stood by his side, Elian's fears lost their grip on his body. The two adanists ran shoulder to shoulder, clearing the one poor Debru that stood in their way with ease. Then they broke through the front line of the battle and found themselves in the relative peace of the other side. Harald killed a few kettu as they passed, but they crossed the remaining distance between them and the Belogs with ease. They reinforced the Hounds' front line, where Tiafel was desperately flinging adani at the Belogs. His attacks lacked any focus, though, and while each individual binding was strong, he accomplished little.

The Belogs, on the other hand, were forces of pure destruction. Their enormous bound swords swept through the adanists, cutting easily through any Hound unfortunate enough to attempt to match their strength against the shadowy giants. The Hounds had responded by allowing the center of their line to bend. As the Belogs strode forward, they permitted the adanists to nearly surround them. Otsoa, kettu, and a few Debru fought to protect their commanders, but they fell against the adanists.

Harald wasted no time consulting with Tiafel. He threw one of his enormous bound spears as soon as he was certain of his aim. The spear ripped over the heads of the defenders and raced for a Belog's skull. The Belog's sword expanded into a shield, which it raised just in time to protect itself. Harald's spear spent its adani against the shield, but the Belog was barely bothered.

Elian glanced over at Harald. A sheen of sweat dripped down his forehead and he breathed heavily. He formed and threw another spear, and although it looked more impressive than the ones most adanists bound, it had little effect on the Belog.

Either these Belogs were stronger than the one they'd already fought, or Harald was near the limit of his strength. Given the shadow eating him up from the inside, Elian had a pretty good idea which was the true explanation.

Elian hurried to shoulder some of Harald's burden. He pulled and cycled adani into his legs and leaped high. He cleared the line of adanist defenders and landed softly on the other side. His arrival attracted the attention of not just one, but both Belogs. They ignored the rest of the gathered adanists and swung their swords at him.

He dove away from the first blade, then hopped away from the second as it sought to cleave him in two. The Belogs advanced, their swords hungry for his blood.

"Aim for their faces!" Harald cried from behind the line.

The adanists took advantage of the sudden freedom Elian's arrival bought them. Golden streaks of light darted for the Belogs' faces, forcing each of them to protect themselves with a shield. They weren't deterred from their purpose, though. Clouds of darkness swirled into existence between the Belogs and Elian, and he cursed as he saw them. He retreated quickly and shouted. "Prepare for spears!"

The adanists in the front line formed bound shields, and Elian leaped up and behind them as dozens of dark spears burst from the clouds and at the place he'd stood just a moment ago. He landed behind the stacked shields and took shelter.

Adanists and Belogs traded their blows all at once, both sides giving it their all. Several adanists responsible for the shields fell to Belog spears that penetrated their defenses, but the Belogs couldn't afford to put their full strength into the assault. Harald, Tiafel, and a dozen Hounds threw as much adani at their faces as they could summon, and thanks to the heart beating beneath their feet, they could summon quite a lot. The ground rumbled with the exchange of adani and shadow, but soon at least one of the Belog was retreating.

"We've got them now!" Harald shouted. "Give it everything you've got!"

The adanists answered his call with a vigorous outpouring of adani. The air turned gold as adanists lashed out with abandon. Elian's heart surged in his chest as he saw the one Belog walking backward. The Hound's lines stopped bending, and Tiafel directed some of his precious reinforcements to the places he felt the line was weakest.

By the time Elian realized not all was as it seemed, the Belogs' plan was already in motion. The Belog which hadn't retreated formed a new shield, big enough to protect them both from most of the spears and daggers thrown at them. The second Belog, which had appeared to be in retreat, stopped and took shelter behind the first. It formed an enormous spear of bound shadow, longer than the monster was tall. It spun the spear in its hands, stopping the spear's rotation when its point was down.

The Belog waited a moment, then stabbed the spear deep into the ground at its feet. Samora's gathering ground, which had resisted the Debru so well for so long, couldn't hold back the focused power of the strike. The grass around the spear died, and for a moment, Elian was sure the Belog had taken aim at the heart of the gathering ground.

He was too far away to do anything but watch.

Then the ground to his side erupted and he heard a loud grunt. He turned to see Harald staring down at the ground, looking like a child surprised during a game of hide and seek. As Elian watched, blood began to trickle out of the corner of his mouth. The blood dribbled down and dropped onto the spear of shadow which had erupted from beneath his feet and impaled him through his stomach.

The spear unraveled, still subject to adani's overwhelming influence within the gathering ground, but its intended damage had been done. Harald sank to his knees as he put his hand over the hole in his stomach.

It seemed as though every eye on the front lines stared at

Harald. The world had gone suddenly quiet, and several adanists stumbled backward as though drunk.

Harald was unaware of the attention. He looked up to the sky, and his lips moved, though no words escaped.

Then the Belogs attacked as one, cutting through the shocked line of adanists and advancing with ease.

34

The only ways Samora kept track of the battle was by listening to how close the fighting sounded and by tracking the number of wounded streaming into the tent for healing. By either measure, they weren't doing well. The battle sounded like it was being fought just on the other side of the thin tent walls, and the line of wounded was now longer than she and Brittany could keep up with.

The line of patients became a blur. She would heal one, only to turn around and find another waiting for her. She didn't allow herself breaks, and the heart continued to aid her, healing wounds faster and more thoroughly than Samora could have dreamed of doing on her own. She felt the tendrils of exhaustion spreading through her body. Her own adani channels hadn't rested since early that morning, but every time she finished a healing her eyes were drawn to the corner of the tent. They'd thrown a blanket over Rakella's corpse, but she still felt the dead adanist's glare whenever she accidentally gave herself a moment to recover.

The only answer was to keep herself so busy there was no time for anything else. She didn't talk, nor did she ever ask a question. Adani found the wounds easily enough. She barely needed to open her eyes, and at times, she went from adanist to adanist without doing so.

When she came out of her healing trances, she heard some of the wounded whispering about her.

"Why doesn't she open her eyes?"

"She won't even ask what's wrong."

"I've never seen a wound heal so quickly. It's not right."

She ignored them. Sometimes, she wasn't even sure if they were real or imagined. Adani guided her body, her hands, and her actions. Wherever she walked, she saved lives, only to send them running back to a battlefield so they could perhaps lose them.

It didn't matter how many she healed, though. There was always Rakella, laying judgmentally in the corner. A dozen lives saved weighed less than the one lost.

Samora finished healing another adanist, but as she moved on to the next a strong hand grabbed her wrist. Her eyes snapped open, and she saw Brittany holding her arm. The other healer's face was pale, and her eyelids drooped, but her grip told Samora exactly how much strength she still possessed, and it was considerable.

"They're calling for those who aren't warriors to flee," Brittany said.

Samora stood in place and blinked.

Brittany explained. "The Hounds' line is about to break, and as soon as it does, the Debru are going to come pouring through the gap. We need to prepare to leave. Heal those who will be well enough to walk."

Brittany delivered the news as though she was telling the nearest kin their family had died. Which she was. Except this was the death of the clans, and possibly all of humanity. If they couldn't fight here, they were doomed to retreat, but where was there to retreat?

They'd gambled it all on this fight, and the Vada hadn't even bothered to show up. It had known it didn't need to.

Brittany let her go and promptly moved on to the next warrior who needed healing, obeying her own orders.

Samora couldn't follow. She stood as though held in place.

They couldn't lose.

If they lost here, they lost everything.

Drawn, as if by instinct, she bent down and dug her fingertips into the dirt, packed solid by the vast numbers of people moving throughout the tent. She let adani drop into the soil and followed it as it got caught in the turbulent currents of the battle. A hundred sensations attacked her at once. Not far from the tent, a line of Hounds pulled desperately on the gathering ground's adani.

She paused for a moment as her senses passed over them. While they all pulled adani, and were no doubt stronger for it, they pulled only a small fraction of what was available to them. The heart had so much more to give, but it wasn't being taken.

A pool of dark shadow stood proudly within the circle of adanists, and though the gathering ground's powerful adani nibbled at the edges of the darkness, the Belogs were plenty strong enough to endure long enough to complete the tasks given to them.

Farther down the line, she sensed a young man's adani flee from his body as his heart gave out. A single Belog fought against the remnants of the Hawks and the Wolves, and it was Karla who stood before the assault, unwilling to retreat even though she was exhausted and the Belog slowly gained the upper hand. Karla pulled deeper from the gathering ground, but even her efforts didn't come close to the buried heart.

Samora watched, a helpless observer, as two very distinct pools of adani, belonging to Harald and her brother, stood against the pair of Belog closer to her tent. Their first efforts seemed successful, but Samora felt the Belog's spear in her own stomach as it stabbed into the gathering ground. It shoved its way under-ground and jutted up again, right underneath an unsuspecting Harald.

Samora cried out, and soon she felt a pair of hands on her shoulders, but she couldn't pull away from the ground. Adani bound her tightly, as though their roles had been reversed. Instead of her weaving the adani, it worked inside her, through no conscious design of her own. The heart beat so loudly she could hear nothing else. It demanded her attention, and she had little choice but to surrender to it.

Deprived of Harald's support, the rest of the adanists broke like a wall built out of twigs. The Belogs advanced as a pair, ripping through the Hounds like a farmer cutting through his field with a scythe. Adani returned to the gathering ground as warriors fell, but their sanctuary had no need of the sacrifice.

The heart had adani enough for all.

It only needed to reach those it was trying to protect.

Following Elian tempted her, but not even he could long survive the attention of two Belogs. She let the heart pull her down as it beat faster than before. Its pulses were strong, but the gathering ground's young adani channels weren't nearly wide enough to accommodate all the heart had to offer. Samora's adani pulsed in time with the heart's, and she felt as it slammed into the narrow channels and stopped. Twice, then three times, her adani was thrust toward the surface, only to have nowhere to go.

Samora's arms trembled as she understood what the heart required. This was a healing, simply on a scale beyond anything she'd ever attempted.

The hands on her shoulders shook her, but she only felt it as something distant. She was too deep in the trance, and Brittany would have to act on her own for a time. The hands pulled on her, but she might as well have been an enormous boulder for all the adani wrapped around her.

Samora took a deep breath and surrendered most of her adani.

The heart and the gathering ground pulled and twisted at it, but within the space of a single beat of the gathering ground's heart she had a sense of all the channels running through the gathering ground. She allowed herself a brief moment to marvel at the wonder, a web of such intricacy no human hand could duplicate it.

The amount of adani needed to widen the channels was enormous, but she had plenty at her command. She gritted her teeth as she prepared her body for what was about to come. There was a very real chance the heart asked more from her than she was able to give.

Not that it mattered. She hadn't saved Rakella, but maybe she could save the clans from suffering a fatal blow today.

That was worth her life and more.

Samora began, first widening the channels that stretched between the heart and the healing tent. Warmth spread from her core, up through her chest, and down through her arms. The process forced her body to channel more adani than it ever had before. It filled her limbs, and at first, it was as though she'd just woken up from the most relaxing nap. Her focus, endurance, and strength were all as sharp as she'd ever felt them. If Brittany had asked her to run to the enormous village so far to the west, Samora would have without tiring.

But as adani continued to flow through her limbs, the warmth increased. Before long, she was sweating, and soon after that her arms burned as though she'd jumped headfirst into a fire. She couldn't move even if she wanted, adani rushing through her so fast she didn't dare twitch so much as a muscle.

A burning inferno erupted in her core as she finished opening the channels between the healing tent and the heart. She lost focus and almost collapsed as even more adani filled her body. She swore she felt her insides burning, but her throat was on fire, and she couldn't call out. Adani cracked her skin, and she bled light, and she didn't know what was real and what was sensed.

Then the heart beat again and pulled some of the adani away. Her arms and core still burned, but at a fraction of the intensity she'd felt a moment ago. Adani flowed smoothly between the heart and the healing tent, and some of Samora's other senses returned. She heard Brittany gasp, but Samora's work was far from done.

As she dove back into the gathering ground with her adani, she felt the Belogs' attention shift away from Elian toward her. Spears of shadow sailed through the air, only to be intercepted by adanists nearing their limits. The ones closest to the healing tent, including Aldrick, were surprised by how effectively they blocked the spears.

Samora could do nothing but trust them and hope that she could act quickly enough.

Strengthened by adani straight from the heart, Samora resumed widening the channels, this time focusing her efforts the channels that terminated adjacent to the healing tent out to the west. Once again, her body warmed until she was certain Brittany had lit a fire underneath her to encourage her to move. But then the channels widened as she finished the weave and the worst of the pain passed.

Again, the Belogs attacked, but their spears were once again held at bay by the adanists, more of whom could now pull straight from the heart. The Belogs' advance stopped, but the adanists couldn't find a way to force them back.

Samora coughed and felt something wet and warm dribble down the corner of her lips. Distant shouts called her name, but she was too far away. Someone tried to send more adani into her but stopped as Samora's body started shaking. Her channels were nearly burned out, but she hadn't yet done enough.

She couldn't open her eyes, but she was certain Rakella still glared at her.

Her life wasn't worth Brittany's efforts to save it.

One more time. The heart already did much of the work. By

flooding the recently opened channels, those nearby widened as well. With one more push, Samora thought she could tip the gathering ground over the edge and flood the whole space with the power of the heart.

The strength in her arms gave out and her forehead dropped to the ground, but she never let go of her connection with the heart. Once more she sent her adani into the heart, and once more it flooded her with the strength required to open even more of the web. Samora's insides turned to ash, but the pain wasn't as it had been before.

Finishing the weave felt as though she was tying a rope around a mountain and pulling it behind her. Adani slipped through her grasp, unraveling as fast as her focus. She desperately clung to one last strand and with a final grunt of effort, pulled the weave tight.

The last of the channels widened and the heart flooded the gathering ground with fresh adani.

The last thing Samora sensed was the Belogs making one last push for the healing tent. She tried to tell Brittany to run, but she couldn't get her lips to form the words. She flopped onto her side as her vision faded.

35

Elian lost all sense of the larger battle. Once the Belogs broke through the line, the surviving Debru all surged at once. He'd been moving toward Harald, but the rush of Debru pushed him away from his friend. He searched for the giant, but he was on his knees and the press of bodies around Elian was tight. Harald couldn't have been more than a dozen paces away, but Elian might as well have been on the other side of a deep valley.

His search for Harald ended when the Debru assault forced him to defend himself. A shadow spear tried to knock his sword away, but he twisted his blade and allowed its edge to cut through the shadow and unravel the spear.

Before he could take advantage of the Debru's sudden opening, an otsoa leaped for his throat. Elian twisted away, gritting his teeth against the burning pain the otsoa's claws left across his side. He ignored the otsoa in favor of the Debru, but that only lasted until he caught sight of a Moka charging for him. He twisted and brought his sword to bear, but the force of the Moka's swing still lifted him off his feet and threw him back.

His feet hit the ground first, but before he could find his

balance he tripped over a Hound's corpse. He landed hard on his bottom, but when he tried to scramble away from the Moka, he found one of his feet was caught between the corpse's arm and torso. He twisted his foot and pulled it out as the Moka brought its sword down. Elian scrambled backward as the Moka's shadow sword sliced through the corpse.

The Moka weaved two bound spears of shadow over its head and sent them at Elian. He knocked one aside with his sword as he twisted, but the other sliced through his left arm, which fell limp at his side.

An errant adani spear caught the Moka in the chest. It lacked the strength to penetrate, but it successfully distracted the Moka for a moment. Elian used his good arm to help him back to his feet. He grabbed his sword from the mud and brought it up in time to deflect the Moka's next cut, which knocked him backward again. He kept his feet, but not by much.

Elian cycled as much adani into his body as he could, but there was only so much it could endure. After a day of seeking out the toughest challengers on the battlefield, he neared the limits of his body's ability. He met the Moka's next two attacks with what felt like the last of his strength, but he succeeded in not giving up more ground.

The Moka's next attack bounced off his sword, and the massive Debru commander blinked as though its red eyes had become clouded. Elian leaped at the opportunity. He was too slow to land a killing blow, but his weak attempt still succeeded at knocking the Moka back a step.

Elian didn't question his fortune but swung his sword again. The Moka blocked each cut with ease, especially once Elian began using his sword more like a club than an edged weapon, but it kept giving up ground.

Elian cut down again, but the Moka retreated, and Elian's swing missed completely. He didn't even have the strength left to stop his sword. It sank into the rich soil, and he cursed. The

Moka didn't take advantage of the opportunity, though. It threw up a shield of shadow.

The sky behind Elian grew brighter and he glanced back to see dozens of spears arcing through the air. They glowed as bright as one of Harald's, but no single adanist could throw so many. Elian retreated quickly as they fell. The spears engulfed the Moka, Debru, and Belogs alike.

Now that he had a moment to look around, he immediately sought out Harald. He let his eyes roam over the larger battle-field. He and the other Hounds were fighting closer to the tents than he'd realized. That last surge of Debru had pushed some of the adanists back into the tents, and only now were they starting to shove back.

The barrage of adani continued, but the Debru shifted their tactics quickly. The surviving Belogs raised shields to protect the Moka and the Debru, which used the opportunity to unleash a blistering counterattack.

The attack broke upon the newly formed line of Hounds, and once more the two sides fought for supremacy of the battlefield. The adanists on the front line were exhausted and cut up, but thanks to the constant rain of spears supporting them from behind, they kept most of the attack contained.

Elian didn't know where the flood of fresh adani was coming from, but he didn't care. All that mattered was finding Harald. If he could reach the big man in time, there was still a chance Samora could heal him.

She had to.

There. Stuck between two groups of adanists fighting desperately to hold the line, a giant lifted himself to his knees. Elian ran toward his wounded leader.

"Harald!" he cried.

The giant shifted, giving Elian a close glimpse of his injury. Intestines poked out of the hole in Harald's stomach even as he held his hand over the wound. Elian knew, as soon as he got that second look, that no matter what he did, Harald wasn't long for this world.

"What are you doing here?" Harald growled.

Elian almost answered, then glanced at Harald's wound and realized how foolish he would sound if he did.

Thankfully, he didn't need to explain. Harald had always known his heart, seemingly from the first day they'd met. His eyes met Elian's. "Help me up, then."

Elian squatted on Harald's uninjured side and hooked his arms under Harald's armpit. He cycled adani and pulled Harald to his feet, ignoring the muttered curses Harald uttered at the assistance.

Together, they stood and watched the battle. The bulk of it had moved past them toward the tents. The Belogs had broken through the lines and hurried toward the tents. Adanists flung incredible assaults at the Belogs and their minions, but the Belogs wouldn't slow their mad advance.

"How did the others get so strong?" Harald asked.

Elian had no answer. He contented himself with standing by Harald's side at the end, for it was the end. Despite the heroic stand, the adanists couldn't last, not against the Belogs' final push.

"I'd like to see Kati, one last time, if I could" Harald said. His voice sounded weak, as though it was coming from far away.

"I don't know where she is." Elian didn't have the heart to tell him there was a very good chance she was among the fallen. The Hawks had been overrun, too.

Harald tilted his chin. "She's that way."

The direction he pointed had a Belog fighting against a small group of adanists. Elian thought he caught a glimpse of Kati's knives, though. He eyed the route, then decided it was as safe as anywhere else. One death was as good as another. They stumbled together toward the battle. Adanists continued their desperate defense against the Debru advance, but the Belog were now well among the tents, and the Debru were wreaking havoc as they passed.

If he had any more strength remaining, he would have drawn his sword and attacked the Belog from behind. He was weak enough now they probably wouldn't even sense him approach. But it was all he could do just to keep his own feet.

They hadn't made it halfway back to the lines when the air rippled with flecks of golden light. The wave started back by the healing tents, then spread until it washed over the adanists and Debru alike. The Debru flinched as though they'd been blinded. The wave washed over Elian, stripping him of his weariness and flooding his body with so much adani he felt as though he'd become a dragon.

His heart pounded in his chest, but he wasn't sure it was just his chest, not anymore. His heartbeat reverberated with dozens of other hearts, possibly even hundreds. The shallow cuts across his body healed, and even though the more substantial injuries to his arm remained, he could feel the way the flesh started to mend together.

Harald shook and almost fell over, but Elian held him up. "What's wrong?"

Harald grunted. "I don't think my body was ready for that."

Elian looked down at Harald's wound, wondering if the wave of adani had somehow healed him. Unfortunately, like his arm, the wound remained as open as before. Some injuries were too much, even for a flood of adani.

Instead of convincing the Belogs to run, the wave of adani made them charge forward, their enormous swords cutting through tents and flesh with equal ease. Adanists screamed as they exerted the last of their efforts, but even with the strength granted to them by the gathering ground and the heart beating beneath, they weren't enough.

"We need to stop them," Harald said.

"You're in no condition to help. The fact you're standing at all is a wonder, but if you start binding adani, the effort might kill you."

"And if we don't, none of us are going to survive."

Elian snarled but nodded. "Still, not much I can do with only one arm."

A moment later he realized his mistake, but before he could apologize, Harald said, "Nonsense. Between the two of us, we've got two working arms, and that should be more than enough. Shall we get their attention?"

Elian took a deep breath, and even without conscious effort, adani flooded into his body, filling him so full he worried he might burst. Unlike before, though, the adani didn't roar through his channels. His body felt wonderful. His arm wouldn't heal for some time, but the pain from it faded. The closest comparison he could draw was that of the dragon's adani, a deep lake of strength he had easy access to. Now it was his.

"Let's go," he said.

Harald raised his hand above his head and weaved a simple spear, blinding in its brilliance. Elian sprinted through the destruction the Belogs had left in their wake as he drew his sword. Harald's spear was so bright it made his running form cast a long shadow ahead.

The rearmost of the Belogs was just beginning to turn when Harald threw his spear. It roared across the sky like a giant lightning bolt, and Elian had to look away as it struck the Belog's hastily erected shield. For the first time that day, the shield lost the duel. The spear punched through the shield and deep into the Belog's chest. It lifted its head to let out a silent roar, and then Elian was there to finish what Harald had started.

Adani pooled in his legs as though it had always been there, and he leaped high enough to bring his sword in line with the Belog's exposed neck. He cycled adani into his arms, wrists, and hands, then cut with all his strength. His sword cut clean through the Belog's neck, and the head and body fell separately to the ground.

The death of its final remaining compatriot caught the last Belog's attention. It turned to carve Elian up with its sword, but Harald had already formed another spear, every bit as powerful as the last. The Belog formed a shield, and once again light and shadow battled upon the plains.

This time, shadow won. Elian didn't know if Harald weakened or if this Belog was the strongest of the bunch. Simply fighting for as long as it had within the gathering grounds had to be exhausting, but it fought as though it had just returned from a long rest.

Elian tried to help Harald, but his efforts were quickly ended by a rush of Debru commanded by a single Moka. Elian carved through the Debru without difficulty. So much adani flowed through him there was no chance for the warriors to stop him. Their bound swords, already weakened by the gathering ground, unraveled into smoke as his own steel passed through. Their bodies barely provided any more resistance.

The Moka, though, was a different story. It formed twin blades of shadow and strode toward Elian, keeping itself firmly between the Belog and him. Another Moka stood behind the Belog, keeping it safe from the bound knives and spears of the other adanists. It seemed to Elian that it was only a matter of time before the Moka collapsed under the weight of the assaults it endured on behalf of its master.

A moment later, the handful of Debru left alive reminded Elian they shouldn't be so easily dismissed. The Belog shielded itself from another of Harald's attacks even as it bound spears of shadow. Those spears launched over the Moka's head and into the press of adanists looking for a chance to bring the last Belog down.

A few of the adanists got shields up in time, but not enough. The spears decimated the lines, and the Moka which had been guarding the Belog's back seized the opportunity to jump into the fray and take advantage of the confusion.

Elian saw it all but could do nothing to help, as his own attention was consumed by the Moka that sought his head. He deflected one cut and stepped away from another, but the uselessness of his left arm proved problematic. The Moka kept striking at his left side, and it was difficult for Elian to defend. It was only thanks to the speed and strength the heart gave him that he stayed alive.

The Belog launched another attack on the adanists, and Elian became convinced that Harald was simply growing too weak to continue fighting. As incredible as the heart was, it couldn't sustain them all. The Belog's black spears ate into the adanists as the Moka cut even more down.

Elian swore, and the Moka chose that moment to attack him again.

Something inside him snapped and it felt as though his body turned white with anger. The Moka swung at his head, but when Elian blocked it, the sword dissolved to shadow. The Moka took a step back, but Elian wasn't about to let it retreat. He cut down, and though the Moka successfully blocked with its other sword, Elian cut through sword and Moka with equal ease. His cut ripped open the Moka from chest to crotch, and the invader died without a sound.

The Belog turned to face Elian, but before it could give Elian its full attention, a handful of spears demanded its shield. The enormous Belog shifted fast, placing itself in such a place that it could block Harald and the other adanists' attacks while focusing most of its attention on Elian.

A small portal of shadow opened in front of the Belog, and half a dozen spears flew at Elian.

Elian was tired of dodging. He sprinted forward, allowing the spears to strike him full in the chest.

As soon as they made contact, they unraveled.

Elian swung his sword, and the Belog took a step back to avoid the cut. It formed a bound sword in its left hand and took a massive swing. Elian braced himself and blocked.

The Belog had the advantage of size and weight, a massive figure towering over Elian's smaller form, but the enormous sword didn't cut through Elian's blade or knock him backward. His feet slid in the gathering ground, but once he found purchase, he matched the Belog's impressive strength with his own. The Belog's muscles in its arm bulged as it tried to push Elian away, but Elian stood strong.

If he'd had a second arm, he thought he might have even pushed the Belog's sword away, but all he had was one arm to fight with. It took every bit of strength he had just to keep the Belog away.

A golden spear sliced through the air and punched through the Belog's shield. The Belog staggered, but still it kept its feet. Harald shouted and threw another spear, but this one bounced harmlessly off the shield.

The giant had given the last of what he had, and it wasn't quite enough.

Then a bolt of lightning struck the Belog on the shoulder, accompanied by several daggers of bound adani. The Belog lost its balance and stumbled backward, providing Elian exactly the opportunity he was looking for. He leaped, the tip of his sword glowing with adani, and thrust it under the Belog's chin and through its skull for the killing blow.

36

After the Belog fell, a dozen spears of adani broke through the last Moka's shield and brought it down. Elian looked left and right for any other Debru, but there were none to be found. A few kettu skittered around, but no sooner did Elian see them than they were pierced by adani spears.

The constant din of battle faded, replaced by an eerie silence. His hearing returned to normal, and he realized it wasn't so much that it was silent as that the groans of the injured were softer than the clash of armies. As he listened to the wounded call for help, Elian thought of Harald and turned around. The giant wasn't anywhere to be seen among the chaos.

Elian cursed and ran toward where he had left Harald. He found the giant man on his back, staring up at the clouds. The hole in his stomach was as large as ever, and now shadow had extended from the wound. It was in his veins, and Elian watched as it slowly spread from his shoulder down his arm.

"We need to get you to a healer," he said.

He reached down to grab Harald, but a motion from Harald's fingers stilled him.

Harald slowly shook his head, but even that looked to be too much for him. His lips trembled as though he was about to speak, but nothing escaped. His hand lifted off the ground and Elian took it in his own. When they touched, he could feel the lack of adani in Harald's body and understood.

He'd spent too much in his fight against the Debru, and certainly too much to help bring down the last two Belogs. He'd left nothing for himself, and shadow had taken over. It was so far spread it even prevented adani from flowing through. No healer, no matter how skilled, could do anything. He shouldn't even be alive.

Harald squeezed Elian's hand tightly and stared straight into him. Elian nodded. "I'll do everything I can, for everyone. I promise."

Harald closed his eyes, satisfied by Elian's oath.

A shadow passed over them both, and Elian looked up to see Kati standing beside them.

"He wanted to reach you," he said.

Kati nodded, then kneeled beside Elian. She put her hand on Harald's shoulder, and when she felt what Elian had, tears sprang to her eyes.

Elian passed Harald's hand over to Kati.

Harald's eyes opened, and when he saw his beloved, the corner of his lips turned up in a smile. He gave the smallest of nods to Elian, who stood, bowed deeply, and left the two alone. He stood several paces away, standing guard in case anything tried to interrupt.

But it was just one tragedy among many, and as such, garnered little attention in that moment. Most of the adanists were searching among the destroyed tents for survivors. Others traced the path of the battle, looking for friends and family who had fallen but might still live.

Elian still felt the heart beating far beneath his feet, its strength still filling him with adani. To Elian, it felt as though the heart was with him, and he didn't understand how he maintained the connection.

For now, it didn't matter. It healed him, and hopefully it would heal many others. It had helped them defeat the Belogs, although barely. He didn't know why the Vada hadn't joined its forces, but he was grateful. He didn't think that even the heart could stand against such a force.

When he turned back to check on Kati, he saw that she was bent over Harald and sobbing. When she moved, Harald's arm moved limply with her.

Elian's throat constricted and he had to look away. His vision swam with tears, but he wiped them away with the back of his hand.

Kati's voice carried to him. "Will you help me carry him back to his people?"

Elian wiped more tears away, then nodded and turned to help. Kati supported one side by wrapping both her arms around his torso, and Elian fit himself underneath Harald's limp arm. Together, they shuffled toward where the Bears had made their camp. Elian had to place his feet carefully, as much of the ground was thick with blood and bodies.

Eventually they reached the tents, and everyone who searched for survivors paused as they passed. Even the injured stopped groaning when they saw their leader carried through their camp. Harald's tent still stood, and Kati guided them in. After a few awkward moments, they were able to lay his body down on his cot.

"He loved fighting by your side," Kati said.

The rock in his throat wouldn't allow any words past, but Elian nodded.

"Would you leave us?"

Elian reached out and took Harald's hand. In death, it felt as though it was so much larger, swallowing his hand whole and making him a child in comparison. He'd taken so much strength from that arm, and still, it didn't seem like enough. He bowed his forehead until it pressed against Harald's knuckles, then let the arm rest gently by its side.

A part of him wanted to stay, but Kati needed her time and there were those he needed to check on, too.

Elian bowed to Kati and left, closing the tent behind him. A few uninjured Bears had gathered outside, and at their questioning looks, Elian shook his head. One of the Bears wailed loudly, and the others looked close to joining in.

Elian needed to think about something else. Anything else. He thought of Samora and Capricia and decided to check on Samora first. The Bears' healing tent was close, and maybe she'd know more about what happened with the heart. He hurried between the tents, then stopped when he took one look at the long line outside the healing tent.

He debated for a moment with himself, then went inside anyway. All the cots were full, and Brittany stood at the entrance, either healing people on the spot or turning them away.

When she saw Elian, she stopped.

That, combined with the fact that he didn't see Samora helping, was all he needed to see to know that something was wrong. The ground shifted beneath his feet, and he stumbled back. Someone behind him caught him and saved him from falling. The moment of weakness passed, and he found his balance again.

"What happened?" he asked.

Brittany asked the first person in line to wait one moment, then pulled Elian deeper into the tent, explaining as they walked. "I don't know. One moment we were preparing to abandon the tent as the Belogs approached, but then she got this distant look in her eyes, and she knelt down to touch the ground. I don't know how, but she was the one who connected the heart to the gathering grounds."

Elian shook his head. Of course she was. Whenever they needed saving, she was the one there for them. "And?"

They reached one of the cots where Samora was sleeping. Her face was pale, but Elian saw her chest rising and falling. She didn't stir as he approached.

"Whatever she did, it hurt. She took on a lot of pain and more adani than any human I've ever felt, and I've spent my whole life around Harald."

Elian took her hand. It felt clammy underneath his own. He couldn't sense any adani moving through her, though.

"It did something to her," Brittany explained. She reached out and put her hand on Samora's covered knee. "I tried to heal her with adani, but it only seemed to make the problems worse."

"What does that mean?"

"It means that for now, I'm beyond my depth. But there's no shadow in her, and although I can't wake her up, she doesn't seem to be in any pain, so I've been focusing on those I can help. When there's time, I'll take a closer look and ask for help, but for now, there's nothing I can do."

Elian looked down at his sister and nodded. "Thank you. Do you mind if I stay here?"

"Not at all, but I do need to get to the others. And you'll need healing, too, it seems."

"Worry about the others first. I'll be here when you have the time and the strength."

Brittany nodded, then rushed back to the front of the tent and Elian wished there was something more he could do to help her.

He turned back to his sister, willing some of the warmth of his hand into her own. She was too cold. He leaned down close to her ear. "Samora?"

There was no response. He glanced over to Brittany, who had her hands full of other patients. He grabbed Samora's shoulder and shook it, but she slept on as though she hadn't even noticed.

Elian leaned back and fought the tears that came to his eyes. He couldn't lose both Samora and Harald on the same day. No victory was worth the loss of both of them.

He held her hand tightly and waited for her to wake.

WARRAN AND CAPRICIA found him at the same time. Capricia entered the healing tent first. She had a bloody bandage wrapped around her arm and looked to be bleeding from her side. When she saw Elian she hobbled toward him, favoring her right leg over her left. Despite her wounds, when she reached him, she threw her arms around him and held him tight.

"Word has already spread throughout the camps. How are you?"

Elian wasn't sure if the word that had spread was about Samora, Harald, or both, but he was too empty inside to care about the answer. "I'm surviving. How are you?"

"The same. Aldo retreated the Wolves earlier than he was supposed to during the battle, so the Hawks ended up taking the brunt of the northern advance. We lost a lot of great adanists."

Elian's thoughts turned, as they had constantly since he'd found Samora unconscious, to his sister and Harald. "Too many," he agreed.

They held onto each other for a long moment, and Elian wasn't sure if he was the one supporting her or if she was the one who held him up. Eventually, they broke apart and took seats next to Samora's bed. As soon as they did, Elian realized Warran had been standing behind Capricia the whole time, respectfully waiting for an opportunity to speak.

Elian clenched his good fist. He knew full well why Warran was here, and he understood why it was necessary, but it was too soon to be thinking about the future. All he wanted was to grieve and wait by his sister's side until she recovered from whatever had struck her down.

"We need to speak," Warran said.

Elian bit back the reply he wanted to utter. "Then let us speak."

Warran tilted his head toward the tent entrance. "I believe it is best if we do it outside while we walk."

Elian tried to glare Warran into submission, but Warran had been Harald's second for years, and there wasn't a single thing Elian could do to intimidate the man. Still, if Warran thought Elian was going to leave his sister's side, now, of all times, he was in for a rude awakening.

Capricia's gentle hand on his arm calmed the outburst before it took form. "I can watch over Samora while you speak with Warran."

Elian swallowed his frustrations and nodded. "Thank you."

He let his gaze linger upon Samora a while longer, then gave Warran a brief nod. He stood, and Capricia took his place next to Samora's side. She offered him a tight smile, and he bowed to her in thanks.

The movement brought a more genuine grin to her face. "You're going to need to wean yourself from that habit."

"Someday," Elian promised.

He followed Warran, though they didn't make it far before they were stopped by a woman recuperating on one of the cots. She caught Warran by the arm. "Is it true?"

He reached over with his other hand and placed it on top of hers. "I'm afraid it is."

She looked away, and though tears gathered in the corner of her eyes, none fell.

Elian squatted down beside the cot. "He gave everything at the end to kill the last two Belogs. If not for him, I'm not sure we'd be here to mourn."

The woman snorted, but her sad smile revealed her true feelings. "That sounds like the way he would have wanted to go. He always said he'd die in battle, I just never thought I'd still be around when it happened."

She directed her next words to Elian. "And how many Belogs did you bring down, young one?"

Elian answered impulsively, before reason could suggest a more measured response. "More than you."

The injured woman stared hard at him for a moment, then barked a harsh laugh. She clutched at her side and groaned as the laughter aggravated her injuries. "I deserve that, I suppose."

"You should rest," Warran said, "Elian and I have much to discuss."

The woman shooed them away. "I'm sure you do. I just wanted to hear the news from your lips. We've got a good one here, though, so take care of him, eh, Warran?"

"I'll do what I can, though I expect he'll make keeping Harald in line seem a simple task in comparison."

They bid the injured woman farewell, then stepped outside the tent. If Elian looked east, it was as if the Bears had just stopped for the night, but when his gaze wandered west, the full horror of the Belogs' destruction became apparent. Not a single tent stood whole. Survivors had stopped searching for the living and now combed through the wreckage searching for anything salvageable. The wandering clans would waste nothing of use.

Elian watched the survivors, and in his head, he heard the injured woman's calm acceptance of Harald's death in battle. Her expectation, now proven true, sharply conflicted with Elian's memory of Harald after they had sparred. His throat tightened, and he had to swallow hard before he could speak to Warran. "How did he do it?"

"Do what?"

"Be so many things to so many people. To me, he was a teacher, a mentor, and a warrior I could always rely on to watch my back. But I also knew he looked forward to a peaceful future. He didn't want to die in battle. He wanted to start a family."

The thought of the family Harald would never have choked Elian up again.

Warran considered, then said, "I don't think he ever intended to be anything more than he was. Every person contains multitudes, and those that choose to follow will see what they will. To some, it is a man who always suspected he would die in battle. To others, it is a teacher." Warran shrugged. "He was all of those things, and more that none of us will know."

Elian nodded but tried to think of anything else. If he thought about all the experiences he'd never have with Harald, he'd be no good to anyone for the rest of the day.

"What's true of Harald is true for us all," Warran added.

"It is?" Elian's exhausted mind couldn't follow Warran's point.

"We all play many roles for many people. You're a son, a lover, an adanist, and now the leader of the Bears. The only way to fulfill all these roles is to be yourself. To try anything else is to ensure failure."

Elian grunted. "You might need to remind me of that more than once."

"Of course."

Warran was no Harald, but Elian appreciated his steadfast nature. It reassured him in almost the same way Harald's presence had in their previous battles. "I'm glad you'll be helping me. Now that you've got me out here, what's next?"

"Well, since the moment Harald died, you, as his second, are now the leader of the Bears."

Elian started at that. Not because he hadn't known it was coming, but because it had already happened. "Wait. Isn't there going to be a ceremony, or something?"

"There will be, but our traditions are strict. One of our first tasks, once the situation is settled, will be to arrange the celebration of Harald's life. At that celebration, you will also be welcomed as the new leader, but that is a formality only. You're already the leader."

"That seems...sudden."

"Many leaders of the wandering clans die in battle. Our traditions ensure we're never leaderless."

Elian rubbed his chin. "What if I had also died?"

"Then I would have become leader. I am third in the clan."

"There's a third?"

"There's a tenth," Warran answered with a smile. "Once you're settled, you can take a look at the order of succession and propose changes at the council."

Elian realized he had much more to learn than he'd thought. For all his time with the clans, there was still too much he didn't know. He almost expressed his doubt but sealed his lips. Warran was leading him through the camp, and it was no doubt intentional. A leader needed to be seen, and Elian had been hiding in the healing tent since the battle. Once again, Elian said a silent thanks that he had Warran here to guide him.

"Beyond that, what else?"

"There are decisions that need to be made, the most important of which is answering the question of what comes next."

"What's the situation?"

"We're hurting badly. The Hounds, Bears, and Hawks all suffered incredible casualties in the battle. We're still working out our final numbers, but each of us is at least halved."

"What about the Wolves?"

"That is another area of contention that will soon become a battle. What I've heard is that Aldo retreated his forces too early, leaving the Hawks to bear the brunt of the Debru assault. I haven't confirmed it yet, but I suspect it's true. The Wolves are more intact than any of the other clans. I've been through their camp, and I suspect there are as many Wolves as there are everyone else."

Elian hoped the news wasn't true, but if both Capricia and Warran thought it so, it probably was. It put Aldo in a position to finally throw his weight around the councils, especially now that Harald was gone. But there were still greater problems.

"What do we know of the Debru?"

"Your guess is as good as mine. Those in the area have been destroyed, but I know nothing more than you."

"We should get a scout in the air to explore our surroundings. Can we do that?"

"If you tell us to."

The newness of his situation struck him once again. "Then, I guess I order that to happen."

"I'll see to it right away." Warran said as much, but he made no move to leave.

"What am I forgetting?" Elian asked.

"Nothing much. However, while I'm giving those orders, you should speak to Kati. We should organize Harald's celebration for tonight, or tomorrow at the latest. If we aren't seen to be moving forward, I don't know how long the clans stick together, especially knowing Aldo's temperament."

Elian looked toward the healing tent, then nodded to Warran. He said a silent apology to Samora, but it looked like it would be some time before he could be by her side again.

THAT NIGHT CAME SO QUICKLY Elian felt as though the sun had raced toward the horizon. The only reason he was able to stand was because of the heart's incredible ability to keep his body flooded with adani. The moment he let it go, he'd be asleep instantly.

He took some small comfort in knowing that he wasn't alone in his exhaustion. Everywhere he looked he saw hollowed out gazes and shuffling steps. They'd broken open a cask of ale, but not even the potent drink could penetrate the exhaustion of the adanists. He almost felt bad they'd moved so quickly, but Kati had insisted. She had claimed that Harald wouldn't want anyone lingering over his memory.

Elian wasn't foolish enough to accept that without question, but he'd said nothing. She shared Warran's concerns that if they didn't move quickly, Aldo would become the new leader of the unified clans. Either that, or he'd break the Wolves off and leave the rest to fend for themselves. And so, they celebrated Harald that night, even though the celebrants could barely stand.

Elian thrust his spade into the soft soil of the gathering ground, then tossed the soil over his shoulder. He was joined by the leaders of the other clans as well as the senior adanists still fit to move among the Bears.

Most adanists preferred to have their bodies lie where they fell, but Harald had requested that he be buried near the tree in the center of the gathering ground. At least, that was what Kati had said, and Elian saw no reason to doubt her. It seemed fitting that his body nourish the same grounds he fought so hard to protect.

When they judged the hole deep enough, they climbed out and lowered Harald's body in. He'd been wrapped in cloths, but there was no mistaking his bulk. It took several of them using ropes to lay his body in its final resting place.

Elian's tears fell freely, and he made no effort to stop them or wipe them away. Meeting Harald had been one of the greatest events of his life, and it felt as though the world had committed a crime to have the man taken from him so soon.

The pain echoed the loss he'd experienced so many years ago, that night the Moka attacked his village. Familiarity with the feeling didn't make the experience any easier.

Once Harald's body was at rest, Kati took a spadeful of dirt and tossed it on top of the body. She bowed deeply to the corpse, holding the bow for several long moments before straightening and taking her place among the Hawks.

One by one, all those who wanted approached the grave and poured one spade of dirt on top of Harald. Each did so silently, and the only sounds in the camp were those of the logs popping on the fire and the that of the soft breeze rushing through the tall grasses outside the camp.

It wasn't long before Harald was covered, and the dirt rapidly filled the hole. When all had taken their turns, Elian, as Harald's successor, went last. The spade sank easily into the loose, rich soil, and he poured it gently over his friend's corpse.

Then he stuck the spade gently in the remaining soil and turned to those gathered. He'd thought long and hard about what needed to be said tonight, and though his words felt insufficient, he hoped they made Harald proud.

He took a deep breath, then spoke, using adani to ensure his words carried to every ear. "It is no exaggeration to say that Harald was one of the best men I have ever known. All of you here know of his strength, which will be legendary generations from now, but he was so much more to me. He was a loyal friend, a courageous commander, and a clever thinker. More than once, when we faced the Belogs, I thought my spirit might break, but so long as he was near, all was well in my heart."

He paused to let the words sink in, then continued. "I mourn his loss today, and will mourn for some time, I think."

His voice trailed off, and for a few long moments, he wondered if he should stop. Samora had once told him that she felt adani guiding her in certain directions, and he wished he had that help now. He tried to still his thoughts and calm the pounding of his heart, but that was a losing battle this night, in this place. All he had was his own intuition, and it was a difficult thing to trust after all the mistakes he'd made along the way. Still, he pushed forward. "While our mourning will last long beyond the sunrise, come sunrise we must prepare for the next step in our long war against the Debru."

Sharp gazes from around the circle stabbed into him, but he continued, "After the losses we all suffered today, tomorrow we must discuss the future of our clans. For now, the Vada waits for us, but it will not for long."

Elian met the stare of every adanist, facing them until they cast their eyes down.

"I won't stand here and claim I have all the answers, but as the Bears' new leader, I will promise you this: Harald left it to me to finish this long war against the Debru, and I mean to see it to its end."

He took another deep breath, then pushed even more adani into his throat so that his voice would carry farther.

"It's no longer enough to simply survive. Today we defeated a force larger than any we've seen in generations. Tomorrow, we begin our campaign to drive the Debru from our lands!"

From different points around the circle, Elian's allies shouted their assent. Warran had helped plan it, but Elian was grateful for them now. The shouts spread like a wildfire, until the roar of over a hundred adanists filled the air.

Not everyone cheered, but Elian didn't expect them to. Aldo, in particular, watched him with a cold and calculating eye, but Elian was prepared for nothing less. There was much work yet to be done, but he would do it. For Harald, his father, and all those whose lives had been cut short by the Debru.

This world was for humanity.

He drew his sword and thrust it high into the air, drawing an even larger roar. As he let the sound wash over him, he swore he'd either fulfill his promise or die trying.

ALSO BY RYAN KIRK

The Legend of Adani

Born of Light and Shadow

From Shadow to Flame

The Ascension of Light

A War of Light and Shadow

Waterstone

The Rise of Shadow

The Shadows Beyond

The Last Sword of the West

Last Sword in the West

Eyes of the Hidden World

A Sword Named Vengeance

Wraith's Revenge

Frontier's End

Song of the Sagani

Legend of the Sword in the West

Nightblade

Nightblade

World's Edge

The Wind and the Void

Blades of the Fallen

Nightblade's Vengeance

Nightblade's Honor

Nightblade's End

Saga of the Broken Gods

Band of Broken Gods

Fall of Forgotten Gods

Rise of the Resurrected God

Oblivion's Gate

The Gate Beyond Oblivion

The Gates of Memory

The Gate to Redemption

Relentless

Relentless Souls

Heart of Defiance

Their Spirit Unbroken

The Sentinels Saga (with Taylor Crook)

Path of the Eternal Sun

A Path Divided

A Path Reforged

Primal

Primal Dawn

Primal Darkness

Primal Destiny

Song of the Fallen Swords

These Fallen Swords

Standalone Novels

The Last Fang of God

Blades of Shadow: A Nightblade Story

ABOUT THE AUTHOR

Ryan Kirk is the award-winning and internationally bestselling author of over thirty fantasy novels spanning nearly a dozen worlds. He lives in Minnesota with his family, where he enjoys long, meandering walks outside even when the snow is high enough to cover his legs. When he isn't glued to his keyboard, he's usually in the woods, either on foot or on bike.

facebook.com/waterstonemedia
instagram.com/authorryankirk
bookbub.com/authors/ryan-kirk